I0553971

THE

DOUBLE MAN;

OR, THE

REVELATIONS OF AN OLD JAILOR.

A Startling Narrative of True Events.

THIS TALE IS LITERALLY TRUE, AND TRANSCRIBED FROM A MANUSCRIPT FOUND IN AN OLD
BRICK HOUSE IN ONE OF THE LONDON OUTSKIRTS.

SPLENDIDLY ILLUSTRATED.

LONDON :

JOHN LOFTS, 262, STRAND, W.C., AND ALL BOOKSELLERS.

THE
DOUBLE MAN;
OR,
THE REVELATIONS OF A JAILOR.

Book I.—The Double Man.[a]

January 1st, 1770.

I AM an old jailor, and in my time I have seen the last of many men; aye, and even the last of many women. You who read the following tale of terror, will perceive it, long and long after I am dead and gone. I have so managed that the paper shall not be found till I have long been laid in the grave. I know that much will not be believed—that my readers will suppose I am romancing, but it is not so—I speak the truth, the whole truth, and nothing but it. Many and many a man have I watched during his last night on earth. I have seen him start in his sleep, and cry out for mercy! I have seen him wake up bathed in perspiration and calling out for water—water for pity's sake! When he has fallen asleep for a little time, only again to wake up, and again to call out for yet more water. I am quite sure that that last night before execution is a far greater agony than the execution itself. I dare say you know that a condemned man is never left alone between his condemnation and his execution, for the prison authorities are afraid that, should the condemned man be left alone, he would destroy himself. Read, then, this awful tale of mine, and believe that it is as true as that you are at this moment reading my words.

a This tale is literally true, and is transcribed from a manuscript found in an old brick house, in one of the London outskirts.

CHAPTER I.

THE GIBBET.

It was a dark stormy night, and the wind went whistling about the dreary heath as though it were sighing for the death of the highwaymen who swung in chains about three hundred yards from the low and sinister-looking public house in which our tale opens.

These executed highwaymen were three in number, and only on the morning previous to the night of which we speak had the third sufferer been placed in chains, and left to rot out in the cold winter air.

For it was winter time, and the snow was on the ground.

There seemed to be some extraordinary excitement going on at this inn, for a traveller might have remarked (had any man, indeed, been so daring as to travel that way after dark and unattended), that lights flashed backwards and forwards in and about the windows as though some unusual cause of excitement was troubling the household.

This moving backwards and forwards of the lights continued for some time; meanwhile all remained solitary and dark upon the deserted heath.

At last the moon rose, and then it might have been seen that the snow was much trampled between the gibbet and the dark, sinister-looking public house.

Suddenly the door of this building opened, and a man stood on the threshold.

"If it don't snow before cock-crow," said he, as though addressing some one within the building, "we shall be blown. The footmarks are all the way as plain as you are ugly, Jabez, from the gibbets to the ken."

"Then hope for the best," said another voice, "and come into the house, for it's as cold as he was when we took him down."

"By the gallows," said the first speaker, "he might have been colder, might Dashing Jack. I little thought he was breathing when I took him in my arms; I 'spose the gent 'ull tip something more handsome now."

"Tip!" said the second voice, which belonged to the man who had been called Jabez, "Dashing Jack 'ull pay you what you ask him, for bringing him once more into the world—why you're as good as a father to him."

"It was an odd go, Jabez, wasn't it?" asked the first speaker.

"What, to be met by a fine lady and get a purse of gold for taking down Dashing Jack out of his chains—if that was odd, I believe you, my boy." And then Jabez gave an odd kind of chuckling laugh.

"Ah," says the first speaker, who was a stout, thick-set man, with a bullet head, "and I can tell you the diamonds she had on her were worth having. Gad—I wonder I didn't make a grab at 'em, though there were hundreds of people within call."

"Who was she, d'ye know, Will?" asked Jabez.

"Not I," returned the first speaker—"not his mother, I'll be bound. I tell you what, Jabez, I believe Dashing Jack is a lord; that's about his ticket, you mark my words."

"Lord," said Jabez, coming to the door, and looking out upon the expanse of snow which was perfectly unbroken, but for the dark line between the gibbets and the house. "I always said Dashing Jack was a cut above all of us."

"Yes, and with plenty of brains," said the first speaker, "or he wouldn't have kept out of the hangman's hands for so long a time. Gad, that was a fine idea of his, to make friends with the hangman, wasn't it?"

"Aye, that it was," returned Jabez; "but Dashing Jack was always a gentleman. Do ye think he'll turn to the road again?"

"I can't say," said the first speaker, "but I should say not. The coves say he made a ten thousand pound job of it, over the crack for which he got lagged, and Dashing Jack ain't the man to work when he can be still."

"Has he spoken yet?" said Jabez.

"No, not yet, but the bleeder we kidnapped says he will in a short time. Hark! don't you hear a horse?"

As the speaker stopped and assumed a listening attitude, the sound of a rapidly approaching horse was heard, loud and yet more loud.

"Douse the glims," said the first speaker, in a low tone of voice, as though he was afraid the horseman might hear him even at the distance he still remained from the inn. "If this is a chicken worth plucking, we must not scare him by having the house all alight."

"I'm fly," said Jabez, and was turning to enter the building, when a shout, uttered by some half a dozen men, was heard to proceed from the interior of the inn, and the next moment these same voices commenced huzzaing.

CHAPTER II.

THE MEETING.

The man who bestrode the horse, the coming of whose footsteps has been recorded in the last chapter, was a gentleman of not more than twenty years of age.

He was exceedingly handsome, and by the light of the moon it might have been seen that his rich black hair hung in exquisite curls about his splendid head. He was tall and broad-chested, and he sat his horse as though he were accustomed to daily riding. Indeed he looked like a trooper, and as brave a one as any in his majesty the king's army. His complexion was dark, while his cheeks were of a rich crimson hue—the hue of health. The great peculiarity of his face was the eyes, which were of an exquisitely light blue. They were not of that blue which is frequently seen, but of that tint which may sometimes be found in rare old china.

No one who had once seen this man could forget this peculiarity of his features, for the dark skin and dark hair contrasted wonderfully with those pale eyes, which were exceedingly soft in expression, and seemed to speak love.

As this personage neared the gibbets he pulled up his horse and gazed at the awful rows of chained corpses.

Perchance the courteous reader may not be aware of the precise manufacture of these chains. Indeed, it might with more truth be said that a man was incased in iron rather than that he was hung in chains—for various bars of iron were riveted about the unhappy criminal, who, after having suffered death, was hanged in this awful condition till his flesh, and even bones, fell away through the spaces between the iron bars.

"Hallo!" thought the stranger, as he drew rein before the gibbets, "some one has taken a fancy to one of these scare-crows since the morning—there is one less than there was Here is the gibbet sure enough, but where is the dead man in his chains. I saw them fastening the poor wretch to his last home as I rode by this morning. So, so ; there must be honour amongst thieves, I suppose, and the poor devil has people who like him well enough to risk their own necks in order to give him decent burial."

The horseman then said a word of encouragement to his horse, and then walked him on towards the inn.

"Strange it is," he continued to himself— "strange it is how one day shall make one man's fortune and end another's. This morning this poor wretch suffered the last penalty of the law, and this morning made my fortune. Ho, ho ! my noble lord and cousin, how will you like to lay down the title and fortune of which you have robbed me, and have to become plain Mr. once more, with no crowd of servants at your call, and your way to make in the world?"

As the young man spoke he took from the breast of his coat a pocket-book, and guided by the light of the moon he opened it, and took from one of its compartments a little slip of folded paper.

"To think," he said, "that this atom of paper will topple my lord from his grandeur, and make me a rich and titled man. My poor mother !—it killed thee to attack thy honour— it was as though a knife struck thee when the whole court laughed at your claim to be the widow of the earl, my father, and could not tell where you were married. Little did I wonder why you murmured when asleep the name of the town where I have now found this evidence of my rights. It was thy better angel, mother, in thy sleep, whispering to thy son the means to prove his honour and thy own. How wondrous it is that the thought struck me to go to Chevley, and search the books of the church."

As the handsome stranger thus mused, he reached the hostelry of which mention has been made.

"It does not look a very inviting spot," the young man murmured, "but I, least of all, never should judge by appearances. They may be honest folks, and true."

"Ho !" he cried, in a loud voice, " house there !"

The candles had all been extinguished with the exception of one or two, before the stranger's horse had reached the gibbet.

"Who disturbs honest folks in the night-time," asked Jabez, putting his head out of the first-floor window.

"A friend," said the stranger, "who claims shelter, more for his horse than for himself."

"We are all honest folk here," said Jabez, once more.

"No one doubts you," said the stranger ; "so quick, and open the door."

"How know I that you may not be a robber, a gentleman of the road ?" added Jabez, pretending to flinch as the stranger started at the word " robber," addressed to him.

"Bah !" said the stranger, "you are more than one in the house, I dare say ; so let me in, I pray you."

"Good," said Jabez, "I will ; but mind you, we are all honest folk here."

A few moments saw the stranger seated in the chief room of the inn on the heath.

It was a dark room, full of odd corners, and contained many doors. A fire was flickering on the great hearth, and not far from this fire stood an immense screen.

The stranger sat down in a chair which stood within the screen, and ordered a bottle of wine, the best the house afforded.

Jabez soon returned with the liquor, and as though to prove that the wine in the house was as honest as the people, he opened it in the presence of his guests.

"Didn't I hear a shouting," said the stranger to Jabez, "as I came near your house ?"

"Far be it from me to contradict your honour," says Jabez, who was the landlord of the house, " but if your honour heard a shouting, your honour did not hear it come from *this* house ; we are all quiet souls in *this* house."

"Hum !" said the stranger, "yet I could swear I heard a great shouting as I neared your house."

"So please your honour, will your honour eat anything ? " asked Jabez.

"No, friend," returned the stranger, " I stopped more for my horse's sake than my own. When he is sufficiently rested we must be on the road again."

"The road," said the landlord. "Will your honour venture to go on the road to-night once more ? "

"Aye, why not ? " asked the stranger.

"There are highwaymen about, your honour," says the landlord.

"Ah," returned the stranger, "if they find no better booty than I can yield them they won't be on the road long, for they will starve to death. I am a poor devil of a captain, landlord, and must start for Spain at six to-morrow. Here ! take my hat."

Till now the stranger had kept his hat fixed low down over his eyes; but now taking it off and handing it to the landlord he saw this latter individual fall back, and stare aghast at him.

"Why—why I didn't know it was you!" says the landlord.

"Why, do you know me?" asks the stranger, stretching his neck and rubbing it.

"And the mark of the rope is gone," said the landlord. Then he added, "why I thought you were upstairs with them; how did you get out?"

The stranger looked hard at Jabez for a moment, and then he said, "Hark you, friend landlord, a joke's a joke; but if you're all honest folk in this house, I don't think ye are all sober ones; and if thou dost not quit the room, I'll thrash thee with the flat of my sword."

Whereupon the landlord returned for answer, "Thou wast always a joker, Jack: thou wast always a joker."

The stranger, at the end of his patience, here started from his chair, and made for the landlord, who drew back, still saying, "Thou wast always a joker," till he neared the door, when saying, "Jack, ring for more wine when thou hast ended that; thou wast always a fellow for wine, and thy dance upon nothing hath not doubtless taken away thy appetite for good liquor."

The stranger looked after the landlord in wondering surprise for a few moments, then shrugging his shoulders he turned to the bottle which the landlord had opened, and commenced drinking the liquor.

All had been silence in the house for a few moments when the stranger once more drew the pocket-book from his breast and again looked at the paper which he had examined by the moon-light under the gallows.

"This is my pass to fortune and to honour," he murmured, and he kissed the fragment of parchment he held in his hand.

Once more he replaced it in his pocket-book, and this he again placed within his waistcoat, and next his heart it seemed.

Now mention has been made of the various doors and recesses which were to be found in this large and repulsive room. Amongst other openings was a door which was quite in deep shadow, receiving on its surface but few rays of light, either from the fire or the lamp.

As the stranger raised his eyes from depositing the pocket-book within the breast of his waistcoat, he raised his eyes towards this door quite accidentally and without thought, and to his utter astonishment he saw his very self before him. There was the fine broad head, the dark complexion, and the blue eyes and curling black hair.

"Is this a delusion of the senses," he asked himself, as he gazed towards the immovable figure standing in the darkened doorway, "or do I gaze upon reality?"

The next moment he recovered himself, and saying, "it must be a looking glass," he caught up the light and walked towards the spot.

But the corner of the carved table caught the ample waistcoat which he was wearing, and tore it open.

The pocket-book fell to the ground, but the owner took no heed of his loss, and pressed on towards the door, where he still saw the figure.

But the next moment a strong puff of wind through this same doorway extinguished the miserable lamp which had only served to show the darkness of the room, and the next moment the stranger was in darkness.

"A STRANGE MEETING," he heard a soft voice say, and then he distinctly heard a door close.

The next moment he was shouting, "Landlord, landlord!" and within a very few moments Jabez was once more in the room.

"Your honor, what is it?" asked the landlord, rushing in; "but where is the lamp?"

"Extinguished," said the landlord. "Quick, fetch another!"

A moment or so more and the lamp was once more casting a feeble glimmer over the great room.

The stranger ran to the spot at which he had seen the mysterious double of his own self, and struck a closet door with his open right hand.

"Landlord," he said, "what place does this door open upon?"

"On the lumber room, your honour, as your honour very well knows," said the landlord, laughing, and then he added to himself, "There's not the least mark of the rope!"

"How should I know, varlet," said the stranger, "I have never been in the house before."

"Ho! ho! that is rich—that is rare! Never been in this house before! egad, I wish I had as many guineas as thou hast been times in this house, Jack."

Thinking the landlord drunk, the stranger once more shrugged his shoulders and bade Jabez prepare his horse.

"What!" said the landlord, "are you going to take to the road again already?"

"Yes—be quick!" said the handsome stranger, and once more flung himself into his seat, and mechanically re-buttoning his waistcoat, little thinking that the treasured parchment lay at his feet; nay, he even stepped upon the treasure and did not know that he was doing so.

"Can there be such things as spiritual visitations?" asked the young man of himself, "have I really seen a vision, or did a real man in the flesh and blood—as like me as my own reflection in a looking-glass—stand in that spot at which I am now gazing. Ah, the door moved!"

He started up once more and ran to the door, but when he laid his hand upon it 'twas as firm as though it were part of the wall.

"I will leave this place at once," he said rapidly to himself, "I have only a few more hours in England, and I do not wish that they should be spent in such a place as this. Ah me! a few hours and I must embark for Spain—but not for long; soon I shall return to claim my own—my fortune, my title, and my Edith!"

"So please your honour," here said the landlord, appearing once more at the door, "your mare is ready saddled, but if I were your honour I would not ride out into the night."

"Peace, fool!" said the stranger, and flinging down a golden piece he strode from the room, leaving his cherished pocket-book on the spot upon which it had fallen when the rough edge of the table had torn open his waistcoat.

The landlord went down to the door, saw his honour into the saddle, bade him "Good night and good luck!" and then barring the door, he returned to the great room on the first floor, and opening a window, looked after his late visitor.

"By the bones of his father he's a brave gentleman of the road," said the landlord; "only out of the irons a couple of hours, and there he is once more in a saddle, and tearing along at a hard gallop."

As he spoke thus to himself the door which the stranger had tried opened noiselessly, and a figure came past its threshold into the room.

He was the very self of the stranger who had so recently left the room—but his face was paler, and the pale blue eyes—(the pale blue eyes which were equally peculiar in both men) possessed less expression than those of the traveller to whom the reader has been introduced.

Indeed, he seemed as though newly risen from the grave; and round his neck was a dark, claret-coloured streak.

Noiselessly he walked to the spot upon which the pocket-book lay; noiselessly he stooped and raised it from the ground; noiselessly he placed it in his pocket; and then as noiselessly he moved up to the landlord and touched him quietly on the shoulder.

Jabez started and turned round.

Even as he turned he heard the retreating sound of the hoofs of the stranger's horse.

"His ghost! his ghost!" the landlord cried, his whole frame trembling.

"No, Jabez; take my hand," said the newcomer, "I am as warm flesh and blood as yourself."

———

CHAPTER III.

THE WAITING LADY.

RETURN we now to our traveller.

It was midnight when he left the hostelry he had twenty good miles before him ere he reached London, and by six he had to be with his regiment; for the gentleman to whom the reader has been introduced was Captain Edgar Trevillian.

Captain Edgar Trevillian was supposed to be the illegitimate son of the late Earl of Milray, and unable to prove his claim to the title and the estates on the sudden and terrible death of his father Lord Milray he had seen them pass to the son of his father's younger brother, and had been compelled to take his mother's maiden name, and by it he was known in the army.

His mother, stunned by the death of her husband, was never able to tell the name of the town where the marriage ceremony had taken place; but, as has been stated, her son had frequently heard her murmur in her sleep the name during the few years she outlived her husband.

Lord Milray died when his son was but fifteen years of age. The countess, his lady, lived to see her son reach his twentieth year, and then she lay down her load of life, and the young man was alone in the world to fight his way to the title and fortune which he knew were justly his own.

It may be asked—why did Lord Milray seek to conceal his marriage with the countess. The reason is easy of explanation: the old earl had threatened to encumber the estates if his son married in his lifetime, and hence it was that Lord Milray kept his marriage a secret. When he assumed the title he would willingly, joyfully have proclaimed his countess as his wife—she whom he had found a simple cottage girl, and whom he had raised to be a peeress of England; but he died within a week of his coming to the title, and rumour did not hesitate to say that his nephew, who in default of sons, was the heir-at-law, knew only too many of the circumstances of the death of his uncle.

Be that as it might, this nephew assumed the title and possessed himself of his uncle's vast estates and fortune, while the unfortunate Trevillian had to endure poverty, contempt, and degradation.

But Captain Trevillian had served the king well, and people said of him that he could fight his own way in the world if fortune was against him.

Return we now to the captain, whom we left galloping towards London.

It was about three o'clock in the morning when he reached the outskirts of the town.

He was drawing rein, for fear of riding down some late sedan or market cart which might be in the road, when his good horse started.

The rider knew his animal too well not to be quite sure that something unusual must have occurred to induce his faithful horse to start, and he immediately looked towards the spot from which the horse had winced.

He saw a figure standing in the shadow of a heavy wall. The figure of a woman—nay, a lady, as far as her dress and posture went—for by the faint lamplight which glimmered in the street, he saw that her robe was embroidered with silver and gold braid, and as her hood lay back a little on her head, the young cavalier remarked that large and perfect diamonds shone in her ears.

She was enveloped in a thick black cloak, which fell almost to her feet, but it was open in front, and Trevillian saw that her breast was white and fair.

As he pulled up his horse and looked towards the mysterious figure, the lady raised her hands and struck them together softly.

The young man, amazed at this act, made no response, but merely looked in the direction of the mysterious figure.

The lady then tremblingly moved forward. Her walk was that of a duchess, more accustomed to the soft carpet of a well lit drawing-room than the cold, ill-paved streets of London, in the dark centre of the night.

As she moved forward she again struck her hands softly.

Still he made no response to the appeal.

By this time she had come up to the horse's side, and as he looked at the little hands he saw that they were covered with jewels.

As she reached his side she started back, and then eagerly peered into the cavalier's face, but he had forced his hat down over his face, and she could not see his features.

"Is it done?" she asked, in trembling accents.

"What, lady?" asked Trevillian, bending in his saddle.

"Is he laid in the cold earth?" asked the fair creature, looking up to the cavalier.

"Who?" asked Trevillian, thinking perhaps the poor woman was deranged. "Pray, lady, how should I know?"

"I was to learn it from a horseman, on a brown horse, and at three. It is now three, and your horse is brown. Indeed I am she to whom you owe this message. Speak—I pray you, speak."

"I do not know what you would have me say," says the horseman, drawing in his steed, which seemed impatient to proceed once more.

"I mean him who was hanged this morning, on the heath—have they laid him in the cold cruel ground?"

As she spoke she raised her hands, and Trevillian saw that they were covered with splendid jewels.

"If you mean the wretch who suffered for his crime this morning, I can tell you, lady—though I much wonder that one so fair can desire to know aught of such a man—I can tell you that his body swings no more in the cold winds. As I passed the gibbet but a few hours past I saw that the body had been removed."

"Thank Heaven!" said the strange lady, covering her face with her hands, "at least he is at peace. I bless you, sir, for the kind news you bring me; and pray let me look upon your face, that I may remember it."

Edgar Trevillian had throughout the interview kept his broad hat low down upon his face, and thus, together with his cloak, of which the collar was up, sufficiently hid his features from the gaze of the mysterious woman.

He hesitated for a moment, and then thought that, perhaps, she was one of those terrible female robbers who cajoled a man, and while doing so murdered him. "Suppose," thought he, "that when I raised my hand to my hat she struck at me with a dagger."

So he answered—"Lady, my face can be of no consequence to you: if you have naught more to say to me I pray you let me pass on, for if my horse moves, as you now stand, he may hurt you."

"Ah!" said the lady, "if you will not let me see your face, at least let me lay this poor hand upon your heart for a moment, for you have brought me the best news I can receive in this miserable world."

As she spoke she raised high her hand, and placed it against his heart for a moment.

With a quick, convulsive action he followed her hand to his heart, and watched it as it once more fell to her side. Then, as though still suspicious, he placed his own hand upon the same spot.

As he did so he started so suddenly, that the horse made a wild plunge.

The rider did not care to govern the animal, for he let the reins go, and madly felt about his breast for the pocket-book which he had placed beneath his coat at the little dark inn on the heath.

"No, no—it cannot be," he cried, leaving open the front of his coat.

But all to no purpose, for he did not find the much wished-for packet.

"And I have no time to return," he cried. "It is now three; the vessel sails at six; and if I am not at the calling of the muster roll shall be branded as a deserter, and, perchance, my life may pay the forfeit. Only three hours! I could not go back in two, even with a fresh horse, and then I should only have an hour in which to return. Fool—madman that I have been! Why did I not see that it was safe when I left that accursed house? The brand of illegitimacy will disfigure me for life if I cannot recover these papers, and I have no power to regain them. On both sides degradation: on one that of illegitimacy, on the other ignominious death. Oh! fool—fool that I have been! What shall I do—what shall I do?"

The lady who addressed him had shrank back as he commenced his wild lamentation, but she now drew near him again; and as he bowed his head, and placed his hands between them, she said:

"What is the matter? Tell me—perchance I can help you?"

If now he would only tell her all, who knows how much benefit she could be to him. But he only weeps more and more, and says to himself—"Fool that I have been; I should never have let the packet pass from my hands except with my life."

Suddenly he started.

"Oh! he cried. "Hope—I see a ray of hope—pale and flickering, but to me a mountain of light. On—on—brave horse!"

As he caught the reins once more with his right hand, he flung back his cloak with the other, and the action also cast his hat upon the ground.

The next moment the horse started forward; and as the high-spirited animal did so, a loud piercing shriek was heard to proceed from the body.

"'Tis he—'tis he!" she cried. "Do not leave me, Holgarth—do not leave me! you cannot—you cannot!"

She staggered as she spoke; but her words did not arrest Edgar Trevillian, who continued on his headlong course. Again and again the splendidly attired woman called upon the horseman to come back, but her words fell upon the night air only, and she fell senseless to the ground, her splendid hair lying in the mud and rain in the roadway.

CHAPTER IV.

LET us now return once more to the little inn. The landlord was sitting near the almost expiring fire, and almost opposite to him was the man who had picked up Edgar Trevillian's pocket-book, and which he still held in his hands.

"By my faith," says Jabez, "are there *two* Gentleman Jacks?"

"No—no, Jabez," said the other; "there is only one Gentleman Jack, and that your obedient servant—who don't mean to die in shoes (a) yet awhile."

"Why," says the landlord, "you might get lagged (b) for one another, and your mother's 'ud hardly know yer apart."

"'Gad!" says the highwayman, "I never had a mother to know me. There, hand me over the stringer-up." (c)

As he did so, the landlord looked at the purse, and said—

"Two slices of luck in one day—yer plants was always good, and now yer luck is—after ye've danced upon nothing in top-boots."

Jabez, when he said Gentleman Jack's "plants was always good," did not allude to any gardening *furore* on the part of the highwayman, but "plant" is the word given to any arrangement for committing a burglary or other robbery.

"Ah!" says the highwayman, taking a small silver pipe from his pocket; "but I danced with a whistle."

"Wonderful!—wonderful!" said the landlord. "When we took it from your throat, and poured a thimbleful of the stringer-up down it, and when we saw yer open yer eyes—by the living jingo, it was as though you was come from yer coffin!"

"It wasn't a bad idea, was it?" answered the highwayman; "a rope may press a fellow's windpipe together, but it can't squeeze the life out of him when he wears such a friend as this in his gullet. They little thought what I wanted this silver whistle for, when I asked

(a) "Die in shoes," to be hanged.
(b) "Lagged," transported.
(c) "Stringer-up," brandy.
(d) "Doing the handsome," releasing him from the gibbet.

them to leave it in my pocket. I've done the beaks this time, and I'll do them again; so hand over the stringer-up once more."

The highwayman's words may appear a little mysterious, and therefore we proceed to clear them up at once. While in jail, and condemned to death, he, upon being searched, entreated his jailors to allow him to remain in possession of a small silver call-pipe or whistle, which they found upon him.

A half-hour before that appointed for his execution, the highwayman took this whistle from his pocket, and, turning away from the jailor—who, as was and is common in all cases of men condemned to death, sat watching the criminal—he knelt down as though in prayer.

He then easily removed the top and bottom of the whistle, put these in his pocket, and then held the whistle in his hand in the shape of a delicate little silver pipe.

Slowly but easily he passed this down his throat and into his windpipe. That the operation pained him was certain by the low sounds that escaped him; but, the feat accomplished, he turned once more to the jailor, and sat with his face turned towards him.

Indeed, this pipe had been given him by a German doctor, whose life he had not only spared, but saved, and in gratitude this personage had given him the whistle, as the most acceptable gift he could offer him, and telling the highwayman how to use it in case of need.

"Hope you feel better, mate," said the jailor, speaking to the prisoner, as the latter turned towards him.

But the highwayman made no reply. In fact he could not. The pipe permitted him to breathe, but would not allow of his speaking.

"Have you grown surly, mate?" asked the jailor; but never a word got he in reply, and not a word more said Gentleman Jack from that moment up to the instant when the public saw him swinging, or rather—as he termed it—"dancing upon nothing in top boots."

The strain of the rope upon his neck of course created insensibility, and in this state the criminal was cut down—in this state he was conveyed to the lonely heath—in this state he was hung in chains, where he remained till Jabez, whose inn was a house of call for highwaymen, had, according to instructions, joined several men in breaking the rivets of the chains in which Gentleman Jack was hung, and in restoring the highwayman to his senses.

Let us return once more to the great room on the first floor of the little inn where Jabez and the highwayman are still seated.

"I say, Jack," says the landlord, "I forgot to tell ye that while we were doing the handsome to you (d) a party of queer cuffins came up, and when they saw us at work, one of 'em bursts out laughing, and says—'Why, he has got more friends now he is dead than he had when living. I say, coves,' says he, 'you're a doing our job,' says he—'I suppose ye'll give him a decent box and six foot of clay?' So says I," continued the landlord, "'of course,' for I was not going to tell him that we meant to get yer a horseback any more. Then says he to his pals—'Come along, mates; the job's jobbed, and as Tom and his brown horse don't seem to be coming, why the namow(a) 'ull have to wait till to-morrow.' And then," continued Jabez, "they wished us luck and moved off. Who was the namow?"

"Who?" says the highwayman, once more taking up the brandy bottle—"why, Milly, to be sure; and thank the stars I've seen the last of her?"

"What! shall you nick (b) her."

"Ah! for her betters."

"What do ye mean, Gentleman Jack?" asks the landlord, thinking the highwayman is going out of his senses.

"You see this pocket-book?" the robber said, raising the article in question.

"Yes."

"Now only you and I know I have got it—only you and I know I am alive."

"And Joe and Bill—don't they know you're alive? ain't they boozing down stairs, and drinking your good health, Jack?"

"No," said the highwayman, coolly taking another sip of brandy; "they're both flat." (c)

"Did you do for them?" the landlord asked, catching his breath.

"Yes," returned the highwayman; "and if I chose I could do for you, and then only myself would know I'm once more in the land of the living. But I like you, Jabez, and while you keep my secret, you may keep your ugly life."

"What—what made you kill Joe and Bill?"

"Because I found this pocket-book."

"What's in it, then?"

"Well, I don't mind telling you.—It contains the certificate of marriage between Lord Edgar Ravensworth (afterwards the Earl of Milray) with Mary Hewson, and also the certificate of the birth of their son Edgar Ravensworth, and who is the real Earl of Milray. This boy, I know, was declared to be illegitimate, and the title and estate went to his cousin, who now holds them, and he could not produce the evidence I now hold in my hand."

"But—but what's all this here to do with yerself, Jack?" stammered the landlord.

"This," said the highwayman, waving his hat—"the man who let this pocket-book fall at your feet was the real earl, and he has lost these evidences of his birth—they are mine—they are mine!"

"Why, they're no more use nor sinkers,"(d) said the landlord.

"They're as good as real flimsies, Jabez. Have you forgotten how the earl and your obedient might pass for brothers? Well, I shall pass for him; I shall make myself the

Earl of Milray, and the road will see me no more. I want a quiet respectable life."

"But the fences(e) will know you."

"Why, they all think I've had my last liquor," said the highwayman, winking at his glass.

"And how will you get over the nob(f) himself?" asked the landlord.

"Oh, as I got over Joe and Will—poor soul! I just "hocussed" their gin, and they went off like infants. Here, drink, Jabez; though it's your own brandy, it's good."

"I'd rather not," said Jabez, looking affrightedly about.

"What ails you, man?" asked the highwayman, "are you afraid I'll do for you? Why, I could have done that if I'd wanted an hour ago. No, no; gentleman Jack don't forget the man who brought him back to life and happiness; for I mean to be happy, my old toper, and if any ill-luck does come, why, I've always this to help me out of it," and he held a very small phial which he took from the lining of one of his boots.

"What—what's that, Jack?" asked Jabez.

"Quiets."(g)

"Oh, save us!" cried the landlord.

"The German doctor gave me this too—he may have been the devil himself for what I know. And quiet enough it is: one or two drops, and a man falls as dead as his greatest enemy could wish him. Gad, it was a shame to waste it over Joe and Will, when a knife would have done the business just as well; only I have a respect for you, Jabez, and I didn't want to make your place in a mess. You should have seen them go off like the snuff of a candle. More brandy, Jabez," he continued, and he was growing intoxicated, "more brandy, Jabez, and call me your grace, and my lord, for I'm the Earl of Milray in spite of the red scarf I wear."

As he said these latter words he pulled down his neck-tie, and brought to view a horrible red line, which went entirely round his neck. It was about half an inch in width, and was of a deep crimson colour.

"Ha!" the highwayman continued, stretching his throat as he looked in the glass, "that very whistle may have saved my windpipe, but it has not my neck; this red mark will stand by me as the German said it would. He was a strange man—his eye seemed fire when he met me in the black forest. Anyhow he has saved my life, and will help to keep my secret."

The landlord here came up to him and offered the liquor. As he saw the blood-red mark he shrank back.

"Don't show the white feather, man," said the highwayman, "at a red neck-tie."

"Will it keep there, Jack?" asked Jabez.

"The devil seize it, yes," said the gentleman of the road. "I must wear my neck-cloth high

---

(a) "Namow," is thieves' English for woman. The word is made by spelling woman backwards.
(b) Leave her.
(c) "flat," dead.
(d) "Sinkers," bad money.

(e) "Fences," receivers of stolen goods.
(f) "Nob," the aristocrat.
(g) "Quiets," poisons.

up, whether it be the fashion or no, or I may frighten all the good company I mean to keep."

Here he arranged his neck-cloth, so as to hide that awful brand conferred on him by the hangman.

"But you're not like the nob that was here out and out," says the landlord.

"Why not? I have his features, his height, his voice; the colour of my hair is the colour of his; my eyes are blue as his are; and my hand is as white and gentlemanly. He too is dark, and so am I."

"Was, Jack, was," said the landlord, shaking his head slowly.

"What do you mean?" asked the highwayman; and, catching up the lamp, he peered

once more into the oval glass which was above the fire-place.

"Why you are as pale as though you was a kinchin, (a) with the bracelets (b) on for the first time."

"I am white," said the highwayman, still looking into the glass.

"And so you have been ever since we took the silver pipe from your throat—you haven't changed a bit. And your eyes look like poor Bess's when she lay stark dead, shot down by the quaker-merchant—they're like glass, Jack," the landlord continued, touching the man's

(a) "Kinchin"—boy thief.
(b) "Bracelets"—handcuffs.

2

hand, " as cold as when you were out swinging in chains on the heath."

" To blab the simple (a) I don't feel my old self," said the highwayman, " I feel as though I was a different man from my old self; I feel as though I did all I do not by my own will but by some one else's. Curse me, if I don't wish I had let the rope do its work!"

For a moment he stood hesitatingly; then he cried out in a loud voice, " Hullo! why, I'm as funking (b) as though I was in the salt-box (c) once more. Here," he continued, flinging a number of golden coins upon the table, and which he had taken from the pocket-book, " here are the yellow boys that will bury Joe and Will—*they're* happy anyhow, for they havn't got their living to get. Where's my horse—where's my horse?"

" So please you he's in his old stable," said the landlord.

The next minute the clattering of hoofs was once more heard in the neighbourhood of the dark and rightly suspected little inn on that dreary part of the heath; gradually the sounds departed in the distance.

Far away he went from the terrible corpses still swinging in the night air—far away from the gibbets, and the inn within which lay the two murdered men.

But he could not ride away from the memory of the singular German doctor who had given him the silver whistle and the little phial of poison.

He could not ride away from these memories any more than he could get rid of the deadly paleness of his face, the cold clammy feel of his hand, the terrible red mark round his neck, and the awful feeling that another being and not he himself prompted his acts and movements.

CHAPTER V.

DURING these events at the inn, a very different scene was being enacted within the London boundaries.

About a quarter of an hour after Edgar Trevillian had spurred away from the beauteous and jewelled woman whom he had left fallen upon the road-way, the caravan of Mr. and Mrs. Naggleton came along that same road towards London.

We have said the caravan of Mr. and Mrs. Naggleton, but we ought rather to have written Mrs. and Mr. Naggleton's caravan, for the lady was of a great deal more consequence than the gentleman, who for that matter was of no consequence at all, as his good lady frequently told him when they were squabbling.

And Mrs. and Mr. Naggleton were always squabbling. They never quarrelled—they were

too good-tempered for that—but they never left off squabbling and carping *at* each other, never *to* each other. Mrs. Naggleton never looked at Naggleton when she said she knew a fool; and Naggleton never observed his infinitely better half when he said he was quite sure he was " acquainted" with a " catamaran." Naggleton never went further than " catamaran," because it was always at this point that Mrs. Naggleton looked about for something to fling at somebody she knew.

It was, as has been stated, three o'clock in the morning, and Mrs. Naggleton had retired to rest within the recesses of the elegant red and yellow caravan, which contained herself, (who took up no small portion of the vehicle) a girl with white hair, whom Naggleton was in the habit of calling " a Halbanian," and a dwarf who got into a house much smaller than a large-sized dog-kennel, and astonished the proprietors by ringing a little hand-bell out of the chimney. Besides these curiosities there were three boa-constrictors, and a scaly armadillo—which latter worried Mrs. Naggleton more than Naggleton himself did, for this animal never saw the good lady but he rushed at and tried to upset her by scudding between her legs; and as all the talking to in the world would not cure him, and as he defied beating, rolling himself up into a ball as hard as ivory, Mrs. Naggleton was reduced to despair; for the only way in which she could " make him feel" was by wrenching the " scaly hedge-hog" open with the poker, which was a dangerous operation, as it might kill this ornament of Mrs. Naggleton's life and damage the receipts of halfpence and pence (3d. was the usual charge) paid to see the exhibition.

Yes—Mrs. Naggleton had retired to rest, but not to sleep; somehow the caravan seemed to have picked out all the large uncomfortable stones it could find in the road, in order to jumble over them, and either shake Mrs. Naggleton out of bed on the left, or crash her up against the wooden walls of the caravan on the right.

Naggleton was, of course, not taking his rest, for he was driving the " cairywan," as he called it, sitting on one of the shafts, and being also nearly jolted off his precarious seat every time Mrs. Naggleton was nearly jolted out of bed.

Mrs. Naggleton could bear it no longer, and she called out from the interior—

" Some people are fools born, and most so when they drives."

Whereupon says Naggleton, " Betsy,"—who was the mare drawing the exhibition, and not Mrs. Naggleton, whose elegant name was Jemima—" Betsy, some people *is* fools, whether they drives or whether they snoozles."

" Which some people couldn't, with other people drivin'—most likely drunk—nohow."

Whereupon says Naggleton, " Betsy— kim up!" and he obliges Betsy with a moderate application of a very limp whip, as a mild punishment for putting her master into trouble.

" Which some people are brutes as well as

(a) To speak the truth.
(b) " Funking"—frightened.
(c) " Salt-box"—the condemned Cell.

fools," Mrs. Naggleton immediately remarks, and a noise is heard as of a lady violently tucking herself up.

"And which *other* people are catamarans," says Naggleton, and smacks his whip loud and high.

This remark shut Mrs. Naggleton up, and the old caravan went lumbering on and on for about ten minutes, Mrs. Naggleton being shaken backwards and forwards even more than before, and Mr. Naggleton many greater chances of being run over by his own Betsy every minute, when suddenly a loud "Whoa-a-a-a!" fetched Mrs. Naggleton straight up in her narrow bed, and brought the "cairywan" to a dead standstill.

"Some people suttingly *is* fools," says Mrs. Naggleton—"and which is more than ordinary fools."

"Which," Mrs. Snaggleton immediately heard her better half say—"which if some people 'ud pass a petticut and come out of the sheets and do summut for a poor feller creetur in distress it 'ud be better than finding fault with other people about nothing nohow."

A plunge was immediately heard; the little window in the front of the caravan was immediately opened, and Mrs. Naggleton's face appeared in the opening; it was a large red face with plenty of cap-border, and altogether reminding one somehow of a very big frying-pan.

"Whatever is it, Teddy?" said Mrs. Naggleton, sinking her dignity in her curiosity.

"Whatever *is* it?" answers Teddy, who can't easily forget his dignity, and who is still seated on his shaft; "some people had better ask whatever *aint* it."

"Then what *aint* it, dear?" says Mrs. Naggleton.

"In the fust place," says Mr. Naggleton, "you pass a petticut and come out of it."

"Teddy, dear, I'll pass two—but what is it?"

"P'raps it may be murder," says Teddy, "*and* p'raps not; anyhow I aint agoin' to give Betsy a chance to go over her; and so I holds her back till you've passed that there petticut and cum out of it."

Mrs. Naggleton took such a little time to "pass the petticut," lower the steps of the caravan, and descend to the common earth, that her better half uttered this remarkable expression,—"Some people *are* spankers when some people chooses."

"Now, whatever is it, once more, Teddy?"

"Just you lay hold on Betsy's head," says the proprietor of the caravan, and his obedient wife, who is six foot two, and who has passed, by the aid of stilts and a long robe, as a first rate giantess, goes to Betsy's head, though in reality she is as quiet as a little lamb.

Thereupon Teddy jumps down and runs a little way before the caravan, and stoops down.

"Jemima," says he to his wife, "no more and no less than a woman. Now, now," says he, as he reaches his infinitely better half preparing to desert Betsy, the mare, "don't let her 'ed go or else she'll be over us, and you'll

make a pretty kettle of fish of it. Yes, it's a woman, and as dead as Queen Anne."

Away lets Jemima go the head of Betsy, for she is a good woman in the main, all but her tongue, and she can be as charitable in the true way as any lady in the land.

Down she plumps by the side of the figure lying in the roadway, and catches up one of the hands, and places her fingers upon the wrist.

"No, Teddy," she says after a pause, "not dead."

"An' *not* far off of it," says Teddy, "or I'm a Dutchman, of which I'm not aweer at present."

"Why, Teddy, Teddy," says Mrs. Naggleton, as she stoops nearer to the quiet figure—"Teddy, what do you make of them things in her ears? And—and look at the rings on her fingers!"

"Why, they're dimonts!" says Teddy, "or I'm a Dutchman, which I'm not aweer on at present."

"I tell you what, Mr. Naggleton; this here's a lady—how came she here?"

"Which," says Mr. Naggleton, "it was better if people thought of lifting other people up and comfiting on 'em, instead of giving mortial lecturs on 'em."

"Suttingly, Teddy," said the lady, who can always be conquered if her kindness of heart be called in question; and, indeed, Teddy knows this well; "suttingly, Teddy."

"Then let me come an' do it," says Teddy, drawing his elbows back. "Stand out of the way."

"You!" says Mrs. Naggleton, "you take a delicut creshure up in *your* harms. No. Strike a light and turn down my bed."

And then Mrs. Naggleton raised the quiet form almost as easily as she would have raised that of a little child, and tramped up the steps with it into the caravan.

A light was soon struck, and then the good-hearted couple had the opportunity of seeing that the young creature, whose life they might possibly be the means of saving, was very young—not more than seventeen—and very beautiful.

Her hair was of a beautiful soft flaxen colour, and her complexion as clear as the noonday light.

"What's to be done now, Jemmy?" says Naggleton.

"Done?—warm a little of our black currant wine—the stove aint out, and then drive on and stop a Charley."

"Which," says the master of the caravan, "a Charley was never no mortial use except to be tossed in a blanket."

"Never you mind that," says Jemima, "you stop a Charley; that's what you've got to do, you know."

The black currant wine was soon heated, and poured into the mouth of the still senseless girl.

The warm liquor caused her to give a sigh as it were of relief, and Jemima immediately afterwards said,

"She draws her breath easier—you drive on easy, too, and mind you stop a Charley."

Very carefully did Mrs. Naggleton tuck up her discovery, and then she sat down patiently waiting for the Charley; in other words, one of the watchmen of those days. A specimen of those antique and utterly useless functionaries was at length met and questioned.

The old watchman came into the caravan, opened his lantern, and peered at the still insensible form.

"Why don't you fetch her to?" asks the Charley.

"'Cos why we can't," says the owner of the caravan, and this seems a sufficiently good reason to the Charley, for he immediately adds, "then take her to the lock-up."

"Why, what's she done?" says Jemima.

"Don't know," says the Charley.

"Then *what* d'ye mean?" asks Teddy, with a kind of property feeling in the young girl.

"Don't know," says the Charley. "Take her to the lock-up—you follow my advice and take her to the Bow Street lock-up—if you don't—*don't*."

Under these circumstances the caravan proprietor says,

"Show us the way," and the Charley answering in the affirmative, he proceeds to do so by calling out to the sleeping population, "Half-past three, and a raw foggy morning."

———

CHAPTER VI.

On rumbled the caravan; Mrs. Naggleton seated with the young girl's hand in hers, and making no more complaints about the jolting of the vehicle.

"Here you are," says the Charley, after they had been rumbling along for some time, and he calls out towards a dark, black-looking building.

His call was answered by a stout, stalwart man, dressed in an odd kind of uniform. He was one of the celebrated Bow-street runners.

"What's up?" this new comer cried; whereupon Mrs. Naggleton immediately treated the official to a chapter on the merits of the case.

"Here, you chaps," said the officer towards the buildings, "lend a hand here."

The next moment the still inanimate form was being carried into the receiving room of the Bow-street lock-up, by several fine, strong men.

A young gentleman was seated near the fire when the group came in. He was so absorbed in his thoughts that he took no notice of the addition to his company, but still gazed into the fire with a despairing look.

"Bring her to the fire," said the officer who had before spoken. "Perhaps the warmth may revive her."

They brought a large cushion from a sofa and laid the beautiful young creature upon it, in the full light of the fire. After a few moments the lips began to move, but still the senses were not there.

"Where do you say you found her, my man?" asked the officer.

"*We* found her," says Mrs. Naggleton, who had no idea of being excluded from her share of the honours—"*we* found her at the end of the Hampstead-road, and just where the houses begin—about a mile and a half away, sir."

As she spoke the stranger started up and looked up at the speaker. He had not noticed the inanimate form.

"And did I understand you to say?" the officer continued, "that she was lying in the road?"

"Yes, right in the middle," says Teddy.

The stranger now roused himself thoroughly, and his eyes fell upon the form at his feet.

"Good heavens!" he cried, "it is the woman, or rather the lady, who spoke to me just before I discovered my loss."

The officer looked sharply at Edgar Trevillian—for it was he, and said "Indeed!"

"Yes," said the young man; "and from the tenor of her expressions I imagined she was deranged."

"I suppose, colonel," the officer continued, "you do not think the young woman stole your pocket-book?"

"Certainly not."

"Then we need not search her," said the officer.

"By no means, on my account," said the young man. "Permit me to add that I should say this is a lady of birth. Her hands are small and obviously not accustomed to work; and if these jewels are real—"

As the young man spoke, he raised one of the powerless hands, and looked upon the rings which encircled the fingers.

"Good Heavens!" he cried, as he started back, and then once more minutely gazed at an embossed gold ring—a coronet, an eagle, and an M—"'tis the seal of a MILRAY!"

The last word seemed to send a magic thrill through the frame of the recumbent figure.

The hands trembled, as did also the eyelids; and the next moment these latter gradually and weakly raised themselves, and allowed the assembled people to see two exquisitely blue eyes.

"The eyes of the Milrays!" said Edgar, to himself; and, indeed, both his eyes and those of the unknown lady were exactly similar in tone.

"Can she be of the family?" Edgar murmured to himself. "The ring helps the supposition to which those eyes give birth."

"Will you speak to her, colonel?" asked the officer.

"Yes," said Edgar.

He then bent over the young girl and said:

"Do not be afraid, you are amongst friends."

Again she started, and then she looked towards the speaker.

Then her entire form trembled, and she raised her beautifully white hands.

"George," she said, "George—not dead—not laid in the cold ground!" and once more she closed her eyes, from which tears were now trickling.

"She is certainly deranged!" said Edgar Trevillian, "and, if I mistake not, a doctor should also be sent for?"

"Certainly, sir," said the head constable, and immediately despatched a messenger for the nearest doctor.

Once more the girl opened her eyes.

"George!" she once more cried, "come to me, come to me!"

"Do you mean me, madam?" asked Edgar, stooping down once more beside the beautiful form.

"Is it you—is it indeed you?" she cried.

"Do you know me?"

"Know you, George?"

"Yes—have you ever seen me before?"

"Seen you before! oh, I must be wandering in my mind! Have I ever seen you before?"

"Yes—where, my poor girl—where—where?"

"Where not?" she cried, suddenly flinging her arms round his neck, "where not? Have I not lived in your love—the love I know you still have for me—have you not?"

"My dear lady, you mistake me for somebody else?"

"Mistake you for somebody else!—can a woman not know the husband of her heart, the father of her child?—no, no, George, do not trifle with me. Lift me up—how came I here?—lift me up, and take me to the home you promised me!"

"My poor girl—my poor girl!" said the young man.

"You need—need *work* no more, and you may live in safety. My jewels were given to me to-night—*to-night.* Oh, little did I think when I escaped, to learn the awful message—little did I think as I put the pearls on that you would be alive to see them. Look!" she continued, "how beautiful they are; those are diamonds—they will bring us enough money to live in peace all our lives. George! George! lift me up, for I am giddy!"

Once more she closed her eyes, and Colonel Edgar Trevillian rose from her side.

"There can be no question of her derangement," he said to the officer, "I never saw her in my life till this evening."

"Humph!" said the officer, looking suspiciously at the young man, who comprehended the officer's doubt in a moment.

"As to my identity," said Colonel Edgar Trevillian, "it can soon be made out by sending a man down with me to the town, where my ship lies ready to drop down with the tide in about a couple of hours."

"Of course, colonel, I can do that," said the officer, striking his keys upon the desk.

"And I presume you believe me when I say that I do not know this lady?"

"I may believe you if I choose," says the officer.

Here Mrs. Naggleton struck in—"She's opening her eyes again, poor dear."

As for Naggleton himself he could offer no comment upon his better half's report, for he had gone to look after "Betsy."

"That I can give a guess at her name," said the colonel, "I will not deny—and here I give it you—but it is merely a guess, and I candidly tell you only made upon the coincidence I find in the colour of her eyes and a ring she wears on her finger."

The colonel then gave a card to the officer, on which he had written these words,—"The Earl of Milray."

"And what am I do with this, colonel?" asked the officer.

"Take it to the earl's residence, and state your case, my man," said Edgar. "I can say no more; if the earl cannot comprehend you my supposition is a wrong one."

"I shall certainly send to the earl's," said the officer.

"And now I must think of departing," said the young man. "Doubtless my regiment is wondering where its colonel can be; I should have been on board last night. The regiment is bound for Spain. I suppose, sir, that I can do no more than I have done towards the recovery of my papers and pocket-book?"

"Rely upon it, colonel, all will be done that can be."

"Good day—I thank you. I can be of no service to this poor girl, or I would gladly aid her. Good day."

But Edgar did not say that he was angry with the poor girl, as the coincidences of the ring and the colour of her eyes suggested to him the supposition that she might be Lady Milly Milray, the sister of his detested cousin, who denied his (Edgar's) legitimacy; who defied and derided him, and who wore the coronet the colonel himself ought to have possessed.

"Good day," he once more said, and was going out at the door, when a piercing shriek arrested his steps.

The young lady had turned towards him, and was gazing with horror-stricken eyes upon him.

"Going!—and without me?"

He turned.

"What can I do for thee?" he asked.

"Where is your love for me?" she asked, wringing her hands. "Am not I always the same to thee? am I not thy *wife?*"

"*Wife!*"

"Yes—thy loving, loving wife!"

He came back to her side.

"Now look me in the face," he said. "Gather your senses together, and look me in the face."

"Yes—yes—yes, George?" she said, eagerly.

"Now, tell me. Did you ever see me before?"

"Oh, George, what have I done to deserve this? what have I done?"

"Great Powers," cried the young man, "am *I* myself mad?"

"I have never wavered in my affection," she continued; "never for one moment. If I did not leave my brother's home——"

"Your brother's!" he said, with a start.

"Thou knowest it—thou knowest it—it was because you were too poor to keep me. If I waited, it was to get these jewels—which are my own—which are my own. Ah! they came too late, since I did not have them till thou—thou wast driven to sin. Oh! when they would have slain thee they little thought that thou wast committing a crime for thy wife's sake!"

"I commit a crime?" said Edgar.

"Ah! thou mayst well shudder, dear, for thou art no criminal; the one fault nearly destroyed thee. How didst thou escape? Where are we?"

Edgar looked at her for a moment, and then said—"Does *he* know where you are?"

"My brother, dear, do you mean?"

"Yes."

"No—no. Oh, you know me again now—I am thy wife Milly—thy wife."

"Yes—yes—yes," he said, hurriedly. "Kiss me and let me go."

"Where—where; not without me, dear?"

"I am only going to—to find a coach to take thee home."

"Oh! I am strong enough to walk,—see here," and she tried to raise herself, but she fell back powerlessly.

As she did so a neighbouring clock rung out the hour—*four*!

"Merciful power!" said the colonel; "I have hardly time to reach the boat."

"Good bye, my poor girl," he said, kissing the half-fainting figure. "I wish thee better."

And breaking away from the frantic embraces of the poor girl, he ran from the office.

With awful strength the stranger rose from the ground, shrieking "George, come back to me. Help—stay him—he is my husband. George—George."

She beat her way past the strong Mrs. Naggleton, who vainly tried to calm her with such expressions as "There's a dear!" "Take it easy." "Let him go if he like—he is not worth looking after," &c., &c.—and she staggered to the door.

"George," she cried again, "I shall be alone—all alone in the world!"

She stopped for a moment and then cried—

"Gone—gone! He has deserted me!"

Again she would have fallen to the ground—but that the showman's wife caught the poor sufferer back to her couch beside the fire.

At the moment the doctor entered.

He went straight up to the patient, and kneeling down, started.

"How come this woman here?"

Mrs. Naggleton told the poor creature's tale in a few rapid words.

"Where is the man?" he asked.

"Gone," said the officer on duty.

"Then send for him back," said the doctor. "I have no doubt this poor's creature's tale is true."

"Send for him—upon what charge, said the officer, authoritatively.

"One of nature and duty,' said the doctor. "This poor girl is about to become a mother."

CHAPTER VII.

THE reader must now be transported to a magnificent mansion in the most superb part of London, and into a morning room, where the great Earl of Milray is being prepared to walk in Pall Mall.

The room was of the most costly character. A rich brocade of green and gold covered the walls; the ceiling was a perfect coruscation of splendid paintings, and the floor was covered with a dark claret carpet of a peculiar pile velvet very little known in England at that day, and in which the foot sunk to the depth of an inch.

The furniture was of white and gold, the coverings of the chairs and couches being of a delicate green satin, embroidered with the most exquisite groups of roses and violets.

The curtains were of lace, which kept out the glare of day from this superb chamber, which was simple, when compared with many of the drawing-rooms in the mansion; and these curtains were looped up with cord of gold. The mantel-piece was of jasper, enriched with emeralds and pearls, which jewels were set in the marble with consummate taste and beauty.

Folding doors opening into the interior apartments revealed a capacious picture gallery. Pendant from its walls hung numerous family likenesses of the noble earl's ancestors, and not the least conspicuous amongst which was a full length by Lely of Sir Hercules Milray, Bart., in a suit of mail, and attended by a poor dependent, his cousin, Keziah Milray, a jester or Court fool of that time. *Apropos* of this calling, many a day has now elapsed since Court or hall has resounded with the noisy laughter which their rude witticisms and uncouth raillery were wont to provoke. The world has grown wiser, if not better, than it was when motley was proclaimed "the only wear." The fool, whether court or domestic is defunct, and his place in society is not quite supplied even by the most celebrated of our stage clowns. True it is the punster is abroad, but though he wear motley in his brain, the fear of "twelve paces" makes him exercise his vocation gingerly; and the vices and follies of his hearers, are not the object against which he directs his never-ceasing double-shotted batteries. It was not so, however, with the jesters of the olden time; if they were not the equals of the after race of wits, in intellect, they were assuredly their superiors in manliness and honesty. To return to the earl's chamber.

In various parts of the room were groups of growing flowers, most of them tropical, and just brought from the conservatory. Many of them exhaled an exquisite perfume, which added another charm to this splendid chamber, which was the Earl of Milray's dressing-room.

Seated before the toilet-table, which was covered with rich lace, was the earl himself, examining his face in the toilette-glass, on each side of which was a cluster of transparent wax candles, ready to be lighted at night time, when the earl would "dress" for the opera and ball.

The noble earl was sipping chocolate from a china receptacle little larger than an egg-cup, while his valet was powdering and dressing his hair.

The earl was a man of about thirty years of age. He was pale and repulsive looking from dissipation, but was not naturally a bad-looking man, but the speciality of the Milray family—the bright blue eyes—were wanting in him ; his eyes were of a dark grey.

The valet was a quick, dapper little Frenchman, who had served various English noblemen in that capacity for thirty years of his life, ten of which he had passed with the earl of whom we are speaking. He had lived long enough in England to comprehend English, and to speak it—after a style. He was deep in the confidence of the earl, and indeed, was more of a companion to his lordship than a valet. He knew all his master's outgoings and ingoings, and there were not wanting people who said that each man could hang the other if they both chose to turn king's evidence.

As they were so they appeared on the morning to which we refer.

"Jules, you have something to say to me?" said the earl, looking up.

"*Oui*, milord."

"Well, then, speak out; you are not naturally chary of your words."

"Certain not, milord—and milord sall know know all ; milord knows my heart is to his service."

"Yes—yes, Jules, we know all about that; what have you to say?"

"The Lady Milly——"

"My sister—what of her?"

"She has left de house."

"My sister left my house!'

"Yes ; she have not return from de ball, milord, of last night."

"Why, where can she be?"

"Sall I make inquiries, my lord?"

"Yes ; yet doubtless she is at her aunt's."

"No, milord,'' said the Frenchman, smiling oddly—"she is not to her aunt. I haf been to Lady Charlotte, and she is not there."

"You know more of this than you have yet told me."

"*Oui*, milord."

"Then speak out."

"Milord, her ladyship puts on all her jewels, dat she haf receive from de bankers, to go to de ball."

"Yes, I bade her do so."

"*Certainement*, milord. And she go to de ball—but that is not all. I also—I go to de ball—dat is de outside of de ball, and I see what I see."

"Yes—yes ; go on."

"I see her ladyship go to her carriage, and then leave him for a hackney coche, and tell de coachman to drive on. Dat is all *I* know."

But you know more, sir—go on, I say."

"Dis morning I rise me early, an I go down

to de street for a little promenade, when I see one—what you call him—one runner of the Bow-street, wid a card in hiꜰ hand. He beckon to me and he say, dis is the Earl of Milray, is it not? I say yes ; and den he says can I see him. An I say his lordship is to de sleep, but if him come at eleven of de clock he *may* perhaps see de earl. *An*,'' continues the valet, "*if your lordship will do me the honour to look from de window* you sall see the beautiful officer on de wait!"

The earl looked rapidly through the window, and turned pale as he saw the uniform of the officer of justice.

"Why sall you haf fear, milord?" asks the valet. "If he come for de affaire of de poor gal Marie, or of the young squire at the Cocoa Tree, (a) or de duel wid Sir James, he would not wait for your lordship *outside*."

"True—true, call him in."

Within a few moments the officer of justice entered the splendid room in which the earl was seated.

"Good morning, my man ; do you want to see me?"

"Yes, my lord," said the man, plainly. "A young woman was brought to the Bow-street station last night, and supposed to be dying. And she *did* die this morning about five, but not before she had given birth to a female child. A gentleman was in the station-room when this young woman was brought in, and then she would have it that he was her husband ; but you see, poor thing, she was raving. *He* gave us this card, and said perhaps your lordship might feel interested in the young woman.

"*I*?" said the earl, in a vacant manner, as though he would say, "What have *I* to do with the matter ;" but he did not know that the sharp detective officer had marked the reflection of his face in the glass, before which his lordship was seated. The Earl of Milray did not know that the common officer had marked his face covered first with consternation and then with rage.

"*I*?" said the earl a second time.

"Oh! my lord," said the officer, "of course I merely bring the message to your lordship. And that is all I have to do—good morning, my lord."

"Good morning, officer," said the noble. "There is some mistake somewhere. *I* know nothing of the young woman—but I may send some one round in the course of the day. I suppose the body will not be buried in the course of the day?"

"Oh no, my lord."

"And pray what has become of the poor creature's child. I think you ꜱaid she gave birth to a child?"

"Yes, my lord ; a little girl."

"Oh, indeed—what have they done with the child?"

(a) A gaming-house where young country "bloods' were only too frequently fleeced of entire fortunes in a single evening.

"It is being taken care off by some show folks, my lord, who found the mother."

"Where did they find her?"

"Close in to town, my lord, and in the Hampstead Road."

Again the officer saw a spasm cross the face of the earl, but then next moment the noble said,

"Oh, the Hampstead Road. Very odd. Good day, officer, I may send round in the course of the day."

"Good day, my lord."

The officer was almost past the door when the earl called after him.

"Oh, by the bye, officer, what kind of a woman was she?"

"Well, we think as how she was a playactor by her dress, my lord."

"Oh! Any money—anything found upon her."

"Not a penny piece, my lord—not a farthing."

"Indeed!—good day, officer. It's very odd the stranger should have put *my* name on his preposterous card. However, I'm curious in the matter. I'll send round in the course of the day. Show the door, Jules."

Once more the officer turned his back upon the room, and again the earl began sipping his chocolate.

No sooner, however, had the door closed upon the officer than the cup fell from the noble's hand, and he clasped his forehead wildly.

"I am ruined!" he muttered, "if this woman is Milly. The family is disgraced—Milly a mother and unmarried. What shall I do—what can be done? And to think that if it is she that she had all her jewels on; they are worth £60,000 at least, and I hoped to raise money on them—my only chance—money and name both gone, or at least one must be lost. If it is she, and if her jewels are upon her, and if I claim her body, how can I explain the matter to the world, for it will be in all the papers. Again, if I do not acknowledge the body I lose the jewels, and with them I lose the money by which I could have staved off my creditors till I could have married the rich city heiress."

As he thus spoke aloud Jules stood at his elbow.

"Milord!"

"Jules!—are you there?"

"*Oui*, milord."

"What do you think had best be done?"

"Milord is frightened at a trifle; if it *is* her ladyship, and if de jewels be wid her, which I mosh doubt, claim her—you sall find a tale for de world and de heiress—but if de jewels are not dere we will say we do not know de poor body, and we will leave it wid de watch."

"Good; go you yourself, Jules."

Within an hour the French valet had reached the station-house; he was soon shown the body of the beautiful sufferer who had laid before the fire on the previous night, who had called so agonizingly after Edgar Trevillian.

He saw in a moment that it was his master's sister, the Lady Milly Milray.

"Is that how you found her?" asked the valet.

"Just so," said the officer, who somehow had taken a rooted dislike to this Frenchy, "you don't suppose, do you, as we'd change her?"

"She don't look as though she was worth much."

"No, she don't—and I suppose she wasn't," says the officer, "or she'd have had a house, and not been a wanderin' in the streets in the middle of the night."

"Ah," says the Frenchman, "she poor ting is at rest: good day, monsieur—my good sire bon jour. I know nosing of de poor gal, nosing whatever."

And raising his hat the Frenchman left the office.

"Poor thing!" said the compassionate officer, "I doubt if she'll have any followers beyond the poor show folk, unless indeed as I walk behind her."

The French valet went home and had an interview with his master.

"What sall you do now, milord?"

"I do not know; it is clear the jewels were stolen from her. Curse on my ill luck," said the earl, after conversing with his factotum for some time.

"Sall I advise to your lordship?"

"Go on," said the earl.

"Den you sall say to de world dat de Lady Milly has set out for Scotland to visit de Lady Elizabet, her aunt—*dat good woman*, to which you sall tell de truth, and add dat she sall tell de world in one little time dat de poor young lady had fallen over de cliff into de sea. Oh, do not start, de Lady Elizabet is much proud, and she will do dis for *de honour of de family*."

"You are right, Jules," said the earl, "you're always right."

And so the earl told the good company he met at the grand houses that night, that his sister had left London for Scotland, on a visit to Lady Elizabeth Milray; and so Lady Milly Milray's sudden disappearance was accounted for.

Of course the letter had been written to Lady Elizabeth, and then the earl tried to forget the mortification of the morning at the gaming-table, which had been his curse through his life, and which had destroyed whatever good and noble qualities he once had.

It was late at night, and the earl was just stepping into his sedan-chair, (a) in order to be carried home, when a letter was put into his hand.

He did not stop to open it.

But when he reached home he remembered the missive, and opening it he read these words—

"MY LORD, or rather SIR, for you are the Earl no longer, I have now the proofs of my legitimacy. I am my father's rightful heir. My father was your father's elder brother. The earldom and its riches are mine—be prepared to yield them up to me.   MILRAY.
Known as Edgar Trevillian."

(a) The "sedan-chair," as need hardly be told, was the common mode of conveyance, in the days of which we write. It was carried on poles by two men.

CHAPTER VIII.

"Now," said Mrs. Naggleton, as she was nursing the poor little mite of humanity which had just come into the world—"now, I have something to live for, and the carrywan may be a palace—that's a house rather; an' it's many a palace as ain't a house."

"Home, home, sweet home! I says ditter to that," says Naggleton himself.

Mr. and Mrs. Naggleton were seated in a little inn-parlour in Drury Lane, near the station, and very happy they looked. If the baby had been Mrs. Naggleton's own—at the same time being Mr. Naggleton's own—they could not have looked much happier.

"What a beauty she will make," says Mrs. Naggleton, tossing the child up and down, but this was only imagination on the show-woman's—we beg pardon, the show lady's—part; for, of course, the future of the baby could not be judged by its present tumbled condition, but

then ladies always know best; and perhaps Mrs. Naggleton judged from the beauty of the mother.

"Poor thing!" says Mrs. Naggleton, "really, when I saw her push her lovely infant—chucksy, chucksy—(this was to the lovely infant) away from her, I thought my heart it would a bust!"

"Never!" says Naggleton, "a good woman's heart don't bust, Jemima; but sometimes it biles over."

"Do it," returned Mrs. Naggleton, "ah, poor thing, to think how she should die and never know her dear daughter; oh, when she pushed the dear away from her I really did think my heart 'ud a bust!"

"Bile over, Jenny!" says Naggleton, cocking his eye and pointing with his pipe.

"As you like, my lad," said Mrs. Naggleton, with a little air of vexation, "but anyhow, done something. Come in!"

"This last expression was adapted to the hearing of some one who had knocked at the

3

door with the unkind importance of a man who meant to knock out a pannel or two with his knuckles.

"Hopen for me," said a voice.

Naggleton dropped his pipe, rose from his chair, and opened the door.

His better-half immediately saw him duck his beard in the most impressive manner. The next moment he turned round and remarked—

"Mrs. Naggleton, my dear, here's a general."

"What do yer mean by general?" said a loud voice, and into the room, and following Mr. Naggleton, came a man mountain.

Mrs. Naggleton was so much surprised that she rose to her feet, keeping however fast hold of the baby.

"What's your name?" asked the general.

This was a coolness Mrs. Naggleton would not endure. She had faced too many crowds at fairs, been on stilts too many times in her life, to be taken aback, even by a general; and she thought he was a general, for he wore a cocked-hat with gold lace, and a gold-laced coat; and now she felt all the bigger for the baby, so she said "What's that to you?"

"It's a good deal for the parish erthorities," said the general.

"Is it, indeed," said Mrs. N., "if some people wasn't fools they'd ask another fool what he meant by it."

Naggleton murmured indistinctly. A quick-eared person, had he been present, might have sworn he said "Kim up, Betsy!" but no quick-eared person was present.

As for the general, he no sooner heard the word fool, than with fatal facility applying it to himself, he said: "Mam—do you know who I am?"

Mrs. Naggleton immediately remarked—"Don't know—don't care."

"Mam, I am the hemmissery of the parish erthorities."

"An' what's that?"

"I'M THE BEADLE!"

Mrs. Naggleton was somehow impressed with this announcement. "Lor, sir, then pray sit down."

"Do—take a cheer," said Naggleton, meaning not applause, but a stool with a back to it—generally called a chair—"an' what will you take with it?"

"Well—no more sarce; when yer sarcy to the parish beadles, yer sarcy to the parish erthorities!"

"Will yer take it hot, sir?" asked Naggleton.

"And strong," says the beadle; and being mollified, he takes off his cocked-hat.

Somehow when his cocked-hat is off, the beadle don't look half such an important man as he was before; but then he looks a great deal more *like* a man.

The bell was soon rung, the something hot was soon in the beadle's hand, and then he *winked*—yes, the beadle actually winked.

Now, how was it that Mrs. Naggleton who was not afraid of the visitor when she mistook him in the dark for a general, was quite polite to him when he announced himself to be the beadle, attached to the "parish erthorities?"

The fact is, that the people at the station, whence the body of the poor woman had been taken to the workhouse, had told Mrs. Naggleton, when she proposed to "mother the little 'un," as she described it—in other words had offered herself as a large-hearted, Christian woman, who would watch over the new-born orphan like a mother—had told Mrs. Naggleton that she could do nothing of the kind till the Board had sat on the baby.

It was when she heard this, that Mrs. Naggleton nobly returned, "Then I don't think the dear baby 'ull want me after they've done it, for the board 'ull squeeze all the life out of it."

Brought up short for this irreverence, Mrs. Naggleton was given to understand the Board was not wooden, but composed of men. Here-upon, Mrs. Naggleton said she begged pardon, and it didn't much matter—she meant what she said didn't much matter—but really her words had another meaning; because, some people are of opinion that a parish Board *is* a wooden affair—some people have gone as far as to say stone-hearted; and one or two persons have put it on record that after their cases had been sat upon by this said Board, they have hardly been able to live after the operation.

So Mrs. Naggleton was, perhaps, nearer right than she thought, when she mistook a board of men for a deal of boards altogether.

The beadle having taken a pull at his glass, with one eye shut and the other on the baby, as though so far it was his property, and the eye of a parish authority must be upon it, thus spoke:—

"The board is a sitting."

"Is it indeed, sir," says Mrs. Naggleton, with an air of extreme interest.

"And you, mam, with the kid, must come afore the Board."

"Must I indeed, sir?" added Mrs. Naggleton, with still more interest.

"I say, sir," says Naggleton, "do you think the Board will let us take the poor little 'un?"

Now the beadle knew perfectly well that the Board was only too heartily glad of getting rid of the poverty-stricken orphans which came on their table, so to speak; but the beadle was a parish authority, so he was not going to commit himself, and he answered: "A Board is a Board—kim along."

Mrs. Naggleton was soon in her cloak and hood, and away she stalked by the side of the "general," who, once more in his hat, excited various passers-by with an insane desire to trip him up into the mud—cocked hat and all; people always did hate beadles.

The Board was not far off, and were having an evening meal, or rather they had come in the morning and had dinner (at the expense of the parish, only it was not with the paupers), then they had squabbled with each other and bullied a lot of old paupers.

Then they had had tea (also at the expense

of the parish), and now they were squabbling before they went to supper, which was also to be at the expense of the parish; and as there were a score of them, and as they met once a week, somebody had sworn they cost the parish almost as much as the paupers. But the Board was too deaf to hear them.

When Mr. and Mrs. Naggleton arrived, baby included, the beadle heralded them in as though he did not know what gin at Mrs. Naggleton's expense might be.

"Yere is the parties," said he.

Whereupon all the Board looked at the "parties," as though they had been trying to commit a burglary at the Bank of England.

Says the chairman to Naggleton, "Step this way, my fine man."

Whereon *Mrs.* Naggleton steps forward with the tramp of a grenadier.

"Oh!" says the chairman, "you're Naggleton, are you?"

And at this very faint joke the Board laugh on and off for about a quarter of an hour.

"Anyhow, yere's the baby," says Jemima.

"And a remarkably fine' un," says Naggleton.

"Not *yours*, I suppose," says the chairman to the showman, who is completely shut up by this remark, and the immense laugh which followed it.

As for Mrs. Naggleton, who never allows anybody to bully her "old man," except herself, she looked at the baby with an air of as much as "if it warnt a baby you'd get it at once."

"Ah!" says the chairman, "and what is it?"

"A gal!" says Mrs. Naggleton.

"What name?" says the chairman.

"No name!" says Mrs. Naggleton.

"She must have one," says the chairman.

"So she shall," said Naggleton.

"Hold you tongue," says the chairman.

"Hold your tongue," immediately repeats the beadle.

"And so you want to keep him," says the chairman to Mrs. Naggleton.

"Naggleton," says that man's wife of his bosom, "speak up."

"Gennelmen all," says Naggleton, looking at the Board—"gennelmen all, though *I* ar'nt a gennelman *at* all, still I'm a man, and a man *is* a man, which—wherefore—and that is to say, if you think you can do better with her, take— I don't mean my Jemima, I mean the baby— if you *don't* think yer can't do better with her, *don't* take. Give her to us, an we'll make a woman of her—that's all."

"Hum!" says the chairman, seriously, thought he knows this is a blessed good riddance of a parish—"hum!—what are you, my man?"

"A showman."

"What's that?"

"The Halbanian, the serpent, the harmadiller, and Mrs. N. on stilts, with the dwarf, when the happence *won't* come in."

"Will you do your duty by it, sir?" says the chairman.

"Shelf me—that is, I will," says Naggleton.

"Well, gentlemen, what do you say?" asks the chairman, looking up and down the Board, all of whom look serious, though they knew, and the chairman knows they know, that it's all humbug, and they've been determined all along to pack the poor little new comer off with the showman, whether he's good, bad, or indifferent.

A little man rises to his little legs.

He was a man considerably below the ordinary size of any individual aspiring to be called a man; and yet he was apparently between forty and fifty years of age. His face was of a copper complexion, and garnished with a pair of skeleton whispers; for, so small amount of them remained on either cheek, that like his few and straggling locks of hair, they seemed to have sustained some injury from recent feminine attacks upon his scalp. His eyes, too, had all the restless activity of a ferret's, and his fromontory of a chin was sustained by a neckcloth of sufficient dimensions to have encircled the entire board. Thumping the baize before him with the palm of his right hand, thus spoke the parish Cicero—

"Mr. Chairman," says he, "I approve of this transfer of said infant on one condition. I am very fond of Skakespeare. I go to see Mr. Garrick when I can. I agree if this man will call the infant Perdita. You know the young female body that is found in Shakespeare was called Perdita ——"

"Hear—hear," says the Board, who always applauded one another—in public.

"Very good," says the chairman. "You agree to this, Naggleton?"

"Oh, yes," says Naggleton; "only we did think of calling her Sally; but, however, if the honourable gennelmen likes we'll call her Pudditer."

"Very well," says the chairman. "Now who was the mother."

A pause—no answer.

At last Naggleton says: "Sir, yer know I think she was a play-actor—'cos why?—her dress was like a play-actor's, and she had a lot o' glass jewels."

Here Mrs. Naggleton struck in, and gave a dozen chapters in no time. The chairman at last fetched her up short—his right hand neighbour having whispered to him that the beef would be over-done, and he added—

"Mr. Naggleton and Mrs. Naggleton, the Board hand over to you the infant, which will be entered in our books as Perdita Naggleton. As to the clothes and imitation jewels found on the mother, we give them to you. Gentlemen, I think the parties can retire.

Which they do, and heartily glad to do so.

"That's a Board is it?" says Naggleton, and the beadle, hopeful of more gin, takes off his hat, smiles, and says: "Yes, that there's the hessence of the perochial erthorities."

Straight to the public-house went Mr. and Mrs. Naggleton and Perdita, as we will now call her. Then Mr. and Mrs. Naggleton went to the station, always accompanied by the beadle. As they went along Mrs. Naggleton bought a very strong wooden box.

"My love," says Naggleton, "what's that for?"

"To put Pudditer's things in.

"Won't they go in yours?"

"No; they're not goin' with us."

"Not a-goin' with us!"

"No."

"Well, but when Pudditer dances at the fairs wouldn't they look well on her?"

"Then we can fetch 'em," says Mrs. Naggleton. "Into this ere box they goes, and there they stops."

"Why," says Naggleton, "you couldn't be more careful of 'em though they was gold."

"So they are—to Pudditer."

"What do you mean?"

"Why, I means as they may some day help to find out her mother; and so ain't they like real jewels?"

"What a 'ed yours is!" says Naggleton.

And thereupon Mrs. Naggleton sails along like a queen.

Arrived at the station, the beadle soon causes the transfer of the poor dead woman's clothes and jewels to the show people; and thereupon Mrs. Naggleton folds 'em up and locks the box. Then she hands the whole to the officer.

"What for?" says he.

"Henter 'em," says Mrs. Naggleton, "and take care of 'em; and you'll do yourself no 'arm."

"All right, marm," says the officer. "I see —identification—you're the right sort, you are; if all mothers was like you there wouldn't be many fools in the world."

"Hurray!" says Naggleton.

"And now we're off," says Mrs. Naggleton to the officer. "Nag and I have paid the undertaker to bury the poor thing—and you jest see he does it proper. We can't stop; Hoggleton fair wants us."

"What! have you paid the berryin'?" asked the officer.

"Yes, o' course," says Naggleton—"you don't suppose as how we could look our Puddy in the face if we had left her mother on the parish. Come along, Mrs. Naggey, or Betsy 'ull bust herself with wonder as to where iver we's got to."

And away went good Mr. and Mrs. Naggleton.

CHAPTER IX.

OUR story must now be carried to a charming little cottage on the south side of the Thames. It was a little, even a tiny house; but it was worth a palace—worth far more than the grand gorgeous palace in which the Earl of Milray lived.

There was but one parlour, but it was so neat, so charming, so "homely," that it was worth all the palaces in the world.

The proprietor of this charming little spot, which stood in its own grounds, was a Mr. Marlow, a gentleman possessed of not much property, but quite enough to keep the wolf from the door of this delightful residence.

His family was not large. One sweet daughter was all he had.

Edith Marlowe was a lovely creature. She was not more than eighteen, and had she been in the world, she would have had hearts beating for her in many a good cavalier's breast; but she was out of the world; her father's house was her universe. She rarely, if ever, passed beyond its walls, and few indeed saw the yellow hair she took such pains to braid; few saw the beautiful brown eyes, which were as lovely as may be found in the wide world.

Mr. Marlowe was a harsh man. He had been ill used in the world, and men who have been thus ill used do not easily forgive. He firmly believed his daughter was better hidden from the world than in it, and so he kept her in his beautiful cottage, and little dreamed she was known to any man who would willingly make her his wife—how little did he dream that she was a wife!

It was a few days after Mrs. Naggleton had faced the board of guardians, that Mr. Marlowe found his daughter cast upon the ground and heavily weeping.

"Edith!"

"Father!" are you here?"

"Yes—you are weeping."

"No——"

Mr. Marlow turned red. If there was one thing he hated more than another it was a lie.

"My dear," he continued, but his voice was far from gentle, "You have a secret from me. Tell it me."

"A secret?"

"Yes, I am sure of this. Tell it me."

"Oh, no—no—no, dear father! I confess I have a secret. I confess I have been weeping; but do not ask me why; do not ask me to tell you that secret."

She flung herself upon the ground, clasped his knees, and looked even still more beautiful than she usually looked, but it did not change her father's countenance one fraction.

"Edith, I bid you tell me this secret."

"I—I cannot."

"Now listen—if you tell me now, I swear to you upon the honour of a man, that, whatever it may be, I will forgive you. I will, upon my hopes of life!"

She hesitated for a moment, and then under her breath she said, "Edgar."

"You do not speak," the father continued.

"I—I must not tell you."

"I warn you once more. Tell me now, and I forgive you all; do not tell me, and beware of me. I have watched you now for weeks; that is I have watched you when in my presence; I have been too proud to spy upon your actions, or set a spy to watch them, but I have seen that you are not yourself, that you are changed. I know not how—I cannot tell how, but you are changed. Now will you tell me your secret?"

"If I might only tell him!" she said to herself—"if I might only tell him! but my oath—my oath!"

"Well?" asked the father, once more.

"I—I cannot."

"Very well; your perverseness be on your own head. I have been merciful—for I feared my mercy would have to be exercised—and you have rejected me. Whatever happens, remember you have only yourself to blame."

He turned upon his heel and entered the house, leaving the poor girl on the ground as he had found her.

"If I might but tell him!—but my oath!" she murmured.

She lay upon the grass till the night came, and then rising, moved towards the house.

She went straight to her little room, and the first thing she saw was a small strip of paper on the table, with the words on it—"I *will* learn your secret."

"I have waited four days for his letter," she said, slowly. "When will it come. How dare I tell my father that I am married—that I am the wife of Edgar Trevillian; that—that—"

The night passed wearily, but day came at last, and the poor girl was looking from the window, when she saw a coach drawn up before the door, and a dark, eager-looking woman descended from it.

She then saw her father leave the cottage and meet the woman half way towards the house.

They entered it together.

Within a very short time she was summoned to her father's presence.

"Edith, I give you one chance more; what is your secret."

"Dear father, I would tell you but I may not."

"Why?"

"I cannot even tell you why I may not."

"Then listen to me. The woman who is just come is a woman whom I set to learn your secret: she will learn it, and then, if it anger me, you are lost. Once more, will you confide in me?"

"Dear—dear father, I would, but I may not."

"Then look to yourself."

The angry father stole from the room, and the poor girl heard him descending the stairs with heavy strides.

That same evening a letter arrived for the poor girl. The spy took it; but instead of handing it to Edith, she sought out the master of the house.

"A letter," she said, "for *her*."

The father looked angrily for a moment, then said: "I will learn this secret by no unfair means—least of all by opening my daughter's letters."

The woman was turning away, when Mr. Marlowe stopped her.

"By the bye, you have not told me your name."

"Death!" said the woman, coldly.

"Death?"

"Yes. Do you find an odd sound in the name?"

"It is not a usual one."

"It is mine," said the woman, "and I go by it."

"But you have another name—a Christian name."

"I have."

"What is it?"

"I shall not tell you, sir."

"Why not, woman; who are you?"

"Was it part of my contract that I should tell my name—and who I am? That has nought to do with my business here. You came to the lock-up house and asked for a woman who could *watch* for you. They call me Death in the lock-up; and you must call me by that or none."

As the woman stood she was awful to contemplate. That she *had* been handsome, and not long before, was evident. She could not have been more than twenty-five—her hand proved that; and yet she had many grey hairs, and her face was hard and stern. She was a dark woman—her eyes were piercing and profound; and, as she spoke, her nostrils dilated like those of a tigress when about to spring upon the bone her keeper is holding without the bars of her cage. Her hands, too, contracted as she uttered her words, as though it clenched and strangled them for daring to pass her mouth.

"You are a strange woman," said Mr. Marlowe.

"I know it."

"You have suffered—Death."

"I have suffered worse than death," she returned, perverting the meaning of her master's sentence.

"How?"

"That is not *your* business," she fiercely returned. "Your business is your daughter's secret. I will soon find it out. I think I know it already."

"Already!"

"Yes; I'm sure I shall know it if I open this letter."

She had her hand upon the seal, but with a cry Mr. Marlowe stopped her—"I am an honest man. I will *not* learn my daughter's secret by any such base means."

"Bah! if you would learn secrets, you must not hesitate at the road to them. Why are you looking so hard at me?"

"Will you tell me your history, Death?"

"Death is my history, and hate and revenge; and I will have it. My life has been ruined—I will ruin *his*."

"*His!*—then you hate some man," said Mr. Marlowe.

"All women are too weak for *me* to hate either of them. I despise women."

"Ah!" said Marlowe; "I see—you have been ruined by some scoundrel."

"I did not say so," she returned, fiercely—

"I did not say so. But I say this: I hate a certain man. Let him hide himself from me—let him defy me as he likes, I will destroy him—"

"You will *kill* him?"

"No—no—no—no. I will see him hanged. I will drag him in the net, laugh at him when he is in its meshes, and tell him, as he ascends the scaffold, at least *one* woman knew how to repay ill for ill, and say to him ' Death is with you !' "

As she spoke she raised her right hand, and so awfully clenched that Marlowe saw the blood spurt from the incisions her nails had made.

"Well, what shall I do," she continued, after a pause. " I am a woman hunter down of men. I dress in all disguises, and go amid all haunts and men to find *him*—and I shall. You came to the lock-up, and engaged me on your miserable business. Bah ! I will find out the girl's secret before to-morrow morning."

"Take that letter to her, Death !"

"As sure as death," the woman returned, and without a word more she left the room.

She found Edith seated in her little room, her face buried in her hands, and her beautiful golden hair sweeping down her fair shoulders.

"A letter !"

And before the poor girl knew anybody was in the room—so softly had Death, as the woman called herself, entered the apartment – the letter was cast into her lap and the woman was gone.

A moment or so and the room was lit up by a beautiful little china lamp, which showed a lovely room with all pink and white hangings—the very room for a pure, spotless girl.

Another moment and the seal was broken. The letter contained only a few words—they were soon read.

"My own—my wife !—I could not dare tell you when I last saw you that I might have to leave England for a few months—not more—when I can *honourably* quit the army. Alas ! I did hope to give you great good news, but we must once more abandon ourselves to hope. You know, I have often told you I am the Earl of Milray. Only this very day on the night of which I write, did I find the proofs of my earldom ; and now—now, when I thought to be within the reach of my most ambitious hopes, I am lost ! My own—my wife, had I not *lost* the packet, by its value I could have honourably escaped from joining in this expedition upon which we are bound. I *lost* them, and I must quit now. Fool that I was to lose them ! But, no matter, I have given instructions to find them, and let us hope they are not irrevocably lost. And now, my own, let me release you from the oath you forced me to accept from you—that you would never tell your father you were my wife till I gave you leave—I do, I bid you, if I may dare bid you ; I say, I bid you tell him you are my own. I think we were wrong from the first not to tell him ; he would have forgiven us. If I *could*

not have proved myself the legitimate son of my father and mother, depend upon it he would have pardoned us. Good bye, my love ; a few months, and we meet never to part again.

                              EDGAR TREVILLIAN.

The paper fell from her hand.

"It has been written three days !" she said, "three whole days ; oh, why did it not arrive before ?—but a few hours ago even ?—and then, without breaking my oath, I could have told my father that I was a wife ! Now—now, who knows how he may treat me ! Oh, had it come but an hour ago !"

As she spoke her attention was called by an extra lightness in the room. The flicker became greater, and looking about her, she found that the letter had fluttered into the coals and was burnt to tinder.

She flung herself down upon the rug and wept heavily. "He's gone—he's gone !" she sobbed, " gone—perhaps I may never see him more ; and even his last letter is a thing of the past !"

A long while she lay on the ground near the fire; at last she rose and moved towards the door, walking stealthily and as though afraid of her own steps.

It was midnight.

"No one is moving in the house," she murmured, "not a soul ; then I may continue my poor work : let me lock the door."

She did so, and took the key from the lock and laid it on one side.

Then she took a heavy shawl, and pinned it across the window so that no light should show through the muslin blind. Next she turned down the lamp and placed a large shade over it.

All these preparations now completed, the room looked almost in perfect darkness, except the small spot illuminated by the feeble light yielded by the lamp.

Then still creeping as though afraid of her shadow, the poor girl went to one corner of the room, opened a heavy press, and brought from it a little packet of fine white cambric.

This was all the secret, but one of which she was heartily in dread !

The cambric was in little shreds and patches, and was not much to look at ; yet she kissed them as she moved them from their resting-place.

Slowly she crept back to the table, and then began her work.

Reader, can you comprehend a poor woman making furtively the clothes of the child who will be her first-born, and of whose existence she dare not speak. Imagine the love, and fear, and hope, and dread that must be within her.

This was Edith's great secret—she was soon to be a mother. She had hid her marriage from her father many a month.

Steadily she worked on and on for more than an hour, at the little white atoms of cambric, and in the little patch of light the lamp gave out.

All the rest of the room was in darkness.

Hist—what is this? Softly, softly opens the door which Edith has locked; the door noiselessly glides back, and Death moves softly into the room. On she came without a sound, without a breath, towards the latter.

She has no need to go very near; she marks the poor girl planning and cutting, and she has the secret.

Softly—still softly she glides from the room, and goes to Mr. Marlowe's chamber.

She strikes softly at the door.

"Who's there?" the master of the house asks, and at once, for he is not sleeping, is not near undressed. He is thinking of his daughter's secret, and, perhaps, in the dark night, he has been weeping.

"Who is there?" he asks.

"Death."

"You here?" he answers, as he opens the door. "Why?"

"Why am I in your house?"

"To—to learn my daughter's secret."

"True—to learn it and to gain money. I want money to follow up my hate."

"Strange creature! Why in the dead of the night do you come to me?"

"To tell you this secret—to be paid my blood money, for it is blood money. I know your face—I know you. To tell the secret, I say —to be paid my money, and to go on my way watching for my vengeance."

"What is this secret?"

"If I told you would you believe me?"

"Yes. Why not?"

"Even if it wrecked your daughter's honour?"

"No, no."

"Follow me—see this secret."

"I—I—" said the father, affrightedly.

"Who questions Death?"

"Direct me," was all the father could say.

"Walk not heavily," she returned, and led the way to Edith's room."

Marlowe hesitated to pass the threshold as the treacherous door opened, but a cruel glance from the mysterious woman drew him on.

Edith was still busily at work, and she was looking almost happy.

"Do you see," whispered Death, "like a good mother she worketh for her child."

The father only uttered an exclamation—he could do no more—but it was enough to wake the poor girl from her half dream of happiness.

She saw all in a moment.

Down she fell at her father's feet.

"Mercy! mercy!" This was all she could cry.

And as he looked down upon her she once more cried,

"Mercy! mercy!"

"All my life has been a blight," said he, "early and late—always, always a blight."

"Who has ruined you?" he said, his eyes growing fierce and dark.

"He is my husband!" she said.

"Husband!—Who is he?"

"I—I will tell you all, father—I would have told you all to-day, but I had sworn not to do

so till he gave me leave; he has, and I will tell you all."

"Have you seen him to-night?"

"No, dear father. The letter was from him."

"Where is the letter?"

"Burnt."

"Burnt!"

"Yes."

"Why did you burn it?"

"It was burnt by accident."

"She lies," said Death.

"Indeed, indeed I do not," said the girl, "it fell from my lap."

"What is his name?" asked Marlowe.

"I will tell you, dear father," said the girl, "but bid this awful woman leave the room."

"She would deceive you," said Death lowly to Marlowe, and as she spoke he frowned, and then he said—

"This woman need not quit the room. What's his name, I say?"

"I will tell it you, father, but only you alone."

With a sudden movement Death seized a black ribbon that was hanging round the girl's neck, broke it in two, and with the ends tore from her bosom a little miniature. As she did so, she said—

"His portrait, no doubt."

But the next moment the room was ringing with an awful cry, and Death's eyes were fixed with terrible force upon the miniature---upon the blue eyes, the white skin, and black hair.

"He has been in England lately then," she cried, "as I was told, and I missed him. Death on me—death on me, I missed him!"

"Who is this man?" Marlowe said, rapidly.

"I will tell you alone."

"No," said Marlowe, "I swear I will never hear his name except in this woman's presence; she has, perhaps, a right to hear it—name him."

The girl rose from her knees, and stood proudly before her father.

"You say, father, you will only hear his name except before this woman?"

"I swear—and further, that you never be daughter of mine, never rest near me or in my house till I have heard it."

"Then you never will!" said Edith.

"His name—his name—that may find him," said Death, her eye still fixed on the miniature, the glass of which she had broken by pressing it with her hard eager fingers.

"I will never say it!" said the girl.

"Never?" asked the father.

"Never!"

As for Death, she did not seem to hear the answer; her eyes were still fixed on the portrait. "His name!" she kept repeating, "his name!—this is his portrait, his very portrait! His name—I never knew it—his name, his name!"

"Go!" said Marlowe, "to die if you will; I have given you two chances, you have flung them away!"

"Father — will you cast me from your home?"

"Will you tell his name?"

"No—never before this woman!"

He raised his hand as though about to strike her, but with a cry she caught his hand, kissed it, and then ran from the room out into the world!

Out into the hard, wide world!

As she reached the threshold she might have heard the cracking of the miniature, which now broke into a thousand pieces under the horrible pressure of the woman who called herself Death, and who now fell forward to the ground foaming at the mouth, but still uttering the words: "His name—his name!"

CHAPTER VII.

THE STRANGE VISITOR.

MRS. SPIKEY had lost her lodger for an entire week. Where was he?—that was the question.

Where?—the lodger who had her first floor, and paid her like a prince. When her lodger was at home she was always abusing him—behind his back, not before his face—when she would almost lay her elegant nose on his instep, so humble and polite was she. Down in the kitchen, she would to her Sally say such things of the captain, that the hearer, had there been one, might have supposed the "capting" was wearing Mrs. Spikey's life away; whereas in truth he it was who kept life within her, for he never looked at a bill and d—d the silver, like many a man who, sooner or later, hasn't a sixpence with which to bless him.

"Sitch a rampageous ruffin!" would Mrs. Spikey say; "sitch a devil! allus a knocking over *my* pails, when they're in *my* passidges, and I varrily believe, a knocking over me, if I was in the way—eh?"

"Yessum," would Sally say.

"Which," the good lady would continue, "which he don't come home hever till day, and then worn out like a man might well be, after sitch; which it's my belief the capting's a gambler."

But the "capting" had not been home for a week, and Mrs. Spikey went about amongst her neighbours, lamenting that fact to such a degree that people began to say the captain must be her son, and pretended to be her lodger to save appearances.

Day after day, and no captain, and then Mrs. Spikey would dissolve in tears, as she recapitulated his good points. "The dear, darlin' capting," she would say,—"he made my 'art come inter me mouth, when he rattled at the dear door—poor feller, of course he ought to have his pleasure, and he did—agoing about like a dear gentleman should. I dessay losin' lots of money, and making every woman go a fallin' inter the bottom of a pit o' love wi' him. Ah! law—law—we shall never see the dear capting again—so much the worse."

The good lady was going on in this strain on the eighth night after the disappearance of her first floor lodger—her feet in a pan of hot salt to keep them lusciously warm—when such a knock came at the door that Mrs. Spikey flew out of the pan as though the salt had been powder, and the knock a lucifer match.

"It's 'im," said Mrs. Spikey; "no un 'ud knock at *my* door like that, except the capting. Sally, let 'im in, and we'll have sitch a supper of tripe and whiskey; let his honour in and ask his honour how his honour does."

Up went Sally with a candle, Mrs. Spikey following in the dark to have a look at her "capting" from the shade of the staircase. The door was opened, and Sally was preparing to "ask his honour how his honour did," but her lower jaw refused its office, and it hung deep down at the sight she saw.

It *was* the captain, and yet it was not. There were his eyes, his face, his stature, but it was not him.

"What's the girl staring at?" asked the new comer, pushing roughly by; "don't you know me?"

Mrs. Spikey, in the background, had also marked the singular appearance of the new comer, also doubted whether the captain *was* the captain, and she was stretching her old neck well out to take another look, when the passage was involved in darkness, for Sally had been confused in so much doubt and fright that she dropped the candlestick, and indeed, nearly fell to the ground herself.

"Mrs. Spikey," called out the new comer.

"Sir to your honour's honour!" says that lady.

"What fool is this?"

"Which, your honour's honour?—if it *is* your honour's honour."

"Has the woman become a fool!" asked the new comer. "Of course I'am your lodger, Captain Holgarth. Be quick with a light—I hate the dark."

"Lor!" says Mrs. Spikey, "your honour's honour *used* not to be afraid of the dark. I'll—I'll go and strike a light, your honour's honour.

"Do, and be quick," said Holgarth.

At this moment a scratch of some grating substance was heard, and the next moment the passage was lit up with a faint blue flickering light.

In these days we should know how to account for such an afair—a single lucifer-match would answer the purpose; but nearly a hundred years ago lucifer-matches were unknown—at all events in England; and as Sally and her "missus" saw the light appear without tinder-box, or steel, or flint, they nearly fell to the ground.

"There's no need to strike the flint," said a soft voice; and as the light grew stronger, Holgarth saw that the man who had struck this light was tall, and dressed in dark cloth.

"Why, how did you come in?" asked Holgarth.

"As you did, through the door."

F. BRETT.

"I did not see you," said Holgarth.

"It does not follow that I did not enter," said the tall, black-clothed man.

"Well, and now you have come in, what do you want?" asked Holgarth.

"First of all you want a light," said the tall stranger—"here it is," and he passed up to the captain, standing on the stairs, an exquisitely white wax-light, which he had lit from the pale blue fragment which he held in his hand.

"And now," added the stranger, "I want to speak with you."

It was a strange sight—Holgarth standing on the staircase, with the light in his hand, looking down on the singular creature standing in the passage.

They were alike, and yet dissimilar.

Holgarth was pale and deathly-looking, but he still seemed somewhat of this world; but the stranger was horrible to look upon—horrible, because one moment he appeared exquisitely beautiful, and the next terribly repulsive;

and in fact it was impossible to say whether he were beautiful or hideous.

His eye was deep, black and searching; his features regular; but his mouth was cruel, and moved in singular curves as he spoke.

"If you want me, follow me," said Holgarth; and, turning, strode upstairs.

The stranger followed; and Mrs. Spikey swore to her servant, almost immediately afterwards, that she did not hear a single sound as he moved up the stairs.

"Nor me either, mum," says the servant.

Let us follow the couple of like yet unlike men, into the drawing-room.

"You have forgotten me," said the stranger.

"Who are you?"

"Can you not guess?"

"How should I. I see too many faces not to forget them."

"Ah! the owners of most of the faces you see seldom or never see yours, captain."

"What do you mean?"

"I mean you wear a mask."

"Yes—when I go to a masquerade."

The stranger smiled and passed his hand across his mouth. It might have been seen that, though the hand was exquisitely white, the nails were long and pointed, and the fingers seemed to meet together terribly—in fact the beautiful white hand looked like a CLAW.

"When you go to masquerades only?"

"What do you mean, I ask once more?" said the captain, starting and turning yet more pale, if that could possibly be.

"I mean, you wear a mask, on the road."

"The captain put his hand to his waist, and placed it upon a pistol.

"Tut—tut!" said the stranger,—"you would only make a noise; you would not harm *me !*"

"Why—why not?"

"When people aim at me, they aim badly; if you fired you would alarm the good woman of the house—don't. And again, it would be ungrateful to fire at me."

"Why ungrateful?"

"I am an old friend."

"I do not remember you."

"Ah! did I not say you were ungrateful?'

"This is some masquerade foolery."

"Were you ever in the Black Forest in Germany?"

"Yes."

"Who did you meet there?"

"A—a German doctor."

"Who gave you a silver whistle and a phial of poison. Not know me, man!—why, I gave you the red necktie you wear."

With a suppressed oath the captain cast his pistol on the ground, and crushed his hands together.

The stranger smiled once more.

"That's well?" he said, smoothing his chin with his terrible hand; "quite well. I like to hear a man swear, though I never swear myself. I like to see a man in a passion, though I never go into a rage myself. Yes, I'm your old friend of the Black Forest."

"You have changed."

"Bah! the world changes, does it not?"

"But old men do not grow young."

"Bah! you saw me by moonlight—now by the light of the candle; that makes the difference. By the by, do you perceive what a pleasant odour there is in the room?"

"Yes; it makes me giddy."

"It is the perfume of my wax candle; it is a noble perfume."

"Who are you?'

"If I wanted you to know I would tell you my name without asking."

"You have come here with a purpose; what is it?"

"Merely to see you after your little affair."

"How, I do not know, but it is certain you are acquainted with all my concerns. You know I am Captain Holgarth here, and Gentleman Jack on the road; you know I have been hanged—you know I have been saved. Now tell me—I am not afraid—are you the enemy of mankind?"

"The what?" said the stranger, slowly and calmly clasping his hands together —"the what?"

"The enemy of mankind," said the resuscitated highwayman, for Captain Holgarth was no other than the dead-alive of our first chapter —"tell me," he continued—"are you *he* who comes before me for the second time in my life? I—I am not afraid. I will make any promise, if you will let me live; let me—oh, let me live!"

"So you believe in Satan?"

"By my life, yes."

"*I* don't," said the stranger, calmly arranging the heavy curls of deep black hair, which fell to his shoulders.

"Why—all men do."

"Except me. Why, if I were Satan, why need I have given you your life? I could have had you fast; you had sinned enough. And yet I saved your life. Do you think Satan would *spare* men?"

"No," said the captain, smiling a ghastly smile.

"No!" said the stranger, with an awful look.

He did not add that perchance Satan might give life to the bad to induce them to *tempt and destroy the good.*

"There is no Satan," said the stranger; "laugh at those who say there is. Holgarth, I am your friend. Do you know why?"

"No; how should I?"

"Because you are brave as a lion. I help and save all brave men. How I knew you were a highwayman I need not tell you; but, knowing it, I knew you would one day, sooner or later, want my silver whistle, so I gave it you. You will *not* want it again—give it me."

As though utterly unable to defy the stranger, Holgarth took the silver whistle from his pocket, and dropped it into the white hand held out for it; the hand closed again like a white flesh vice.

"Will you take the poison too?" asked the highwayman.

"No," said the stranger; "you may *want* that."

For a few moments the stranger looked calmly and smilingly at Holgarth, then he continued, "Ah, I have to ask pardon for having stayed so long; you must be tired after your last night's adventure. I must wish you good bye, but I will watch over you. If I can help you I *will.* I will be near you in your greatest need; have no fear. By-the-bye, *have you got those papers safe?*"

"What papers?"

The certificate of marriage of the late Earl of Milray to the woman who is supposed to have been his mistress only. The earl's *will*, and *the other papers.*"

"How do you know that?"

"Bah! I was at the old inn on the heath, last night."

"*You* were?"

"Yes; why not? an inn is as much a house of accommodation for one man as another, if he bring money in his pocket."

"Water—I want some water," said the captain.

"Bah!" said the stranger, "water is not your drink. Brandy, whiskey, usquebagh—those are your liquors. Good bye; we shall not be long before we see each other again. I shall remain in England for some time. Do not hesitate at *anything*. I will help you. By the bye, I suppose you know your wife is dead. Oh, she *was* your wife, though you called her your mistress."

"How do you know *that?*"

"Bah! I am tired of answering your questions. Good bye, once more. Yes, your wife's dead, and you have a child born to you. Good night."

Before Holgarth could speak, so much was he astounded by the awful information the stranger seemed to possess, the latter was at the door, which he noiselessly opened.

In a moment or two the highwayman rang the bell, and almost immediately Mrs. Spikey appeared.

"Has that gentleman gone?"

"Gone, your honour's honour—isn't he here?"

"No, he left a few moments since?"

"Not by the street door, your honour's honour. I have been standing at it."

"Nonsense, woman, he must have passed you without your seeing him. What are you coughing for?"

"Yer honour's honour will parding me, but the puffume is so very pecooliar that I can't help it."

"Fetch me some brandy. What was that?"

It was an odd clapping sound to which the highwayman referred.

"I don't know, yer honour's honour, but it seemed like the clapping to of a door, I thinks. So your honour's honour wants a go o' brandy, does your honour's honour, an' ye ought to have it, for I *never* saw your honour's honour look so mortial pale—like a sheet—and which my fust floor gentleman was alus looking a likely honourable man for a gal to drop her eye on. Sally shall fetch the brandy, yer honour's honour, and happy it's I am that your honour's honour's here, after eight days again, and the Lord he knows I feared you was a-gone for good. Yer honour's honour don't speak."

"I'm not well."

"Nor do yer honour's honour lookut."

"Go; and take away that candle, and bring up others—it sickens me. And leave the door *open.*"

CHAPTER XI.

THE POISONED BOUQUET.

OUR tale now takes us to the exquisite palace of the Earl of Milray.

The earl was sitting in one of the gorgeously furnished rooms. Could many of the poor shivering wretches in the streets have looked in upon the nobleman, how they would have envied him—how they would have thought the splendid room an earthly paradise! And yet not one of them but was happier when a halfpenny or a morsel of bread was thrown to him than the gilded nobleman seated in his palace.

It is certain that happiness does not depend upon riches. Far be it from the writer to say that riches do not tend towards happiness. They do. It is to be doubted whether people driven for the means of living *can* have many happy moments; but this is a very different affair from the belief that money of itself constitutes happiness.

Happiness consists in three great facts which, combined with easy circumstances—that is, the power of paying the way, and being pretty well sure of the morrow's dinner—constitute pure happiness. These three great truths are—truth, a good conscience, and honourable duty in that station of life to which it has pleased the great God to call us. With these three blessings, a man may indeed be happy, if his means are well. Nor is it to be said that without means he shall be unhappy, possessing these three qualities. But under this latter condition his happiness will be mingled with pain—will not be that peace "which passeth all understanding," which makes the world light when it is dark—brilliant, when to other days it is but poor daylight.

Look at this earl and surroundings.

The room is hung with golden and coloured paper; the noise of the streets is shut out with double windows; when one walks across the flowered carpet the foot sinks deep in the downy pile. The nobleman is dressed in satin and fine linen; the food that is before him is the rarest in the world, served to perfection.

And what is he thinking of as he sits listlessly gazing at some beautiful birds, encaged and yet happy in each other's society, and billing and coing with the freedom of unsinning creatures?

He is thinking of death, and poison, and safety for himself.

Compare this man with the poor mechanic a few hundred yards off perhaps—the mechanic who has finished his dinner before the nobleman begins his breakfast. His face is open and friendly; and the homely meal finished, he lifts his little ones to his honest father-breast, and kisses them. Is not this gentle and beautiful. Far be it from the writer to say that all noblemen are bad—all working men good fathers, but he wishes to point out that very frequently comparative poverty (for a healthy working man is *not* poor), is a far happier lot than one of immense riches.

Let us return to the apartment of the Earl of Milray.

It has been said the nobleman was seated full of angry, nay criminal thoughts, surging in his brain.

Suddenly he struck a hand-bell, which was near him.

In a moment a footman, splendidly attired, appeared at the door.

"Send my valet here."

"Yes, my lord," says the obsequious servant, and soon the valet made his appearance.

"Jules."

"Me lord."

"Look at me."

"Me lord has bad work for his poor servant to do dat me lord will not do for himself. Of whom does me lord think?"

"Can you not guess?'

"No—the pretty Fanny, the orange girl?"

"Confound it no. I am not thinking of women at all;—talk of Fanny some other time. By the bye, have you arranged a meeting for me with that little baggage?"

"Yes, me lord; she pouted, but she consented."

"So much the better—though I am getting tired of women. Now guess again what I think of."

"I am too humble to seek my lord's thoughts."

"Look at my eyes."

"Ha! me lor—may me lord's servant dare say dere's murder in me lord's eyes?"

"Yes—you may dare say that."

"Who does me lord think of?"

"Who did that letter come from?"

"Mr. Edgar Trevillian."

"Do you think I can let him live, Jules?"

"No. Was me me lord, I would assassinate him."

"You see—he speaks the truth—he *is* the earl. *I* am no one."

"De more reason to keep de earldom," said the French valet, laughing.

"I will keep it, Jules. You have lived in Italy?"

"Almost all my life."

"You know, perhaps, something about the poisons they use."

"All about dem."

"Ah! I suppose if you chose you would kill me in a moment."

"In a moment, me good lord."

"That is if it would pay you."

"It pay me, me lord, bettare to have you live."

"I've no doubt—and it will pay you better to have me continue to be thought the earl."

"Certain, me lord."

"Then help me to destroy this Edgar Trevillian."

"Certain, me lord."

"Can you poison him, Jules, so that no trace of the poison can be found?"

"Yes, easily. He sall smell to a bouquet—he sall die."

"When?"

"When me lord likes."

"We must invite him here—we must *kill* him here."

"Yes, me lord, and wid de bouquet. My poison sall leave no trace, and de doctor he sal say, him die of de fit, poor fellow. He, he!"

"I will make it worth your while."

"Oh certain, me lord."

"Then I may now arrange my plans. I must first ask him for a week in which to consider his claims."

"Yes, me lord; it is always well to have time to you—you get from him de week."

"Exactly; and now what shall I do with myself."

"Sink, me lord, if de little Fanny—de little Fanny's a fruit dat should be plucked."

"Oh!" said the earl, "I can't go to pluck it—bring her here."

"*Oui*, me lord," said the obsequious valet.

CHAPTER XII.

THE FLOWER GIRL AND THE BOUQUET.

COVENT GARDEN was much in those days what it is now, if we except that whereas the "swells" of this day walk about the market peaceably buying flowers, a hundred years ago they fought with the market people, chucked the market girls under the chin, and generally made themselves as low as they could.

Amongst the girls who were known or pretty at Covent Garden, at the date at which our tale now stands, was one Fanny—as pretty a wench as any ever seen. Her hair was of a bright auburn colour, which all her female enemies, to say nothing of her female friends, said was a clear red; but for all that Fanny showed as much of it as she could under her handsome new cap.

She was quite a sight standing behind her basket of oranges—for she sold oranges from the first moment they came in till the last moment before they went out, and her enemies and friends did say this was that her character should not be lost of *the* orange girl.

Yes, she was a sight as she stood behind her little basket, whether by day or night. Her handsome white and red skin looked still more handsome in contrast with the oranges when the sun was shining on them all, and of a night she exhibited a new beauty. For in those days orange-girls used to light up their orange-baskets with a candle surrounded by a crimson paper, and the red reflection which was thus cast upon her pretty features, caused many a man's heart to beat, and his lips to open as he saw the charming sight.

Fanny knew her power, but she had managed to keep herself straight—not perhaps so much from a desire to do so as by the help of Strongarm Will, as he was called.

Strong-arm Will was a market porter, and the swells, when having a "real row" in the market, used to avoid Will with extreme alacrity.

He was as strong as a horse, and a good deal more willing.

He had loved Fanny, with all the strength of his strong nature, for years—long before his beard began to grow—long before the "bloods" (a) had made bets as to who should have Fanny to himself first.

And he kept on loving her, long after the beard had come and his chin showed blue from the constant shaving, which in those days was imperative upon a man if he wished to show that he hated the "Frenchies,"—not that the Frenchmen of those days wore moustaches, but the people of Covent Garden did not know to the contrary.

But Fanny would have naught to say to him. She didn't say no—but she certainly didn't say "yes;" and so poor Strong-arm Will looked and longed, and tried to work off his passion by carrying heavy loads and slaving like a horse, but all to no purpose; and his old mother would condemn Fanny and say she it was who caused her boy to toss about night after night without sleep, and raging and perhaps cursing as he lay through the long hours between the evening and the dawn.

At last poor Strong-arm Will went nearly mad with love; and let me tell my readers that even in these day men and women go mad with love, aye and sometimes die of it—and it is perhaps better to die of love than never catch the complaint.

And so the doctors told Will that if he did not wish to lose his life or his reason that he must go away, and so at last Covent Garden knew Will no more, and they said he had gone into the north to work as a miner.

Anyhow Fanny did not fret much about him; she laughed and chattered with her customers just as easily the day after he went as the day before, but somehow when she got home after the orange-selling was over for the days she cried as though her heart would break.

"The coward," she said, "to run away—a big strong man like him to run away from a poor girl like me; what harm could *I* do him?"

Though perhaps Fanny knew that the only thing from which a brave man may run with honour is love—all-conquering love.

But Fanny was not going to show the "other girls" that she was hurt; so next morning she dressed herself as smart as usual, and polished up her little gold earrings as much as ever; and you see could well afford to wear gold earrings, for the "bloods," when they bought an orange of Fanny, did not care what price they paid for it, so that in giving the money they could press her hand.

Many a time had Will felt inclined to rush at one of these customers, as he had seen the gentleman's hand press that of the girl he (Will) loved better than all the world.

Indeed, to go further than the earrings, it was said that Fanny had managed to save quite a little heap of money in the few years she had "sold" in the market, and this must have explained the meaning of her words as she put

the earrings in her ears: "He shall never have a farthing of it now."

Well, to market she went, and of course the "bloods" were soon talking to her. *They* had heard Strong-arm Will was gone, and they grew more daring in their talk than they had ever been.

Poor little Fanny, instead of taking this as a warning, felt that *now* she ought to be less sorry than ever that Will was gone for good.

The oranges went off well that day—better than ever; and the night was just falling, when a plain, French-looking man came up to the basket.

"Good evening, sweet Mees Fanny—air you vell?"

"Quite, Mr. Jules."

"How beautiful you shall be," said the new comer.

"Nay, Mr. Jules," said the girl, "how beautiful I *am* people talk about."

"Hey," says the Frenchman, whom it need not be said was the spurious Earl of Milray's valet—"hey, but I mean when you are the countess ——"

"What do you mean, Mr. Jules?—and you've not told me—how is his lordship?"

"Me lor is dying."

"Of what?"

"Of you."

Here Fanny laughed.

The next moment her eyes were sparkling with delight, at something the Frenchman had dropped into the basket.

It was a diamond earring—only *one.*

"Oh!—how beautiful!"

"Not so beautiful as you, Mees Fanny," says the Frenchman.

"Is it yours?"

"No, yours, if you will get to de oder."

"Where is de oder, as you say?"

"Near de earl's 'art."

"Oh, bother," says Fanny, picking up her basket, but still holding the diamond earring in her hand.

"Sall I tell you somesing lovely, Mees Fanny?"

"Yes—yes."

"De earl loff you more dan de rest."

"Bah!—they all say that."

"But him speak de truth."

"What else does he say?"

"He say he marry you when your sall will."

"What, make me a lady?" says Fanny, setting down the basket and looking at the diamond earring once more.

"Yes, he sall make Mees Fanny a beautiful countess, and she sall come to de market in de silks and de laces, and buy de orange and de flower her pretty belle self."

"Oh, that would be lovely," says Fanny, shaking the jewel in the remaining light, and seeming fascinated with the sparkle. She was not the first woman who had, or has been, fascinated with diamonds. Nay, it *is* said that in very hot countries *men* even have such a passion

(a) "Bloods"—the young gentlemen about town.

for them as has been seldom equalled among women in our colder climate.

"Yes, none of the other bloods have said—come and be a lady, Mees Fanny."

"Oh! I don't know that," says Fanny.

"Well—well, you sall come to get the oder earring."

"Why can't you bring it to me?"

"Oh, de earl vish to give it you, Mees Fanny."

"Then why can't he come," says Miss Fanny, straightening herself, and arranging her little cap.

"De poor earl is too weak tinking of you, Mees Fanny, to come to see you."

"Poor fellow!" says Fanny, and here she *kissed* the diamond earring. And she thought, "Well, though this nasty little Frenchman has brought the ring, I do hate him, that I do! I always did and always shall—the nasty sneering creature!"

She little thought what was passing in the nasty little Frenchman's mind—little thought that he was sighing for her himself, and that he had sworn to possess her if he died for it.

Jules could do as he liked with his master the earl—could turn that poor creature round his French finger, and *did* often.

Here was his scheme:

He meant to betray the orange-girl to the earl, no matter by what means; and then, when the earl was tired of her, take the poor thing himself. Monsieur Jules was not delicate,—he always wore second-hand things; so he did not regret that his master should win Fanny ere he, the vassal, should have her in his power.

So it is in this world: often and often the servant is the master—often and often the footman swinging on behind my lord's carriage, has my lord within completely within his rough power.

"You will come, Fanny," says Jules.

"I don't say that."

"Fanny, I do know you do not loff me, but I do moch for you; you come wid me to de earl."

"What do you mean, Mr. Jules?"

"Mees Fanny, the earl is dying to make you his countess. I haf prepared a parson, and when he see you, and when you laff at him an make him rage, I sall say, me lor, dere is de minister—sall he come for to make you de man and de wife?"

Here the orange-girl started.

"Are you really my friend, Mr. Jules?"

"Yes."

"Then—then I will come. Are these real diamonds?"

"As real as your eyes are bright."

"And the parson is there?"

"In the drawing-room, vaiting for you."

"Where is the earl?"

"Vaiting in his chamber, white and pale, sighing for you."

"I'll come," said the girl.

"Vhat, sall you not go with me?"

"No, I'll follow."

"Ah, I see, you vood see Master Vill?"

Here the girl started and blushed.

"Ah, you sall like Master Vill perhaps better than you sall like de earl. De earl would loff you and put de diamonds in de ear himsel, and de Will sall make you to make de fire. How happy you sall be wid Will! Good bye—adieu, Miss Fanny. I will giff you de one diamond you haff to remember the earl by, till de Master Will him make you sell it for de gin."

For a moment the girl hesitated, then she said: "I won't come with you—all the girls would laugh."

"What sall a countess care for the laff of a poor lot of orange-girls."

This touched the girl's vanity in the quick, and she said, "I'll come," and she raised her basket.

Of course, all the other market-girls were watching this long talk between the earl's valet and Fanny.

"Oh, leaf your basket."

"But my oranges?" says Fanny.

"Vhat sall a countess want with oranges."

"But they will see me leave my basket, and they will guess."

"Vhat sall that mattar, Mees Fanny—de countess? Vhat sall de countess care for de opinion of de orange-girls."

"True," said Fanny, and left the side of her basket.

"Come, Mr. Jules," said she, clasping the diamond earring tightly, "I will follow you."

"Nay, madame," says he, "I will follow madame de countess as I will haff to in a few days."

Poor Fanny turned red—then white—Jules offering to walk behind her was such an immense honour.

"No, not now," says she; "walk by my side now."

"Nay, madame," returned the valet; "madame must allow me to walk behind—I dare not to disobey de earl's express orders."

So Fanny walked from the old market with the valet, who had so often purchased oranges from her, walking behind her. All the men, and women, and girls stared, as well they might, but no one interfered.

Now had Will been there, beyond a doubt he would have sent Mr. Jules rolling in the mud as easily as he would have snapped a stick of sealing-wax.

Little did Fanny, as she sailed along, know the valet's thoughts. "Ah!" pondered the French scamp—"ah! now she has left her basket—now she has shown herself walking before me, and I obsequiously following, she will not dare show herself in the market again. The earl will soon tire of her, and then—"

Here the valet smiled, and one of the market girls, a remarkably ugly girl, who had never sold an orange to bloods but once, when the young noble said, "stop my vitals—but you are the ugliest wench in Christendom." This market girl, seeing the valet smile, said—"And vell he may."

But neither she, any more than Fanny, could look into the dark brain of that false serving-man.

———

CHAPTER XII.

IT was growing dusk, and the earl, as we will call him, was nearly drunk.

He had been drinking all the afternoon with a companion who was dressed like a clergyman.

In the times of which we speak clergymen were a very different body to those which now exist. Far be it for the present writer to say that there are no bad clergymen now—the newspapers often prove to the contrary. Far be it from the present writer to say that at the date of this tale there were no good ministers of the blessed gospel; but he does say this—that whereas the majority of existing clergymen of the present day are respectable men, the masses of the clergymen of England a hundred years ago were infidels, drunkards, roués, (a) and scamps.

There sat the earl's companion, in his flowing black gown, his ponderous wig thrust back off his head, his glass in one hand, and his pipe in the other.

The worthy couple had just been finishing a worthy song, the purport of which may be guessed by the following concluding lines—

"All means are fair,
In earth or air,
To court the fair,
And lay them low.

Well may we be spared from quoting the entire poem.

As the song ended the door of the splendid chamber opened, and a footman brought in a fresh supply of punch.

At this time there was a peculiarity in serving punch; it was brought to table in flames—real devil's drink it would seem, would it not? Nor was there much sense in this custom, for to a dead certainty much of the spirit was lost—burnt, by this means. But it was the fashion, and fashions are not always sensible, as the most fashionable reader will admit. But stop, it may be there was some sense in it. The less spirit in the punch, the less chance there was for the topers to be made drunk, and therefore there was some sense in making the punch weaker every moment it stood on the table. And it must also be added that one authority states that burnt punch has a far superior flavour to unburnt. We have tried the ex-

periment, but found the result uncommonly nasty. Whether we made mistakes or not it is impossible to say, but if the flavour was a correct one, we wonder every man who took half a pint of this abominable mixture did not want a doctor to cure him of the attack.

"Well, Tom, how are you now?"

"I—I feel as tall as yourself, my lord," returned the earl's companion.

"When the devil is Jules going to return with the wench? Don't drink too much, Tom, or you'll be reading the wrong service—instead of mock-marrying us, you'll be mock-christening us."

"Why the devil, my lord, do you want any mock-marriage at all? She won't be the first flower-girl ruined without the help of a minister."

"Bah! my dear old Tom, you know nothing about the matter. A woman who supposes herself a wife is more stimulating than a poor devil of a girl who flutters like a bird in a cage. When my blood boiled perhaps I loved caged birds, but now I'm past that kind of thing. No—no, I'll have the mock-marriage, or you won't have the ten pounds I've promised you for the job."

Then the mock-clergyman sighed.

"Gad!" says the earl, "I mustn't drink much more, or I shan't look interesting, shall I? Have you ever done this kind of thing before, Tom?"

"What, Milray?"

"Why, mock-marriages."

"No."

"Ah! then you must get your hand in. I'm often married. It's a pity I didn't have you before. You make a devilish good parson. I could almost swear you *were* a parson, Tom,—were you ever bred to the trade?"

"Yes," says Tom—and a more attentive listener than the earl might have heard Tom, the jolly companion, sigh—"yes, Milray, I was to have been a regular one, and I can tell you that once on a time few men had better prospects than I had."

"Ah! there's no prospects equal to punch. Have another glass."

"Curse me—drown care," says the mock-minister, and *does* take another glass.

"How long have I known you, Tom?"

"Three months."

"Hum! Three months is it since you saved my head from being broken in the flash ken? (a) Mighty obliged I was to you for saving it."

"Ah, my lord, I wish I could look after myself as well as I have looked after others."

"Tom, you were to have been a regular jaw-parson, once, was you?"

"Aye, Milray, and if I'd looked out sharp I might have been a bishop."

"Then, old boy, you would have been a greater rogue than you are now."

In the midst of the laughter with which the

(a) "Roué" comes from the French word "rou"—a wheel. Criminals in France used at one time to be broken on a wheel as the means of execution. Hence a Duke of Orleans, when Regent of France (and who was the worst rake who ever existed—he died, the feeble wretch, while endeavouring to rob a poor girl of her honour), declared that all rakes ought to suffer death on the wheel, and so he christian-named them *roués*. In the course of this work it is possible we may have to refer to this detestable Prince of Orleans, as our tale will carry us to France.

(a) "Flash ken"—one of the most frequented of low drinking houses.

earl greeted his own stupid joke, if joke it could be called, the door opened, and the valet, Jules, entered.

"Me lord."

"Hullo, ugly—is that you? Where is the girl?"

"Down stairs."

"How does she look?"

"Frighty, me lord, but you sall make her smile, me lord; me lord must go to his room, 'cause he ill again."

"All right," said the earl, and a close observer might have observed that the veins of the neck of the lascivious nobleman had swollen immensely since he had heard that his pretty victim was below. Indeed, the only real ecstatic moments of his present life were those which immediately preceded and followed the destruction of a girl.

"Here, Tom, just you make this place look as sober as a church," continued the earl, rising and dashing his head into cold water.

Within a few moments the room had assumed a very different appearance to that which it had been wearing. Instead of the pipes, punch-bowls, and glasses scattered in all directions,—instead of the earl and the jolly mock-parson, pipe in mouth, and unbuckled waistcoats and undone necktie—instead of the roysterers, stretched upon a couple of sofas, laughing and enjoying the coming acts of wickedness, were to be seen an orderly, well-arranged room—no pipes, no punch. The mock parson had pulled his wig forward—a heavy book lay on the table before him, his spectacles were on his nose, and by the faint light he looked a holy man, who was diligently studying theology.

Meanwhile the earl had gone into his adjoining bedroom, put on a dressing-gown, powdered his face, and seated himself in a large heavy chair near the fire. He looked a man who was very ill, and who required a very skilful doctor to bring him back to life.

"Is me lord ready?"

"Quite. Cut along."

Down stairs went the valet, and into the room where was waiting this beauty.

She had already taken airs upon herself, and she was walking up and down the room angrily, and flinging about a hoop, before which the largest of modern ones would have seemed a mere trifle.

And she had taken out one of the gold ear-rings, and replaced it with the diamond jewel with which the Frenchman had first tempted her, by dropping the same into her orange basket.

"How dare you keep me?" she asked.

"Me ladie," says Jules, "when I told de earl you was here, he faint dead away, and we haf take de time to bring him to. Will me ladie come up stair? de earl is dying to see me ladie."

"Lead the way," says Fanny, looking more beautiful than ever.

Up stairs she followed Jules, and she smiled as she thought all this grandeur would soon be hers—was as good as hers now.

Entering the room where the orgy had taken place, she saw the minister deeply engaged in reading his book.

In accordance with the prevailing fashion, she made him a low courtesy, and bent her head lower.

"Good day to you, my child," says the mock-minister.

"Good day, sir," says Fanny, and she says to herself, "there, sure enough, is the minister."

The next moment she saw the earl.

She started and stopped, and as the earl saw her, excited as he was by the punch he had been drinking, he nearly leapt from his chair towards her.

He had long waited for this moment, but, as may readily be comprehended, he was a miserable coward, and till this time the strong hand of Strong-arm Will had saved the poor little orange girl.

The earl had not wasted much time after the departure of the strong lover. He had been determined to be the first in the field, and truth to tell, much was the rage and anger caused by the knowledge learnt by many bloods that Fanny had been snatched from their grasp.

The earl, however, repressed his wish, and merely rose totteringly, and came towards the beauty, who leant against a table, and began toying with her cap-strings.

"Fanny—dear Fanny."

"Ah! you don't mean it, my lord."

"Not mean it, Fanny!" Here he took her hand, and again such a thrill went through him that he nearly caught her to his arms.

She tried at first to disengage her hand, and then she pressed his in return.

Again the earl nearly ceased to be master of himself, but, by a superhuman effort, he saved appearances.

"How kind of you to have pity on me. I have been dying for you, Fanny."

"I don't believe you," she said.

"Look at my eyes," says the earl,—"and feel my heart."

He took her other hand, and now it seemed as though an electric current was passing from self to her, and back to him again. Fanny had never looked so beautiful, nor he so handsome since they had known each other.

"How—how your heart beats," she said.

"For you—for you."

"You do not now seem as though you had been ill."

"No, you have come—and you have saved my life."

As he spoke, he drew her past the threshold of the larger room into the smaller.

Jules closed the door.

The next moment the earl pressed his lips to hers. She could not speak—she could not move. She could only return the pressure, and feel as though a new life was given her for ever.

She lived years in that moment—in that deep ardent kiss such as she had never yet felt. And he—he felt the soft pressure of the silken

E.L.BRETT.

flesh, and knew he could have destroyed her at that moment.

"The earl sall spare you, monsieur the minister," says the valet.

"I hope he will," says the minister.

"Why?" asks the valet.

"Silence, my man—that is my business."

The next moment the earl called—"Reverend sir, are you at liberty."

"Ah! it must be then," said the mock-minister, in a low tone—so low that even the valet did not hear him.

The next moment the minister passed the threshold of the inner room, and stood in the presence of the earl and his victim.

"Reverend sir," says the earl, "perform your holy office."

And the next minute the sacrilege was being committed—the mock marriage was progressing.

Let the particulars at least of this scene be passed over in silence.

The mock-marriage ended, the earl gaily

saluted the orange-girl, and embraced her saying: "Ah, at last, charming Fanny, you are my wife."

As he spoke he leered at the mock-minister, who, to speak the truth, was looking uncommonly serious.

"Good night, my lord," he said—"I am going."

"This here is for your services," says the earl, taking a couple of notes from a little casket. "I hope soon to see you again, reverend sir," says the earl, with a grin.

The mock-minister, still looking grave, took the money, bowed, and moved towards the door.

"What does Tom mean by all this solemn business?" thought the nobleman; but the next moment he had forgotten this personage as he looked upon the pretty Fanny, who stood hesitating and doubtful near the earl.

"What, my pretty bird—are you trembling?" he asked, and laughingly took her hands.

5

"Good night, my lord," once more said the rev. Tom; and the solemnity of the words once more made the earl wonder what on earth had come over the spirit of Tom's thoughts.

Now Jules had passed from the room, through the folding doors, a few moments before Tom said the second " good night."

The dusk had grown night, and the large room had not been lit up—only the small chamber in which the marriage ceremony had taken place had been illuminated, therefore it was not to be supposed that the mock-minister could see the valet, who in truth had passed out before that personage, in order to have a little chat with him before he went his way.

The valet, seeing Tom appear, was about to speak to him, when the meaning of the latter stayed the Frenchman's tongue.

"Oh!" said Tom, in a low tone, but loud enough for the Frenchman's quick ear. "He —he little thinks he *has* been really married to her;—little does the earl think she is really the countess. He would have the ceremony—and —and I wanted the ten pounds."

After a pause he continued—

"Confound the door—where is it, Jules— Jules?"

But never a word in reply made Jules, who got behind a screen, and so kept out while the earl, swearing, asked what was the matter, and while his lordship came and showed the *real* minister to the door.

The earl having returned to the inner room, Jules emerged from behind the screen.

"So—so, his *real* wife! Ho, ho! Monsieur Jules, you sall have a countess for your leetle mistress!—ve sall see vhat ve sall see."

CHAPTER XIII.

FANNY'S FIRST DRESSING.

THE next day poor little Fanny, known only to two men as the Countess of Milray—or rather known only to two men as the wife of the man supposed to be the Earl of Milray—was duly dressed for the countess's post.

M. Jules, who could undertake any part and play any character, had found a tire-woman, an abigail who was willing to wait upon my lady the countess.

Let us see what the poor little orange-girl had to go through.

When preparing for Covent Garden Market, she had to tuck up her hair as naively as possible in two or three pretty bands, then she had to plant her little cap on the back of her head, and so much for that portion of her costume.

As to her face and neck, she left them as nature made them.

Then she only had to put on a short dress over her shorter petticoats, thereby showing a smart pair of legs in a smart pair of red stock-

ings, ending in a natty pair of high-heeled boots, and she was complete—with the exception of a small cotton handkerchief passed over the shoulders and crossed over the breast, a natty straw hat perched on the top of her head—and there she was.

Now, then, dressed as the countess, let us see what she had to go through.

When Milly came to her bedside on the following morning to that of the supposed mock-marriage, she made a low curtsey, and then asked my lady if she would pass her smock.

This was an immense flannel garment, into the embraces of which Fanny resigned herself.

Indeed, Fanny would willingly have had a good chatter with this hand-maiden if she had dared—for she had not talked to one of her own kind for many hours; and truth to tell she wanted to talk naturally, but she remembered she was the "countess," so she held her tongue.

"Will me lady have blue powder or white?"

"What?" says Fanny.

"Will me lady be powdered blue (a) or white?"

Fanny could only guess that Milly referred to her hair, so she thought for a moment, questioned herself, and then said: "What's your name, my dear?"

"Milly, me lady."

"Then, Milly, I don't think I'll have it blue."

"Don't, me lady—it's horrid. Shall I begin, me lady?"

"Oh yes," says Fanny, thinking that now indeed the honours of an aristocratic position were beginning to be assigned to her.

The first proceeding was to take all Fanny's hair straight up from her forehead, and as the late orange-girl, seated before a glass, saw the sight, she opened her eyes even wider than the operation of "lifting" her hair had pulled them.

Then the hand-maiden produced from a bag a cushion about the size of a large pudding of these days, but not quite in the shape.

This was laid on and about the head of the new countess, and her pretty bright hair was stretched over it, tucked in, and all made comfortable.

This little operation altogether lasted about an hour and a half—perhaps two hours.

Fanny all this while had said not a word, but had quietly sat staring at herself in the

---

(a) We need not tell our readers that at the period to which our tale refers, powdered hair was worn by both ladies and gentlemen, but we may possibly be allowed to add that "blue" powder, to replace white, was attempted to be introduced, but after a little time became a signal failure. Yet it is a positive fact that English men and women powdered their hair blue in the last century. To be sure the powder was not so blue as the paint with which the early Britons picked out elegant devices on their martyred bodies; indeed it was rather the colour of starch, or what is called blue writing paper; but only imagine hair of this colour, and you can imagine what hideous "guys" many of our ancestors of the last century looked when dressed for a party.

REVELATIONS OF A JAILOR.

glass, and wondering whether the headache she was getting—the first for some years—could become any worse than it already was.

At last, when Milly made an admiring pause, and drew back and admired her handywork, Fanny said—"And now I suppose you've done, Milly?"

"Done, me lady!—why I've hardly begun!"

"But—but I shan't have to go through all this every morning of my life?"

"Oh no, me lady, your head 'ull last three weeks!"

"What!"

"I don't mean your head, me lady, which let us hope will last a hundred years. I mean your head of hair will last for three weeks!"

"What—like this?"

"Oh lud no, me lady; it ain't half finished yet, me lady."

"And do you mean to tell me, Milly, that my hair's to be kept up like this for three mortal weeks?"

"When it's finished, me lady."

"But how am I to go to bed?"

"With it."

"What like it is?"

"Like it will be when it's finished."

"And I'm not to have it combed out for three weeks?"

"Yes, me lady, unless you like to keep it up for a month—some ladies do, me lady. Shall I go on, me lady."

"Yes, Milly."

"Then me lady had best put on her mask."

And here the serving-woman produced a delicate little mask for the face, with glass eyes.

"What am I to do with that?"

"Put it on, my lady."

"Well—but I never saw ladies wear such a thing, and besides—"

Here Fanny hesitated and stopped. She was going to say she thought her face too pretty to be hidden by a mask.

As for the serving-wench, she could barely repress a laugh, but she kept a serious face because she saw the "countess's" eyes upon her in the glass.

"If you please, me lady, I want to powder you."

"But what's that to do with the mask?"

"Why you see, me lady, if you don't hold the mask before your pretty face, the powder will fly into your ladyship's eyes, and nose, and mouth, and your ladyship will be blind for an hour, and sneeze all your hair down again."

"Ah, to be sure!" says Fanny, and up went the mask.

Then the powder was rained upon her little head in pounds, it seemed to her, out of a machine very much like an exaggerated pepper-box, and until Fanny thought her head would drop under the weight.

The hair, while being brushed over the cushion, had been greased, and so the powder adhered easily, and when the little countess removed her mask she immediately looked into the glass.

"Oh my," says she—"how pretty."

And, truth to tell, she did look more charming than ever.

The fashion of bewigged and powdered hair was a miserably troublesome one, nay it was almost a torture, but it was charming in the extreme—a delightful mode to look at: and so perhaps we may excuse those ladies who, when they went to court, rather than not have the hair done by a fashionable hairdresser (and of course just before a court day fashionable hairdressers were in great demand), would undergo the operation the day before, or even two days before, and set up all night, nay, even two nights, that the beautiful effect produced by the hairdresser might not be spoilt.

But to return to Fanny.

"Well, Milly," says she, and the capital effect Milly had produced made her new mistress much more confidential than she had yet been—"well, Milly, and now I suppose you really have finished."

"Oh dear no, me lady, there's the ribbons and the knick-knackery," says Milly, and, diving into her bags and boxes, she produced half-a-dozen ribbons, and—and a most extraordinary thing.

This latter was a little coach-and-six in coloured glass.

"Oh! what a pretty little thing," says Fanny.

Milly then produced other glass toys,—a boat with half-a-dozen sailors rowing her—a queen seated on a throne—a huntsman seated on his horse—a four-post bedstead with crimson hangings, and a golden-coloured wheelbarrow full of red hearts, wheeled by a flesh-coloured Cupid.

"Oh! the dear little toys!" says Fanny; "what are they for?"

"Which would me lady like?"

"Oh!" says Fanny, catching up the flesh-coloured Cupid, "I should like 'em all, Milly."

"Oh, lud! me lady," says Milly,—"why, they would knock together, and go smash."

"Lor! Milly, what do you mean?"

"Oh, lud! me lady, your la'ship can't wear 'em altogether."

"Wear 'em! I mean to put 'em away, and take care of 'em; hasn't me lord bought 'em and sent 'em to please me?"

"Oh, no, me lady. Me lord's sent your la'ship a beautiful 'talian greyhound, and he's waiting to see your la'ship (a)—the hound, I mean, not me lord. I've brought these—which will your la'ship please to wear in your la'ship's hair?"

"Wear these in my hair?" (b)

"Only one of 'em, me lady—because, as I said afore, if your la'ship weared two at a time, they would go smash."

(a) "La'ship" was the correct way, in those days, of pronouncing "ladyship."
(b) This is a fact. It became the fashion to wear all manner of odd objects in the hair. A coach and six was quite a common object, and a flesh-coloured Cupid, wheeling a golden wheelbarrow of red hearts, was at one time quite the rage.

"Very well," says Fanny, after a little consideration, "I think I'll have the little boy and the barrow."

And thereupon Milly lifted up the glass god of Love, and soon he and his barrow were dangling in the powdered locks of the new Countess of Milray, as we will call the poor thing.

"And now I suppose my head is done," says Fanny.

"Oh! no, ma'am, the patches."

"Oh! to be sure," says Fanny, who had often seen the patches (a) on the ladies when serving them with oranges—though, to be sure, the greater part of her customers were gentlemen.

"Which will your la'ship choose?"

"Oh, the dear little round ones—I have tried 'em with bits of black paper cut out of printed letters, and they looked beautiful."

"Oh, me lady, but the sun patches will not do alone, you know; the ladies now wear pictures."

"What's pictures?"

"Oh, me lady, you can have a sun or a moon on your forehead, to represent the sky, but you must have something below on your cheeks."

"Oh, what fun!" says Fanny, and immediately began turning over the little box of patches Milly produced.

There were lots of little things stamped out in the black satin patch-plaster, and looking much like the shadow pictures which children buy in the toyshops.

"Oh! here's another little boy with a barrow," says Fanny. "I'll have that."

"Excuse me, me lady—but your la'ship has a Cupid in your hair, already, and your la'ship must not have a Cupid on your cheek. Suppose your la'ship has a coach and four; and which does your la'ship like best—night or day?"

"La! I'm sure I don't know," says Fanny, blushing.

"Because if your la'ship likes day best, why then you must have a sun patch on your forehead; but if your la'ship likes night best, why

then you must have a moon patch on your forehead.

And the next moment the patches were stuck on.

"Oh, how beautiful?" says Fanny; "and now I suppose my head is made, isn't it?"

"Oh, yes, me lady, and now for your la'ship's dress."

Far be it from the present writer to go into the particulars of the hoop, but he may be allowed to say this, that the dress of the fashion of the date of our tale was about five times as cumbrous as the most cumbrous of the most fashionable dresses of our times.

At last the dressing was complete.

It had lasted four hours.

"Oh, dear me," says Fanny, rising from the glass, and standing once more—"how heavy I do feel." And indeed she looked about four times the size she had appeared as an orange girl—as though she had grown once more as large as her old self for every hour she had sat before the glass.

"Why," says Fanny, Countess of Milray, "I can hardly walk. I actually waddle."

"And now your la'ship is complete—except the 'talian greyhound, and Mr. Jules will bring him."

"Milly," says the countess, "do you like Jules?"

"I never say no ill of my fellow-servants, me lady," says Milly.

"But supposing you did," says Fanny.

"Then, my lady, I should like to wring his ugly head off his ugly neck. I hates him, an' the way he patteronizes us, why, it's enough to make my hair fly off my head. Why, what's he—only a Frenchy—and what's a Frenchy? nothink, me lady,—and as Strong-arm Will—"

Here she was interrupted by a cry from Fanny.

"What is it, me lady?"

"Do you know Strong-arm Will?—I've heard of him."

"Lud, me lady, he corted me once, till he fell in love with a bit of a horange girl."

"You don't know who she was, Milly?"

"No; and if ever I finds out, I'll scratch her eyes out."

"That is if she'd let you, you know," says Fanny, and Milly would be able to see that her lady was blushing, only Milly had laid the red and white paint on so thick that really no blush could show through it.

"However," says Milly, "I'm saving money, and when Will comes to his senses I suppose we'll agree, and open a pub. together. Will your la'ship have your la'ship's hound?"

"Oh, yes."

"I'll go to Mr. Jules. He always bows to me; but I know him, for all his bowing and scraping; he don't catch me, don't Mr. Jules."

Away sailed Milly, and got outside the door. She said to herself, "Well, the new—lady is not a bad-looking wench—I wonder how long me lord will keep her."

Milly had assisted at the inauguration of too

(a) These patches have almost wholly gone out of date, though we do sometimes see them used by ladies. It is surprising the beautiful effect that is produced by one or two small patches judiciously placed upon the face. Let any lady reader try this experiment. Take two fragments of black plaster, one the size of a large shot, and another the size of a pea. They must be pretty round. Now let her place the large one on the right cheek bone, and the other near the left hand corner of the mouth, and then contemplate the effect in a glass. If she is pretty, they will make her prettier. If she is plain (if any of the lady readers of this work can be plain), she will still find that the patches improve her. Mind, these patches must be perfectly round. Let them be square, and the effect is lost. It is for this reason that round moles on the face are called beauty spots, and shapeless ones on the countenance of a woman are so hideous. In the last century, men as well as women wore these charming and inexpensive additions to comeliness; but towards the end of this fashion it deteriorated. Instead of the patch being round, it was shaped in numberless curious fashions, not one of which approached the real "sun" patch, as it was called, except the crescent shape, or "moon" patch, which was very pretty. As to many of the shapes we refer our lady readers to the continued conversations between the countess and her maid.

many Countesses of Milray not to know who and what poor little Fanny was supposed to be.

M. Jules was not far off.

Milly found him, playing with the Italian greyhound.

"Good morning, M. Jules."

"Me angel, you sall find yourself vell, I do hope."

"Quite as vell as you can vish me," says Milly, imitating the French valet's accent, and going down in her skirts as though she had been suddenly cut short.

"I sall am moch glad to hear dat."

"When you've *quite* done with me lady's dog, me lady will take it."

"Oh!" says Jules — "you air de lady, de queen—I vish you vas my queen."

"I don't care a crown, M. Jules, about being married to—to any one."

"Ah, you air a pure—you dof not know de delights of married life."

"If you've quite done wid de dog, M. Jules——"

"Certainly, Mees Milly," says the valet, and he hands over the dog, which immediately responds to that attention, and all the others which the valet has shown his dogship, by snapping at that worthy Frenchman's fingers.

Somehow dogs seem to have a private and peculiar knowledge of good and bad men.

Such is dog life.

The Frenchman said—"Ah, you wicked one," quite gently ; but he gave the dog such a look, that if he could gave read human countenances (and it is possible dogs can), he would have determined never to take a piece of meat which M. Jules offered.

"Vill you ask to my lady?" says Jules, "vhen she sall see me lord? he vant to see her much particular."

"I'll ask me lady," says Milly, and flounces away.

"Ah, madame," mutters the Frenchman, as Milly departed—"if you vas Madame Jules, I vould clip de petticoats — I do hate high women."

Little Fanny was only too glad to see her lord, and she gave Milly a vigorous message to that effect.

Milly, carrying it to Jules, that inestimable man bowed low to the serving woman, and said he would take me lady's kind vords to me lord, and then he bowed himself out of the ante-chamber, in which he had been waiting with Fauchette the dog, who, by-the-bye, made friends with her new mistress at once.

"Ah!" muttered Jules, "me lady is to be made use of at once. I know—I know."

CHAPTER XIV.

THE POISONED BOUQUET.

JULES went straight to his master's room.

"Me lord."

"Well—I'm as weak as a rat, give me a glass of kirsch."

"Me lord," said the Frenchman, pouring out the required liquor, "me lady's ready to see me lor."

"Ah! then it's more than I am to see my lady. How is she?"

"Widout doubt well."

"Hum!" said my lord, and took a pinch of snuff, as much as to say it would be odd if she was not well.

"Me lord."

"D—n man, you have something to say—speak out."

"Me lord, last night, after me lord vas no more vant me for de night, I go for de leetle valk to de house where de Mr. Edgar Trevillian lif—"

"Well."

"He is not a fool!"

"Who?—this infernal Trevillian?"

"He is clevare, me lord."

"But not so clever as *I* am."

"Me lor!"

"And you as well, Jules—of course I mean you as well. He's not so clever as you and I are."

"No, me lord."

"Ah! he must be got out of the way."

"How?"

"Bah! I'll run him through, or have him shot. I'll manage."

"Me lord had bettare let his poor domestique manage."

"Why?"

"Because dis Trevillian is a devil. One Mistress Spikee and her mam'selle, Sally, dey say dat he fight like a solger of de guard, an dat he haf always de pistol to him vaistcoat."

"Bah! I will shoot him down like a dog."

"But—but suppose him shoot you down like to de dog de fust."

"Nonsense, Jules—I wasn't born yesterday."

"Nor was dis Trevillian. Me lord had bettare leave de affair in de hand of his faitful domestique."

"What do you mean?"

"Did not your lordship say de oder day to me, dat I had been to de belle Italy?"

"Yes."

"And dat I knew de poisons?"

"Yes—yes."

"Vell, me lord must not risk him life—de poor Mr. Trevillian must die by de poison."

"Bah! he would not eat in this house."

"I haf not say he vould."

"But you say he is to be poisoned?"

"Yes—but I haf not say he sall eat."

"Then how shall I manage?"

"I haf not said your lordship sall manage."

"Confound you—what *do* you mean?"

"When haf you receive de letter?"

"The night before last."

"Good—an I haf been to dat dear gentleman, and I see him, and I say to him, 'de poor lord pray you to come to see him ; he is vary ill vid de news you gif him, and dat it is true, he knows dat, and he is de more ill because of de poor countess dat know nothink of all dis misery.' And he come to-day at two of de clock."

"Well, and when he has come what shall I say to him ?"

"Noffin at all. You sall not see him, nevvare."

"Then how is he to be managed ?—you have said you will not end him."

"No : de countess sall do dat."

"Fanny !"

"Yes : Fanny."

"How can that be ?"

"Why the poor little thing sall know noffin of it. She sall kill him widout knowing it, and she sall smile as she kills him."

"Hang me if I comprehend you !"

"Me lord, I did not say you could. Look here, me lord. I haf a poison which if you only smell to him you die. I could kill you, me lord, so vile I shave you if I like to set some on de shaving brush. De poison must come near de nose for two seconds or it is not no use."

"You terrible fellow !" said the earl, looking eagerly at the waiting man. "Go on."

"I sall put some of this poison on a bouquet, and den I sall manage dat de countess give it to de man."

"But perhaps she will smell it."

"Oh de flower gals hate de smell of flowers, and nevare smell to 'em."

"Take care—don't injure Fanny."

"Ah, me lord loff Fanny—jest at present."

"I shall for years—I feel sure of that."

"So my lord say. Me lord, vill you leaf all in my pore hands ?"

"Yes, yes—you know I must."

"No, me lord," says the Frenchman, bowing humbly, but there is a cruel smile on his face, "no, me lord, not *must*, but you ought to *bettare* leaf de ting in my pore hands."

"Do as you like, but damage Fanny and I'll slice your ears off."

"Ah! me lord," says the valet, "if no one evare do her no more harm dan me Fanny would be a happy gal."

The nobleman started, but he said not a word.

At the same moment a sedan was brought up to the door and one of the bearers rapped a thundering rap at the door.

"'Tis he," said the earl, looking from the window, and marking a pale-faced, handsome man walk from the sedan, "is it not ?"

"*Oui, milord, c'est lui,*" said the Frenchman.

"And you are not prepared ?"

"Pardon, me lord, I am quite prepared."

The visitor was shown into the dining-room, and his card taken up to the earl.

The card bore these words :

THE EARL OF MILRAY.

And they were surmounted with a coronet.

"Already," said the earl.

"It is de first of dem cards dat he use, and de last," says the valet in a low voice to the earl, when the footman had left the room, "leaf all to me, me lord—Mees Fanny sall come to no harm."

But the Frenchman did *not* add that he was about to make Fanny the unconscious perpetrator of a murder in order to have more power over her when the poor girl should fall to his ugly share.

Swiftly the valet went to his own room, where was standing a bouquet of exquisite flowers in a glass of water.

Swift almost as thought the man went to a large press, took from it a little black box, and opened it with a key which he took from some concealed place in the chimney.

Opened, it showed a little array of phials of different colours.

"The blue," said the valet, and raised a phial of that colour from the box.

He took out the cork, holding the bottle away from his face, and poured *two drops* into the very heart of a trumpet-shaped blue flower. The flower quivered for a moment, and then seemed to bloom more freshly than before.

"Prepared," the man said lowly, and swiftly corked the bottle, locked the box, put it away in the press, and once more hid the key.

The whole process had not taken half a minute.

Then he swiftly ran towards Fanny's chamber and softly tapped at the door.

Admitted in the room, he walked as softly as though he could not run, and laid the bouquet on the table near which she was stretched on the sofa.

"Is me lord coming ?"

"No, me lady, not yet ; he is a little ill."

"Ill !—shall I go to him ?"

"No, me lady ; he pray me lady to wait for him. Does me lady like her dog ?"

"Much, tell my lord. Will he soon come ?"

"Soon, me lady ; and—"

"Yes."

"And will you receive a friend of his—Mr. Trevillian—till his lordship can come ?"

"Oh certainly, Mr. Jules ; why, what have you got there?—Fauchette, be quiet!—flowers?"

Fauchette, the dog, had growled at Mr. Jules.

"Yes, me lady, flowers."

"The idea of bringing flowers to me, Mr. Jules !"

"No, not for you, me lady ; I would not insult me lady wid flowers, but I sought me lady would be like a lady, and give de flowers to Mr. Trevillian ; it is de custom for de ladies to do dis."

"Oh yes—give them here."

"Do not smell dem, me lady, dey might make you sick."

"Oh, I never smell flowers ; I have had too much of them," and she put the bouquet down on the table near her.

"Sall I tell Mr. Trevillian to enter ?"

"Yes."

Within a few moments, Holgarth—for it need not be said that the visitor was he—entered the room.

He was pale, as on the previous night but one, when he alarmed Mrs. Spikey and Sally her maid.

Fanny rose and made her best curtsey, and Holgarth, fired at once with the charms of the creature before him, bowed low, keeping his blue eyes on her all the time.

"What a pretty (a) fellow," thought Fanny, as she gazed at the visitor.

"Dis is de countess," says the Frenchman.

"Indeed!" says the visitor, "I did not know his lordship was married."

"Yes, lately," says the Frenchman, and goes out leering.

"Pray sit near me, Mr. Trevillian."

He sat down near her.

"Are you a relation of the count's?"

"Yes—he has not told you my business here?"

"I—I do not talk much with him," says Fanny uneasily, and she was blushing, though the paint hid the fact.

"Ah, I would I had no business with him now that I see you, my lady!"

"He is a pretty fellow," thought the countess.

"Oh!" she says suddenly, "I forgot; pray accept this bouquet."

"Why, my lady?"

"Why, it is the fashion for the lady of the house to give a bouquet to her visitor."

"Is it?" said Holgarth, and as Fanny held it towards him he stretched out his hand; "I love the perfume of flowers," he added, "and shall inhale the perfumes of these with extra delight." The compliment so flurried Fanny that she dropped the flowers on the sofa.

Fauchette made a start at them directly and seized them with her teeth.

The next moment the dog, still holding the fatal flowers, plunged motionless and dead to the ground.

"Oh! my poor dog!" said Fanny, picking up the animal, from which the flowers now fell, "the scent has killed her—the nasty things!" and taking them up petulantly she cast them into the blazing fire, where in a moment they were consumed.

Holgarth laid his hand upon his sword for a moment, as though he would draw it, and his eyes were still upon Fanny; but as he saw her in tears, repersuaded himself he was wrong, and resigned his arm.

"Did me lady ring?" said the valet, putting in his head; he started as he saw the visitor still standing.

"Oh, Jules, come here; Fauchette seized the flowers and she is dead!"

"It's a leetle fit," says the Frenchman, "Fauchette often has dem."

And as he spoke he saw that the visitor had half drawn his sword.

CHAPTER XV.

THE PEER AND THE HIGHWAYMAN.

THE false Earl of Milray was standing near the door of his chamber, listening for any sound which might reach him from the chamber in which he knew the terrible scene of the bouquet was being enacted.

Not a sound—not a threat.

Suddenly he heard a footstep.

Nearer and yet nearer.

"Ah!" he thought, "that is not the footstep of Jules."

Indeed it was not. The Frenchman moved softly, and almost without sound, like a social Jesuit as he was. This step was strong and powerful, as though it was tramping away all opposition as it were mere show.

"Who is it?" the earl asked himself, and could not move from the spot on which he was standing when the sound first approached.

Nearer and nearer came the steps, and then, with a wild effort, he tore himself from the spot to which he had been rooted as though by enchantment, and flung himself into a seat.

As he did so he heard a second footstep; he recognised *that* in a moment—it was that of Jules.

"The bouquet has failed," he thought, "now who is to blame for this: can that Frenchman have sold me?"

Thus it always is with guilt.

The criminal is ever fearing that his brother criminal will betray him: this is the curse the wicked ever carry with them—"fear of the wicked and therefore fear of themselves."

The next moment the door was opened, and the voice of Jules was heard, saying—

"This is the gentleman, my lord."

The earl rose and bowed.

The visitor simply moved slightly forward.

"Leave the room, Jules."

"Me lord, yes," says the domestic, but having closed the door he runs round by passages and galleries, and is soon near the two enemies.

"My lord," says the visitor.

"My lord *to you*," says the earl, bowing.

"Not yet," returned the visitor.

"Pray be seated," says the earl.

And with mutual bows the two men seat themselves smiling at each other, although they are the bitterest enemies, and although no one is near to mark their comedy.

Thus it always is with enemies who are accustomed to anything like society: such men are not violent in any time of the world's history.

But in the age to which our tale refers, "gentlemen,"—that is to say, men whose position allowed them to have white and exquisitely soft hands—were in the habit of killing each other with all the politeness in the world.

The French and English army meeting, neither side, under the direction of the "gentleman" officer, would fire first, and history does not tell us who *did* fire first.

When "gentlemen" quarrelled and finished with a duel, they smiled as they crossed swords, and when the unlucky duellist fell mortally wounded, instead of sending some last words to mother, sister, or wife, in many instances they

---

(a) "Pretty" a hundred years ago had not the meaning of to-day—it meant well-made and handsome.

gave their entire attention to dying like gentle-men, with a smile upon the face, so as to convince the world they were " gentlemen in death."

Thus it was that while the acknowledged earl, and the man who declared he could wrest the title from him, sat face to face, determined to destroy each other, and yet smiling at each other in the most charming manner.

Such was the custom of gentlemen at the date of our tale.

The visitor, the assuming earl—the resuscitated highwayman—knew that his life had been attempted by the earl ; the earl knew that the man opposite was aware of that attempt, and yet both men sat smiling at each other like the politest people upon earth.

" Well, my lord," continued the earl.

" You see, my lord, I have lost no time."

" *No* time."

" I am a man of action."

" A lord, you mean."

" Pardon me, my lord ; till I have wrested the title from you I will forego the honour of being called ' my lord' by you."

" You are polite."

" I am of your family, my lord."

" I am willing to admit that—in private."

" Oh you are willing to admit that I am the son of your elder brother, and therefore that I am really the Earl of Milray."

" I am willing to admit all that—in private."

" My dear lord, if you see the matter as I do you will never have to admit the affair in any other way than in private."

" I do not see your drift so thoroughly as I recognise in you the family resemblance."

" You *do* then recognise the family resemblance ?"

" Thoroughly—you are the very likeness of your father, *my* father's brother, the Hon. Mr. Trevillian."

" The Honourable Mr. Trevillian was a gay man I believe ?"

" Nay, sir, do not condemn your own father."

" Very gay."

" Very."

" They say, my lord—do they not—that he had an illegitimate boy very much like his son Edgar ?"

" Yes, I have heard something to this effect ; but what has that to do with us ?"

" Really nothing, my lord," says the visitor, smiling.

" No, nothing," says the noble, taking a pinch of snuff delicately with his white left hand.

" Therefore, my lord, let us change the subject."

" Let us change the subject." reiterated my lord, in the softest and most charming manner.

To have heard them you might have supposed they were politely talking of some affair referring to a third party, but had any one *seen* them, narrowly watched their eyes, the conclusion would have been different.

They did not take their eyes from off each other for a moment, and each had his right hand concealed ; the one in the breast of his coat, the other under the cushion of the sofa on which he was sitting.

" Most happily will we change the subject," said the lord.

" Yes," said the other, " let us return to my former suggestion—that the affair need not go beyond ourselves."

" Ah ! I cannot understand the proposal."

" I suppose you can guess that *I* will not give up my claim."

" I can understand that," said my lord. " The Milrays do not give up a subject on which they have set their mind—do they ?"

" No, my lord."

" Hence it is that I also am determined to maintain a strenuous opposition to your, may I say it, preposterous claim."

" So, even if I show you that I am the legitimate holder of this title you usurp, you will not give it up."

" I will not give it up."

" I expected this, my lord."

" I am prepared to go into the law courts."

" And to bribe the judges, my lord ?"(a)

" And to bribe the judges, Mr. Trevillian."

" Ah ! shall we change the subject again, my lord."

" As Mr. Trevillian pleases. I am totally at his service, for as long as he likes."

" I would speak of the lady Milly."

" You know her."

" I know her, in society. She is just of age, is she not ?"

The highwayman knew this well. Had he not waited two days for her to come to his lodgings with her jewels. It was with the proceeds of these he had intended to commence an action against her own brother in order to recover the title. But she had not come, and so he had conceived the plan to which reference has been made.

" She is just of age," said the noble.

" A charming lady."

" My sister is most charming ; we hope to find a great match for her."

" That is, my lord, if she has not already determined upon one for herself."

(a) In those days the judges were not so noble-minded and upright as those of these more fortunate days. We firmly believe that a judge of the year 1860 would rather die than accept a bribe, or be found dumb, but only so short a time as thirty years ago, a judge enlivened his judicial duties by the introduction of a bottle of wine. This was only thirty years ago. A hundred years ago things were not what they now are, and when people say, " Oh ! the good old times !" it would be wiser to utter the sentence with an emphasis on the "Oh"— thereby intimating that they *were* times, which happily have passed away, for ever. As an instance of what the times were at the date to which the "Condemned Cell" refers, or rather, in this instance, a few years before it, it is a fact that a clergyman (very clever) being desirous of obtaining a bishopric, bet the Duchess of Yarborough, the Dutch mistress of King George the Second, that he would not gain a certain bishopric. He did get it, being recommended thereto by the duchess herself, and he lost the bet, which was many hundreds of pounds ; he gladly paid them, for the bishopric was worth thousands. Such was life in the last century.

E. BRETT

"Indeed, Mr. Trevillian; do you know of any such match? you say you know her."

"No—but I heard something about a match. It struck me that, perhaps, *you* had heard of it, and had set your face against it."

"Oh, dear no!" returned the lord, "I love my sister too well to oppose her plans in any way. You believe me when I say this; I can have no object in—in lying to you!"

"You honour me, my lord?"

"I am desolate to think I cannot pray my sister to do herself the honour of seeing you, but she is not in town."

"No, my lord?"

"No, she has left for Scotland; she is going to her aunt's—but I need not trouble you with her whereabouts."

"No, my lord, not till the private arrangement of our affair to which I have referred is settled."

"Dear me," returned the lord, in his most winning voice, but his eyes were fast upon the highwayman, "dear me, we are returning to that subject again, are we? and just, too, as we were getting so sentimental over Lady Milly. Poor Milly! it was, perhaps, dangerous to send her unaccompanied into Scotland."

"Very dangerous, my lord; *did* you send her quite unaccompanied?"

"With the exception of a few servants of a friend of ours; I could not spare my own people. The *roads* certainly are unsafe."

"Very, my lord. They say since Gentleman Jack was hanged, the night before last, the gentry of the road have sworn to kill every man and ravish every woman who fall in their way for the next month."

"Horrid! I wonder what a highwayman's life is like?" asked my lord.

"I wonder," returned the visitor.

In the pause which followed the fall of a light footstep was heard.

The earl knew it in a moment; it was that of the French valet. "Is he plotting this

6

man's destruction?" thought the earl; "is he in some way about to rid me of this rascal?" his next thought was, "he is listening—he will know too much." And then followed the thought, "this man, Jules, must die."

"What noise was that, my lord?"

"A rat."

"Kill him."

"I would," returned the lord, "but rats get out of the way."

A pause of some seconds followed.

"Well, my lord, shall we return to the question of a quiet means of settling our differences."

"Ah! you said something of settling this affair of the earldom with reference to those detestable law courts. I had almost forgotten the reference; pray let us hear more of it."

"You are determined not to yield the earldom?"

"Determined as death."

"As *death*, my lord?"

"As death."

"Then," returned the highwayman, "suppose we make it a matter of life and death."

"Oh, as you wish," said the earl, but he turned as white as innocence, and heartily wished that Jules would come to his aid.

As he wished the door opened, and Jules appeared bearing a tray, a decanter, and two glasses.

The valet came up to his master, and by an expression pointed to one of the glasses—the one nearest the earl.

The earl looked, and saw a few grains of fine white powder at the bottom of the glass.

The menial filled the glasses, both from the same bottle on the tray, and put the glass in which the powder had rested near the earl. Jules then took the other and placed it near the visitor.

"Some choice hock," said the earl—"it is my practice to have it poured out for myself and visitors, even if I do not drink myself."

"Do, my lord," says the highwayman, "if *you* drink I will, but I dare not drink in the presence of your lordship unless *you* set me the example."

"If me lord drink it will do him much good," says the servant significantly, so significantly that the earl raised the glass to his lips and was about to drink, when suspicion haunting the guilty mind, he hesitated.

Suppose Jules had turned on him—suppose the powder was a poison, while the other glass was unpoisoned. Perhaps Jules saw the way to make more money by this Edgar Trevillian if *he* were earl, than if he, the thinker, still wore the coronet.

Fool! it did not strike him that the weaker the master the safer the power of the servant. It did not strike him that Jules knew he could do as he liked with his present lord, and might not be so sure with a future master.

Lastly, and most unusually, he did not think that the powder might be an *antidote to the portion of wine his glass held, and that the re-* *mainder of the wine in the visitor's glass and in the decanter contained a deadly poison.*

Idiot that he was, he set the glass down untasted, saying—

"Jules, I do not feel equal to my work this morning."

"What—you do not drink, my lord," said Holgarth, with a sneer, "then nor can I. I will not drink until my lord has drank; or I will not drink at all."

"I fear, my lord," said Jules, steadily taking the glass, "dat me lord find de wine is not so good as it is in de usual way—me lord vill allow me to taste him."

Quite as steadily as he had raised the glass he put it to his lips, and drank half of it.

"Me lord, I tink it is as good as it is de usual."

"Is it, Jules?" says the earl, "let me see," and taking the same glass as that from which the domestic had drank, he tasted the liquor.

"I was mistaken," he said, and drank what remained in the glass.

"You will now do me the honour of a mere sip of this poor wine?" asked the earl.

"My lord, I am honoured," says the visitor, and stretched out his hand to the glass.

As he did so the wide cuff of his coat caught the top of a chair, and the glass was upset.

The cover of the table was in a small measure pale green, and the visitor saw that when the wine had run on the table the pale green had turned to a faint red.

He had spilt too much hock in his riotous time not to know that this was odd.

"Ah! another glass for Mr. Trevillian," said the earl, immediately.

"Pardon me," returned the visitor, bowing, "I am unworthy to drink in your presence having overset this glass of wine—and, and destroyed the *table cover - see, the pale green* has turned to *faint red*, and it would seem that it is turning to *blood* red."

The earl started.

Not so the Frenchman. Nothing made that cold-blooded man forget himself for a moment.

"Ah," said he, "I haf nevare see de vine do dat wid de table cover before - nevare."

"Nor have I," said the visitor, and moved the hand which was in his breast.

"Leave the room, Jules."

"Me lord, I obey."

The next moment the two men were once more alone.

Suddenly the aspect of the highwayman underwent a complete change.

He got up from the sofa, flung one handsome leg over an arm of it, and cocked his hat on one side, so that he looked like Captain Macheath in a boozing ken. (a)

---

* Thieves' drinking pothouse. The word "boozing" is Saxon, and certainly means "to enjoy whilst half asleep." The word "ken" comes from "kahn," the principal inn, a title which in all probability was introduced by some eastern beggar or scamp, who applied the term used in his native land to the English "inn," whereon it was swiftly adopted as being new, easily said, "knowing," and not known to the authorities.

"Don't you think we've had enough of this, Milray."

The earl looked astounded for a moment, and then said in the same tone he had adopted all through the conference—

"I think so—to what are you alluding ?"

"D—n it, man, cut the polite—you know you're as g eat a scamp as I am."

"I—I thought you were Mr. Edgar Trevillian !"

"Well, I am, to you and the world, and I mean to wear your shoes if I wear them for the next month or so."

"Hum! you will soon hoist me out of my title it would seem."

Here the highwayman took a pistol from his breast, and flung it with a loud crash against the opposite wall.

A moment more, and the pistol which the earl had concealed beneath the pillow of the sofa was pointed at the highwayman's breast.

"You have been rash, Mr. Trevillian."

"Bah !"

"I can take your life.'

"Bah !"

"But my hand is on the trigger of the pistol !"

"It will make a noise if you fire it—won't it, my lord ?"

"Doubtless ; but a pistol fired off is no such wonderful occurrence ; there is a pistol gallery a few houses away."

"Bah ! why do you not fire ?"

"Because I want a little talk with you."

"Speak away ; but you will no more shoot me than you succeeded in *poisoning* me."

"Poison, Mr. Trevillian !"

In answer the visitor pointed to the stains on the cover.

By this time the stains were *blood* red all of them.

The earl did not look to the table, he was afraid to take his eyes off the man whom he now believed in his power.

"Why, my man," he returned to the highwayman, "the noise would make no stir, and if it did, before the neighbourhood could be alarmed, Jules, the Frenchman whom you saw and who is devoted to me, would have removed your body, removed the signs of blood on the carpet, and I should be safe !"

"You have reckoned without your host, my lord."

"How do you mean ?"

"Look from the window."

The lord did not move.

"Ah, I see you will not look ; I will for you. I see an officer of justice."

"Well ?"

"He came here with me, knowing me to be the Earl of Milray."

"What do you mean ?"

Here the wretched man's hand and pistol trembled.

"This : I showed the authorities at Bow Street my proof ; I told them I was desirous of having a private arrangement with you, and

prayed that an officer might be sent with me, to—to protect me, my lord."

"You wanted little protection."

"Pardon me, my lord, I wanted much. You see I have persuaded the police I am amiable, would treat fairly with you, but that I am a little afraid of you—so the officer watches over me. I told him if a pistol-shot came from this house to break in at once ; he has half-a-dozen men round the corner."

"Great powers !" said the earl.

"Fling your pistol down, my lord ; fling it down, it is useless."

The lord in a kind of rage flung the weapon from him, and then equally disposed of his cool fashionable drawl.

He started up now, and then these two men faced each other, no longer drawling humbugs, but men face to face ; if infamous, courageous —if actually wicked, certainly defiant.

The highwayman still sat on the sofa-arm, but his eyes and face were full of the workings of courage and will.

The earl's was equally full of determination.

"Now, my friend, how is this to end ?" said the earl, "quick !"

"Spoken like a man," returned the other, "I did not think you had so much pluck in you."

"Go on."

"I spoke some time back—before the wine came on—of an arrangement whereby we might settle this arrangement amicably—that is, to the satisfaction of each as far as possible."

"Go on ; though the officer could not hear the thrust of a knife if I stabbed you ?"

"If he did not hear this whistle," and the captain held one up, "he has instruction to break in at the end of an hour. Our interview will have lasted an hour in five minutes more ; so if you stab me you must be quick about it, and about removing the blood stains. And then you would have to account to the police for my disappearance."

"I would say you left by the other side of the house."

"Bah ! In the first place you have to do the deed ; and in the second you won't attempt it."

"Go on—what about this private arrangement ?"

"This ; we will neither of us give way. One of us must die, and within the five minutes."

"A duel it would seem."

"No, my lord ; a duel would be inconvenient to the survivor. Near relatives may not by the code of honour fight duels ; and I doubt much if the survivor would not be *hanged* under the present state of affairs. You know since that scandal of the colonel's the Government are hard on duellists ; and what would the Government be on me or you fighting a duel—we near relatives—without witnesses in the house and under such equivocal circumstances."

"Then what do you propose ?"

"One of us must die, and must appear to the officer outside to have committed suicide. The thing is quite simple, my lord. If you are the victim, the death will be explained away by saying that you were so convinced of the reality of my claim that in despair you destroyed yourself. Whereas, if *I* am the victim, you can say that in a paroxysm of grief at your proving to me that my claim was ridiculous I sent a bullet through my heart."

"But, how do you propose to arrange the chances?"

"Oh, if I have arranged the entire plan I have not forgotten the chances. Here is a brace of pistols."

As the highwayman spoke he produced a brace of most exquisitely worked, silver-mounted arms.

"They are both loaded; call your man Jules and let him extract the ball from one of them. May I summon him?"

"Certainly!"

Clearly and sharply, like the sound of fate, rang out the little summoner.

The next moment the man entered the room. He gave his master a searching look, but he read no responsive look in his eyes.

"Extract the ball from one of these arms," said the highwayman.

The serving-man began his task it was one at which he was an adept.

"By the bye, cousin Milray," said the highwayman, "would you like to see the proof of my identity?"

"No," said the earl, quite calmly, "I am sure you are the son of my father's elder brother, no other man's son can you be; and, therefore, I am sure you are his legitimate son, or you would not come here on this desperate errand."

"Good!"

"De pistol is unload," said the Frenchman.

"Let this man retire," continue the highwayman.

The valet looked at his master and comprehended the plain nod he received for an answer to quit the room.

No leave-taking did these two men, the Frenchman and his master, seek the one of the other: their attachment was that of the wicked—the entirely wicked have no affection.

"Now," continued the highwayman, "one of these pistols is loaded the other not. I place them under this table-cover which your wine stained blood red. Now, I move them backwards and forwards—do you do the same."

"I think I comprehend your drift, do I not?"

"I think you do. You will take one of these pistols, I the other; each will stand on one or the other side of this table, each will place the pistol he withdraws to his own breast over his heart, and at the word fire! each will fire; he who escapes will be the Earl of Milray, he who dies will appear to have committed suicide; what do you think of my plan?"

"Ah—what is this?" the earl's face lit up with a delight; *as though he was saved from death and reigned the earl once more.*

The highwayman saw the illumination of his enemy's countenance, but he did not appear surprised by it. Indeed, an observer would have marked—an observer, Jules to wit, did remark—that he seemed as though he knew the expression would pass over his face.

At all events it caused him to assume the fashionable air once more.

"Now, Mr. Trevillian, take your choice of weapons; place you first your hand below the cloth and take *your* choice."

"No, my lord, I could not."

"But I insist, Mr. Trevillian."

"Oh, then I obey; I am too polite to *disobey* the direction of the most noble the Marquis of Milray. Do you know, my lord," continued the highwayman, placing his hand below the cloth, "I *thought* you would be polite enough to give me my choice."

And as he does so he smiles a remarkable smile.

"I am a polite man, Mr. Trevillian."

If a rogue meet rogue, who will win?

"See, my lord, I have chosen a pistol," and he showed his weapon.

"Then the other is for me," said the earl.

"Now, my lord," continued the highwayman, "you place your pistol upon your heart as I do mine upon mine. Thank you, my lord, that is right. Now, when I call three we both fire; is it not so agreed?"

"Yes, so agreed."

"One!"

A pause.

"Well, Mr. Trevillian, why do you stop?"

"My lord, you haven't your pistol well over your heart. If the bullet does not hit the mark it will cause you pain; if the *heart* be hit death will only be like sleep."

"Thank you, Mr. Trevillian, you are a gentleman."

"Oh, my lord."

A pause.

"Two!"

Another pause.

"That is right, my lord, "you have the pistol *exactly* over the heart."

A pause.

"Three!"

A second after the word passed the man's lips two reports were heard, but in that moment each treacherous wretch had turned the pistol upon his adversary.

They stood looking at each other for several moments, each clasping his pistol tight in his hand.

Which was dead? one of them must be.

"You have lost, my lord!"

As he spoke the noble fell forward on the table, the blood pouring from his mouth and dying the other portion of the table-cloth at once and awfully a deep true blood red.

The next moment the highwayman caught the right hand of the nobleman in his, and turning the pistol within it upon the breast of the dead man he pressed it down hard and firm upon his breast.

As he did so Jules was standing by his side.

"I knew you vould kill him, me lord."

"My lord!"

"I haf heard all."

"Yes—I knew I would kill him, friend, as surely as you tried to kill me."

"Do you vant a faithful servant?"

"Yes. Are you one."

"Vas I not faithful to him?"

"Yes, it would seem so."

"I will be so to you, me lord."

"Good—and I knew I should kill him. The engravings on the stocks of the pistols were known to me—one is engraved in little circles, the other in little squares; I saw you unload the square engraved one, and I knew your master would be polite enough to give me first choice when he had thought of shooting me. I had first choice, and I felt for the square chased pistol, and I found it."

"You are me lord," says the Frenchman, bowing low his head.

All their conversation had passed most rapidly, so rapidly that it was finished as the door opened and the servants came streaming in.

"Jules, hide the other pistol."

"Yes, me lord."

And the serving man thrust it in his breast.

"Your master has committed suicide," said the highwayman, taking his hand away from the arm of the deceased nobleman.

The arm remained in the position in which the highwayman had placed it, the pistol, a ball from which had *not* killed him, pressed lyingly against his breast.

The scurrying of the servants backwards and forwards was soon interrupted by the entrance of the police-officer to whom the highwayman had referred as watching over him—the triumpher in the bloody struggle of life and death.

"Oh," says this man to the highwayman, "I was afraid he'd done for you, my lord."

"My lord!" said two or three of the servants as the police officer thus addressed the highwayman.

"My poor—poor master!" says Jules, "to tink dat he haf kill himself because he haf lost de title!"

"What title?" says a servant.

"He was not de rightful earl!" says Jules, "I hear all. *Dis* gentleman is a lord," pointing to the highwayman, "and my poor master he so mad he kill himself!"

"Ah!" says the officer, "my lord, I really thought as how it were you as was popped at; an' sez I, my lord—Lord! sez I, yere we shall have a dance upon nothing (a) out of this, as sure as my name's Charley White!"

"Take the poor gentleman to his room," says the highwayman.

"Yes, my lord," say the servants, and obey the order of the new lord.

Meanwhile, poor Fanny was below wondering what the pistol-shot meant, and why the people

(a) "Hanging."

seemed to be hurrying backwards and forwards all over the house.

CHAPTER XVI.

THE CARAVAN CONTAINS ANOTHER INMATE.

FOUR days had passed since Mr. and Mrs. Naggleton quitted Drury Lane, and the caravan was not jumbling, it was quite still. The dwarf was asleep, the white-haired Albanian was pulling the hair of that sleeping dwarf, the most good-tempered little man in the world; and the armadillo was "gruffing about," as Mr. Naggleton himself would term it—"like a babby with his high teeth cutting."

Besides the little girl who had become part of Mr. Naggleton's company, was another girl who was far from little; in fact, she was nearly six feet, and she had such a babyish face that though Mrs. Naggleton had her *fears* upon first seeing her the day before at the statute fair, that she might drop the dear "Puddy," as she called Perdita—she looked so very awkward, she could not say "no" to this young nurse, when here Naggleton pointed out that she might be shown as a baby giant, a child four years old six feet high.

So this rustic beauty, who goggled like a guy as she was, became raised so high in the world as the caravan stood above it, and also she became endowed with the baby, which, to say the truth, though light, weighed upon this sylph like a ton weight: Tiny—this was the young giantess's little name—was so afraid of letting the dear treasure fall.

Yes, the caravan was drawn up for the night, and somehow, though it was only a poor wandering showman's old ramshackle cart, it looked, it *was* a home—a cheerful, happy, God-given home—in the midst of the heath upon which Naggleton had commanded "Betsy" to "whoa." The reader will please to remember that "Betsy" is the horse—not the wife, not Mrs. Naggleton—who went through the world with the tender name attached to her of Jemima.

Yes, the caravan was a *home*, and as much cannot be said for many palaces, so called. Now, somehow this was a palace, and the king was Mr. Naggleton himself.

Not much of a king to look at was Mr. Naggleton, for he was a mild-looking middle-aged man, with sandy hair and sandy whiskers, and eyes very much the colour of boiled gooseberries; but a king for all that, who reigned with much gentleness, and of whom in her heart Madame Jemima was very proud, though she did "reckon him" up now and then; and indeed, the dwarf could tell of a time when the "missus" flung every available article at her king, who guarded them off with one elbow and one knee; and indeed she was only fetched up when she fell upon the dwarf, and was about to pitch that curiosity at her well-beloved lord and master,—fetched up by the dwarf exclaiming

"Missus! whatever you does don't send me to glory!"

The gentler intimation that Mrs. Naggleton was about to "do for" Mr. Naggleton fetched Mrs. Naggleton to her senses, for she immediately put a black wig on the Albanian, so that the public should not see his white hair for nothing; clapped some charcoal on his white eye-brows to the same end, and then ordered him to go and fetch a bottle of rum and a half-pint of shrub.

The shrub Mrs. Naggleton warmed, and made her lord and master drink every drop; she helped him drink the rum.

But, dear me, all this was long and long before Mr. and Mrs. Naggleton found the poor woman lying in the road, and it is very cowardly of this present writer to say anything about it.

Well, to get on.

The caravan was pulled up for the night on the heath—on the heath in preference to the village, because Naggleton had learnt the experience that if he located on the ground the boys got up on the wheels and peeped in at the windows all for nothing, and so the receipts were damaged, to say nothing whatever of the injurious effects it had upon the belief of the villagers in the show-people to see those worthies buy such every day things as bread, and butter, and even candles.

So Naggleton never would buy anything in a small village till he was about to leave it, when the effect might be just what it liked, he having wrung every penny out of the place that could be got by all the talking means in his power.

Well, Mr. and Mrs. Naggleton were having their supper.

As has been said, the dwarf was asleep, and the Albanian (a) boy plaguing that good-natured little man. Tiny was nursing the baby.

Now mark. They had only had Puddy four days, and yet this was Mr. Naggleton's remark,

"My dear Jenny, how that there child does grow!"

"You certingly have a eye!" says Jemima, and approvingly hands the pot of beer to her lord and master.

"Grow! why, bless my knee-breeches, if I don't see her grow;" and it is certain that if Puddy did grow Mr. Naggleton had a chance of seeing her, for he never took his eyes off the little charge except he was asleep, or entreating people to walk up, or looking after "Betsy," who always went down on her knees if she was not jerked up about every twenty seconds.

"It was almost a pity we left them there glass things at the police-station, wasn't it? Ye see, my Jenny, Puddy 'ull soon be growed up to the stilt-business, and then she would look well in 'em. My eye! didn't they blaze in the light, just like real! Ah, my little beauty!" continued Mr. Naggleton, shaking his clasp-knife with which he was cutting his beef, at the little infant, "ah, my beauty! I lay my life your mother was a stunner on the stage, and reg'lar knocked 'em all over. Why she was out on that there road on that there night is more than this here man can say."

"Take another pull," says Mrs. Naggleton, once more approvingly.

Mr. Naggleton was about to do so, when an extraordinary sound so surprised him that it was a wonder he did not resign eating and drinking for ever. This remarkable sound cannot easily be reduced to paper, but such as can be made of it—here it is.

"K-h-t-chsey—k-h-t-ch-ch-chtshz!"

"Why, wot's that there?"

"Why, Tiny, what are you at?" asks Mrs. Naggleton; whereat Tiny replied in the broadest Yorkshire tongue—"Makin' yoongster looaf!"

"Making my beauty laugh!" says Mrs. Naggleton.

"Turn her into a red Ingin, Mrs. Nag," says the proprietor of the caravan, "and our fortune's made. If that there wouldn't do for the war-cry, why what would?"

Here Miss Tiny uttered the same remarkable sound, which caused the baby to give quite a horrified leap, as though she'd been electrified.

"Dammy, Mrs. N., turn her into a red Ingin!"

Mr. Naggleton did not mean a red engine, but a red Indian; the remarkable cry had suggested the idea of an Indian war-whoop.

"Oh, dear no, Nag," says Jemima, "she

(a) Albanian really means white—not a native of Albania. It comes from the Latin word "albi"—white. It need not be said that an Albanian, as seen in exhibitions, is a human being whose hair is perfectly white, whose skin is unnaturally colourless, and whose eyes are generally red. Albanians are to be found in all countries, and amongst all men, from the North Pole to the equator, from the swarthy gipsey to the fair-haired Saxon. The scientific mode of accounting for this phenomenon is thus given;—The philosophers say that in a perfect human being there is always a certain amount of colouring matter in the body—this becomes intense in hot climates, weak in cold climates—hence we have the negro of Africa and the fair Dane or Swede. The colouring matter gives the entire tone to the complexion, and especially to the hair and eyes; the dark centres of the latter are entirely formed of this pigment. Now, in the Albanian cases this pigment, or paint, (from pale yellow to deep red-black) is totally, or almost totally absent—hence it is that the hair and skin is white, and the eye naturally red, for there is no natural paint to hide the blood which is circulating in the pellucid orbs. The most singular part of the matter is that animals have this peculiarity not only in common with men but possess it infinitely more frequently. It is said that this defect arises from the fright of the mother, whether woman or animal, while bearing the child; and it is a singular fact that the animals who are the most timid—evidently therefore the animals most liable to be frightened—are those which most frequently give birth to these singular creatures. We barely ever hear of a white lion, though such a thing has been known; and we seldom hear of a white elephant, though such things are, and fetch in eastern lands an im- mense price; but such timid creatures as hares, rabbits, rats, and mice, are continually producing these creatures. And the fact may be added that Albanian men are peculiarly timid and weak, and as a rule have been, or are, the children of one or two weak parents. In conclusion, white animals must not be confounded with Albanian creatures. A white hare is not necessarily Albanian—a Polar bear is always white—but in both these cases the eyes are almost always black. Albanian men and animals are known by dead whiteness and red eyes, though it is a curious fact that cases are on record of Albanian men with perfectly blue eyes; but these cases are wondrously rare.

ain't got enough spirit; she'd break down and cry, and then the people 'ud smash the cair wan."

"Well, there's summut in that," says Naggleton.

"No, she must remain the infant giantess, and we must cut her hair shorter and make her clothes shorter, and then she'll look about five. Lor, look at her, looking at that dear hinfant—why she don't look four and a half."

And indeed, to speak the truth, Tiny did look like a very little girl seen through a very large magnifying-glass; for she was, as it has been said, full six feet high, and Mrs. Naggleton had dressed her in a light blue dress, which came half way down her legs, with a little pinafore over that, and all her hair cropped down to about four inches long, and then violently curled with a pair of tongs Mrs. Naggleton always carried to throw a wave into the hair of the Albanian. Tiny looked at the baby just as a tiny girl would.

But she started when Mrs. Naggleton, her majesty of the cairywan, actually said her clothes must be cut shorter still.

If Tiny had the look of a child she was in years almost a woman, and she understood that "shanks" were parts of a lady that ought not to be shown, whether she be infant-giantess or charming young woman.

"Whoot mum, coot ma petticoot shorter? why, thull coot it awa altogeether!"

"Go along!" says Mrs. Naggleton, talking to Tiny as to a child, "go along, and take care of baby!"

"Why, so I a doo; but a caant have noo tricks played wi petticoot, wi winter a coomin on!"

"Go along, I say!" says Mrs. Naggleton.

"Whar go to?" says Tiny.

"Go—go to sleep!" says Mrs. Naggleton. "and here's your supper; give me the darlin'!"

"Oh, you beauty!" says Mrs. Naggleton, "you're my own!"

"Ah, Mrs. N., I wish she was your own."

"An' ain't she as good?"

"Well, Jenny, she's as good as gold."

"Yes, Nag; and now the cairywan's complete—there's a baby in it."

"Suppose, Mrs. Nag, we said as how this here spanker's ours—no one would know to the contrary—suppose as how we tell her we're her father and her mother, then she'd love us all the more, and we won't love her none the less; and lor! won't it be a merry-go-round. 'Walk up! walk up! and see the lovely hinfant phenomener dance a hornpipe in stilts like a hangel!'"

"Oh! you god-king of a man!" says Mrs. Naggleton, and fetches out a gin-bottle.

"Mrs. Nag, your health!"

And now Mr. Nag, being full of food, spirits, smoke, and good-temper, thought fit to ask Tiny a few questions.

"Tiny, I want ye to tell me summut."

"Fust measter; is it aboot my pore petticoots?"

Then she stroked that article as far down towards her ankles as it would go—it was not very far.

"No, Tiny, it aint."

"Second, measter and missus, yere not a gooin to mak ut shorter; cos if ye doo a'll roon away."

"You will?"

"A' will!"

"Very well then," says Mrs. Naggleton, "you shan't have another tuck up," and Mrs. Naggleton said to herself, "neither, my dear, shall you have another tuck down, and as I'm convinced you're growing, why it'll be all the same in a month or two.

"Now, Tiny, tell yer master where are ye from."

"Yoorkshur!"

"What place?"

"Hooggooltoon-toof."

"What was you a doing near London when we tuk you?"

"Noothin."

"Well, what had ye been about?"

"Sarvant-galling."

"Where?"

"Near city, wi' Mrs. Spikey's married sister."

"Oh! Why did ye leave?"

"Cos measter said I was allus a toomblin over he, and missus her zaid as I never got oot o' the way o' she, an ut's true a was allus a toomblin over booth of 'em—them was very smool people, and a 'um not smool, Mr. Naggooltoon?"

"So then ye went away?"

"Yes; I lefted 'em booth oop an shoo'k 'em, an then a went away."

"You clever girl, you! and then ye went to the statty (a) fair at Richmond?"

(a) We suppose it is necessary to say what a servants' statute fair was and is, for in some parts of England these detestable periodical hirings take place—generally in the North of England, and especially in Yorkshire. At the period set apart for this "hiring," all the servants, males and females, of the *lower* kind stand in rows in the market-places, and would-be masters and mistresses walk along the ranks and inspect the "offers" as they would a pack of sheep, hogs, or vegetable barrows. These purchasers stop, make inquiries, sometimes of not the most delicate nature—for many a thriving north-country farmer's wife has stood "in the statty" once on a time herself—and then the hirer passes on to the next article. The girls wear no distinctive mark, but we have heard such questions asked by young half-drunken farmers of the most dashing girls present, that it might be supposed that some of the girls did carry some distinctive mark by virtue of which such questions were put to them. It may be added that we are very frequently inclined to rank the morality of country life above that of town, but anybody who attends a "statty" fair of even these ameliorated days will hear enough to make him open his eyes if he keeps his ears wide open. But if the girls wear no perceptible badge of the kind of service for which they chose to be hired, it is different with the men: these latter wear such insignia (if the term may be employed) as tell their wants without their speaking. A general farm labourer wears a straw twisted round his hat; a man who wishes a place as ostler, or horse overlooker, wears a wisp of horse-hair in his cap; while a clever sheep-shearer and dairy manager carries a pack of wool. Thus the master can tell the man's wants without speaking to him. It is to be hoped that the advance of education and the spread of human dignity will soon do away with these degrading and animal-like exhibitions, the effect of which cannot but be ignoble, and a proof of this may be shown in the fact that the miserable shilling which binds the man to the master for the year

"Hey, a did; an thar ye see me, an a' the gals an their chops a grinnin at me, and I'd a clean a knoocked em doon if ye had not coom to tuk me off rank."

"Ah! an made a giant of 'e!" says Mr. Naggleton.

For all response poor Tiny looked at her legs.

"An now, Tiny, I tell you; if you'll swear never to cut us, we'll swear never to cut you—now, what do yer say?"

"Poon me loife I doon't unnerstand," says Tiny.

"Look here; you say as how you'll never hook, cut, give leg-bail, go away from cairy wan—we will swear never to turn yer out of it."

"What, keep I here allus?—wull, rally."

"Yes, allus."

"And not mak I wear shorter petticoots?"

"Jest so," says Mrs. Naggleton.

"A' sweer—hard," says Tiny.

"So does I," says Nag.—"never, so help me never, while I has a crust of bread an' a pipe o' bacca, shall you want, you Yoorkshire Tiny."

"I backs the master," says Mrs. Naggleton ; and she literally does so by thwacking her hand hard down upon that showman's shoulders.

"Oh! how joolly," says Tiny—"I'se gotten a hoo-o-ome at last! Please, Mrs. Naggultoon, tak baby."

Mrs. N. made an immediate plunge for the little treasure—she saw Tiny was overcome ; and no sooner was Tiny quite sure the treasure was safe, than she set up such a roar, that Bob, the dwarf, was shaken up out of his sleep as though by an earthquake, and he came tumbling forward like a very drunk dwarf indeed.

"Holloa! Tiny, you've woke up Bob."

"What's the row?" says Bob.

"We been a swearing never to part."

"Then hand over," says Bob, and held out a fist quite large enough for any man towards the great pot of beer.

"Yere's 'er luck and yer luck, an all frens round St. Paul—hurray!"

Here the armadillo could stand it no longer, but unrolled himself and scudded forward—of course right between Mrs. N.'s sainted legs, as

(the mere use of such a pledge is an instance of the implied want of good faith between the parties) is almost immediately spent in the nearest beer shop. Perhaps the feeling of low degrading inhumanity in this matter of statute fairs is not better shown than in the fact that the "statty" fairs for "hirings" are quoted just like other fairs. We have now at our side a north-country paper of a few months back, a journal most advanced in opinions, of large circulation, appealing to the great mass of the people, and directed by a most Christian gentleman, which contains this shameful sentence :—"Northallerton, Yorkshire.—The supply of cattle was good, prices firm. The supply of farm and other servants was small in quantity—prices ruled high, and not many contracts were completed." Does not such a sentence as this carry its own condemnation. We repeat—we hope the day is not far distant when such scenes will only be traditionary. At one time the "statty" fair at Richmond was one of the most important in the kingdom. We do not know whether hirings still take place there ; for the credit of a town so near the metropolis let us hope not.

usual. But the armadillo was not a sympathetic anamal, so after sniffing about for a few moments back he went to his blanket in a kind of huff.

"An who knows," says Naggleton, excited with beer, tobacco, gin, and philanthropy—"who knows but praps as how Bob 'll marry yer some day, and ye'll both have a show of yer own."

The idea was so good that Bob hurrayed again, like a Trojan.

And the idea was also so good, that Mr. N, equally, if immodestly, applauded his own little remark, and the two together made quite sufficient noise.

When they had quite done a lull succeeded.

Then Mr. N. was going to speak up again, when Mrs. Naggleton said—"Hush! I thought as how I heard a voice."

"Some people is wrong," says Naggleton.

"And some people aint," says Mrs. Naggleton. There, didn't you hear it again—didn't it say help, jist as though it was under the cairywan?"

"Lor, yes."

"Here," says the dwarf—"you take the poker and get behind me : if he passes me use yer poker—but he'll find my fists tough uns."

"The moon's up," says Mrs. Naggleton—"you'll easy see him."

"Now, who air yer?" says the dwarf, flinging back the door as bold as a lion.

"My lor!" says Naggleton, looking over the dwarf—"my lor! Jemima dear, if it aint *another woman*."

And there, sure enough, leaning upon the wheel of the caravan—or rather *one* of the wheels, because it has four—was a pale-looking handsome girl, and who was looking up to them, and who now, in the voice which Mr. and Mrs. N. had heard, said—"Help, help!"

———

CHAPTER XVII.

MR. AND MRS. NAGGLETON MEET WITH ANOTHER SURPRISING ADVENTURE.

"WELL," says Mr. Naggleton, when he was quite sure a woman was near the wheel—"well, a go's a go, and ain't this a go, Jemima?"

"Go along," says Jemima ; not using those words to the stranger, but to her Naggleton.

"A woman," says Naggleton.

"Some people is fools," says Mrs. Naggleton, who always lost her temper when she was mystified.

"And it's a good job," says Naggleton, "as how some people ain't."

Meanwhile Tiny got behind the dwarf, who armed himself with a heavy boot, and the Albanian trembled in every hair of his precious white head. The armadillo of course unrolled himself, came to the door, and sniffed ; whereupon that animal being for some unknown reason absolutely and utterly disquieted, retired to the extreme limits of the "cairywan," coiled himself up, and went to sleep directly.

E.BRETT.

"Who's there?" says Naggleton, in a loud voice.

"Some people 'ud frighten other people with their wices," says Mrs. Naggleton.

"Wices, Jenny—what, am I wicious?"

"Some people don't mean other people's wices as wices, but the wice of the other people's throat."

Then in a much softer voice Mr. Naggleton remarked—"What is the matter with thee, dear."

"I have lost my way—and I'm fainting," was the answer, in a sweetly soft voice.

Now the present writer has forgotten whether he has said that the Naggletons cut off their communication with the outer world when they had done showing for the day, by the very simple means of hooking up the steps which led to the machine *under* it, therefore when the stranger was discovered at the wheel, Mr. and Mrs. Naggleton were above her.

Now Mr. Naggleton, after hooking up the steps, and padlocking them, (for on one occa-

7

sion the steps had been stolen and all the caravan was in dismay) was in the habit of having a chair handed down to him, by which means he ascended, with some difficulty, to his small palace; the chair was fished up after him, and all was complete till the next morning, when a descent similar to the ascent was made.

But now Mrs. Naggleton made "no bones" about steps or chair, and no sooner did she hear the pitiful expression "I have lost my way and I'm fainting," than she took a leap like a diver into water, or rather like an angel down to earth, and arrived with a crash upon the ground.

Down came Nag after his wife, like a dutiful husband as he was.

"My dear," says Mrs. N.—"where is thee going."

"I don't know."

"Where is't come from."(a)

(a) In those times, "thee" and "thou" were words very freely used by all Englishmen as well as Quakers.

"From—from my father's."

"But why hast thee come from thy father's?"

"Some people is inquisitive," says Nag.

"And others, too, more hidiots; which they had much better let down theirselves than try to let down their wives, which they're allus at, an' afore lady strangers." Then she added: "My dear, which humble is, an' ever was an' will be, but still welcome—henter!"

Mrs. Naggleton's idea of entering was odd; she just picked up the stranger and carried her in.

"Another!" says she, "and like the other—which if not in her face in her natur, and this is curus!"

"What! a—?" says Naggleton.

And Mrs. Naggleton seemed to understand him, for she said "umps!"

"Oh, I am so ill!" says the stranger.

"Lor, moom, doantee tak on so," says Tiny, looking down on the stranger, a beautiful girl, apparently about seventeen.

"Ah, deary," says Mrs. Naggleton, "I fears as how you'll be wuss afore's yer better."

"I must see a doctor," says the young lady.

"Yere!" says Mrs. Naggleton to the dwarf, "go and fetch a medikul man imeget."

"What—with my legs?" says the dwarf.

"Why, yer fool—yer wouldn't go with any body else's?"

"Why, missus," says the dwarf, "I should be hours on hours—sha'n't I, missus?"

"Yah!" says Mrs. Naggleton, not by any means desiring however to say "yes,"—though "yah!" may mean "yes" in the German tongue. "Yere, you!" this was to the Albanian, "you go for the medikul genelman."

"La, missus!" says the Albanian, "what show me all for nothink? and I ain't a going to a medikul man; praps as how he'd play tricks with me like that there doctor as turned my eyes about till I didn't know whether I seed or whether I didn't."

"Which," says Mrs. Naggleton, "this yere's rebellion, an' yer ought to be beheaded and yer head a top of Temple Bar!" (a)

Here the dwarf squinted and the Albanian made a tremendous grimace.

"Naggleton, go yourself!"

"My dear—"

"Go yourself, I ses!"

"But, my dear—"

"Oh, laws-a-mercy-me, what a man it is; what does he mean?"

"My love—suppose we all goes?"

"What, for the medikul man?" says Jemima, in a regular screamer voice, "why, he'll think us the gentlemen of the road and blunderbuss us all!"

"Now, I say, Mrs. N.—hanswer me this—how long should I be a going to the williage?"

"Well, if yer was a man ye'd be half an hour; but if yer was a willain—and I don't say yer are—and a poor feller-creature in a fix, yer'd be a hour."

"Wery well—which it ud be a hour a goin' and a comin'."

"Well—what then?"

"Well, Mrs. N., and suppose as we all go, why the medikul man ull see her in twenty minutes."

Mrs. Naggleton was taken quite aback by this brilliant reasoning—"Well," says she at last in a low voice, and looking admiringly at her husband, "you are a genus, Nag; that's what you are, yer know!"

"I does know it, Jemima," says Naggleton, and adds, "Betsy!"

The horse, which was eating a circle of grass round the pole to which she had been tethered, as though she was quite sure that the grass must be better at the length of the rope than any of the grass nearer the centre, immediately uttered a loud neigh, as though she understood the business, and quite willingly abandoned the circle of grass, which would induce all the unknowing villagers who came that way to declare it was a "fairy's ring!" (b)

Within a few minutes the caravan was rumbling on towards the village, Mr. Naggleton at the horse's head, and Mrs. Naggleton at the stranger's, which she was bathing,—she herself

(a) It is a fact that not more than a hundred years ago—that is to say in the very memory of some few still alive, who boast more than their hundred years and a memory which "the Lord hath kept green,"—yes, it is a fact that not more than a hundred years ago the heads of rebels, whether hanged or beheaded, were affixed upon spikes and arrayed in horrible symmetry above the Temple Bar in Fleet Street under which we now daily pass. Hence Mrs. Naggleton's remark. We talk of the good old times, little thankful that we are for the blessed advanced times in which we live, when life is more sure and starvation less likely than in any other age; and we do not think that amongst the advantages enjoyed, or rather endured by, our grandfathers and great-grandfathers, the privilege of seeing a dozen men hanged every morning for killing a man or stealing a sheep—it was all one—and after taking a walk through the City and smelling the hideous effluvium which emanated from the heads above Temple Bar. Now happily the chief use of that division between the City and the Strand is to be used as the name of a charming and cheap Magazine to which we refer our readers. One word more with respect to these ghastly heads and we have done. They were generally affixed on poles and placed above the Bar reeking from the body—(the very stains of blood and corruption still are to be seen on the stones of that building)—but it was for some

time the practice to boil these heads in pale tar, when the features assumed a less ghastly appearance, and gave to the Bar the idea that the heads of decapitated Moors were grinning their ghastly grins upon the roving world below. Sometimes the entire body of the criminal was spiked to the common gaze. Under these circumstances the body was always boiled in tar, otherwise the spectacle would have been only too ghastly. Yes, this was one of the benefits of the good old times. For our parts we prefer the Bar new times, however bad they may be.

(b) "Fairy's ring."—Doubtless, many of our readers do not know what a "fairy ring" means. It is a black perfect circle sometimes found in the middle of a field. For some hundreds of years (in the good old times) people believed the fairies made this ring, and used the space enclosed as a ball-room; and this belief was more fully believed, because shortly after this black ring appeared, and which continually grew larger until it disappeared, (they said when the circle was very large the fairies had visitors), a very fine new grass grew on the spot—"the fairies' carpet," said the learned. Will it be believed? in some parts of Devonshire and Cornwall, people believe to this day that the fairies do make this ring; and we have conversed with an intelligent countryman in Cornwall who has told us he has seen the fairies dancing. Now, at the risk of being tedious let us explain best knew why—with strong vinegar and water.

"Don't you mind Naggleton, dear."

"Why, what's the matter with him?"

"He may seem a brute, dear, but he's a good 'un; that's what Naggleton is!"

"He seems a nice little man."

"He is," says Mrs. Naggleton, "but, lor, if I didn't put the bridle on he'd be a wicious 'un, I can tell you."

Here the stranger moaned.

"Lor bless thee heart, don't moan," says Mrs. Naggleton, who, by the bye, had two styles of conversation—one which she learnt in the young country days of her life, the other which she had picked up in the caravan. "Thee'lt see a meddikul man soon. Hullo! what's up now?" continues the show-lady in show language, "I should werry much like to know what's *he* hup to now. Nag, what is it?"

This was from the window.

"Why, Jenny," says he, "I've got a hi-deer."

"Then hold fast on to it, for you may never get another," says Mrs. Naggleton, who has not kept her promise so far as words can go to love, honour, and obey, "what's yer hideer like?"

"Why, where's we a going?"

"To the meddikul man s!"

"There's a hideer," says the showman.

"And what's your's, Nag?"

"Why, go to the *hinn*!"

"Oh!" says Mrs. Naggleton in a blank voice, "ah – yes," but she recovered the next moment, and remarked, "there, praps, you'd better go on!"

"Why, aint I?" asked Nag.

"Yah!" says Mrs. Naggleton; and so far from meaning "yes" "yah," certainly meant "no," and a very fierce one in this instance, and Mrs. Naggleton smashed to the window as though glass had no value whatever.

"Kim up, Betsy!" said Naggleton, and that was all he said till he reached the village.

Here he once more drew up.

Meanwhile within the caravan a very touching scene had taken place.

Tiny, as we have hinted, was retiring; and

upon the introduction of the young stranger into the caravan, she retired with her baby behind that curtain which generally hid the 'entertainment' from mortal and uninitiated eyes till 'all in to begin!' was a certain fact announced by the shutting to of the door.

Suddenly the little Puddy, as babies will, burst into a scream.

The stranger started. "Ah! have you a baby here?"

"Yes, dear," says Mrs. Nag.

"Oh, give it to me—let me nurse it!" says the stranger, "I—I—"

"Oh, I understand—I'm a mother myself, you'd say—yere, Tiny!"

Whenever the Yorkshire giantess emerged from behind the curtain, her head touched the ceiling, though her boots (beuts she called them) were a long way off in the corner.

And thereupon the young stranger seized the little infant and caught it to her breast; and as though the little atom of mortality knew every thing was now all right, she ended her riot, and lay sobbing upon the white fluttering breast of the young stranger.

Mrs. N. shook her head.

Then she shook her head again, and she said, "Ah!"

"There was a good deal in Mrs. Naggleton's "ah!" It meant—"you're deserted, my poor dear; you've been ruined and wronged like many a gal afore yer, and like many a gal as ull come arter yer, poor thing!"

But the stranger made no reply, she only pressed the little treasure closer to her heart.

"What's yer name? if I may make so bold," says Naggleton.

But the young woman made no answer.

"Some people, perhaps, don't like to say their names," says Mrs. Naggleton, after a lapse of about five minutes, "and some people is right."

Still the visitor made no reply.

Mrs. Naggleton put her rough right hand upon the stranger's delicate white shoulders, whence had fallen the red cloak in which she was wrapped when found.

The stranger started and looked her hostess in the face.

"Mrs. ——, I beg thee pardon, me dear, but I don't know thee name."

"My name?"

"Oh, not for uniwerses if thee don't like, me dear."

"My name is—"

But at this moment the vehicle was drawn up with a tremendous jerk, and Mrs. Naggleton swayed like a tenderling orphan.

She was at the window in a moment.

"Does some people want to break other people's necks?"

"My Jemima, yere's the pike."

"Then pay it."

"And, my Jemima, yere's the village."

"Indeed!"

"And, my Jemima, yere's the *hinn*."

"Oh," says Jemima, and opening the door,

---

the fairy rings. Under certain circumstances a certain wondrously small *mushroom* is made to grow by the Grower of all things in a given spot. It comes to perfection in a few hours, and dies in scattering its seed around it. These seeds grow and also die in scattering their seed, and so the vegetation goes on till a great circle is formed, when some change in the air destroys the vegetation and the ring vanishes. "The fairies have moved," used to say our ancestors. But, it may be asked how it is that there is only a ring of black, and how it is the interior of the ring is a brighter green than that without? All this is easily explained. The seed will not grow upon the ground which has recently produced this vegetation : hence the spread of the circle; and as this little mushroom destroys the blades of grass—*not the root*—while it is living, fresh grass grows after the fungi are dead ; and as these latter have manured the ground the new herbage is beautifully green and fine. Is not this a simplification of a mysterious affair? The spot on which horses are tethered often looks like a fairy ring. It is of course no such thing. A genuine specimen of this latter can always be told by looking for the minute dark brown mushrooms which compose it.

behold Nag is already there, ready to hand the queen of his soul to her mother earth.

"An' a good thing too," says Mrs. Nag, "my dear, she's in sitch a state; I didn't say anything a fear of frightnin her, but I knows what's what, and let me tell you I wants looking to myself."

"Why, Jenny," says Naggleton, slapping his right hand on his right thigh, "you don't mean to say as how arter all these yere dismal years as how you goin' are to have—"

"Some brandy—yes, Nag, I am," says Mrs. Naggleton, in a remarkably soft voice, "that's all, Nag, I'm goin' to have some brandy."

"Oh, lor, is that all?" and he very disconsolately pays the tollman, who has been looking on this scene with great disgust—the tollman's wife's niece had once been run over the leg by a caravan, and so the tollman hated all "that there lot."

"Which is the hinn?" says Nag.

"Drive on!" says the tollman.

"Right or left?" asks Nag.

"Drive on!" says the tollman.

"Good night, old boy!" says Nag.

And "Drive on!" returns the tollman.

On, straight-a-head, went Naggleton, and very soon the village inn shone out through the night.

Mrs. Nag, still much subdued, did not return to the vehicle, but marched in the mud by the side of her little man whom she had taken for better or worse; "and a good deal the betterer," as Nag would say.

———

CHAPTER XVIII.

THE OUTCAST FINDS A FRIEND.

ON went the caravan, and soon the village was reached.

Only one inn was there in the village, and here there was great distraction, for a carriage had arrived, which was creating an amount of inn-keeper's attention.

It was a large carriage of the period—an immense machine, which in these days would be indicted for a nuisance—a coach in the interior of which a country dance might almost have been achieved.

The occupants of the interior were an aged lady and her daughter; while outside were the coachman, of course, and the blunderbus-man, who always accompanied a carriage while travelling through the country.

This blunderbus was a preposterous firearm; it was short, thick, and so heavy, that few men could aim with it; and, when they did, little good was achieved, for it was a peculiarity of the blunderbus that it sent bullets any way but straight. So the highwaymen were not very much afraid of blunderbuses.

So, when the caravan drew up before the inn-door, with quite as much noise as the carriage itself had done, there was no more notice taken of it than though it was still out on the common.

But Mr. Naggleton was not the man to be put down—except by his Jemima. He coolly elbowed his way amongst the servants and attendants who surrounded the door, and roughly asked, "Is this the hinn?"

"Yes, young man," said the landlady, who had no sentimental nonsense about her—"yes, young man; and full we are—and full we ever should and would be to sitch as you."

"Oh!" says Mr. Naggleton, "ain't my pence as good as anybody else's?"

"Go along, young man!"

"I shan't!" says Naggleton: "there's a feller-creetur in distress, and I shan't!"

The landlady couldn't speak. She turned to her ostler and made a motion indicative of chucking the insolent "young man" into the horse-pond.

"And," says Naggleton, "a feller-creetur as is a woman; and, when a feller-creetur is a woman—why—why—why," continues Naggleton, as though now he had got it—"why, she is one."

"Go along!" reiterated the landlady, who had now recovered her breath—"or you'll go to the round-house (a)—that is where you'll go to, you know!"

Now, the elder of the two ladies had been not an uninterested spectator of this little altercation, in which apparently Naggleton had got the better, if we may judge by the kind glances all the chambermaids and wenches hanging about had thrown upon him; and she now came forward.

"My man, what is it you want?"

"A bed—"

"Straw?" says the landlady.

"And a doctor," says Naggleton.

"What, for yer sel?" says the landlady.

"Any how, mam," says the showman to the landlady, "if I had the doctoring of you, I'd shut you up for a month!"

Here a maiden tittered. The landlady looked round to give her a month's warning on the spot, but all the maids were as grave as death.

"Why do you want the doctor?" says the lady.

"Mam," says Naggleton, pulling down his head with his right hand, by grasping all the hair he could find with that member—this he called making a bow—"Mam, yer honour," says he, "I found a poor woman outside my cairy-wan in a state, so my Jemima says, as, when a woman, wants the kindness of other women, an' not their tongues; and so I took her inside my cairywan, and, as that warn't enough, and she wanted a meddikul man, why, I brought her yere—yere she is—and that's all."

Here he gave his head another pull down, and winked at the landlady through his lovely locks.

"Poor thing," said the lady. Then turning

(a) The "round-house" was the station-house of that day. Why round-house it would be difficult to say, for those that remain are every one as square as four sides can make them.

to the landlady, she said : "Can you not let the poor woman have a bed here ?"

" Lawks, me lady—two, if she wants them."

" Bravo !" says Naggleton—" an' praps you can find two doctors near if she wants them—but she don't, mam. She only wants *one* bed and *one* doctor, and you to keep to yourself, mam."

Meanwhile, the lady had gone out into the dark night, and tapped at the door of the caravan.

Mrs. Naggleton immediately opened it—in fact she had been standing at the door and trying to hear all without opening it, for fear of the cold air coming in.

" Me lady !"

" Is the poor girl here ?"

" Me lady—jest."

" Can I come up ?"

" Suttingly, me lady."

And the grand lady, who travellled in her own carriage to the town, thought she was not degrading herself by going into the caravan.

Indeed, as a rule, and a very flat one, for every body must by this time know it, those women who at first sight appear ladies, and who give themselves any airs whatever, are precisely no ladies at all.

The found girl was leaning against one side of the caravan—her eye fixed upon nothing, her senses far, far away.

She had not the least idea any one had entered the vehicle, and she still remained vacantly gazing into space, as it were, when the lady touched her upon the shoulder.

The girl started, and in a moment her natural expression came back to her eyes.

" My dear !"

" Madam ?"

" I hear you are in trouble ?"

" Yes, madam."

" Who am I speaking to ?"

" Oh ! there's no need to tell you who I am, madam."

" I will tell you who *I* am. I am Lady Harriet Seymour."

" Indeed, my lady."

" You have something weighing on your mind, my poor girl."

" I am alone in the world, my lady."

" Alone ?"

" That is, at present. I have lost my husband."

" You are very young to be a widow."

" I—I am not sure that I am a widow."

" No ?" said the lady, a little coldly.

After a pause she tried to resume her previous frankness, and said—" He has deserted you."

" I do not even know that."

" I am afraid," said the lady, a little coldly, that you are not willing to be at all confiding to me — perhaps you are not in want of a friend ?"

" Indeed I have not one in the wide world."

" Oh ! doant'ee say *that*," says Mrs. Naggleton.

And thereon the grand lady looked at the showman's wife, shook her hand, and smiled. " Leave me to manage," she whispered.

" Have you no father ?"

" Yes, lady."

" And you have left him ?"

" He forced me to leave him."

" Why ?"

" He thought me—lost."

" And he did not think rightly."

" Indeed, no—I am married to one of the best gentlemen who live. Why I have not seen him I cannot tell. He was to have seen my father, and told him all, the very night before that on which my father drove me from his house."

" Drove you ?"

" Yes. He demanded the name of my husband—indeed, indeed he is my husband—before a mad infuriated woman he had taken into his service. This woman seemed to hate him ; why, I know not, and I would not name him before my father. He would not hear it, except through her, and so he drove me out into the wide, wide world."

The lady looked grave for a little while longer, then she asked—

" Why did your husband—I am sure you speak the truth—why did your husband wish to keep your marriage secret from your father."

" Oh ! lady, the world said he was illegitimate," said the poor girl ; " and he knew as well as I that my father was an honourable man, and would abhor an illegitimate son-in-law. So we waited while Edgar——"

" Oh ! his name is Edgar ?"

" Yes, my lady — while Edgar sought to prove his legitimate birth : could he have done that, madam, he would have been an earl. But all his attempts were hopeless, and the very night before my father drove me from his house, he was to have come and told all, and prayed my father to forgive the blot of his birth—for, lady, my husband is such a good, good man."

" How long is it since you left home ?"

" I do not know. About a week I think. I have been wandering in my head, I fancy. If Edgar writes to my father all will be well." Suddenly she started. "No, no—all will not be well. If he writes my father will tell Death his name, and she will *murder* him ! I did not think of this—oh, I did not think of this !"

And heavily she fell to the ground, happily senseless, for a time.

Mrs. Naggleton had the poor form up in a second, and Mrs. Naggleton herself carried the poor girl to the inn bed-room and the bed which had by this time been prepared for her.

And by this time Naggleton had made friends with the landlady, for he was drinking her " werry good health " in some of the worst gin in that county.

Within twenty-four hours another child was brought into Peggle-cum-Wog, as the village was called in which the angry landlady lived.

The child was a boy, and even the landlady herself was moved to admiration by the superb size of this little creation : "Wouldn't he make a fine landlord!" says she, "if he grows oop as he's born!"

The grand lady and her beautiful daughter, Constance, were still at the inn.

As for Mr. and Mrs. Naggleton they were not *rich*, but they were not so poor as to be unable to live a day without exhibiting the dwarf, the Albanian, the armadillo, and Tiny, who, by the bye, had created a gigantic amount of interest in Peggle-cum-Wog. No sooner did she appear than little boys whooped after her in the most frightful manner, and then ran away in fear. Whereas those cries of derision sank into Tiny's heart, and very frequently tears would fall upon Puddy's little face under these circumstances : for Tiny was tender-hearted, as nine out of ten of very large people usually are ; she had a heart as large as her body.

So Mr. and Mrs. N. determined to stop in Peggle-cum-Wog for some days ; till, as Mrs. Naggleton remarked, they could see "which way the cat jumped," or in other words, they saw what was what.

Mr. and Mrs. Naggleton were seated at tea on the third day after the birth of the child, and truth compels us to state that Mrs. Naggleton had spoilt her tea with brandy, when again a tap came at the door, and again Harriet Seymour stood at the door of the caravan.

"Good evening !" said her ladyship, "may I come in ?"

"Down came Naggleton in a bump," as he afterwards expressed it, and in the space of no time the steps were arranged and the lady once more entered the friendly old show.

"Now look here, friends."

"Oh, me lady, a deal too humble," says Mrs. Naggleton.

"A *deal* too humble," says Naggleton.

"*Some* people is too fast," says Mrs. Naggleton—who, alas ! has been drinking *that tea* and wishes to manage this business.

"Kim up, Betsy !" says Naggleton, under his breath.

"No, no," says Lady Harriet, "all kindly people are friends, and so you and I are. Now, tell me, do you think the show would hold any more ?"

"Well," says Naggleton, looking about, "I don't want to say any think wenemus, but though we ain't azakly boilin' over, we ain't far from it. Tiny ain't a morsel, an' for a dwarf, *the* dwarf takes up a mighty lot o' room ; and the Albanian must have a place to comb his hair in."

"Now, look here ; the doctors say the poor girl must not suckle her child."

"Right they are," says Naggleton.

"Much some people must know, any how, about that !" says Mrs. Naggleton.

And apparently this time she has won, for Mr. Naggleton doesn't say a word—in fact he blushes.

"Now," said her ladyship, " do you think you could make room for a baby ?"

"Well, a baby, me lady, don't take up more nor a foot of room—but a baby's a baby," says Mrs. Naggleton.

"Why, what were it if it weren't," says Naggleton, looking towards the dwarf, who was peering out from behind the curtain.

"Now, look here," says the venerable lady Harriet, smiling and talking far more pleasantly than would many a woman in a far lower sphere than herself, "I want you to take care of Edith's child—she has told me her name's Edith. I will pay you."

"Oh, me lady, we ain't been a harsking for coppers, me lady," says Mrs. Nag.

"No, not if I knows it," says Nag, himself.

"I will pay you liberally ; and I prefer to leave the child with you to leaving it with a stranger, for I know you are good, if rough people. The child is not delicate, and roughing it with you in the pure open country will make him grow up a strong man. Now, what do you say to that ?"

"But," says the showman, "what does the young woman say ?"

"As I do—she knows that it would be selfish to keep her child with her—for she has no means of supporting it."

"But it's hard, ain't it, me lady, to lose yer child ?" says the showman's wife.

"Yes ; but hard things are sometimes our duty to perform. Edith knows she must *work* for her living. From what she has told me I am convinced that her father will not yet receive her, and therefore she must depend upon herself ; her child would impede her, and her child would suffer. She understands this, and she is perfectly willing to let her boy go with you. Will you take him ?"

"Yes, dammy !" says Naggleton ; and then, covered with confusion as with a garment, he stuttered, "Me lady—begs your pardon !"

Meanwhile Mrs. Naggleton was wiping her eyes, and saying as how she wished she had the dear boy to kiss him, that she did.

"Which as how," says Nag, "we haccepts your lady-me-ship's offer, 'cos we're poor ; but lor, we'll take care of that boy like—like as though he was ourselves, and—and," says Nag, looking at the well-spread tea-table, and the brandy bottle, "we takes care of ourselves, we does !"

"Very well," says her ladyship, taking her purse from her pocket, "here's my first instalment," and she laid a bank note upon the table.

"Oh, my lady, not afore we looks arter the little un as if he was ourselves !"

"Nonsense !" says the lady ; "now start with your show and come back in a month ; the child will then be given to you. Good night ! I am going to-morrow."

"Good night, me lady," says Mr. Naggleton, "but will your ladyship excoose me if I ask yer ladyship what's to become of her ?"

"Oh, I thought I told you ; she is going to be my daughter's companion."

"Why, heny fool could a told that," says Mrs. Nag.

"Good night !"

"Good night, me lady," says the showman, "and it's yourself ought to have pleasant dreams and pleasant days, for yer're a good woman from top to bottom."

Lady Harriet Seymour laughed merrily, descended the caravan, and went happy into the inn.

For your good deeds are better for the body than the physic of the wisest doctor on earth.

CHAPTER XIX.

A CONVERSATION AT THE "COCOA TREE."

ALL London was in indignation. An English ship had been taken, her crew made prisoners, and the vessel burnt.

Nor was it our habitual enemies, the French, who had effected this degradation. The *Gorgon* (this was the name of the ill-fated ship) had been found drifting near the Spanish coast, and partly burnt.

Being an English ship, the news of her discovery was soon carried to Gibraltar, the Governor of which immediately instituted an investigation. It resulted from this inquiry that the vessel taken was the *Gorgon*, and the probabilities were that the vessel in question had been taken by Algerine pirates, and then fired and sent adrift. This conclusion became almost certainty, by the discovery on board of an Algerian sabre.

The news was received in England with equal astonishment and incredulity. How was it possible that a vessel, carrying several companies of an English regiment too, could have been attacked and overcome by a horde of lawless and ill-regulated pirates? Yet still the fact remained, that the vessel was discovered stranded and half-burnt; that she contained an Algerian sword; and that she had quitted England ten days or a fortnight before with English soldiery on board.

The public opinion soon resolved itself into a settled belief that the regiment must have been attacked with fever, or dysentery, or some other epidemic; and having thus exculpated British pluck, the public became rather desirous that the subject should drop—for Britannia, the queen of the waves, does not like to remember that she is sometimes conquered on her own element, though it is a fact; that in the last century a good many British ships fell into other than British care.

"Oh," said a young blood (a), on the morning when this news arrived—"we shall hear no more of Trevillian and his hopes of the Milray earldom."

"No—Milray need not quake in his elegant shoes now," said a second.

"Did he ever?" asked a third.

This conversation was taking place at the

Cocoa Tree, the gaming-house to which we have frequently referred. The gentlemen were trying to refresh themselves with gin, in which rue had been steeped. This bitter drink was a favourite with the blood of that day.

"Ever?—yes; I should say so," said the first. "Why, don't you know that Trevillian is the son of the elder brother of Milray's father? Trevillian has always sworn his mother and father were married; but he could not prove the marriage, and Milray came in for the title and estates."

"While *he*, poor devil!" says the second, "is, in all probability, by this time sold to some infernal old Mahomedan, and working as a slave. Curse Fortune!—what a futile jade she is. Here's a man who had his chances of a rich earldom, and who has dealt to him a slavery in North Africa!"

"*I* can't make out clearly," says the third aristocrat, "why you are so sure the *Gorgon* was taken by those Algerine beggars. Why should they burn her?"

"My dear Wilmot," says the first, "can't you comprehend that the Algerian scamps could not have taken the vessel past the straits? Our fellar at Gibraltar would have been sure to discover the business; so they burnt her; and all our poor devils have been slipped under the very noses of the garrison; and, perhaps, by this time Trevillian has been bastinadoed, and—and, perhaps, made a eunuch of !"

The laughter which this brilliant witticism created was at its full height when a gentleman ran hurriedly into the gilded and luxurious chamber.

"Good God!" says he—"have you heard the news?"

"What," says the gentleman whom we have referred to as the first speaker, and who was Lord Alchester—"what, has Billy Natherton got an idea?"

"No, no, Alchester—be serious! This news is too horrible for laughter.

"Why, he's as shocked as a maid!" says Lord Alchester. "What should a maid be shocked at? Ah! I know—the duke has ordered over from Hanover a new German mistress, more hideous than the last—if that's possible, and I don't believe it is—she hates me, and I love her quite as much?"

"What do you think has happened to Milray?"

"Arrested?" asked Alchester.

"Arrested!" returned Natherton, "as though that was any news! Why Milray never took a chair(a) but he ran the chance of arrest."

"Took—expected," continued Lord Alchester. "Why you talk of the man as though he were past away."

"And, by Jove, that's the truth," says Atherton. "Here, give me a glass of brandy," he continued, turning to a waiter.

(a) "Blood"—aristocrat.

(a) "Chair," "sedan-chair," the vehicle carried by two men, one before the other behind. "Sedan-chair" was the Hansom of that day.

"What!—dead?" asked the lord.

"As Queen Anne," retorted Natherton. "Shot clean through the heart." .

"By Jove! who's the scoundrel who has murdered him?"

"Well," retorted Natherton, looking round him anxiously, " if *he* was a scoundrel he has been shot by one."

"Why, hang it, man," continued Lord Alchester, "you don't mean to say Milray has shown the white feather, and shot *himself?*"

"By Jove he has."

Here the aristocrats looked at each other, and each man's face was pale, for all, with the exception of him who brought the news, thought that his *debts* had driven him to commit self-destruction, and each man knew he himself had debts, and if he grew pale it was as much by asking himself the question — "Shall I ever come to such an end?"—as by any feeling of sympathy for the late earl.

"Why?' at last asked Alchester.

"Why," returned Natherton, " he had cause. Trevillian has proved his legitimacy."

"Trevillian!" said several gentlemen.

"Yes. You all start. I suppose you have not forgotten that Captain Edgar Trevillian always maintained that he was the real earl."

"But he left with his regiment in the *Gorgon*, the ship found on the Spanish coast half burnt, and which, it is supposed, was boarded and taken by Algerine pirates."

"You're wrong, Alchester ; luckily Trevillian missed the vessel, owing to his being detained while seeking for the proof of his mother's marriage with the old earl. By Jove, he *must* have given sufficient proof, or Milray would not have ended the contest in this way."

"And when did this occur?" asked Alchester.

"That's the most extraordinary part of the business—nearly three weeks ago !"

"I tell you what, Natherton—you're drunk!"

"In the first place, Alchester, perhaps you're not able to judge whether a man be sober or drunk ; for you're never either one or the other. I say again—the suicide was committed three weeks ago, or nearly. I ask — has anybody seen him for three weeks?"

A silence ensued.

At last it was broken by Alchester, who said —"By Jove! when I come to think of it, *I* havn't seen him for about that time ; but, really, in our kind of life men drop out from amongst us so often, that a man is just missed, and that is all—especially if he's not flush of money : and, as for Milray, he certainly had wrung the very last bank-note out of the estate —poor devil ! so he's shot himself—and three weeks ago !"

"I thought he'd gone to Scotland, with his sister, Lady Milly, as they call her—but I protest she has no more right to be called "Lady" than my old housekeeper has. Yes! I'm quite sure some fellow told me he, Milray, had gone to Scotland."

"Natherton," says Alchester, suddenly, "have you seen Trevillian?"

"Yes, by the most singular chance a Frenchman asked me to go up and see the new lord."

"More mystery!" responded Alchester—"go on."

"The whole affair is most extraordinary. You know my man bought a ring of some poor devil, who had picked it up Hampstead way. I happened to see it on my gentleman's finger, and at once recognised the crest on it as Milray's. I took the thing, and thought I would call on Milray with it."

"Ah!—I see!—so you went to the house."

"And when I got there, and asked to see Milray, I was shown this Frenchman of whom I have spoken, and who gave the startling news that Milray was dead, adding—" *The new lord has never got over the shock.*"

The gentlemen who heard the history here exhibited various marks of surprise. Mr. Natherton continued—" The French valet asked me if I knew Mr. Trevillian?' 'Mr. Trevillian?' I returned. 'Yes,' he added, 'the son of the old earl, to whom the late earl, his nephew, succeeded?' I answered—'That I had seen him riding with his troops. I had never spoken to him."

"Nor I—nor I," several voices exclaimed.

"As for me, I once spoke to him," said Lord Alchester ; "but I was so drunk that I don't remember what he said, nor how he said it. I only remember one thing, that he didn't wear his hair in powder—that it was a fine black ; that his skin was as white as a woman's, and his eyes as blue as the sky above us."

"The Frenchman denied me to see his master," continued Natherton, " and added the information that Milray had destroyed himself in a fit of despair upon seeing the proof of his claim to the title and estates which Trevillian brought with him. The catastrophe, the Frenchman told me, created such an effect on Trevillian that he had been unable to move since, but kept his bed. He further said that the fright had affected the new lord's memory, and he could not remember the face of old friends."

"Well, for that matter," urged Alchester, "as far as I know, I don't think he has many friends to number ; for most men fought shy of him with that brand of bad birth on him."

"And now comes the most singular part of the history," Mr. Natherton continued. "I went up to Trevillian's room. It was he beyond a doubt. I question if there are two such men in the whole kingdom — nor the whole world. There was the white skin in combination with the black hair and exquisite blue eyes ; but, by Jove, gentlemen, he looked like a man raised from the dead."

"Well, I've no doubt it is a shock to see a man shoot himself," said Lord Alchester. " As for me I doubt whether I should ever get over it at all."

"He didn't know me," continued Natherton, " nor did I expect him to ; but he did me

the honour of confiding his wishes to me. He said that he had exerted his influence to prevent the affair being known, and had gladly allowed it to be supposed that Milray had gone into Scotland, and more especially for this reason—the disappearance of Lady Milly, the late lord's sister."

"Lady Milly lost!"

"Gone: Milray stated she had left for Scotland. She never left London, that is clear, and Trevillian fears that Milray played her some foul plot. Hence he desired to keep things quiet, and to that end he actually obtained a certificate of death—had Milray's body removed into the country—and he is buried!"

The gentlemen present started, but they were too eager to hear what was coming, to utter a word.

"Now, however, he has come to the conclusion that he has done wrong in hiding the matter—indeed, he tells me the safety of Lady Milray herself calls for an investigation—and

by Jove! gentlemen, the end of it is that a coroner and jury are to sit on the body of George, Earl of Milray."

Again, the aristocratic gentlemen started, not so much in compassion for the fall of George, Earl of Milray, as the conjuration of coroners sitting upon their bodies, should they make similar endings to that which they supposed Milray had cast upon himself.

"Another word, and I have done," continued the narrator. "There can be no doubt that Milray did send a bullet through himself in sheer despair at the certainty of the proof Trevillian brought to bear against him. Not only does Trevillian give this statement, but the Frenchman, who, it seems, was watching the interview, is thoroughly prepared to corroborate it."

"By Jove!" said Alchester—"if I had been in Milray's place, I would have flung the gauntlet down, and have fought Trevillian for the earldom."

8

"What—cousins fight?" said a gentleman— "that is against the laws of nature?"

"By Jove! I forgot that," continued the lord. "Well, poor devil! perhaps, after all, it was the best thing he could do; and let us hope we should have the courage to do the same thing if we got into any mortal fix. Well, Natherton, have you come to the end of your tale? By Jove! you've made half an hour slip away like half a minute."

"Yes—that's enough for one time," continued Mr. Natherton. Then he added, after a pause—"No: there's another piece of news. As I was coming down stairs from Milray's room, I heard some odd, wandering screams, apparently from a woman. I really could not prevent myself from asking what was the cause of them; when, with a shrug of the shoulders, the Frenchman returned, that it was a poor little girl who had been Milray's mistress, who had been thrown into a fever by the death of her patron. I added, that she must, then, have been very fond of him; whereupon, with another shrug, the Frenchman returned, that she had only possessed him during a day before his death, and that she was so fond of the late earl that she swore he was her lawfully wedded husband."

"Well—you've made a morning's work of it, Natthy," said the lord, who then turned towards his companions and said carelessly — "I suppose we shall receive Trevillian at once—there can be no doubt. It won't look well to wait till he has legally proved his claim. Let's call him Milray at once, and have done with it."

The affirmative answers were unanimous.

And these gentlemen rose and went about their various engagements, determining to give the hand of friendship to the new lord, whom they no more dreamt of being a clever highwayman, than they expected to become royal princes before the day was out.

CHAPTER XX.

THE BITER BIT.

THE new earl and Jules were seated in the beautiful dressing-room in Milray House, to which the reader has already been introduced; and which at that time was occupied by the late earl.

Holgarth, or rather the earl—for we must now call him by that title—sat in the very chair once occupied by his predecessor; and before him was the very same antique china chocolate cup, which the late earl had used when the news of Lady Milly's disappearance—now a month ago—was given to him.

All was going well with the new earl.

Trevillian's claims, which had long been known to the legal world, were speedily recognised and accepted; and as he sat opposite the Frenchman, he knew that in a few days he would be inscribed upon the rolls of England as one of her earls, and would take his place in the House of Commons.

What had he to fear?

He knew that Trevillian had been taken prisoner by some power, in all probability an Algerine pirate.

He knew that he ran no risk of being identified as the highwayman called both Dashing Jack and Gentleman Jack, for was not this man notoriously hung? was not his body placed in chains?—and even if it had been removed this was a circumstance too common to create much attention.

And as though it were not enough that the real owner of the title was safe out of the way, and that he could not be recognised as himself; it was in all probability certain, he thought, that Lady Milly was dead; so he was safe from being denounced by her as not being her brother.

As for the friends of Trevillian, whom he soon learnt were very few in number, he determined upon maintaining his assertion, that the shock of seeing the earl murder himself had, in a great measure, destroyed his memory

So he was sound and safe at all points except one—Jules, the Frenchman.

This he *knew*.

Mr. Jules also *knew*.

And both men knew that either they must agree utterly and wholly, so that one could not fight against the other without both falling; or else the one must become the victor over the other and destroy him.

Each man had measured his own strength and chances; each man saw that union was better than divison.

Holgarth saw that Jules would be a very useful agent in his wretched imposition. Jules saw that Holgarth was more valuable to him alive than dead; *at all events for many years to come.*

So as the two men sat opposite each other in the splendidly furnished room of that magnificent mansion, each watched the other, but each was quite willing to come to terms.

"Jules!"

"Me lord?"

"D—n, sir!—there's no need of ' me lording' it here!"

"Oh yes, me lord; for I might forget it another time."

"Hum—Jules, do you know what I'm thinking of?"

"Perhaps."

"What?"

"Wezer you sall kill me."

"Well—that was about it."

"Yes; and I have sought of killing you, me lord."

"Have you; and what conclusion have you come to?"

"Zat you sall better live."

"That's to say, it would pay you better to let me live than to kill me *if you could?*"

"Jest so, me lord."

"Well, that's just the conclusion I've come to with regard to you."

"I am ver glad to hear it."

"Look here; if I die you cannot benefit by it."

"No; unless, me lord, I sall marry de viddow of de earl who sall have one leetle boy—den my son-in-law sall have de earlom ven you die."

"Hum—but Milray has no widow?"

"Oh, no, me lord."

"Then don't talk nonsense. Now, see here: you benefit more by my life than death. I could *not* benefit by *your* death, and I shall by your life."

"Oh yes, me lord."

"Yes; for you will gladly do my dirty work if I pay you for it?"

"Jest so, me lord, pay me for it."

"You like money, Monsieur Jules?"

A change passed over the countenance of the French valet—"it is de only sing I *do* lof," he said.

"Except yourself?"

He grasped his hands one in the other and answered: "My money *is* me; when it is mine it is part of me!"

"Very well. Now I'll pay you £1,000 a year to sell yourself to me body and soul, to do my bidding, no matter what. To do as I tell—to *kill* for me, to lie, to cheat, to rob for me, to do all I *will* have done?"

"I am your's, me lord; vid money you can twist me round your finger; all men can conquer me vid money."

"Then if a man offered you £2,000 a year to destroy me and serve him you would do it?"

"Me lord, I sall always now tell you the truth, for I am to you body and soul. Yes, I vould keel you if I was paid."

"And suppose I don't pay you regularly?"

"You sall!"

"Hey-day, these are great words."

"You—you *vill*, I am sure you vill, me lord."

"You are right," said Holgarth, shaking his head, "I will; I shall make you worth £1,000 a year."

"Den it is settled?"

"Settled."

"May I take me lord's hand to seal de bargain?"

Highwayman as he was, heartless criminal, as he sat in the splendid golden chair, he was ashamed to give his hand to his miserable partner in guilt. As he did give his hand even *he* blushed.

Jules saw the repugnance but he did not show his knowledge; shook the hand humbly, and then sat down again.

"May I ask a question, me lord?"

"Yes."

"Vat vas me lord?"

"I told you you might ask a question, I did not tell you I would answer it."

The man bowed low, and rubbed his thin, greedy-looking hands.

"And now, me lord, I'll tell your lordship a secret—a great secret!"

"Go on," said the highwayman, sipping his chocolate.

"De Lady Milly *is* dead!"

"How do you know that?"

"I know de Lady Milly is dead."

"How long ago?"

"De very night dat she vas missed."

"Where?"

"She die in de road, and her body vas taken to de Bow-street Station."

"Do you know why she went where she was found?"

"No, me lord; only dat she have gone to de place to meet some one."

"Who?"

"I do not know, me lord; but dere is something more to be told. Her ladyship came of age de day before she die."

"Yes, I know that."

"Ah, me lord know den de Lady Milly?"

"No!"

"An' on dat day me Lady Milly take her jewels—vich vas hers ven she became of age—from de bankers, an' certain she wear 'em ven she go from de house. I have seen de diamonds shine ven she pass to de carriage."

"And these jewels, where are they?—they are worth £20,000."

"Oh, me lord know dat too!"

"Go on, sir!"

"Vell, me lord, she leave de house vid 'em; but ven I see her body dere vas no jewels on it, dey vas gone."

"How came you to see the body?"

"De earl, he learned all about it, and send me to see; de earl vanted de diamonds of de poor Lady Milly."

"Where was Lady Milly found?"

"Near de place dey call Hampstead."

Holgarth started, and took from his little finger the ring with the Milray crest on it, which had been given him by Mr. Natherton.

"Jules—Lady Milly *did* wear those jewels on the night of her death?"

"Me lord?"

"I am sure of it—you must go to the station and make inquiries; perhaps they are there—find out."

"Me lord, it is no use."

"Go, I say!"

The Frenchman bowed humbly and left the room; but he determined at that moment to learn who and what his new master had been, and by what means he knew of Lady Milly and her jewels.

Obediently he went to the station.

The officer on duty was the very man who had accepted the box of clothes and jewellery, and the key from great-souled Mrs. Naggleton. He knew the Frenchman in a moment.

"Hullo!"

"Good day, mistare; you remember me?"

"Oh yes," says the officer, Charley White by name, "never forget such toppers as you."

"Haf you found anysing aboot dat poor woman?"

"No."

"Nosing?"

"No," says Charley White, "the poor thing was a hactor—that's what she was!"

"Poor sing; she vas beautifool!"

"Well, that's more than I can say for you, your honour. Now, what do you want?"

"Nosing dat you sall object to, mistare. I sink I know de poor gal; sall I tell?—vell, yes, if I see de close—de poor commedienne's close—vich you sall show me."

"Now, look here," says Charley White, aged about forty-five, "now, look here: a joke's a joke, and what ain't one ain't one, you unnerstan' that. An' I don't see what yer're droppin' about our office for; but I ain't a bad sort o' chap, an' as I likes to oblige, I will; but on conditions, monseer."

"Yes, mistare."

"That after ye've seen the clothes and the bits of glass gimcracks, you'll not come a showin' yer wery winegerry face here again?"

"I sall promise, mistare," says Jules, with great alacrity, "everysing dat you sall vish, if you sall show me de close of de dear dead darlin'!"

"Very well," says Charley, "that's a bargain any how; an' if yer don't keep it, yer won't keep ole bones in yer bit of a body; and if twas dinner-time I'd be down on yer!"

And, thereupon, he lugs down from a shelf the identical box, takes the identical key from a bunch he carries in his pocket, opens it, throws open the beautiful silken robe, opens the paper in which the jewels are wrapped, and tosses the diamonds up and down.

The Frenchman saw in a moment that these were the jewels he had now sought for two masters.

He immediately began sobbing: "Oh, my poor sistare—oh, my dear sistare! dey sall be hers!" and he was going to touch, whereupon says Charley White:—

"Yes—but they shan't be yours!"

"Dey vas to my sistare."

"Yes, but they shan't be to yours, unless you can prove 'em to be yours. Look here, my hadmirable Frenchy," continued Charley, screwing up the jewels, rolling up the clothes, putting them all back in the box and fetching down the lid with a bang, and locking all up with a clatter—"this yere box and what's in it was confided to my care, and I mean to care for this yere box and what's in it; and take your change out of that."

"And you sall not gif to me my sistare's poor jewels?"

"No, not till you can prove ye're yer sister's brother."

"I sall go to de judge."

"You may go to the devil if you like!" says Charley, and puts up the box in the old place.

Jules marks this, and thinks the box might be easily stolen.

"Good morning, mistare!"

"Good mornin', mounseer; dessay you was werry fond o' your sister, but you won't be fond of her clothes if I know it!"

And away went Jules.

Now this attack upon the clothes and "bits o' glass," as Charley called the valuable jewels, raised Charley's self-will.

"Which," says he to a comrade, "they was not confided to me erficially; then why should I mind 'em erficially? why should I mind 'em yere?"

"Why," says the comrade, "won't they be more saferer here than elsewhere?"

"No," says Charley, "which why? I ain't allers yere, I ain't allers at home; but Mrs. W. she's allers at home; and lor, wouldn't that woman have 'er eyes on 'em!"

"Which and praps, Charley, her fingers," says the comrade.

"Oh, I keeps the key allers; and, besides, Mrs. W.'s a woman with no curosity."

"Ain't she; then show her in a glass case."

"I say, Tom, none o' that; Mrs. W.'s Mrs. W., and I can't stand a bit o' that there!"

"All right!"

"An' now—shall I take that there box from here, or leave this here box there?"

"Ask Mrs. W."

"Good, I will; she know's a thing or two, does Mrs. W., I can tell you. I'll take the box to Mrs. W."

And sure enough that is what Charley did do, putting another similar box in its place to make all ship-shape.

Now, when Jules reached home and told his master the entire particulars, the highwayman started; and, after a moment's consideration, asked the exact position of the box.

Jules gave it him; and after some further conversation he returned to his own room.

Then he turned over in his own mind the reason why the new lord wished to know the position of the box.

The Frenchman could make nothing of it, but he stored his memory with the fact.

The next day all London justice was scandalized by the rumour and the truth, that Bow-street Station had been broken open in the dead of the night.

Why, it seemed impossible for justice to say, that nothing was stolen but an empty box. The parties came to the conclusion that it was done for bravado, and possibly by the highwayman, who, as it appeared, stepped into the shoes of the rascal called Gentleman Jack, who—and the justices congratulated each other on the fact—had swung at Tyburn.

This new chief of highwaymen was called, it was said, Captain Strong.

As for Charley White, he was triumphant. "Wasn't I right?" he said, "about that there Frenchy? He done it, or some of his gang. Wasn't I right to take that there box from this 'ere place; and wasn't Mrs. W. right when she said 'Charley, put it under the bed; we never was burglared, and we never will be burglared!'"

But another man had something to think over in the matter of this box.

After leaving his master at the termination of that conversation, he watched the false earl all day; and at midnight saw him leave the mansion. He followed him, but lost sight of him.

Four hours after he saw his master return *with a box*.

The sharp wits of the Frenchman told him all in a moment. *His master had been a highwayman.*

Next day not a word about the box said Jules to his master. Not a word said Holgarth to his companion in crime.

"Had he the jewels," thought Jules, and was determined to learn that secret also.

CHAPTER XX.

MR. AND MRS. NAGGLETON ONCE MORE.

THE "cairywan," containing, as usual, Mr. Nag., his Jemima, Tiny, Perdita, the dwarf, the Albanian, and the armadillo, was progressing at as slow a pace as was compatible with going at all.

It was night-time; but Mrs. Nag. had not retired with Tiny and the baby to her portion of the caravanserie.

By-the-bye we have not described the internal sleeping arrangements of "Naggleton's None-such." This was the name given to the affair, and in tender blue and chocolate letters. The sleeping arrangements went as follows:—

The interior was divided into three portions by two curtains. At one end, and behind one curtain, slept the dwarf and the Albanian—viz., that is, they slept when they were not cuffing and kicking each other, which was their usual mode of passing the night. In the other portion, at the other end of the vehicle, slept and snored Mrs. Naggleton, Tiny, and the baby.

Upon Tiny joining the establishment her length created a vast deal of confounded contemplation. She was so long that her knees reached the bottom of the bed, and both her legs stuck out in a way anybody would have given "twopence over" to see.

It was decided that there could be no more bed imported. "That 'ud make the carrywan *all* bed," said Naggleton at the time. So Tiny had to put a box for her legs, and cover them up with an old rug, under which circumstances she had the air of a gouty subject, and had to endure the extreme merriment of Mr. Naggleton himself.

In the third, or middle portion of the concern, slept Mr. Naggleton himself, and many a time, and before Tiny had been in the caravan a month, had contemplated her legs sticking through the curtain which separated him from the wife of his bosom.

Yes, it was night-time; but nobody had gone to bed.

At last Mrs. Naggleton, indignant at the slow state of things, put her head out of that window which has already figured in our story, and clapping an eye on the mare, she remarked—"Kim up, Betsy."

But the horse did nothing of the sort. "Her kimmed slower," as the dwarf said.

"What's the use o' sayin' kim up to Betsy, when I'm blest if the willage don't seem to be slipping away, which it's a most hexterrer-ordernary thing for a willage to do."

"Some people is fools—yah!" said Mrs. Nag., as brisk and vigorous as possible.

"Some people is," says Naggleton in reply, "and some hosses is not; for if this animal don't know as how she's got to get there to-night, why what animal does?"

Mrs. Naggleton might have said more; but the weather was not sultry, and the wind was impatiently playing with Mrs. Naggleton's locks; so, with another "yah!" Mrs. Naggleton smashed to the window, and sat down in the jingling conveyance.

On went the conveyance—for hours it seemed to Mrs. Naggleton—and Tiny had almost pitched forward and flattened the baby many times, when Naggleton yelled out—

"Yere it is—just like it was when we went away."

"Why, drat the man," says Mrs. Nag., "does he think it 'ud change in a month!"

"Betsy," says Nag. to the mare, "Betsy—she's toothy to-night—that's what she is about—kim up, my lovely."

"Exactly," says Mrs. Naggleton, showing out upon a wicked world once more; "exactly, make Betsy kim up, *and* live up in *a* style."

Here Betsy herself, without any more talking to, saw how things were—perhaps saw the dull lamps of the town, for she suddenly started off at a trot, thereby casting Mrs. Naggleton back upon Tiny, and never once left off till she found herself in the town, and before the inn, when this remarkable mare pulled up as suddenly as she had started, and then looked about with all possible coolness.

"Yere we is, and there they *are*," says Mr. Naggleton, receiving his wife in his arms as she jumped from the caravan; "yes, yere we is, and there they are. Do you think we'd better have in the baby?"

"No," said Mrs. Naggleton, speaking with an air.

"Cos I think Puddy's sick'ning for the measlums(a), and then don't ye see, Teddy," says Mrs. Naggleton, with a brilliant sense of the true in her, "then they'd be sick of us."

"Well, that's as plain as you are, my love," says Nag.

"Speak for yourself, my man, speak for yerself," say Mrs. Nag. "and don't be so plain-spoke out."

"Now then," says the sharp landlady, of

(a) "Measlums." Why, it is impossible to say, but most people in the last century, and many even now called the "measles" the "measlums."

whom we have spoken, coming to the door, and with an eye on Mr. Naggleton's turn-out; "now then, go along—we don't take in show-folk."

"Ah! but you do gentlefolk you know, as they finds out, my dear, when you 'ands 'em the bill."

"Go along," shrieks the landlady.

"Go along o' *you*," says the showman, and coolly marches into the hotel.

"Is an honest woman's house not her castle?" says the landlady.

"A *honest* woman's house, praps, is; but—I want to see Lady Harryat."

Here the landlady was so indignant that she caught up a hot water-can near her, which was not empty, and was about to hurl the machine at the head of the offending man, when Mrs. Naggleton made her appearance—flew at the landlady, and a fine hand-to-hand encounter took place.

The noise fetched out two gentlemen from the side path.

"Damn it," says one—"two to one on Blazer."

"Done," says the other.

And the next moment madame the landlady was knocked through her own back door.

"Damn it—Blazer's lost," said the first of the gentlemen.

"Then, stop my vitals!(*b*)—pay up," says number two.

The noise also brought Lady Harriet Seymour and Constance to the head of the stairs.

Lady Harriet at once recognised Naggleton, and she called to him, and asked that gentleman to come up stairs.

The landlady, who, in picking herself up, had found a pitchfork so convenient to her hand, that the devil himself might have placed it there, now came running in, making a charge at Mrs. Naggleton, intending to spit her against the wall; but no sooner did she see Mr. Naggleton shaking hands with the lady than the truculent woman let fall her fork, and began bobbing about like a Chinese mandarin.

"So you've come?" says Lady Harriet.

"Yes, me lady, through 'ail and snow, and the wind that do blow!"

This poetic way of putting his statement was not new. Naggleton had used it any time these eight years, when speaking of the armadillo's coat of mail, which he thus described:—

"Through 'ail and snow,
Though the wind that do blow,
Gentlefolks all, yer must know
His shell it keeps so!"

This poetry was Mrs. Naggleton's own, and she was as proud of it then as ever. When she belaboured Nag., he had only to repeat Mrs.

Nag's poem, and she was as smooth as cream in a moment.

"Come this way," said Lady Harriet, and she led the way into a room, in which was seated Edith and her little child.

Mr. Naggleton's poetry had been so successful that he thought he would try a little more, so he stooped down towards the baby, and thus expressed himself :—

"It's a month agone
Since you was borne!"

Mrs. Nag. wasn't so pleased with this poetry. You see it was not her own, and she was like other people, she didn't like rivals.

Mr. Naggleton neatly went through the chair the lady was so kind as to offer him, instead of sitting down on it—he was so over-powered by the honour. The second chair, offered to Mrs. Naggleton, was refused by that lady, who triumphed in the act; and she looked down upon her husband as though by this time she had crushed him completely in fashionable and polite knowledge.

"Let me see; you know what you agreed upon now more than a month since?"

Mr. Naggleton could not forget his poetic victory; he, therefore, tried to improve upon it, by adding, "Just to a T, and," pointing to his better half, "so does she!"

Here Mrs. Naggleton went down as though suddenly hit under the knees, and then plumped up again like a good cork.

"That you are to take the little child, and let us hear from you once a month, and see you twice a year."

"That's it," says Nag.

"Every bit," adds his wife, who has been thirsting to show that she also can make rhyme.

"I will look after the mother—her name is Edith; she will be mine and my daughter's companion, and, as I have said, you will take care of her child."

Here Edith stooped over her child, and kissed him.

"Doan't 'ee take on," says Mrs. Nag., "because if yer do I doan't 'ee know how we'll be able to take 'ee off."

"Edith," said her ladyship, "you must know that what I propose is for the best."

"I know it—I know it, my lady," said the young mother.

"Then, chirrup," said Mrs. Naggleton, and thwacked her own hands together.

"He has been named Harold," said the lady, "and, of course, you will call him by that name."

"Which, as godfather and godmother, we will—we will," says Nag.

"Which, like a mother, *I* will," says Mrs. Naggleton, and she looked about as though she decidedly had the best of it *this* time at any rate.

"You will be paid monthly, Mr. Naggleton."

Mr. Naggleton once more tried to show off—
" Nay, lady, nay—I wants no pay."

Whereupon Mrs. Naggleton, not to be behindhand—"Nay, lady, nay—we wants no pay—HURRAY."

"Nay, lady, nay," was the beginning of a popular song (c)—the remainder was Naggletonianism.

"But you must be paid, my good Samaritan; and do you know," the lady continued, with a smile, "I have offered to pay you—and the show may not always be so successful as I see it may be.'

"Ah!" says Nag.

"So you'll agree to accept my terms—say £50 a year till the child is five years—"

"Oh, madam!" exclaimed Edith.

"Now, Edith, you have told me your tale, and you are worth more than £50 a year to Constance and me; and now, I think, there is an end to the business—I hate business—so, if you like, I will order the supper."

Mr. and Mrs. Naggleton were so overpowered by this last condescension, that they did not know their feelings, and then they burst out in protestations. "What!—heat before a lady bred and born?—no—not if they knowd it!—no—not a bit!"

"Nonsense," said the lady; "you are the guardians of my god-child—mind you take care of him."

It was a pretty sight to see the girl Constance fondling the child Harold. She was a girl budding into seventeen years of age, when the girl is changing into woman—when, perhaps, the most delightful period of woman's life appears to the contemplation of the other sex. It is beautiful to see the new-born womanliness struggling with the girlishness which will be no more in a few months.

Constance was a charming brown beauty. There was no pre-eminently lovely feature; but every atom of the countenance was good, and the whole face beautiful. It was a good sight to see the young girl bending over the infant.

Here the lady touched the bell, and in another moment the supper was on the table.

It would have been great fun to a cruel looker-on to see the trouble poor Mr. and Mrs. Naggleton were in. The knives kept flying over the forks, and the forks kept scratching all over the plates, and, as for glasses, Naggleton broke one at the very first going off, and he never recovered the smash.

"And now, I suppose, Mr. Naggleton, you will go off immediately into the country?" said Lady Harriet,

"Well—no, me ladyship."

"No!"

"No—we're agoin' just to London."

"Dear me—why?"

(c) It ran
" Nay, lady, nay,
Turn not away,
Thy soft eyes from thy lover, &c., &c."

"Puddy's jools."

"What are they?"

"Puddy is Puddy—our baby, the baby, as Mrs. Naggleton calls her hown."

"I do—I do," says Mrs. Nag.

"Puddy's mother was a hactress; that's what Puddy's mother was about."

"You mean the child you have with you in the caravan?"

"The very hidentikul, me ladyship."

"Pray tell me her history."

"With a will, me ladyship," says Naggleton, clatters up his plate, and commences his narrative, and with so many remodellings, try-backs, and corrections, that he ended precisely where he began, after giving all the particulars in various ways.

"So you think she was an actress?"

"Certingly, me ladyship," says Mrs. Naggleton—"or why should she have had all them there glass jools on?"

"What did the jewels consist of?" asked the lady.

"Lor! me ladyship, you'd better ask me what they didn't consist of—bracelets, necklaces, earrings, thing for the waist an' the 'ed, me ladyship, and brooches, and rings. Lor! they must be worth pounds on pounds—p'raps five."

"And that's all Puddy's fortune—eh?"

"All, except her legs, which we mean shall make 'er a living."

"Oh?" asked her ladyship.

"Yes, me ladyship, she's to be a dancer; an' on the werry fust day as she performs in public she shall wear every one o' them jools, and, too, won't they sparkle, jest like real uns—only—" Here Mr. Naggleton shook his head.

"Only! Mr. Naggleton?"

"Only I wish they was all marked R, instead of M; then they'd agree with her name now, yer la'yship. Why there's M's all over them there jools; an' them there jools I'll have, as Mrs. Naggleton naterally says."

"Yes, me lady," says the show-woman, " them there jools—we calls 'em jools in the perfession, though they is only glass—is as good unner our own eyes as unner those o' Charley White in a box—which leastways I don't mean that Charley White's in a box, but the jools is in a box—and out they shall come." Here Mrs. Naggleton made such a movement that one might have supposed the jewels a tough back tooth, and Mrs. Naggleton a strong-minded female dentist.

"Yes, me ladyship," says Naggleton, " we left them there jools with the perlice officer, Charley White, and now we're agoin' to get them there jools to-morrow."

"Very well," said the lady, " we'll all go on to town to-morrow."

And so the curious spectacle was seen of a lady's carriage and a caravan keeping company for about twenty miles.

They were crossing a heath when Lady Harriet, who, for the novelty of the thing, was riding in the show, looked through a window and saw a sight which thrilled her to the very heart.

It was the row of gibbets on which the criminal dead had been hung.

"Ah, me ladyship," says Mrs. Naggleton, "I suppose ye won't look out again?"

"No, indeed; it was a frightful sight!"

"But if you did, me ladyship would find that one of them gibbets is empty."

"I wish all were, my good woman."

"That gibbet ought to be full, and gov'ment's offered twenty pounds to have it full once more.'

"What do you mean?"

"Me ladyship, one of the greatest highwayman as ever lived, Gentleman Jack, Dashing Jack, ought to be there."

"Did he escape?"

"No, me ladyship, he was hung by the neck till he was dead; and then he was put in chains, and then he was stolen!"

"Stolen!"

"Sto—len, me ladyship, as you jest say. Taken down, buried they say; they say a great lady paid to have him stolen, me ladyship, and that's all."

"Poor wretch!—then he had somebody to love him."

"Lor, me ladyship, we all has something to love us; no matter how small we is nor how large we is, which it's all the same."

"Have we passed those dreadful gibbets?"

"Yes, me ladyship, and it's a good thing the wind don't set this way; if it did, me ladyship would not want to see 'em to know they was there—they knocks yer down, me lady, wi'out touching yer." (a)

"Close the window, Mrs. Naggleton, for heaven's sake!" said the lady. "Do the poor creature's friends often steal the bodies?"

"Often, me ladyship."

The conversation continued for some time on this subject; but London was reached at last, and the caravan and the carriage were to part company.

The parting of the mother from her child must be passed over. There are some things the novelist cannot manage, and this is one of them. Who can tell what a poor mother feels when parting with her only child.

She knows that she lives only for that little fragment of life, and yet she must quit it.

She knows that no one can care for and love it as she can care and love it, and yet she parts from her darling.

So it happens in this unlucky world. There is always a great war of hope, and sorrow, and despair, in which to fight.

Edith knew that if she kept the child—if the servants and visitors saw her touching it, scandal would be busy, and, perhaps, even with Lady Harriet Seymour and Constance; yet she

could not bear to part with the little fellow, even to Mr. and Mrs. Naggleton, without whose honest, plain-dealing charity the poor child would never have been born at all—he and his mother would have perished on the heath.

Lady Harriet knew that Edith would be more willing to part with her child to the Naggletons than to any other people. You see, Lady Harriet had lived and suffered, and she knew what to do best.

All happiness is the result, more or less direct, of suffering. Those who have not suffered are not happy in the real acceptation of the word.

"Come," said her ladyship, who by-the-bye, had prepared a quarter of Harold's yearly cost. "Come, part with him at once—the hope of seeing him will be as great a joy, or almost as great a joy, as having him lying in your arms."

So Edith laid her little charge in Mrs. Naggleton's arms, and then humbly asked Lady Constance to take her to her home.

The show once more itself—that is to say, the show being itself, it jogged on towards Bow-street.

Arrived there, Charley White was down on them like a bullet.

"Hulloo! what's up?"

"How are you?" says Naggleton.

"Well, tol-lol—what's up?"

"Them jools!"

"Have yer heard?" asks Charley White.

"What?"

"How them there jools was tried to be stoled."

"Stoled!" says Mrs. Naggleton, tearing open the door behind which she had fixed herself, that she might delicately hear without being seen.

"No, mam," said Charley White, who didn't seem at all astonished to see her, perhaps he knew from Mrs. White at home that ladies are (were,) that is fond of using the ears they were born with—and if not what is the use of ears?

"Not sto—len?' says Mrs. Nag, even then remembering her grammer as taught her by Lady Harriet.

"No, mam, not stolen; but as near as a toucher—mam, that's about it, mam. Charley White has a high, and Charley White was that there high. Charley White has two highs, and Charley White uses those two highs—and when the French party highed the box, I hooked it off. It's at home under my bed—do you want it?"

"I do," says Nag, like taking a solemn oath.

"Some people is—what they always is," says Mrs. Naggleton, looking down on her lord.

"Kim up, Betsy!" says Nag., and as the horse was going to progress he immediately countermanded the order with a whoa-a-a!"

"Then come home and see my old woman," says Charley, and he jumped into the show—being off duty, and just hanging about.

During this short transit, Charley "hit up" the dwarf, took stock of the Albanian, and wrenched

E.BRETT.

open the armadillo, who shut upon his approach as though he was a thief and had good reasons for disliking a constable; and Charley sent Tiny into a state of "skirry," as she afterwards called it, before they arrived at Mrs. White's second floor lair.

Within five minutes the two families were as intimate as the circumstances would admit of; and the young Whites had had a gratuitous view of the dwarf and white-haired Albanian.

Then Charley had out the box and handed it over; and Mrs. Naggleton made this speech: "Luck—thank'ee—wont forget'ee!"

Then Naggleton had a little private conversation with a young White, and was preparing to exit, when Charley White says to his younger self, "Hullo, my lad! what have you been stealing a gold sovereign? Now, I tell yer what—if yere don't take this 'ere back to the owner I'll ta e yer up and chuck yer out o' window; and look yere, I don't want to see

9

where it come from, so I'm going to turn my head."

Charley did, and soon delivered back the coin to Teddy Naggleton, who was so overcome that he really dropped the jewels.

"Mr. White—sir," said Naggleton, "if ever there was a man as was a man why then that man you are. If ever a man, and sich a man, knows the want of another man, why then that man I am!"

Whereupon Mr. White returned—

"A man when he's born is born to be a man, and if he isn't, why then he's unmannerly; which therefore, comrade, I take what yer says as yer meaning, and wish yer jolly well."

So then the two men shook hands, looked that mutual esteem they could not or would not express, and parted; Mrs. Nag of course kissing the young Whites till all that small fry began to fancy themselves nothing but sounding smacks.

So Nag started to go about the country showing the dwarf, the hinfant giantess five year old (which she was), the Albanian, and the armadillo (Lady Harriet's allowance unbroken into in his pocket), while Charley White remained to watch for that Frenchman, in order to be "down on him like a bullet directly he hove in view."

CHAPTER XXI.

THE NEW EARL IN SOCIETY.

"JULES!"

"Me lord?"

"Dress me well this morning, I am going into the world amongst the best people."

"Me lord, if me lord dressed bad, he vould alvays look me lord."

"By the bye, who lives up-stairs in the top floor?"

"Me lord, have me lord gone to de top floor?"

"Yes, why not? This is my house, I pay you a good rent for it, my man; and a man has a right to walk over his own house."

"Vraiment, me lord."

"Well, who is she?"

"She?"

"Yes, it is a woman!"

"Mees Fanny, me lord," said the Frenchman, smiling a sic ly smile; "if me lord sall say any more, I sall bloosh."

"Jules, you're lying; you do not care for women—who is she?"

"Sall it be necessaire to say?"

"I will know!"

"Den, she is—Mees Fanny is—de lady of de late earl!"

"By Jove!"

"Oui, me lord, Mees Fanny have had a great fever; at present she is veek, ver veek, and I guard her."

"Let me see," says the earl, touching his forehead, "did not one of the fellows who came here yesterday say that Milray married the day before he died? Yes, I remember quite well."

"Married, me lord; yes, as me lord married often before."

"Ah, you mean a mock marriage?"

"Oui."

"Poor devil! is she pretty?"

"A leetle."

"And why have you kept her out of the way?"

"I have no wish, me lord, wid de leetle Fanny."

"Hem—it seems you like de leetle Fanny?"

"Oui, me lord," says the Frenchman, after a pause.

"Now, you know, Jules, you and I must have no secrets. What is your arrangement about Miss Fanny?"

"Me lord say dere is no secrets to us."

"Yes."

"Me lord, I vish — I vill marry Mees Fanny."

"If she'll have you; for my part," muttered the earl, "I think she'll have confounded bad taste if she does."

"I sall make her have me."

"Bah! pour out my chocolate."

Little did the earl dream as he saw the obsequious Frenchman at his elbow that he was weaving such a plot about him as he might never release himself from. Little did he think that the Frenchman was contemplating the day when he—the valet—should seize the revenues and grand domains of the Milrays.

As the nobleman (for by this time he was recognised a nobleman, and must, therefore, be called one)—as the nobleman stepped into the sedan, he little thought the ferret eyes of the Frenchman were upon him.

A little crowd at the great gate of the house impeded the advance of the sedan for a few moments.

During this stoppage, a singular-looking man, dressed in heavy black, saluted the earl.

Some one in the crowd noted that the earl shrank back—he could not grow paler than he was—and he cried out, "No one's going to hurt you!"

Next moment the sedan was in motion, and the black-clothed gentleman replaced his hat upon his head.

Many of the usual occupants of the Cocoa Tree were present when Holgarth entered. He was superbly dressed in pale blue and white velvet, and many diamonds sparkled on him.

A gentleman immediately advanced to meet him.

"Glad to see you out, Milray," said the gentleman.

"Thank you, Ashton; I have had a narrow escape. I have been desperately ill. When you called the other day I was so bad that I could not remember you, and even now I remember very little of our old acquaintance."

"Indeed, Milray," continued Lord Ashton, "I assure you that did I not know you by your face, of which no man could doubt a moment, I should say you were not yourself; you don't even shake hands as you used to—your hand is cold and dead."

"I know it, Ashton; and I ask myself sometimes—shall I ever recover my old self. I have paid dearly for this earldom."

All this was said loud enough to be heard amongst the company.

"Ah, Alchester!" said Lord Ashton to a passing gentleman, "this is Milray."

"Glad to see you, Milray—glad to see you in the place of that ass, the late Milray—wish you'd told him who you were long before, and so have let him shot himself years ago; he was a blot in aristocracy—all he could do was to ruin women; as to fighting or hunting, don't believe he knew what they meant!"

"His death was lamentable, good Milray."

"Oh, I never should have thought he would

have had the courage to do such a deed; permit me, this is the Hon. Mr. Natherton."

Within a few moments Holgarth had been introduced to a score of the highest aristocracy in England as "Milray"—meaning thereby the "Earl of Milray."

"I feared at one time that I should not gain the day so easily," said Milray, as they were talking in a light easy manner of his succ ssion.

"Oh!" returned Lord Alchester, "the fact of Milray killing himself was the best proof you could have had of your claims."

"Then again," said Lord Ashton, "how fortunate it was his French valet was watching you; his evidence as to the suicide, and Milray's admission of your claims, was superb."

"Yes, it gave me the earldom," said Holgarth.

"Still, Edgar," said Ashton—"and I shall call you by that name—still you are not the same old Edgar; you are changed! I never could have believed illness would have changed a man so utterly. However, wl ether or no, I still have the scar of the wound which, without your help, would have been fatal."

Here a gentleman rapidly entering, Alchester said, "Here is Gentleman Jack Mudberry: do you know Mudberry?"

"No," said Milray, who could scarcely support himself in the chair.

"You are ill again, Milray," said Ashton.

"It will pass off."

"Do you know about Mudberry?" said Alchester; "he was stopped by that infernal Gentleman Jack; the scamp forced him to sup with him, and Mudberry talked so much about the adventure that we have christened him Gentleman Jack Mudberry."

Here the individual in question came forward, and seeing Holgarth, started, and said, "Gentleman Jack, by Jove!"

Holgarth tried to look unconcerned, but he appeared ghastly.

"Go along, Mud," said Alchester; "this is the Earl of Milray; Captain Edgar Trevillian that was."

Mr. Mudberry still kept looking at the highwayman.

"I believe," said Holgarth, "that the highwayman you refer to was hanged about two months back."

"His very voice," Mudberry continued—"can two men have existed so much alike?'

At this moment another gentleman entered the gaming-house—the black-clothed man who had raised his hat in the street to Holgarth.

He came calmly in, looking to neither right nor left.

"Who is that?" asked Holgarth.

"A queer fish," Alchester returned; "we don't know much of him, but he loses his money handsomely, so we wink at his questionable character."

Slowly the man looked up, started as he s w Holgarth, and smiling in a manner which was much more repulsive than his natural appearance, he said:

"Captain Edgar Trevillian!"

Milray started.

"Surely I met you, sir, when your regiment was in Germany."

"Ah; I remember you."

"I have long had a message for you."

The gentlemen about moved away from the seated earl, who had no power to rise.

"Sir," said the stranger.

"You here?"

"Yes, why not?"

"What have you got to say?"

"You owe me your life once more."

"I know it."

"Your resuscitation is suspected—do not start."

"Who suspects it?"

"I will tell you."

"I will kill him!"

"You must NOT kill him: you must bribe him, destroy his soul!"

"What is his name?"

"No matter."

"When shall I know?"

"Soon, when I choose to tell you. Remember you owe me your life once more; for the man who has accused you will soon be cut of your path. People will say he has been mad in accusing you."

"Why, oh terrible man! do you favour and yet persecute me?"

"Because I admire you, Holgarth."

CHAPTER XXII.

FANNY.

TURN we now to the poor deserted Fanny. For day after day, week after week, she had lain tossing on her bed, fever-worn and at times very near death.

She had been moved from the grand portion of the house very soon after the news of the suicide of the earl had spread through the house. Taken from the gilding, the velvet, and the luxury of the drawing-room of Milray's house to a dismal up-stairs garret.

For days she remained utterly unconscious of what was passing around her.

The old woman Jules had calmly appointed to watch over the fallen girl, sat by the bedside day after day, slept on the same bed as the sufferer, night after night, and still Fanny raved unintelligibly.

Every day Jules came creeping into the room, and asking questions. If the girl were asleep, he would come and look on her wolfishly, and smile at some passing thought to which he never gave words.

So day after day went on.

The earl had been slain about ten days, when the nurse, who was dozing, was startled by the inquiry: "Why, where am I?"

She looked up, and saw that the patient had once more the light of reason in her face.

"That's all right, me dear," says the woman.

"My dear!" says Fanny, suddenly remembering that she was a countess, "my dear! what do you mean by such a word?"

"Only, me dear—me dear," said the old body, nodding her head, and smiling like a hideous aged vampire as she was, for she had heard from the servants that Fanny was only the late lord's "miss," and as the late lord was dead what need was there to be polite to Fanny?

"How dare you—" Fanny had proceeded, when she fell from weakness upon the bed.

"Ah!" says the old woman, "you must keep your strength up, me dear. What was your drink in the Garden?"

"What garden?'

"Covent, me dea'."

"Who dared to tell you I knew Covent Garden?"

"—Market," says the old woman.

"Why, why am I here in this hole?" asked the poor girl in a few moments, and as she passed her hand over her forehead—

'Cos yer is," was the remark of the hideous old nurse, who now produced a gin bottle and two glasses.

"Yere," says the old woman, "take a glass; I dessay you did in the Garden.'

And here she held out the liquor.

Fanny pushed the dose away---had she taken it, in all probability it would have killed her--- and took no heed of the old party's grumbling to the effect that it was "spiled and spilt," but stretched her hand towards that part of the bedstead where she expected to find a bell-rope.

"What were you looking for, duckey?"

"The bell-rope; I want my maid."

"Oh, ain't we made o' pride!" says the nurse, tossing off another glass of the gin, which, at that time, was exceedingly cheap; the Chancellor of the Exchequer was not in the habit of putting extra shillings on the drink every time Parliament met.

"How dare you, woman?" said poor Fan.

"Woman!" says the old crone; "honest woman if you like, and that's more than some trulls are. Woman me no womans, madam."

"You shall be punished for this," said Fanny. "I'll let you know before long that you are speaking to the Countess of Milray."

"Humph! there may be a countess, me dear, but she has not got red stumps for hair."

Poor Fanny looked still handsome, but far from the blooming beauty who, only a few weeks before, was a healthy and happy orange girl. She was thin, very thin; her eyes were sunken, and all her bright beautiful hair had been cut off, that her head might be kept as cool as possible.

The reference to her appearance caused Fanny to start She bade the woman to bring her a glass; and, rather from a desire to see the misery the poor girl would endure, than from a desire to obey her patient, she brought the miserable guttering candle, and a cracked mirror, to the bedside.

Fanny looked into the tell-tale glass, and burst into tears.

A few moments calmed her. Then, turning to the nurse, she said, "Who is your master?"

"Yours!"

"Who is that?"

"The hearl."

"The earl!" the girl eagerly said. "I thought he was dead."

"Oh, when a hearl dies another springs hup, me dear."

"Who is he? what is he like? how long have I been lying here?"

He? a gemman; I haven't seen him; an' yer'll have been on yer back, me dear, down in the screaming fever a fortn't cum next Toosday.

"Why, am I here in this garret?

"Why, says the old woman, losing all patience; "why, because you're only a servant of a kind, me dear, and so you are in a servant's room. Why, good lor', yer don't suppose as how the new lord want you a scrieling out about the place like a wild Ingin from America, and you only the hold glove of the hold earl; whichways he warn't hold, but hold I calls him."

"Then, am I not the countess?"

"Me dear, no more than I."

As the woman spoke Jules entered the room softly. He heard the last question and the last answer.

Down fell the poor girl; and, when she once more moved, she was again raving. The fever had returned upon her.

A delicately-nurtured woman would have assuredly died under this attack; nothing could have saved her: but Fanny had been hardly bred; up early in the market, struggling for the living she had acquired, she had become strong and able to cope with illness, such illness as would have killed a delicate woman.

Again days and days passed, and she was a raging maniac; she grew still more pale and thin, and the gin-drinking old harridan of a nurse wondered how it was she did not die.

At last, on one miserable night, she again became as much her old self as she would ever be.

No longer was she the petulant, the defiant Fanny, but a broken-down woman; all her energy past away, and weary of the life that was in her.

The cry she gave, when once more she knew herself, awoke the old nurse.

"Heydey, my dear! yere you are agin."

"Good evening! I remember all."

"That's a dear!"

"Let me see, you told me I was not the countess?"

"No more nor I ham."

"Then who am I?"

"The earl's lady!"

"And not his wife?"

"No, me dear: leastways, if you was, why did Mr. Jooles, who knows all about the late count, send yer up yere, me bird?"

"Oh! Mr. Jules sent me up here?"

"Yes; he is a fine man for a Frenchy, isn't he?"

"But—but I was married, I declare to you, ma'am."

"Yes, me dear, so we all is, unner such circumstances, and them there men—them there men!"

"Where is Mr. Jules, ma'am?"

"Oh! you needn't say mam to me; I am only a miss. Mr. Jooles is down stairs. Would you like to see Mr. Jooles? A fine man for a Frenchy!"

"Yes, miss, I dont know your name."

"Ann Baggett is my name, an' Hingland is my nation; Old Pancras is my dwelling-place, and well I knows me station."

"Mrs. Baggett, will you be good enough to ask Mr. Jules to come and see me!"

"I say, me dear, yer speaks wery like a lady for a horange gal!"

"Oh! My father was a gentleman, and my mother was unfortunate. He gave me a governess for a little time, only being in the market altered me. Now, now I seem to be, as I once was, ABOVE the orange girls. Well, you tell Mr. Jules I want him."

"Yes, miss, and I wish yer was my lady, for yer'd make a good 'un," said Mrs. Baggett, nurse, for sometimes a lady-like tone, even when the speaker is not a lady, will put down cruel insolence and vile impertinence.

While Fanny talked to Mrs. Bagget in the Govent Garden style, Mrs. B. was impudent; when she spoke to her more in the manner of her early days—a manner which she had long forgotten, and which had been brought back to her by reason of her illness—Mrs. Bagget was actually polite, or, rather, as near polite as she could be.

Mrs. B. was "going to go" to the door, when she fetched herself up with a jerk, for there was Mr. Jules, as she described it, "all in a heap a lissunin' with all his years."

"Good even, Madame Baggett: you sall be von vell, I hope."

"Vell, I don't know," said Mrs. Baggett; "praps yes, and praps no—but that depends on vhich vay the cat jumps; an' its a werry ill wind that doesn't blow summun good, and summun to Jericho."

"Oui, Madame Baggett; go down de stairs."

"Mounseer!" says Mrs. B., who was fond of driving her little store of French.

"Descend de stairs," says Jules.

"Oui, mounseer," says Mrs. B., and did descend, but not unaccompanied by her lovely gin bottle.

"Good even, me lady."

"Oh, Mr. Jules, you know I am no such thing."

"I know dat? I do NOT know dat."

"You can't mean to say I'm really the countess."

"I do."

"Then why am I here?"

"Because no one but me know dat you air me lady!"

"The minister—"

"He have died."

"Then—then only you know I am married."

"Only me, me lady."

"Then I am in your power."

"Oui, me lady."

"And you will help me, will you not, to prove I was married to the Earl of Milray?"

"That sall all depend on de circumstances, me lady."

"Who is the new earl?"

"My new master, me lady."

"Who is he?"

He vas a captain in him Majesty's army; now he is me lord and master."

"Ah, then, if you are his servant, you will stand by him, and I and my unborn child, perhaps, are lost."

"No, me lady. If I no wish you to be call me lady, why call I you me lady?"

"True."

"Me lady, I will save you on one condition."

"What is that?"

"If you sall become de moder of von leetle boy, he is de earl."

"Yes, I know it."

Jules smiled cruelly as he said, "Oui, I know dat, also; and den de new earl sall be drive from de house.

"Why not? he would drive me."

"But all dat sall take time and money."

"I cannot wait, and I have no money."

"You sall vait, and I have mosh money; mosh more than I vant."

"And you will help me?"

"On von condition."

"What is it? quick!"

"Do you know my leetle secret?"

"No; what is it?"

"I loff you!"

The rascal did nothing of the kind. He never loved anybody beyond himself during his lifetime, but he saw that the nearest way to his end was to touch the best portion of her woman's heart.

"You love me!"

"Oui, I have always loff you, even when you haff been the poor orange girl; but what chance haff I had; for I was a poor valet—you a pretty beauty. Now dat you are poor an' in trouble, Fanny, I say I loff you, I vill marry you."

The poor girl turned away in disgust from the repulsive Frenchman.

I vill make you good husband—be good father to your child, and den he sall have de chance to be de earl."

She started at these latter words, and looked him narrowly in the face.

"Oui, Fanny; do you no comprehend? if you marry me, I sall haff de right to see dat vou sall, me say, be known as de countess, and de young child as de earl; sall you answer me?"

For full five minutes the poor entrapped girl lay turned away from the cruel clever tempter. She ran over all the facts of the case in her mind. If she repulsed this man, what was she to do? She could not go back to the Market again. Her savings would soon be swallowed up; and even if she worked elsewhere, could she earn enough to educate her son, if one were born to her, as the son of the Earl of Milray should be educated! Then again, even if she could earn enough to educate him, would not her boy be ashamed of her as he grew up?

But she was not conquered.

Then another moment's thought told her that she was perhaps standing in her child's way by opposing, in any manner, the only man who would aid ⅃er in establishing her child's claim to the earldom; so, as quick as the thought struck her, she determined to accept Jules. Turning to that ugly valet, she said:

"Mr. Jules, if you desire to marry me, I am willing to be your wife."

The Frenchman started, his face became red, partly from lascivious passion, chiefly because he saw a wide open road to the successful end of his ambition; and he stooped down, took the fragile form of the girl in his arms, and kissed her lips.

"I vill make your fortune and mine," he said, and in the same moment he thought, "If she has a son, I vill ruin him before I give him the earldom, and then that earldom will be as good as mine."

He had barely kissed the pale lips of the beauty, when a loud "bravo!" sounded behind him.

He turned, and saw the earl, his new master.

"Good evening, Mr. Jules. So this is the manner of your conduct when you are out of my presence!"

"Me lord—"

"So you are going to make your fortune and hers, are you?"

"Me lord, dis is de young lady dat the late lord—"

"Yes, yes! I know all about it; you are not particular when you rat."

The Frenchman's eyes sparkled at the insult, which he fully comprehended; but he bowed his head, and once more said:

"Me lord."

"So you are going to marry her, Mr. Jules?" asked Holgarth.

"If me lord will allow me."

Oh, certainly, it's nothing to me."

If the earl had looked at the Frenchman, and if he had read his face, he might have perused the words, "It's ALL to you."

But the earl was not looking at the Frenchman, but at the sick girl, whom he was languidly admiring.

"You'll make a pretty couple."

"Sir—my lord, says Fanny.

"Well, my bird."

"Do you know I was married to the late earl?"

"No, my poppet, I do NOT know that you were married to the late earl."

"I was indeed: I can prove it," said the poor girl, hoping, perhaps, to move the pity of the earl, and thereby trusting to avoid a marriage with Jules, which she had consented to, believing that she was thereby doing her duty to her unborn child.

"How do you prove it?" said the earl in some alarm.

"Jules," said the girl, looking at the Frenchman.

The valet gave her one of his worst looks, for he guessed the way her thoughts went, and said, "Me lord, I know nosing of what de dear girl say!"

"Of course not," said Holgarth, reassured. "Evidence, my pretty wench; do you think to show evidence of your being the countess by letting your late husband's valet kiss you a month after the earl's death, and by promising to marry him?"

Then turning to the valet, he continued— "I was anxious to see this fancy of Milray's you told me about, so I've found my way here, my man. Seeing her, I can only wonder what on earth he saw in her."

Thereupon the earl turned upon his heel, and left the room.

The valet then leant over the weak, unresisting woman, and said to her; "Never mind, ma mie, ve vill ruin him; he sall lick de dust from our boots."

———

CHAPTER XXIII.

MRS. WHITE, wife of Charley White, was much above living altogether upon her husband. Mrs. White made a little money—not much— by playing with little bits of thread and about five hundred bone handles, on a pillow like a sofa cushion. This playing she termed lace-making. We do not see much lace-making in London in our days; but to this day they work hard with the little bits of thread, and the cushion, and the slips of bone; and, indeed, so poor is the task, that the fingers that twirl these bits of bone are almost as thin as they are.

But Mrs. Charley White's fingers were as fat as good living could make them. She only played, not worked, with the bones, and when she went out to tea she always took her pillow, done up genteelly in brown paper, so that she might clatter her tongue and her bobbins at the same time.

Again, Mrs. White did the most profitable kind of lace work. She mended lace, and she charged a pretty stiff price; and as she worked for the aristocrats, s e altogether made a good thing of it; and as she informed her friends (when Charley was on duty) her husband had never bought a stitch of the things on her back, and which, though it was neither here nor there, the "me dears" knew of a long stocking with something even better in it than a handsome leg, "me dears."

Well, amongst other customers, Mrs. White worked for the housekeeper at Milray House—had worked for her during many years. Mrs. White gener..lly turned up once a month "to lace" the household, as she termed it.

Well, about the usual day, Mrs. White rung the area bell of Milray House, and in about five minut s after she had curtseyed to the housekeeper, shook the head housemaid's hand, had a word with the coo, and even given a nod to the scullery-maid, who never had lace mended or unmended, and was seated near a roaring fire, her feet on a hassock, and a fine glass of punch not a hundred miles away from her right hand.

Mrs. Pannetty, the housekeeper at Milray House, was a little, dignified, sharp woman, not above flattery, and Mrs. White was a big jolly woman, not above turning out good strong doses of flattery, which, however, were never too strong for Mrs. Pannetty.

" Well, Mrs. White, and how does the world use you ?"

"Things is coming round," says Mrs. White. This was a modest way of alluding to the stocking. And it is certain that Mrs. White herself was coming very round indeed.

"That's good," says the housekeeper, who had also got a stocking. People who have heavy stockings are, somehow, always very amiable togeth r when they talk of these agreeable household goods.

"And how is White ?"

"White is well, M s. Pannetty, and so's White's children. Those children shall some day know the vally of a stocking, me dear, which is handsomer than as though it had the finest leg in it!"

"Ah!' says Mrs. Pannetty. It was not much to say, but there was a great deal in that " ah."

"And now what's the news you've got, Mrs. White ?"

Mrs. W. took a touch of the punch and commenced. "The most curious haffair I know is White's own, and the sham jewels."

Now Mr. Jules was fond of listening where he had no right whatever to listen. His private room was next to the housekeeper's parlour, in which sanctum it need not be said Mrs. White was taking her punch.

And some time back, long before the death of the late earl, Jules, feeling lonely by himself, had walked into a large cupboard in one corner of his room and made a small hole into the corresponding cupboard in Mrs. Pannetty's room.

Now Mrs. Pannetty was fond of showing off her china, (her own property) so she had had the door of her cupboard removed, and everybody who came into the room, saw four shelves of handsome china ; nobody saw the hole just below one of the punch bowls.

Whenever Mr. Jules felt lonely, and knew that Mrs. Pannetty had company, he just walked into his cupboard, from which HE had removed the shelves, shut the door, pulled out the plug from the little hole, and had his eye at the hole in a moment. Then he would glue his ear to the same aperture, and learn quite a much from Mrs. Pannetty's visitor as Mrs. P. herself ; and learn far more of the housekeeper than ever the sharp little body ever intended to make public.

Mr. Jules had seen a good deal in that room, and he knew that at any time he could put a little spoke in Mrs. Pannetty's w eel, if that lady opposed him ; for instance, he witnessed the interview between Mrs. P. and a young fifteen-year stable-boy, who forced himself into the lady's presence, and there made a declaration of his love. Mr. Jules also witnessed the lady's tremor, and her avowal that she would think of it, in a few years, perhaps.

Well, on the very morning that Mrs. White touched the punch, Mr. Jules, coming into the room, heard voices, and was in the cupboard in a moment.

Now, Mr. Jules had also made a hole in his cupboard door, that he might have his eye in his room while one ear was at the hole.

His astonishment may easily be guessed, when he heard the visitor's expression — "White's own, and the sham jewels !"

He knew the name of the constable White, as well as he knew the value of the jewels.

He panted for the next words, but they were of little value, for Mrs. White said—" My dear " —she was softened by touching the punch— "my dear, which shall I do fust ; the tippet or the muffettees ?"

Then followed such a discussion on lace in general, and Mrs. Pannetty's in particular, that Jules felt inclined to thrust it all down their throats.

"But," suddenly said Mrs. P., what about the jewels, my dear ?"

"SHAM jewels, my dear, which we kept under the bed, and which little Tom broke open the box with a poker, the dear little love! and when I came home, there he was with a necklidge, shining like real dimunts and the blessed light o'day, round his hinfant neck !"

At this moment Jules heard the door of his room open, and peering through the hole in the door, he saw his master enter.

The earl looked about, and then murmuring, " Perhaps he is in his bed-room," called out, " Jules."

No answer made Jules, and he heartily hoped, if the earl determined to look for him in his bed-room, that he would turn round towards that chamber, and go towards it.

No such luck, however, for Jules this time.

The earl came straight towards the cupboard-door.

But Jules was not caught.

An inner cupboard opened within the receptacle in which Jules was standing,(a) and when the earl opened the first it was empty, for Jules had, of course, shut the intervening door.

The earl muttered an angry oath upon the Frenchman, and was just about to close the door again, when he heard these words :

"Found, my dear, dead in the road, with all her sham jewels on her, my dear."

The earl started, and stood still.

Meanwhile Jules remembered that he had not plugged the hole, and he thought that if either of the women noticed the light streaming through it by reason of the cupboard-door being open, there would be an end to the secret.

But this danger was soon obviated.

The earl started, saw the hole, placed an eye to it, hesitated another moment, then ran to the door of the room, locked it, returned to the cupboard, closed it, and took up the very position which Jules had held.

As the Frenchman heard this state of things he bit his fingers in rage till the blood came, for he could hear nothing of the revelations; the earl was hearing them all, and he, Jules, dared not speak.

"Lor, madam," says Mrs. White, "the most wonderful history; the poor girl, a hactress, me dear, was picked up, with her sham jewels on her, and what do you think happened to the dear, me dear, at the station-house ?"

"Oh," says Mrs. Pannetty, "never mind, dear, what happened to her, tell me after you've told me about the jewels."

It was at this moment that the French valet, hidden in the inner cupboard, began to mark an odd state of things. He heard an odd singing in his ears, his temples began to throb, and great specks flew before his eyes.

"The jewels, me dear," continued Mrs. White—"the sham jewels was left at the station arter she wanted 'em no more."

"What!—was she sent to Bridewell (b) then !"

"No, my dear; she was sent to glory."

"What do you mean, my dear ?"

"She became a corse."

"And, then, what became of the jewels ? you know we have suffered about jewels. Lady Milly, who, I say, has 'loped with some low creature, no doubt—perhaps a stable-boy, them creaures is so haspiring—Lady Milly came o' age the day she 'loped, and she had on jewels worth £100,000 ; (c) she only had 'em given her that day, because she came of age.

"What became o' the jewels ? Why, they

was left at the office in Charley's care ; an' what do yer think ?"

"What ?"

Here Jules, in his concealment, became aware of what was the matter with him; he was being slowly stifled for want of fresh air.

"What ?" said Mrs. White, in her excitement taking a long touch at the punch, and immediately coughing, to show that she wasn't used to it. "What ? why a rascally Frenchy comes to the office hinquirin' after them there jewels—sham jewels ; an' says Charley, who's a clever un, 'them there jewels is there,' pintin' to the box, and then says he, 'they's in my care, and they goes to my home,' and home he brought 'em."

Honest Mrs. White couldn't see the smile that stole over the earl's face, as he heard this revelation. "The jewels are mine once more," he said.

"And home they are, I 'spose, now, Mrs. White, me dear."

"Oh, no ; that's the curousest part of the story : home they're not ; White gived 'em up."

If Mrs. White had not seen the smile that passed over the highwayman's face, it was well for her that she did not see the frown which overcast his countenance at her last words.

"Give 'em up ; who to ?"

"Why to the showman that took the hinfant ; Mr.—dear, dear ; what is that good Samaritan's name ? Mr. Ted—Ted—no, Ted was his Christian name ; Mr. Tag—I don't think it was Tag. Gag—Mag—Nag—oh, I've got it—it was Teddy——

At this moment the French valet, unable any longer to endure his confinement, tore open the door between the cupboard, and fell against the earl, who, thus assailed in the darkness of the cupboard, naturally shouted.

Striking at the door, it gave way ; and the two women frightened at the various unexpected voices, uttered scream upon scream.

"You—Jules !"

"Me lord, yes ; pardon me."

Still the women kept screaming.

The rapid run of several men towards the housekeeper's room seemed to cause the earl and valet to regain their senses.

"What is to be done ?" asked the earl.

"A moment—a leetle moment, me lord," said the valet, and the next moment he ran to a screen, and laid it lightly on the ground.

"Thieves ! rape ! robbers ! murder !" the two women cried—"in the next room—quick !"

The footmen ran to the valet's room, and flung open the door.

The earl was seated near the fallen screen ; the valet was standing obsequiously near him. The cupboard was not open.

"What does all this mean, pray ?" asked the earl. "Has the entire household gone mad ?"

"Oh, me lord," said Mrs. Pannetty, "me and Mrs. White didn't know your lordship was

(a) In old houses this arrangement is frequently seen. It is generally supposed that the one cupboard opened from the other to obviate the use of a number of doors in the room, while two separate supboards were formed. The inner cupboard was generally used for lumber.

(b) Bridewell, situated, we believe, near St. Bride's Passage, Fleet Street, was the prison to which wanton women were sent. At this jail the women were unmercifully beaten in the good old times.

(c) Mrs. Pannetty made a slight mistake. The value was £60,000 here. We heard a terrible noise like the falling of a house."

"It was de screen, Mistress Pannettee, which I let to fall nearly upon me lord, and for which I scream like de devil because I fear dat me lord sall be kill."

"Clear the room," said the earl; and the servants obediently followed each other from the room, but Mrs. White and the housekeeper regarded each other with looks which plainly said—"It was no screen, and that Frenchy couldn't shout like an Englishman."

"Well," said the earl, looking at the valet.

"Me lord." So answered Jules.

"What were you doing in that cupboard?"

"Leestening to de ladies."

"Hum!—you often listen."

"A leetle—when I am tired of my own poor company."

"Hum—your company's not the best in the world. Don't bow and scrape now we're alone—we know each other too well for that."

"Know, me lord?"

"Yes. We'd cut each other's throat if either could benefit by the other's death."

"Me lord!"

"Ah! that look was the truth. Now, what did you hear?"

"Me lord comes to my poor room jes ven I commence to hear. *Vat did me lord hear!*"

"My man, that's nothing to do with you."

"Oh!—*oui*, all to do wid me."

"Then you won't hear it. Don't look at me like that, or I'll crush you like a beetle under my foot."

"I could hang you, me lord—like a rat."

"Bah!—you were an accomplice, and would hang with me."

"No, me lord; not if I turn me to be de informer."

"You could do nothing alone, and the probabilities of my story are so great, that I have only to say you trumped up the history because I turned you away, and the judges would believe me, and you would end your days on the hulks."

The Frenchman looked at the earl for a moment as though he were foiled, then he continued—"I sall not harm me lord; vill he pay me my tousand pound pare year."

"Very well. Now you won't know what I've heard — depend upon that," said the earl rising; "and remember, the higher you climb the greater will be your fall when your time comes."

The earl left the room, went down the stairs, and stepped into his sedan. Meanwhile, the valet stood in his private room, looking towards the door through which the earl had passed, and biting his fingers.

"*Prend garde!*" he kept muttering to himself—"*prend garde! ou je te tuerai.*"

CHAPTER XXIV.

THE NEW EARL.

LADY HARRIET SEYMOUR and her daughter in a charming room in their house.

In this room was to be found no reproduction of the extreme extravagance of Milray House. And yet the Seymours were very rich, and the last Milray and the present usurper were far from wealthy. Thus it frequently happens in the fashionable world. Only too frequently, where we see grandeur and unhesitating luxury, there are bailiffs at the door, and heavy care at the heart of the master; while at a neighbouring house, where there is no pretension—where the owner has a plain dark-green carriage, and a few unpretending servants —the owner might eat off gold, and fling sovereigns all day long at passers by, and yet not feel the loss at the end of the day.

This latter house keeps its tenant; the grand house to which we have referred only too frequently changes its occupant, who not unusually exchanges his preposterous splendours for a poor lodging in Boulogne, or an infinitely worse in the Queen's Bench.

Of this we may be certain, that expensive living is no criterion of great or, rather, lasting wealth.

Lady Harriet Seymour's little room was charming, and yet not expensive. It might have been in the house of a man possessing but a few hundreds a year.

The pretty chintz was a pink and white flowering on a drab ground; the walls were plain, yet beautiful; and the carpet—a deep claret— gave a quiet tone to the room, which altogether seemed to soothe a visitor as he entered it. (a)

Her ladyship was quietly dressed in plain brown silk, and had not an ornament about her. Constance was dressed charmingly in a high-necked muslin dress, below which, and on the neck, was to be seen a sparkling gold and diamond chain.

Each lady was performing some piece of legerdemain with a bit of embroidery, as they pleasantly chatted.

"If Edith grows no better, she must be sent to Harrington;—the waters will soon set her up."

"Oh! mamma, I know what would set her up; the sight of her child and her husband— both at once, you know, mamma!"

"Ah! my dear, she will, I fear, never see her husband more. Of this I am convinced — he *was* her husband. She showed me one of his letters, from which she had cut off the name. It was written as no mere seducer could write, but with a strength of love and honour which told me, without a particle of doubt, that she was married to him."

(a) Doubtless readers have remarked this fact, that while many splendid rooms are irritating and discomforting, many common rooms are cheerful in their poverty; while many moderately expensive rooms seem the perfection of homes.

"Has she told you his name and hers yet?" asked Constance.

"No."

"Don't think me curious, mamma, but—but do you not think she would be happier if she confessed all to you?"

"I think she would; but she tells me that she doubts if she has a right to inform me."

"How so?—I may ask," said the younger lady, blushing deeply,—"you know, mamma, I love Edith already, and I feel more interest in her life than I would have believed possible a little while since."

"My dear, I do not like to pry into Edith's secrets; she will tell us when she thinks she may honestly do so. I will tell you what she has told me. Her father is a cruel harsh man, whom she believes to have suffered terribly in his early days by the licentiousness of some unprincipled man. Edith was beloved by a gentleman whom she calls Edgar. This gentleman universally had the stain upon him of illegitimate birth, he knowing all the while that his name was as untarnished as any man's in the kingdom. Edith, like a true woman, believed her lover's protestation that he *was* the legitimate son of the earl his father, but she dared not tell her father of her engagement, because she knew he had a hatred of illegitimate children—a hate which grew out of the curse upon his early life. So they remained secret, and were married secretly; and by the force of some singular belief, Edith took an oath that she would never divulge her husband's name till he gave her written permission to do so. Her father discovered her married condition before that permission was given her; but it arrived only an hour before her father drove her away from his home—if home it could be called."

"Indeed, no!" said Constance, looking round the comfortable room and then towards her good mother.

"She would then have told her father her husband's name, but he demanded it in the presence of a singular woman whom he had engaged to watch Edith, and who recognised him as one she hated by a portrait Edith was wearing. Edith refused to yield the name in the presence of this infuriated woman and she was driven out into the world. Such," continued Lady Harriet, "is the unhappy story of the poor girl to whom we have given a home."

"But why does she hesitate to tell *you* the name of her husband?" asked Constance.

"Oh, she has an excellent reason. She says she took an oath never to divulge her husband's name till he gave her permission; the letter she received bade her only give up this name to her father—so she reads the letter—and therefore she considers her oath binding upon her with respect to all other people."

"How strange!" said the girl, dropping her hands and gazing before her.

"Hush!—here she is!"

The door opened and Edith entered.

She was very pale; her long flaxen hair lay soft and close to her white cheeks and neck, and her great grey eyes looked sadly and gently towards her benefactresses.

"Good day, Edith; I am glad Constance persuaded you to keep in bed for an hour or so; are you better?"

"Oh, much; a week or so and I shall be quite myself."

"A week or so, and you will see your little boy."

"Oh, yes," Edith said, looking gladly for a moment, "I shall see him for a day."

"Oh, Edith, come and help me with this troublesome rose," cried out Constance, holding up her embroidery, "or I shall never finish it."

Edith went to her young friend with a lightened step, sat down, and began at the embroidery.

The conversation had changed to general subjects that continued during ten minutes, when a tremendous summons at the door of the house drew Constance to the window.

"Oh, mamma! it is the lord we met at the ball last night, and who paid you such attention."

"You, my dear, I think," said the lady.

"What a very handsome man he would be if he were less pale, and if he had more expression; he looks like one raised from the dead."

The next moment a servant entered and announced "The Earl of Milray!"

"Milray!" Edith said, yet so lowly that no other soul than her heard the word; and then she thought: "this is the man who is keeping my husband from the earldom, me from happiness, and our son from his rights. I dare not meet him! I dare not—dare not meet him!"

As she thought these words, she rose.

"Edith, where are you going?" asked Constance.

"To my room, Constance."

"Why, will you not stop and see the great earl who paid me, your friend, such compliments only last night?"

"I am weaker than I thought I was; and again, I do not know him. I should be in the way."

"Oh, do—do stop!" urged the young lady.

Edith sat down again; but Lady Harriet said—"My dear, you are thoughtless, and therefore cruel, without intending it. I am sure Edith would infinitely rather go to her room than remain here. Go, my dear Constance, and I will come to your chamber when the earl is gone."

Edith started up as she heard footsteps without the great door, and barely had she left the room by the small door in one corner, than Holgarth entered the apartment and bowed to the ladies.

Still pale as death—still a man of death among the living.

After a few passing remarks, Lady Harriet said—"My lord, you are ill?"

"No."

"I am glad to hear it; but you certainly look

ill. You must allow an old woman like myself to say so—what think you, Constance?"

"I should say Lord Milray is very ill indeed."

"I would I were," Milray continued, smiling, "for I would gladly be all that you think me, Lady Constance."

He smiled as he spoke, smiled again as he marked the young girl's blushing at his compliment; but the smiles were not well to look upon.

"I may tell you, Lady Harriet, that the shock of my cousin's death gave birth to a heart disease, to recover from which I shall require long years of peace and domestic happiness."

As he uttered the last two words he looked towards the young lady, and once more he saw her bow and become confused.

"We have of course heard, my lord," continued Lady Harriet, "of your terrible illness: is your memory growing better, my lord?"

"Not much. I am still saluted by old friends whom I do not know; but the doctors hope the best for me. I have refused to see my old doctor, the gentleman who attended me while in the army: I had long grown convinced that he was not an adept in his profession."

"Oh," continued Lady Harriet, "we have heard something about that, too, my lord. You see, we women are so fond of hearing the news. I believe the doctor vows you are not the same man."

"Indeed, in one sense, I am not; I do *not* seem to be the man I was previous to my elevation; but I need not say the doctor's scandal is laughed at."

"Beyond question," said the lady, "your lordship has too remarkable personal qualifications to be mistaken for another."

"I believe that, Lady Harriet; I think it would be difficult to find another man like me."

"I am sure of it."

"My poor cousin recognised me in a moment, though I had not seen him for fifteen years. The poor fellow admitted my proof at once—his death by his own hand proves that."

"It does, indeed, my lord," answered Lady Harriet.

"How fortunate you were to escape from the fate of the Gorgon, my lord," said Constance, in a low voice.

She had been furtively looking at him while apparently engaged upon her embroidery, for some minutes; and, indeed, she seemed to be fascinated by the visitor.

"Very fortunate," said the earl, "the ship is a wreck—all my old companions dead or in slavery. I am most thankful I am not amongst them."

"All your companions!" said Lady Harriet, "no, not all; a sergeant escaped, it seems—I read it in to-day's paper—and is in England."

"Indeed!" said the earl, turning, if possible, yet more pale than he was habitually, "where is he to be found?"

"In hospital, poor fellow," answered Lady Harriet, "the paper says he is quite deranged; this madness was brought on by the agony he endured while on the water. How is it you are forced to come to a poor woman's humdrum to learn the news?"

"I do not read much," said Holgarth—he did not add because he was sickened at the narrative of the executions, to which his eyes always turned when he took up a journal.

"I trust I may have the honour of re-seeing you, Lady Harriet, before I leave town," said Holgarth, speaking to the elder lady, but looking towards the younger.

Constance raised her eyes rapidly.

"Are you going to leave town so early in the season?"

"Yes, I must go down to my Wilts estates."

"Are you not afraid?" asked Constance.

"Of what?" he continued.

"Of highwaymen—they swarm in the west country!"

"Bah!—I don't believe in half the stories told of highwaymen. I should like to see one," said Holgarth, looking in a mirror, "I wonder what the fellows are like?"

"Savage wretches!" said Constance.

"By the bye, I hear of a new celebrated highwayman," said Lady Harriet Seymour, "a roadster who is to become or has become as famous as the poor wretch they hanged a month or so ago. Let me see—what did they call him?—Dashing—Dashing, or else Gentlemen—ah! I have it—Gentleman Jack!"

"Odd name for a thief," says Holgarth.

"Nay, but they say he really was a gentleman in manners; and they actually add that he was the son, in a certain way, of a great nobleman."

"Ah! I've heard something about it. I remember that at all events—yes, to be sure—Gentleman Jack was hanged—the blackguard! Pity he couldn't be hanged twice, Lady Harriet. Pray, who is the new scamp who seems to have bought up Gentleman Jack's shoes?"

"Oh, they call him Captain Strongarm, my lord," said Constance.

"Indeed!—another odd name for a highwayman."

Now all the time, during which the conversation about the highwaymen was proceeding, the false earl had been nervously twisting his hands about one within the other, nor did he mark that in doing so a ring he wore fell to the ground.

This jewel was the signet ring handed to Holgarth at the Cocoa Tree by a gentleman, who said he had found his servant wearing it, and knowing the crest on it to be that of the Milray family, had paid the man for it, and learnt that he had picked it up in the roadway near Hampstead, where he had been visiting his mother.

The ring was really one worn by Edgar Trevillian on the night of his meeting with Lady Milly. In grasping his hand she quite unknowingly bore the ring from it. It fell to the ground, and there lay till picked up on the following morning by the serving-man to whom reference has been made.

Many a time and oft had Edith seen the ring upon her husband's finger.

The conversation between Lady Harriet, Holgarth, and Constance, after continuing for some little time longer, was ended by his rising and bidding the ladies good day.

Lady Harriet shook him heartily by the hand—"Come here, my lord, as frequently as you like. The Seymours and the Milrays were always good friends, and let us be as amiable as our old forefathers."

"Willingly," said the earl, looking towards Constance, whose eyes fell as his encountered them.

The earl had barely left the house when Constance discovered the ring on the ground.

She picked it up saying—"Oh, mamma! the earl must have dropped this ring."

Taking it Lady Harriet said—"Unquestionably, this is Milray's ring; I really think this looks like the legendary Milray ring which opens and shows a turquoise bearing the motto "Honour and Perseverance."

As she spoke she touched a spring, and the turquoise was brought to view.

"The very same," said Lady Harriet; "my dear, wear it till he comes again."

"Do you think he will come again?"

"I am sure of it."

With a rapid movement the girl flung herself upon her mother's breast, and in that action told a secret of which she herself was hardly aware.

Holgarth had fascinated her.

She loved him.

CHAPTER XXV.

THE GERMAN DOCTOR.

HOLGARTH left Seymour House with as light a heart as he could wear in his black bosom.

He knew Lady Constance was attracted by him, he knew he had gained her love.

And her fortune.

For Constance was rich. Her fortune was the talk of the gaming-houses, and many an unknown longed to call her and her treasures his own.

Holgarth had made about £10,000 by the robbery for which he had suffered, in the full belief of the nation, the full penalty of the law. He and his fellows had robbed a Government waggon proceeding from Manchester to London w th money.

The escort's drink had been drugged, and the treasure secured. Holgarth's share was £10,000; but barely had he put it in safe keeping, than the ministers of the law were upon him, and he was carried to prison, which he left only for the gallows.

After his fortunate escape he claimed the money of an aged man—a receiver of stolen goods, in whose care he had left it, and in whose care it still remained, when he came to claim it, for without honour among thieves even thieves could not live, and so the money was safe.

Not so the receiver.

Holgarth could not afford to let him live. Before he left the house he had seen him lying dead.

So now only old Jabez was alive of all who knew that Gentleman Jack was still alive.

But what was £10,000 to the Earl of Milray; it would not last a couple of years, and Holgarth had determined to make a good match, such as he, by his acquired position, might easily make.

He soon learnt at the Cocoa Tree of Constance's wealth, and he determined to obtain it; hence his attention to Lady Harriet and her daughter.

Leaving Seymour House, he was carried home to his own palatial domain. As he was borne along the streets he smiled at his good fortune. All those who could have done him harm—all those who could have extorted money from him, were swept from his path; he who could have disputed the title to the earldom with him had disappeared. None of his old comrades believed him risen from the dead. All the great world of fashion recognised in him the Earl of Milray, whose estates, once relieved from the heavy load of debts laid on them by several representatives of the title, would yield a great—a magnificent yearly income.

All seemed smiling before him—all seemed promising, bright, and successful.

Arrived at his dwelling-house, he was met, almost on the threshold, by Jules.

" Me lord."

" Well."

" Me lord have a visitor."

" Who ?"

" I know not."

" Where is he ?"

" In me lord's private chamber."

" Why there ?"

" He walked dere of his own will; and I have not say no, because he says he's de great friend of me lord."

Without a word more Holgarth turned and ascended the stairs.

His face had become a blank, if that term can be understood.

He entered his private room, and as he did so, his visitor rose.

He was a tall man, dressed in black. It was impossible to say whether he was handsome or horrible to look upon. His looks were unearthly—defiant—captivating.

He held his hand out to Holgarth. This hand was white and soft, and really beautiful, and yet it looked like a claw.

" How do you do ?"

"Who—who are you ?" asked Holgarth.

"Bah! you know the German doctor. Have you forgotten me again? You forgot me at your old landlady's—you have forgotten I saw you at the Cocoa Tree.'

"I—I forgot."

"Yes," said the visitor, smiling a ghastly smile—"yes, you tell the world you *forget*—you are not a bad pupil of mine—but how you forget. You forget about the wife, and—and your child."

"I—I have forgotten," said Holgarth.

"Ah! I wish I could improve your poor memory, but I can't. It's very lucky Lady Milly's dead—is it not."

"Yes—she is dead."

"Quite—now you can marry Lady Constance."

"You know that also?"

"Why not? People will talk—servants are people. Your marked conduct was seen at the ball—people whispered—servants talked—and to *my* servants, and so I hear the news. By the bye, I approve the match."

"Indeed!—why?" asked Holgarth, licking his parched lips with his tongue.

"Bah!—I admire marriage. Without marriage there would be no world worth caring for. Marry, my pupil—doubtless you will be happy. Why, you are trembling—Gentleman Jack, the bold highwayman, is trembling."

"Not that name here, in the name of Satan."

"Satan," said the visitor, with the comeliest of smiles, and arranging his thick, curling black hair, with one of his white claw-like hands—"Satan—who is that? Ah! I remember you asked me once if *I* were that personage. Let me say again, I don't believe in him. Pray, what is Satan like—is he like me, for instance?"

"How should I know."

"That is true," said the stranger, smiling—"how *should* you know?"

"Why have you come here?"

"You are unpolite to a visitor who saved your life."

"I would you had not saved it," said Holgarth, spitting angrily upon the ground.

"Why, are you not happy?" asked the dark visitor, with another smile. "I try to make all my scholars happy—and you are a favourite scholar of mine."

"Happy!—how can I be happy?" the highwayman asked.

"Nay, why are you *not* happy?"

"How can I be?—I am always afraid of discovery."

"Who shall discover you?"

"You, perhaps."

"Bah! you were happy just now."

"I had forgotten you."

"You are polite; but if you feel happy in forgetting me, pray do so."

"You torture me," said Holgarth, looking towards the German doctor.

"You torture yourself—you are not tortured. Some men make their lives a perfect hell; and yet fear hell itself more than most men."

"Why have you come here, I say?" said Holgarth, looking once more towards his visitor.

"To compliment you on your marriage. By the bye, I have told you—have I not—that your child is dead?"

"What child?"

"Bah! what child!" said the German doctor, smiling. "Why, Lady Milly's. Yes, the poor child is dead; so you can marry Constance—I beg your pardon—Lady Constance, with a better conscience than ever."

"You say you came to compliment me?" said Holgarth.

"And I do," added the stranger, heartily. "Marry Lady Constance; but—but *watch her.*"

As he spoke these words the stranger became horrible to look upon.

"Watch her?" said Holgarth.

"Yes," returned the stranger.

"Why?" asked the highwayman.

"But I have said enough," answered the other: "women are women—that is quite enough to say. Watch her—and be *happy.* You ought to be happy—no man more so. You have riches, health, a title; you are going to have a rich and beautiful young wife; and you may smile at misfortune."

The terrible cruelty expressed in the stranger's face, and which was utterly at variance with the words that accompanied that expression, if not with the tone in which the words were uttered, was perfectly lost on Holgarth, whose eyes were directed to the ground.

"Good bye!" the stranger continued, after a pause—"good bye! *for the present.* You have nothing to be unhappy about—except—ah! yes, you have one thing to be unhappy about, my lord?"

"What?" the miserable false lord said, looking up at his calm tormentor.

"Death!"

The stranger uttered this word with awful emphasis.

The highwayman shrugged his shoulders and said—"Why should death make me more unhappy than any other man? All mortal things must die!"

"So they say."

"Is it not so?" asked the highwayman.

"Bah! I know nothing about it. But I do not speak of King Death; I speak of *the woman Death.*"

The highwayman sprang from his seat, and almost leapt upon his visitor.

"Be calm!" returned the latter—"calmness alone conquers all things. Yes, the woman Death is upon your track!"

"How near to me is she?"

"I do not know."

"Is she in this city?" asked the highwayman, the sweat streaming from his forehead in large drops.

"I do not know," returned the stranger, whose calm impenetrability was terrible in comparison with the other's agitation.

"Tell me," the highwayman continued—

" tell me, you who seem to know all things, will she discover me ?"

"I do not know," once more returned the dark stranger ; and, rising from his chair, and moving towards the door, he said—"Marry Lady Constance, and be happy; and receive this consolation—should the woman Death come near, my lord, I will warn you."

A moment, and he was gone.

Meanwhile, the earl could barely support himself. He caught at the back of a chair, or he would have fallen. His lips were ashy pale —his mouth beating as it hung open—so great was the earl's fear.

But suddenly he started, and the pale ghost of a smile illumined his face. "Ah!" he muttered. "I forgot; she will not seek for me as the earl, but as—as—"

At this moment he saw Jules standing at his elbow.

The valet had entered noiselessly, and was standing near his master.

"Me lord must dress for dinner."

"I am ill," returned Holgarth ; "I cannot dress—I am ill—sick—a doctor—a doctor of great fame and skill—I am ill—the place seems rocking."

———

CHAPTER XXVI.

THE RING ONCE MORE.

MEANWHILE a singular scene was passing at Seymour House.

The two ladies, their little sentimental scene over, sought out Edith.

She was lying on a couch, her face concealed in her hands.

She roused herself to receive her kind benefactress ; but it was clear she was miserably ill.

"Is your visitor gone, Constance ?"

"Yes, dear Edith," the girl returned. "Lord Milray has gone—he has been charming."

"He is a gentleman," added Lady Harriet; "and all real gentlemen are charming, let their faces and figures be what they may."

"He is very handsome, though very pale," continued Constance. "Tell me, Edith—describe to me your dear husband, whom I am convinced will one day return and proclaim you his lady wife."

Softly smiling, Edith said—"He had perfectly black hair."

"So has Lord Milray," the girl threw in.

"Blue eyes," Edith continued.

"So has my Lord Milray," the girl continued. "How very strange—because, you know, men so seldom have blue eyes, and especially with black hair. How *very* strange. Well, and what was his complexion ?"

"A dark brown," said Edith.

"Ah!" returned Constance, "there we differ. Lord Milray has a magnificent pale complexion."

"Magnificent!" said Lady Harriet; "there you are wrong I think Lord Milray's complexion spoils him ; it is deathly, Edith, as that of a corse."

Edith only shook her head, as she recalled to mind the rich, dark glow of health which mantled on her husband's cheek.

Suddenly she started, as she saw the ring upon Constance's finger.

"What ring is that, Constance ?"

"Lord Milray's."

"Lord Milray's!—impossible."

"I assure you; he must have dropped it just before he left the room."

Lady Harriet and Constance saw Edith put her hand on her forehead, and say—"Impossible!" but they little guessed what was passing in her mind.

"Could it be possible ? Was it indeed he ? Had he deserted her ?"

Such were the questions that raged through the poor lady's brain, as she looked upon the ring, which she had so often touched while on the hand of the only man she had ever loved with a woman's whole affection.

"Edith, what is the matter with you ?"

"Nothing, madam, I assure you—or almost nothing. Did you say, Constance, that—that that Lord Milray dropped that ring ?"

"I suppose so," said Constance.

"I am sure of this," said Lady Harriet, "I know the ring ; it belongs to the Milray family. I saw it in the hands of the father of the last Milray. If you touch the spring—"

"The stone will fly back," continued Edith, "and discover a turquoise, on which is carved the motto—' Honour and perseverance !' "

"Great Powers !" said Lady Harriet, " she knows the ring as well as I do. Constance, leave the room."

The young lady immediately obeyed.

"Better—b tter," Edith returned. " Oh, give it to me, for it is my husband's ring."

"Edith !" said Lady Harriet.

"Oh give it to me—give it to me !" the girl continued ; " it is, indeed, my husband's."

"Then he is, or was, a Milray."

"Why do you say was ?" asked the girl.

"I hardly know," returned the lady. " Tell me, when did you see the ring last ?"

"About two months ago."

"Where ?" asked Lady Harriet.

"Upon my husband's hand."

"I ask again, Edith, was he a Milray ?"

"You force me to say *yes*," the girl returned.

"What was his Christian name ?"

"I refuse to tell," Edith replied.

An angry flush passed over the face of Lady Harriet, and she thought that Edith had hid that she was *not* married, and that the father of the little child was the late earl, who had probably worn the ring, which had descended to the present lord, and who had, perhaps, frequently shown the ring to Edith, his mistress.

"Edith," the lady continued, " I trust you

have spoken the entire truth to me when telling me your history."

"I have, madam, indeed."

"You have told me that your husband suddenly ceased to visit you."

"Yes, madam," returned Edith meekly, "that is the truth."

"And it is about two months since you last saw him?"

"About that time, my lady."

Lady Harriet shook her head as she said to herself—"Why the history is as clear as daylight. The late earl was the husband; his visits, of course ceased when his life ended on that fatal day. She must have seen the ring on his finger—that ring he passed to the possession of Edgar." Then speaking aloud she asked—"Edith, where were you married?"

"Madam, I scarcely know. My husband has the papers—I only know for certain that he and I, and his friend, went in a coach together to a little church in the centre of London. I might be able to tell it again, but I am not quite sure—I never thought it would be necessary to know the spot."

"You were married in a church, then?" continued Lady Harriet.

"Oh, yes; a very small, odd-looking church. I remember it struck me that it did not look like a church at all!"

The lady started; and now her doubts became certainties. The momentary thought that if the late earl and Edith had been really married, their son, now in Naggleton's caravan, was the veritable earl passed from her, and she convinced herself that the late misfortune each had imposed upon her by a false marriage and had pretended to be his own cousin, the Captain in the army, in order to prevent her making inquiries amongst the higher classes. This," thought she, "accounted for the secret marriage, the oath not to name him till she had his permission, the disappearance in fact, explained away every difficulty of the case."

"My dear Edith," the lady continued, "are you quite sure about this ring?"

"I am quite sure that the owner is my husband."

"The owner is Lord Milray," said her ladyship.

"Then," retorted Edith, "I am Lord Milray's wife."

"Impossible!—he is unmarried!"

"Does he say so? has he said so to you?"

"No," returned Lady Harriet, "but it is well-known in the world that Lord Milray is a bachelor."

"He does not speak the truth—nor has he ever spoken the truth—he told me he was seeking to obtain the Milray peerage, which was justly his. He never said he was the undisputed owner of the title."

"My dear," says Lady Harriet, "you have been shamefully deceived. Many a girl has been equally deceived before you—many will be equally deceived after you and I have passed away. Whatever has happened, you, I know—

I am sure, are innocent. In my eyes you are as innocent as you were while suckled in your mother's arms. Be then assured that neither I nor Constance will ever desert you, whatever has happened, or whatever may happen."

During this speech the change which passed over the face of the poor girl was terrible to witness. First, her features expressed blank astonishment, then alarm took possession of them; and then, as the full force of the shameful, yet kindly meant, words struck home to her very heart, the red curtain of shame upon her cheeks and neck was as deep as the colour of her very blood.

Lady Harriet — her best, her only friend, believed her an unmarried mother—believed her a lost woman, though she declared her innocent.

For some moments she could neither look nor speak to her benefactress. At last, with great command over herself, she steadied her voice, and spoke.

"Allow me, madam, to swear that I am the wife of the man who called himself my husband. Had he deceived me his love for me would never have remained so pure, holy, and respectful as it ever continued to be. His passion for me was not the result of an impure nature, but the effect of a pure and holy love. A woman may be deceived into believing a man loves her, but she learns the truth after she has yielded herself—after he has taken possession of her. I know—I am certain the man whom I called my husband was married to me, *for he loved me more after marriage than he did before.* No libertine ever loves his mistress thus. No, madam, however inexplicable *my husband's* conduct may have been since last I saw him, of this I am certain, that, in keeping away from me, he was forced to do so—he was absent by no will of his own; and if I have not had a letter from him, it is not because he has not written, but because his letter has been lost or stolen. Believe me, madam, I could not speak with this earnestness if I did not utter the truth. I am married, and my husband cannot come to my side, or he would. You must believe this—you must indeed, or how can I, being an honest woman, remain in your house. Did I stay here under your suspicion, I should not be worthy to inhabit your dwelling; so you must—*you must* believe I am married, and that I am not a deserted wife (for I am not), but a poor, houseless, hapless widow, only happy in finding such a friend as you, dear lady."

She flung herself upon Lady Harriet Seymour's bosom, and wept so, and heartily.

"I do indeed believe you, Edith — indeed, indeed I do," said the lady, after a time, and when the unhappy young mother had become more calm and able to bear consolation.

But during the storm of tears the lady had come to the conclusion that Edith was indeed a widow. "Yes," she thought to herself, "that man Milray—that coward, who met misfortune with a bullet, which he cast into his own breast—that poltroon was not as bad as we painted him. He could love, and he did this girl; but he had not courage to own the fact. Why? A moment's thought yielded her an answer. Had he not numberless creditors, and was it not currently reported that he he kept them at bay by promising to marry a rich heiress; and was it not notorious that, in consequence of this promise of his, his *hand* had been refused by the fathers and guardians of several rich, but untitled, young ladies, who were ready enough to barter away their thousands to be called "my lady;" but who did not desire to be laughed at as "Milray's receipt," as the earl's intended wife was called amongst the clubs and gaming-houses.

"Now," thought Lady Harriet, "shall I tell her at once that she is a widow, or wait till she is calmer?—and then she thought what a coward must this man have been to meet death without a thought for wife and child?"

"Tell me, Edith, did your husband know that you were about to become a mother?"

"I did not tell him, and he did not ask me."

"You are quite sure the earl is your husband?"

"Quite, if that ring is his?"

"But—but the earldom has changed hands lately."

"Indeed!" she cried, as she remembered *the letter* she had received on the fatal night when she was driven from her father's house. Could he indeed have become the earl—could he really have deserted her?

"And, Edith," returned the lady, "when earldoms change hands, I need not say that death has been busy."

The girl trembled slightly—that was all.

"The present earl has been thought illegitimate all his life till lately," the lady continued, wondering that Edith showed more curiosity than terror.

"He has till recently been in the army—a poor soldier."

Again Edith started.

The lady continued—"But recently he gained the proofs of his birth, showed them to the then earl, who was his cousin, older than himself, but the son of his father's younger brother—"

"Yes—yes—yes," Edith said rapidly.

"The earl, you know, would have all the family jewels," continued the lady, desirous of preparing her protegée for the catastrophe; "and when he saw the proofs of the present earl's claims—be prepared, Edith—he—he *shot* himself."

The girl started once, and then said—"And then the plain captain became the great earl?"

Lady Harriet was at a loss to comprehend the manner in which her statement had been received. Cou'd she, she thought—could she still be deceived?

After a moment's hesitation, she said—"Yes, the poor captain became the earl, and remains one."

"Describe him to me," continued Edith. "Is he dark—dark hair?"

"Yes."

"Blue eyes?"

"Yes; you—you seem to know him, Edith," said the lady, forgetting that Constance had depicted the earl.

"And what was his name when a poor captain?"

In great amazement the lady said—"Captain Edgar Trevillian."

Edith looked before her wild-like and confusedly.

"Edith, what ails you? Speak."

Lady Harriet then heard her weeping, and, stooping down, heard her say—"Deserted—Edgar—your wife!"

"Edgar Trevillian your husband?" cried Lady Harriet, catching the girl by the wrist.

"Yes, my husband—I would he were not."

And without another word she fell heavily back, happily senseless for a time.

———

CHAPTER XXVII.

THE FALSE EARL AND THE REAL COUNTESS.

SEVERAL hours had passed since Edith had for a time happily forgotten her griefs.

She soon came to herself once more; and, as it almost always happens, the temporary stupor which had overpowered her had become, as it were a restorative. Once more returned to her senses, she seemed to be far better able to bear her new misfortune, as she thought it, than she would have been had she not lost her consciousness for some minutes.

Constance was sitting by the side of the bed on which the suffering lady was lying.

"Oh, Lady Constance, you still believe, I trust, that I am an honest woman in intention, if not in deed."

"I do, I assure you, dear Edith," the young lady returned.

"I am utterly unable to comprehend this affair, Constance. He was always so kind, noble, affectionate. Can he have suddenly changed?"

"But, after all," continued Constance, "there may be some mistake; he may not be your husband, for I am sure you are married. So is mamma sure. Those letters you have, signed 'Edgar,' are not those of a mere lover; they are the loving words of a true husband."

"Indeed—indeed they are," said Edith; "but the ring!"

"True!" returned Constance, "that is at present inexplicable. What do you intend to do?"

"Go to him," returned Edith quickly—"go to him, and end my terrible doubts. All things point to him as my husband, except my own belief."

"That is right. I also would go to him if I were in your position."

Here Lady Harriet entered the room. She seemed agitated. "My dear," she commenced, "the earl has sent to inquire for his ring. Here is a letter from him, brought by his French valet."

"A letter!" said Edith. "Let me look at it."

Lady Harriet quite unhesitatingly handed the letter to the suffering lady. She tore it open and then flung it down with a cry of joy— "It is not he!—this man is not Edgar Trevillian—he is a cheat!"

"What can you mean?" asked Lady Harriet.

"This, my lady—compare this letter with mine," said Edith, taking the well-loved packet of letters from her pocket. "All mine are signed Edgar—is this the same?"

They certainly were *not*; but Lady Harriet looked grave.

"Why do you not speak, Lady Harriet?"

Lady Harriet Seymour hesitated for some moments, then she said—"My dear Edith, I am so convinced of your honour and truth that no quantity of evidence would make me doubt you; but why may not you be mistaken? Men are men. Sometimes those who seem all honour and truth, are only too frequently bad at heart, and utterly devoid of honour. I am bound to tell you I *must* believe the present Earl of Milray to have been Captain Edgar Trevillian. Scores of men who knew him, recognize him. It is true none of his late companions are to be found—for a good reason."

11

"What reason?" asked Edith, for she did not know all her misery.

"No matter," said Lady Harriet, guardedly, "it is also true that he has an odd impossibility of remembering his friends; but the forgetfulness arose from the shock he received at witnessing the late earl destroy himself in fear. The great German doctor, an odd, tall, black-haired man, says he has known many similar cases, and he takes a great interest in his lordship. I must say, Edith, you have been deceived."

"How, my lady?" asked the girl.

"The man who married you was *not* Edgar Trevillian. There is no blame to be attached to you, Edith; as I have said my house shall ever be yours. But I fear you have been the victim of an unprincipled villain."

"Oh—no, no, no, Lady Harriet!" cried Edith, "he was so good and noble. You should have seen how proud he was of me; and I have seen him give to the poor so gently. No; there is some great mistake, but *he* is innocent!"

"I hope so, Edith," said Lady Harriet, a little coldly.

"I will go to this man," said Edith, rising, "if you will let me, my lady."

"I think you can demand it as a right," said Lady Harriet. "Take back the ring; I wish you all the success you wish yourself, Edith."

"Good bye," said Constance, hesitatingly; for have we not said she loved Holgarth, and therefore she could not anticipate much pleasure if Edith *did* discover the earl to be her husband—"good bye, Edith, for a little while: whatever happens I know we shall not be enemies!"

"Never!" said Edith, returning the kiss.

In a few moments Edith and Jules were moving towards Milray House.

"Madame look a leetle white," said the Frenchman.

"I am not well," returned Edith, with a smile, "neither do you look in health."

"No," returned the Frenchman, "I am much in agony. I vatch all de day by de bedside of de dear dat sall be my own vife—a poor gal dat have de fever."

"Indeed! where is she?"

"Oh, to de house of de carl."

"Poor girl!—I should like to see her."

"Oh, me and me dear sall be happy to see you to de bedside of Mees Fanny."

Edith still continued talking about the sick girl, in whom she took an interest as a suffering woman, and therefore like herself—for Jules, for what purpose will be seen hereafter, thought fit to tell Edith the whole particulars of the orange girl's history as they were *generally* known.

Arrived at the mansion, a footman informed the French valet that his lordship had not yet returned.

"Ah, then I will wait for the earl near the poor girl's bedside," said Edith.

"*Certainement*," said the Frenchman, and led the way up stairs.

Fanny was still very weak, and lay faint and pale upon the garret bed.

She seemed a little frightened at first of a visitor brought by Jules, but she soon recovered herself as she saw the smile and heard the voice of gentle Edith.

"I hear you have been ill?" said Edith.

"Yes, mam," returned Fanny.

"Oh! pray don't say ma'am to me," returned Edith, "I am only a kind of servant."

The voice was so kind, the manner so tender, that Fanny turned towards her visitor, buried her face in her hands, and burst into tears.

For you see she was still very weak.

Jules remained in the room and meant so to do; but in a very short time up came a footman with the message that my lord had come in and wanted his valet.

"Sall I show you to downwards?" asked the Frenchman of Edith.

"Oh, no," returned that lady, "tell my lord I will be with him in a few moments to deliver up the ring."

For to tell the truth, Edith was afraid to see the earl—afraid that her worst fear might be confirmed—feared this in spite of the difference in the hand-writing.

Jules bowed and looked round for the nurse, thinking that if *she* were present there would be little chance of Fanny making a confidant of her newly found friend; but that hideous old woman, though present, might as well have been absent, for she was fast asleep; and, in fact, drunk asleep near the fire, and lurching so much, that even she, bad old woman as she was, must have had a good and guardian angel, or she must have inevitably pitched in amongst the flaring coals.

The Frenchman bowed and left the room.

"I—I hope you don't think I am like myself as I am now?" said Fanny.

"No; you have been ill!" returned Edith.

"Yes, I was pretty once: it seems years ago. Look here—this is my portrait," and she pulled a little miniature out of her pocket—"this is my portrait when I was an orange girl. The gentlemen bought lots of oranges of me; and I was very well off, and happy, then. I wish I had remained an honest orange girl! Strong-arm Will would have had me; and he would have made a good husband."

"What a pretty portrait!" said Edith, taking it up, and looking on the bright auburn hair, and pleasant features, and the face, above the painted basket of oranges—and which work of art Fanny had had done some months before, little thinking of what an important part it was destined to play in the drama of her life.

"Yes, very different from me now—isn't it?"

"Yes," said Edith, who could not utter an untruth; "but, doubtless, you will soon become well again."

"Never!" said Fanny, fresh tears rising to her eyes. "Oh! don't give me my portrait back: pray keep it—if I may ask you."

"But would you not like to keep it?" asked Edith.

"Oh, no!—I should like you to have it; for yours is the only kind and true voice I have heard in this place; and I should like you to remember me by taking it. I do not, indeed, want it; it would pain me to keep it."

"Then," said Edith, "I will keep it till—till *some one asks* me for it."

Edith meant by "some one" Fanny herself; but the sick girl took the words literally.

"Yes, promise me that—keep it till some one asks you for it : you will promise to give it up to the first person who asks you for it ?"

"I do promise—I swear; and now I must go. I may never see you in this house again; but if you think I am your friend, and if you are in trouble, come to Lady Harriet Seymour's. Good bye!"

"Good bye!" says Fanny; and the next moment Edith was leaving the room.

Her heart beat heavily as a footman pioneered her to the room in which the earl was awaiting her.

She entered.

For some moments she had no power to raise her eyes.

"Well, my dear—let me look at you," said a voice.

"Not him!" she cried aloud, as she heard the voice, and raised her eyes.

The next moment she uttered a piercing cry. "Edgar! she cried. "Husband — dear husband!"

The earl himself was startled, so powerful was the appeal made by the woman before him.

"What ails you, my dear?" he asked.

She felt herself falling, but, by a powerful effort, she continued standing, and, indeed, walked close to the false nobleman.

Eagerly she peered into his face.

For full a minute she peered into his face—then suddenly caught up his right hand, and looked at the back of it.

She flung it down.

"You are *not* Edgar Trevillian!"

He started—trembled even—but he soon regained his composure.

"The world says I am."

"Then, why did you tremble when I said you were not?" asked Edith.

"I thought I was in the presence of a mad woman—perhaps I am. And, again, I have been ill."

"No," Edith returned; "you trembled with conscious guilt. Where is the blue uneradicable cross on your right hand which the real Edgar placed on *his* right hand when he was a boy? You are a traitor, and I will unmask you!'

"Oh!—a blue cross on his right hand?"

"Yes."

"Thank you—I know it—I have the blue cross there."

"You lie; your hand is white."

"With paint — we gentlemen paint our hands."

He did lie: he had no cross upon his hand.

"You say that you are Edgar Trevillian?"

"No; I say I am the Earl of Milray. Pray who are you?"

"No matter; you have lost a ring?"

"Yes; at your mistress's, I presume. Sure you are sent with it, my tragedy queen. Come, be good-humoured, and we may be friends, my dear."

"Where did you get that ring?" asked Edith.

"Well, my queen," continued Holgarth, "you are pretty enough to answer; and I would answer you, but I cannot. The ring has been in the Milray family three hundred years."

"I know it," Edith returned. "You have not had it a hundred days. I—I saw it on the hand of the true owner, and true earl, not three months ago."

"Bah! Give me my ring."

"And suppose I refuse it."

"I will give you in charge for endeavouring to extort money, and have you whipped in Bridewell."

"You are right," said Edith, taking the ring from her finger. "At present you are the conqueror; but it shall not always be so. Take it. Do you believe you can keep an oath?"

"Yes, my beauty."

"Well, then, I swear that if you can read me the secret of the ring—the secret every true Milray knows—I will acknowledge you as the true earl."

"What is your name?"

"Edith Milray"

"Oh!—a namesake of mine, it seems. Well, this is what I read on the ring," he continued, taking up the jewel, but little dreaming of the secret spring, the turquoise, and the motto. "I read on the ring—'I love you, Edith—the Earl of Milray is your slave.'"

She only smiled.

"What does Edith answer?" the earl asked, continuing to look upon the jewel.

"Honour and Perseverance!" returned Edith.

"Honour—that is my motto—that of the house of Milray."

"No; that is *my* motto, for *I* am of the house of Milray," continued Edith, moving to the door.

"Are you going?"

"Why should I remain, *my lord*."

"Are we to be enemies, fair Edith?"

"Yes."

"If I am your enemy I may do you harm at Lady Harriet's."

"I defy you."

"And I may harm your child, Edith. Ha! ha! you blush. You see I know the whole history."

"Lady Harriet is too wise to be swayed by such as *you*," said Edith, with infinite contempt.

"Lady Harriet *knows* me to be the Earl of Milray; and her family and mine have always been friends. I have you in my power. Are we enemies?"

"Yes," returned Edith undauntedly—" truth

and honesty do ultimately win ; not to be *your* enemy would be to exist neither truthfully nor honestly. I *am* your enemy."

"You can gain nothing, Edith, by opposing me - gain much by propitiating me. If I were not a Milray, should I be so much like— Edgar."

"Ah ! then you are not Edgar ?"

"Let us suppose so. Let us suppose that I am his cousin—that I am next of kin after him, and that he is dead. Do not start—all this is mere supposition between you and me, cousin Edith. Suppose that this cousin could not claim the estate, because a *crime* forbid his appearance amongst English gentlemen—and suppose he had the opportunity of personating his *dead* cousin Edgar."

"Dead !" said Edith.

"Let us suppose he did sail in the *Gorgon*— you knew he was going to sail."

"Yes."

"Suppose he and all his companions were wrecked—that they are all dead : suppose no one can prove me any other than Edgar !"

She would have fallen senseless at this recital of the terrible news, but something whispered her that if she lost herself for a more minute, this unalterable man might ruin her in the time, so she held her ground and steadily faced him.

"Then," she returned, after a silence of some duration—"then my son is the Earl of Milray."

"If he is legitimate."

"Oh ! I can prove that."

"No. The church in which you were married is burnt down—with it the register, and I hold your marriage certificate."

"Great Powers !" Edith cried.

"As for your child, I would destroy him *in the showman's show*, and remove the last obstacle from our path. All this is supposition, Lady Edith, Countess of Milray."

"You would not kill him, would you ?"

"No—not while you are silent."

"Oh, you admit I could do you harm," said Edith.

"Yes ; because slander always does harm."

"Slander !" she cried, starting.

"*I* should call it slander, and it would be, for all I have said is supposition. Now Edith, cousin, how do you decide ?"

She thought for a few moments. Time— that was what she wanted—time. So she turned, and said—"What do you propose ?"

"Have you discovered me to Lady Harriet ?"

"Yes."

"Then you must clear me—admit that you were mistaken in supposing your husband to be me."

"I promise," said Edith, and whispered to herself—"Time—time !"

"Do this—promise not to mingle my name with yours more, and I promise to leave your child alone."

Edith thought for a moment. "Does he

know Naggleton ?" she asked herself. Then she said—"You know the showman who has my son ?"

"Yes."

"Do you ever see Drummond ?"

"Sometimes," said the earl.

"Oh !" thought Edith, " he does *not* know the showman's name, and he never will, for I will entreat Lady Harriet and Constance to keep the name to themselves. Now I only wait for time." Then she said aloud—" I promise."

"And I'll be your friend."

"Good day, my lord," said Edith, over whom a great calm—the death stupor of misfortune—had fallen. " You cannot read the secret of the ring ?"

"I shall before long. I shall make you love me enough to tell me."

Edith was too broken down in her grief to let her cheek and neck reveal the anger and hatred she felt. She answered—"HONOUR AND PERSEVERANCE !"—and turning left the room.

To go home ; and do what ?

To exculpate this thief and robber—to admit to the best of friends she had in the world, and whom she would have gladly laid down her own life to shield, that the man she had declared was her husband was the earl, and then fling herself upon her widowed bed and weep tears as precious as blood for the lost husband and father.

Meanwhile Holgarth had called for his valet, and commanded him to prick with a fine needle a cross upon his right hand, and this torture over—and it *was* a horrible torture—he bade the serving-man rub the terrible drawing first with warm water, in order to remove the congealed blood, and then to rub the infinite number of small wounds with Indian ink. Then out came the black cross of which Edith had spoken.

He smiled as he saw the convincing sign— smiled as he thought he would take his glove accidentally off, and exhibit the sign of his being Edgar Trevillian ; but he little thought that by this act he was weaving a fragment of a net about himself, such as all bad men *do* weave.

In the rapidity of her expression, Edith had made a mistake, which might one day aid her greatly. She said Edgar had a black cross on his right hand. She meant to say, and thought she said—black ANCHOR.

As little did Holgarth dream of this truth, as he did that the Frenchman, true to his nature, had been endeavouring to witness the interview between his master and Edith.

He *had* overheard some of the expressions uttered both by the lady and the false earl ; but he could give them no connection ; he only came to the conclusion that Edith had, or desired to have, some power over the earl, and that he defied her.

And yet there stooped the scoundrel valet before his master, laboriously, nay servilely attendi g to his wants, and in his innermost soul la ing up a store of vengeance for every menial act he performed.

———

CHAPTER XXVIII.

IT was a dark night, and old Jabez had said so more than once to his elegant company. The winter had been long and hard, and as yet there were few signs of returning spring.

" Gentleman Jack," says Jabez, sweeping his pipe round him like a sceptre—" Gentleman Jack—mates, I no more knows where Gentleman Jack is nor I knows how to fly—if he isn't in heaven he's in the other place."

" Stow that," answered a merry gentleman in the corner. He was a highwayman who joked those he robbed, and who always kissed the pretty girls he robbed. People did say that some of the pretty girls had taken quite a liking to him, but certainly the old parties held this gentleman generally called the Count, in utter abhorrence, for he never stopped a stage-coach without having out every old or stout woman and bumping her. This operation was effected by this unceremonious performance. The sufferer was taken by the shoulders and bumped against the wheels. And what for —simply because they were either old, or fat. He was a very merry highwayman, the Count. " Stow that," said he, " you know, Jabez, they say you've said Gentleman Jack 'ull live to have another dance upon nothing, and die in a pair of boots not yet made."

" Nix—I never said any blab that way."

" Easy, Jabez," said the count, " we know all."

And here Jabez turned pale and looked about. " I swear, mates, for all I knows to the contrary Gentleman Jack's in a bed he can't turn in if he tried.'

Now in reality the Count and his companions knew nothing about the end of Gentleman Jack beyond the fact that old Jabez always trembled in his ugly shoes, whenever this subject came up, and as he always protested that Gentleman Jack was dead, of which the robbers had not the least doubt, they pretended to doubt the highwayman's death in order to divert themselves at Jabez's expense; and besides, the Count had discovered that, whenever Gentleman Jack was referred to, the liquor which came up after the conversation was always of a better kind than that which had preceded it.

For only three men knew that Gentleman Jack still lived—namely, Holgarth himself, old Jabez, and the German doctor But stay, was this latter personage a man? Could man be so cruel, cold, heartless, hopeless ? Was he something worse than man and still less near God than all human creatures ?

It is true that Jules knew his master, the earl, had been a highwayman, or something very like one, but he could not identify him

with the notorious Gentleman Jack, who till recently had been as much talked about as Jack Sheppard himself.

Old Jabez had had a miserable time of it since that evening when the highwayman was resuscitated He being a bad man, lived in continual fear of death - death suddenly and awful as a vivid flash of lightning. He continually feared that Gentleman Jack would repent him of his mercy, be sorry that he had let the old scamping landlord live, and return to ' quiet' him with the terrible poison, by means of which he had stilled the life in the frames of the two men who had just previously helped to aid in once again causing the blood of life to circulate in his veins.

Hence it was that old Jabez was so very desirous of proving Gentleman Jack dead that the frequenters had got into a habit of pretending to believe the highwayman was alive.

They little thought how real was their pretence—little thought how one day their pretended belief in his existence would tell against the mock earl.

The conversation had continued some time in this strain, and Jabez's pipe was as cold as his own feet and lips—he was in such a fright when the Count, seeing it was time to ask for the super good wine, proposed another bottle.

" Certainly, certainly, mates," said Jabez.

" Why, man, you're shaking like a namow(a)," said a black-looking gentleman of the road, who had been quietly smoking in a dark corner— " why you look as though your last cap was over your eyes, and saw the devil all the same before you."

" Mates, I've got a touch of the ager on me."

A loud laugh saluted this explanation, and in which Jabez covered by calling " Jonathy."

Obedient to the summons a stout, well looking lad appeared. " Two bottles from the salt-box bin," says the landlord.

" Aye—aye, my master," said the boy, winking on the highwaymen, " did you say three."

" Yes, Jonathy," said Jabez, " three—three for their honours."

" Certainly, my master," continued the boy, with a broad laugh on his face—" four for their honours from the salt-box bin."

" Is that your new tapster, Jabez ?"

" Yes, my mates—a queer cuffin, with no more dad than I picked up in the road. The clothes he had on then don't fit him now—he's pulled up, mates, he's pulled up.

" He'll make a pretty piece of humanity when he's shot up another inch or so," said the Count, " and he won't keep at apster all his life, and die in the sheets. Mark my words, he'll stride something higher than a beer barrel before he's twenty, and if you live five years longer, Jabez, you'll have to wait on him as one of your best customers."

" Mum, mates, here the kinchen is."

The boy entered the room—the very chamber

(a) " Namow" a woman.

in which Trevillian had lost his pocket-book—at no slow pace.

He had grown pale during his absence, but yet he did not look frightened.

"Master, your cellar has something in it besides spirits."

"Jonathy—Jonathy," said old Jabez, "what do you mean, lad?"

Old Jabez would speak to the boy as though he were an honest landlord, for the boy had not yet been formally let into the secrets of the little inn on the heath; and, however much he might guess the character of the place, he had not yet been allowed to mingle with the highwaymen.

"What do I mean?" returned the lad; "what do I mean? why, I mean to say that you keep *bodies* in the cellar!"

Down fell old Jabez's pipe, and his face became as white as it could be.

"Ha, my lad!" said the count, "and that's why you showed the white feather!"

"White feather!" said the boy, "who talks of white feathering to me!" and catching up one of the bottles he had brought into the room, he flung it straight at the highwayman.

Had it hit him, the consequences might have been frightful, for the bottle was heavy, and the strength with which it had been thrown that of a man; but the Count had been too well used to 'dodge' bullets, not to be able to escape the missile, which crashed against the opposite wall, and stained the dark brown distemper, a blood red with the dark crimson wine which the bottle had contained.

The next moment, half-a-dozen pistols were pointed at the lad's head and breast. He did not flinch.

"Now, my kinchin, suppose I blow your head off?"

"I don't care! What did you say I showed the white feather for?"

"There," said the highwayman, making a click—"there, the pistol is cocked. Now, down on your marrowbones, and cry peccavi (a), or by St. George you'll have more lead in your brains than you'll like."

"I shan't," said the boy, looking fearlessly at the highwayman.

"Then confound me," said the highwayman, flinging down the pistols, "then we'll shake mawleys, (b) and drink another bottle between us."

Within a minute or so the boy was instructed as to the character of Jabez's guests, and was seated and helping to drink the wine he had brought up from the cellar.

"Ho—ho!" says the Count, "may I never kiss a trim wench again if I'm not fly to Jabez's hornpipe with his bacco-pipe when we talk of Gentleman Jack. Confound me, Jabez, why he's below in Jabez's cellar!"

"Yes," said Jabez, after a start, "yes, you're right, Gilly—yes, it's Gentleman Jack.

I was paid a few shiners to get him out of his ornaments, (c) and as I did'nt know where to stow him I boxed him in the cellar. How did you find it out, Jonathy?"

"Why, my master, I did'nt find it out, but the rats did; and as I wanted to know what they found I looked, and so it was, my master."

"Poor Jack!" said the count, "he was a fine fellow, and they do say, a real blood over the broomstick. (d) He made a good king of the road, didn't he?"

"Who's king now?" asked the boy.

"Ah—who is?" asked the Count, "eh, old fellow?" and he looked towards a portrait sketched on the bare wall over the mantlepiece.

It was a sufficiently good portrait of Holgarth to be recognized as his.

"That's all that's left of you," the Count continued, addressing himself to the rude portrait. "Gad, you little thought when you forced the artist to draw your mug, that that 'ud soon be all that was left of you: gad, Jack, you had no widow or wench to mourn for you, and there you are all alone. Who's king now, Jack?"

"Who?" said Jabez, "why the gentleman they call Sir Strong-arm, to be sure."

"I knew a fellow called Strong-arm," said Jonathy—"Strong-armed Will; he was a porter in Covent Garden."

"They say he struck a horse that wouldn't stand still dead with his fist, one night last week," said the Count.

"Though why he hasn't tasted my claret yet I don't know," said Jabez.

As though obedient to the demand, the sound of two horsemen coming across the heath was immediately heard.

The highwaymen immediately started to their feet. "Douse the glims" (e) said one, and immediately the room was in darkness.

Nearer and nearer approached the sound of the hoofs of the two horses, and soon the riders pulled up before the house.

The night was quite dark, and the highwaymen clustering at the window could not see who were below them in the road.

The noise of a whip handle beating against the door was immediately heard.

"What, ho!—house!"

But no sound was returned.

The summons was repeated several times, and then, and not till then, did the cautious old Jabez lift a window, and make a reply.

"Who's there, waking honest people in the dead of the night?" he asked.

"Does CLEM live here?" asked a voice.

"CLEM lives—" returned Jabez.

"Then ST. CLEMENT'S IS OVER THE WATER," returned the voice, to which Jabez returned in

a "*Peccavi*"—I have sinned.
(b) "Mauleys"—Hands.

(c) The chains in which the highwayman had been hung.
(d) "Blood over the broomstick"—an illegitimate child of an aristocrat.
(e) "Douse the glims"—put out the lights.

his usual key—" All right, mates, he's blabbed the passwords, sparkle the glims." (a)

Down stairs Jonathy, under his master's direction, went, and opened the heavily-barred door.

" Out of the way," said a heavy voice, pushing past the lad.

" Hands off!" returned the lad, returning the push, " the passage is wide enough for both."

" How many ? " the lad continued.

" Two," the voice returned, and the lad counted the four footfalls.

He closed the door, arranged the bolts once more, and led the way to the large room in which the highwaymen were sitting.

They reached the apartment as the candles were being lighted, and as they entered, the room was in darkness, but for the red glare of the fire—for the candle the boy had taken down with him to the door had been extinguished the moment the air met it.

As the lights illumined the room, Jabez looked towards the new comers.

" Three," said he, " 'twas only two."

For there stood a third man in a heavy black cloak.

The highwaymen once more started to their feet, and seized their pistols.

" Good evening, gentlemen," said the intruder, upon whom all eyes were turned, " don't be alarmed. I know the next password— " DEATH."

As he spoke, the highwaymen looked about with more satisfaction in their countenances, but still suspiciously.

But the effect of the password on one of the other of the new comers was tremendous.

He was slight for a man, and dark and eager looking. As the word passed the stranger's lips, he ran forward as though he had been suddenly shot.

" Gentlemen, let me pay my footing," said the stranger, and he flung a handful of gold upon the table.

" What red gold," said Jonathy, and the highwaymen seemed to think so by the expression upon their faces.

" Bah!" said the stranger, that is the fault of the mist, not mine. Oh, don't move from the fire on my account ; I do not care for heat."

" Well, mate, who are you ? what's your handle?" (b) asked Jabez of the leader of the three new comers.

" I'm Sir Strong-arm, as they call me," said the man, who was colossal, and seemed to have the strength of a giant. As his arms moved one could see the great muscles gliding backwards and forwards with the motion.

" Full glasses to Strong-arm," said the Count, filling his own glass and handing the bottle to the stranger who had flung down the gold.

" I never drink," returned the stranger.

The awkward pause which followed this statement was broken by the boy Jonathy suddenly calling out, as his eyes rested on the massive highwayman, " Why, you are Strong-arm Will, the Covent Garden porter."

Quick, almost as quick as thought, the Herculean highwayman fell upon the lad, caught him up as though he were an infant, cast him over the back of a chair, and began breaking him by crashing down the spine on each side of the edge upon which the boy's back rested.

" You coward!" said the boy, and uttered no other sound.

But the word touched the highwayman. He being a strong man, and not long since an honest one, felt the sting the word conveyed.

The next moment he lifted the lad up as tenderly as though his own child, and setting him down said, " I hope I've not hurt thee, lad."

The boy shrugged his shoulders and turned away, spitting blood as he did so.

The strange man went up to him. " You ought to thank me," said he to the lad—" I put the word coward in your mouth."

" Did you ?" returned the boy, " well, I did wonder what made me say it."

" I am a doctor," the stranger continued— " a German doctor ; and I can put words into the mouth of a man—and you are a man in thought and feeling, if not in years."

The tempter himself seemed at work, so cruel looked this mysterious personage as he saw the strong boy's eyes lit up at the flattery.

" Give me your strong hand," he continued, " I like brave men—and you are one, and you have a friend in me."

The boy heartily took the hand of this self-styled friend, but he drew back as he touched it, for though soft it was cold, and the boy felt the long nails enter his very flesh and cut it ; and as he took his hand away from the horrible embrace—his right hand—he felt it burn, and within it, the hand, a desire to do some cruel deed.

Long and long afterwards, when he was angry, the right hand began to burn, and he felt it pressed by the soft cold hand, and he felt the long claws like nails entering his flesh.

" Yes, I am Strong-arm Will," said that personage, " and I mean to make some feel my arm before it's tied to my side." (c)

" Bravo ! " said the stranger, putting his hand on strong-arm Will's shoulder.

" Hands off," said Will ; " and where the devil you sprung from, I don't know."

" I was near the door, and was about to knock when your horse's hoofs stopped me, and I waited."

" Hum," said Will, " here's your health ; " and looking over the glass, he added, " Long life to you."

The next moment the glass from which he was drinking fell from his hands.

(a) " Sparkle the glims,"—light the candles.
(b) " Handle"—name.

c This was a reference to the time when he should be hanged ; and then, of course his arms would be pinioned to his side.

The highwaymen, looking at him, saw his eyes fixed upon the portrait of Holgarth over the wall.

Now Strong-arm Will had learnt that the destroyer of the girl he loved so well—poor Fanny—was the Earl of Milray; and since he had taken to the road, he had entered London, and waited to look at the earl, whom he determined should one day fall beneath his hand. He watched at Milray house, and saw Holgarth carried from the court-yard in his sedan. He could have shot him as he saw him, but something seemed to stay his hand—not pity, neither fears for his own safety, for he had no wish to live, but an indescribable feeling which suddenly possessed him. He had no knowledge of the death of the actual Earl of Milray, and therefore naturally concluded that Holgarth was the man upon whom he must revenge himself.

His surprises may therefore be easily comprehended when he saw the portrait of the man whom he hated the worst in the world, whom he supposed to be an aristocrat, sketched on the wall of the drinking room of a highwayman's house of call.

Amongst others to look in the direction of Strong-arm's eyes was his companion, the slim, dark, eager-looking man. As he masked his features, a low cry escaped him. "At last,' he murmured—"at last I am near you once again."

"Whose portrait is that?" asked Strong-arm Will, his eyes still on the features.

"Whose?" returned Jabez, "why, the countenance of a friend who's drunk his last *claret* here below in *this* here world—them there is the feechures of Gentleman Jack, who died as elegant as any gentleman on the road, in scarlet pants, a blue velvet coat, and a bucket of flowers (a) like a colly flower!"

"Can there be two men so much alike?" asked Strong-arm Will of his very soul, "it *must* be the man!"

"Dead!" muttered Will's companion, turning pale and reeling—"dead! then my vengeance will never be achieved."

"Dead as Phayry,' said Jabez, who did not in the least know who Pharoah was, "and that's his portrait."

"If," muttered Will—"if you are the man I will tear you limb from limb."

Here the strange mysterious being who had taken the boy Jonathy by the hand, came up to where the slight-looking highwayman was standing.

"Death."

The man started, but did not answer.

"Death, why do you not answer?"

"How—how do you know me?"

"No matter," the mysterious being returned, "suffice it that I do. DEATH, *he is not dead— he waits your vengeance!*"

(a) In the last century it was quite the fashion for a darling highwayman, when going to the scaffold, to wear a new and splendid velvet suit, and carry a beautiful bouquet; these expenses were always borne by his friends

"NOT dead!"

"No—living happy, a great man, about to become the husband of a lady of title."

"He shall never live to wed her," said the highwayman, nor did he hear the mysterious person mutter—"He shall, he may not die yet." The next moment the highwayman, whom we have described as slight-looking, fell to the ground in a fainting fit.

Strong-arm Will turned immediately; "Hollo, mate!—what, playing the woman! Hang me if I don't think you *are* a woman; for never a wench do you notice, and the younger they are the more you seem to hate 'em."

"Would you save his life?" asked the mysterious stranger lowly in Will's ear.

"What do you mean, mate?" asked Will.

"If you would," continued this strange being, in still lower tones, "do not tell him the name of the nobleman who resembles Gentleman Jack. Should you disobey my directions, the hour in which you do so he will die, and you be cast in prison!"

CHAPTER XXIX.

EDITH'S LETTER.

EDITH's life had now become a torture.

Had Edgar deceived her, or had he not? Was he really Captain Trevillian or not? These questions perpetually surged within her brain, but they never gained a long ascendancy. Soon returned the calm unhesitating belief that the man who was her husband was a true gentleman, and that if he were dead, he died as he had lived—nobly, and therefore honestly.

When she most thought of him, she most wished to take in her arms the child she loved the best of all created things, but she was too unselfish to desire to remove the child from the friendly and healthy control of Mr. and Mrs. Naggleton; and again, without Lady Harriet's aid, she could have done nothing, and therefore she felt it would be ungrateful, and even cowardly, to ask that lady to alter her plans respecting Harold.

Yet many a time in the night-time she would wake from a dream of nursing her little one, to stretch out her arms, and find only vacancy by her side. So naturally her life became melancholy and cheerless, yet she always showed a smiling face to Lady Harriet her patroness, and to her daughter, Lady Constance.

Upon her return from Holgarth's princely mansion, she had arranged her plans. What good could she do by declaring that she was sure he was an imposter? Could she prove it? and did not everything seem to declare he was the earl, and also Captain Trevillian? If she herself, during the time it occupied her to reach home actually questioned herself, she, the wife of Edgar Trevillian, if the earl did not tell the truth, how could she prevail on her mistress, or Constance to believe in her story. So she de-

termined to declare that "a great mistake had been made." This did not commit her to the lie of saying that she supposed Holgarth must be the earl, but at the same time it allowed lady Harriet to think the better of Edith for her candid admission, and to be more friendly to her than ever.

All Edith asked was, that she might be allowed to retire from the room when "his lordship" called. This permission was readily granted, and so, on the very day following her visit to Milray House, she shrank from the drawing-room when a footman entered with the card of the "Earl of Milray."

She went up to her bed-room and laid her head in the white counterpane of her bed and wept sorely. She, with her woman's instinct, saw what was happening. She saw Constance's eye light up when the earl was announced; she knew the girl loved the man who, she was convinced, was an arch scoundrel.

Yet how could she prove that he was not the noble gentleman he pretended to be. If Edith had opened her lips upon the subject once more she might have irrevocably offended Lady Harriet, and yet not to speak was to allow the girl, for whom she had such a sisterly love, to fall into the grasp of a cruel monster. For Edith saw the shallow eyes Holgarth possessed —saw them in all their cold cruelty, *and knew him for what he was.*

The next day Holgarth came again. On the following day he renewed his visit, and so a couple of weeks sped on.

During this time Edith had sought many plans by which she could set Constance on her guard—but she abandoned them all as uncertain, and even hopeless.

Yet she never abandoned her determination to find some means of causing Constance to test Holgarth without she, Edith, apparently having anything to do with it.

She was sitting by herself one day, while Holgarth was sitting below her saying soft nothings to the poor girl he had resolved to make his wife, when the plan entered her brain complete and clear.

She took a sheet of paper and wrote in a disguised hand:

"My lord—You are deceived. Lady Harriet Seymour is almost penniless, and Constance quite so, for Lady Harriet has lost all her fortune and that of her daughter's in a speculation which has failed. She of course wishes to hide this from you, and desires to marry her daughter well, hence her extreme attention to you—but I respect your family, in whom I am much interested, and therefore, set you on your guard. Try her in any way you may think fit.

"STELLA."

Edith blushed as she wrote this communication, for an honest woman will always be ashamed of writing a nameless letter, even if she does it with the best purpose in the world.

When she had finished her work she left the house, took a coach, and was driven to the south side of the water. There she posted her letter and then returned home.

Edith in writing this letter had counted upon Holgarth's character, as she thought. She persuaded herself that he would at once make public enquiries about Constance's fortune, that these enquiries would reach the ears of Lady Harriet, and that then this lady would take means to ascertain whether the earl's attentions to her daughter were prompted by mercenary motives or by real affection.

Two days passed, and Edith heard nothing of her well-meant scheme.

She was about retiring for the night when Constance burst into the room, holding up an exquisite diamond and turquoise necklace.

"I shall be married in this," she said; "and I'm sure it's the most beautiful necklace in the world. Who do you think gave it me?"

"Who? Constance, dear," said Edith, taking the shining ornament.

"Lord Milray—Edgar. We—we are to be married next week," said Constance, hiding her head in Edith's lap.

Edith dropped the jewel as though it had stung her.

This then was the end of her attempt to break off the pending marriage between the daughter of her dear benefactress, and the man who was usurping the title and estates of Edith's own husband. *She had forced on the marriage.*

"Yours has been a very short courtship, Constance."

"Yes, Edith—but he is so good—so true a gentleman that I am willing to be his wife with all my heart—oh, he has acted so noble."

"He—nobly?" stammered Edith.

"Yes, Edith. I must tell you the noble truth. It seems some cowardly creature has said that I wanted to marry the earl for his fortune and title—especially for his fortune —and that I and mamma were only schemers."

"Oh, nobody said that, Constance, I am sure!"

"Oh, yes, Edith, in an anonymous letter, which was dropped in a club-room, and which was picked up and read by everybody. The earl came in and some drunkard read it to him. He was so enraged that he offered to champion me with his sword; and when no one accepted the challenge, he said he would prove the calumny of the letter."

"Indeed," said Edith, "what did he do?"

"He sat down," continued Constance, "and wrote a letter to me, saying he had been arrested for a debt of £2,000—that he could not pay it— and that he prayed me to do so. This, you know, Edith, was to test me, and see if I were mercenary or not — to ascertain whether I wished to marry him for himself or his fortune."

Edith started. She saw Holgarth's counter-scheme in a moment. The villain had seen it would not do to ask openly about Constance's money, and had, therefore, pretended an arrest to test the girl's power of helping him; for, it need not be said, Holgarth knew she loved him, and was quite sure that if she had the power, she possessed the will to send him any sum of money he might demand.

"Did he send the letter to you, or to Lady Harriet?" asked Edith, thinking that if he sent it to the younger lady, he was one of the most cunning scoundrels she had ever heard of.

"To *me*," said the girl. "That was so generous of him. He did not apply to mamma, whom he might be sure had money, but to me, without knowing I had much money, and because he was gentle enough to think that, as I am soon to be dearer to him than mamma, he ought to ask me in preference to her. Why," continued the girl, "he paid a man a guinea to place it himself in my hands; and he did."

"What did you do?"

"When the letter came mamma was out, so I could not speak to her."

"Then, why did you not come to me?"

"I came to your room, and knocked several times, but you did not answer; and so I guessed you were out, perhaps, with mamma."

Once again Edith started. Had she seen Constance, she might have counterplotted yet once more the earl, who it seemed to her was aided by power beyond that of this world; and the girl had actually come to seek her, and yet so deeply had she been preoccupied in thinking how she might save her young mistress, that *she did not actually hear her summons on the door when the poor girl actually came to ask her counsel.*

"Why did you not come in?" asked Edith.

"I don't know I am sure," said Constance.

"What did you do?"

"Why, you know I had received all my rents only on Tuesday last, and as the bank-notes still remained in the house, I put them in a parcel and sent them to the club by the messenger himself. There were *more* than £2,000 worth."

"Can I believe my senses!" thought Edith— "I have aided this man in endeavouring to injure him, more than he could have aided himself."

"And now what do you think?"

"I cannot think, Constance," said Edith, taking Constance's hands in hers.

"Why, he exhibited the bank-notes amongst the gentlemen at the clubs—challenged once more any gentleman who questioned my honour and honesty, and then replaced the notes in the paper, went to a jeweller's, and bought this exquisite necklace, and sent it and the money—all for me—to dear mamma, with an entire explanation, saying that he had used the pretext of an arrest to prevent scandal in the clubs, and to prove that I was not the mercenary woman the cruel world had made out. But you look confounded, Edith."

"No—oh, no!" she returned.

"Shall I go on?" asked Constance.

"Yes—what else has happened?"

"While mamma and I were trembling with happiness he came in, and in a few words asked me as wife from mamma, and mamma put my hand in his, and we are to be married——"

"But how comes it that you are to be married so quickly—there will not be time sufficient for preparations," said Edith, thinking that any delay, however small, gave still greater chance of the false earl's detection.

"Oh, Edith!—Edgar—do not start so—Edgar is so plain and unpretending, for all he is a great lord, that he desires little or no preparation, and indeed he desires the wedding to be private."

"But you, Constance, would like it public," said Edith, who guessed that Holgarth had capitally good motives for a private wedding—the more people there were with their eyes fixed on him the less greater the chance of his detection.

"Yes. I should like a public wedding," said Constance. "I should like to say before thousands that I would love, honour and obey him all my life; and but for the affair of the anonymous letter, I would have insisted upon a public wedding, but now I wish to be as obedient to him before my marriage as I shall be after, and so I am determined that the wedding shall be private, as he desires it, and I will wear this beautiful necklace. Oh, Edith, there is blood upon it," said the young creature, in sudden alarm, and sure enough a drop of blood shone deep red on the greatest diamond in the necklace.

"How came it there," said Edith, turning pale, but the cause was soon apparent. In the agony of her suppressed feelings, Edith had driven one of her nails into the flesh of her hand, and the oozing blood had stained the bride's jewels.

It was a bad omen.

"Good night, Edith," said Constance, kissing her companion—"I wish you would like to be present at the wedding, but I know you would rather be away—would you not?"

Edith thought for a moment—then she said, "On the contrary—if you will let me, I will be present."

——

CHAPTER XXX.

MR. AND MRS. NAGGLETON ARE DELIGHTED AND FRIGHTENED.

MR. and Mrs. Naggleton had had a little "brush."

Mrs. Naggleton, the early spring morning being a little fresh, was not honouring the "cairywan" with her presence, neither was Tiny, the child giantess. The giantess was also airing little Horace as well as herself, and Mrs. Naggleton was chucksey-chuckseying Puddy up and down till the dear child might have wondered when she ended and all the rest of the world began.

The vehicle was moving towards London, by the North Road, and as Mrs Naggleton had her earrings on, it was clear she was going out to tea. Not that Mrs. Naggleton was dressed by no means. But she never went out to tea without her earrings—they gave the tea an extra flavour, and as she was very much distracted by the way in which those ornaments kept hitting her up, she always "put 'em then in of a mornin'" to grow accustomed to the ornaments by tea-time, otherwise she would have misbehaved herself and have been taken for a fool.

Yes, Mr. and Mrs. Naggleton had had a little "brush."

A butcher's boy, as polite as butchers' boys usually are, seeing the procession to belong to a show, took a look at it, and thus addressed himself to Tiny—"Don't drop him" (referring to the baby) "my female hellerfont; for you'll not be able to come all the way down and pick up the pieces."

This address so frightened the female young elephant, that she "scrouged" on to Mrs. Naggleton immediately.

This lady, having that natural objection to being run down from behind which all ladies, in common with all gentlemen, have felt from time immemorial, turned round and "digged" Tiny in the side, thereby causing the ear rings to swing about like live fishes at the ends of fishing lines.

Whereupon, the boy said—"I wonder whether she had 'em both together—one arter t'other—wery 'medtate!"

Whereupon, Mrs. Naggleton immediately called upon Naggleton to "whip the saucebox into nothing."

Naggleton apparently didn't see it, and probably he knew that when a man has a contest with a boy his only chance of victory is a corner, whereas there were no corners in the Great North Road; and so Naggleton said—"Kim up, Betsy!" which, as may have been before remarked, did not refer to his Naggleton, who went through the world a Jemima, but the mare who dragged the entire caravan community from morn to dewy eve, and always went to sleep when Naggleton entreated people to "walk up!—all in!—to commence!"

"Not only," says Mrs. Naggleton, thereupon, "was some people born fools, but some people is agoing to remain fools all their showy lives—yah!"

And Naggleton thought he could do no better than remark—"Easy, Betsy! don't be frightened—and gently over the stones!"

And, thereupon, Mrs. Naggleton rampaged along the road like a unicorn.

However, when they reached town, Mrs. Naggleton was a little mollified—not much.

"Is he a goin' to stop to-day?"

Still the caravan proceeded, though Mrs. Naggleton had pulled up—Tiny dutifully fetching to behind her.

"Hi!" says Mrs. Naggleton.

Which remark seemed to spirit Betsy to further display of power.

"Yere, take the churrub!" said the lady, almost pitching Puddy nearly on to "Horatio," as Naggleton, when classically inclined, would say of Horace; and then Mrs. Naggleton flew after the machine, fell upon Betsy's head, and fetched the affair up with such a jerk, that the Albanian and the dwarf, who were having a quiet fisticuff inside the caravan, were both knocked over in a moment, and, as each afterwards vowed he had floored the other, they had another fisticuff to prove it.

"Nay—you, you—" Mrs. Naggleton was beginning when Teddy put her down in a moment by the quiet dodge as he called it. He patted the mare and said, "Steady—Betsy—steady—you're a hanimal as is too valiable for her to do it. Don't jib, it's only her jibberish, an yer head's as safe as the monyment o' Lunnun—so, steady, Betsy, steady, and show a woman what a mare ken be if that there mare she chooses it."

"Teddy, dear, I wants to freshen up."

"Betsy—mare, she can."

"Teddy," says Mrs. N., "don't have a stiff hupper lip—whatever yer does, don't have that."

"Betsy, mare," says Mr. N., "what's the use o' row—no use—then why fore row?"

"Teddy, dear—you're right."

"Then, Jemima, drop it."

So the brush was over, and Mrs. Naggleton and her Teddy were one again.

The fact is Mr. and Mrs. Naggleton were going on a visit to Lady Harriet's, and the lady of the caravan had laid in a stock of properties wherewith to deck herself, and which she now proceeded to do. Over her handsome new hoop she spread her crimson petticoat, then she put on her "green paduosoy taffetas" over that, and looped it up handsomely through a kind of pocket-hole, as the fashion was, and when she had added her blue boots and her pink hat with a ginger coloured feather in it, she looked quite a picture.

Tiny said she never had seen anything like it, which was indeed the truth, and so taken aback was Naggleton when he looked in at the door, that the first thing he could say, was, "Yere, missus, don't you come out a walking in that figor—they'll take you for a May Queen;" though in his heart of hearts, Mr. Naggleton perfectly well knew that the queen of his soul and partner of his show ran much greater chances of being saluted as a November Guy.

When the caravan reached that stable in Drury Lane in which it first rested in the commencement of this story, Mr. Naggleton bundled his wife into the coffee-room of the tavern as rapidly as he did the Albanian and the dwarf. Indeed, she looked a bit to be seen for a "apeny."

Then Mr. Naggleton dressed, and inasmuch as he put on a flaming calico waistcoat with red roses as big as saucers, and yellow tulips as large as the corresponding cups, perhaps he had no right to be so ashamed of Mrs. Naggleton when she proposed walking in state to Seymour House, her arm in her husband's, and Tiny traversing behind, in a blue sash, which the boys cruelly pulled into a draggle, and little Horace close up in her arms—we say perhaps Mr. Naggleton had no right to shrink from this public display of Mrs. Naggleton's dressy charms, and propose a coach to that lady, in fact, shield her from the public gaze till she sunk back upon the seat with the expression, "Well, Naggy, you are a fine gentleman after all. I see, you've treated me to a coach, my Teddy, because you see I'm too fine for the street."

"That's it," said Naggleton, pulling down that astounding waistcoat; "Hang me, Jemima, but you jest have hit it."

When they arrived at Seymour House it became clear to Naggleton that he had guessed rightly as to the effect Mrs. Nag. would have created, for a milkman passing at the moment of her descent, he was so staggered that if his pails had not balanced him upright nothing could have saved him from the area steps from the top to bottom at one fatal plunge. Even the footmen looked aghast at Mrs. Nag.

Let us pass over the meeting of Edith with her child. There are some things neither men can describe, and there are only women imagine, and amongst them is the wondrous love of a young mother for her first child.

Imagine Mr. and Mrs. Naggleton seated in Edith's own room, the baby on his mother's lap, and Mrs. Nag. spread out like a peacock.

"I am so sorry Lady Harriet and Lady Constance are away this evening; they have gone to the opera, with—with the Earl of Milray."

Mrs. Nag. was sorry to hear that, she would have liked to air herself before her ladyship in the blue boots, and, indeed, she was only sorry she couldn't wear the hat and ginger-feather in doors.

Here a servant came in with a delicate china service and a silver pot of chocolate.

Mrs. Nag. had guessed she should have a fine cup of tea—but what on earth was this, she asked herself, as she saw the chocolate being poured out.

Edith was too much taken up with her little treasure to ask whether Mrs. Naggleton preferred tea, and so she gave the footman the cups to hand round.

Now Teddy saw the handle to the delicate china cup he took in conjunction with the saucer below it, but though he tried a round dozen of times to get his fore-finger into it, he could not achieve his purpose, and at last, as a desperate effort he " overed" the brim with his entire hand, and took the dose at a gulp.

" Mr. Naggleton," said the wife of his bosom, "you shocks me," and as she *had* thrust her finger through she proceeded to sip her chocolate in a ladylike way. She made surprising faces over this new drink, which our showman nor wife had never seen, but her obvious distaste was as nothing to Naggleton's, who seemed about to collapse, and who kept wiping his mouth with his coat-sleeve in the most energetic manner, as though to get rid of the flavour.

Mrs. Naggleton, after the first dozen sips, was fain to desire to set her cup down, but the fates were against her—she had got her finger in the handle, but she could *not* get it out, and she had to finish the dose (in sips to be genteel), and then pull the cup off her finger as though it were a tight ring.

" Will you have any more?" asked Edith, smiling.

" Thank you,"said Mrs. Naggleton—"no more soup."

The footman who stood behind, to wait, burst into a guffaw, but Mr. Naggleton was too far gone to be angry, and indeed, beckoning to that official he whispered to him—" I say, mate, have yer got a drop o' summet short?"

It need not be said that our Edith soon came to herself, and in a very short time Mr. and Mrs. Naggleton had a capital meal, such as they liked, before them, and Edith was seeing that they had all they wanted. The honest folk enjoyed themselves amazingly.

CHAPTER XXXI.

STRONG-ARM WILL.

WHILE Mrs. Naggleton was enjoying that tea which she loved, and which replaced that "soup" which she detested, she suddenly clicked the saucer and cup together, in such a manner that her Teddy looked up and thus adjured her, " Steady."

But Mrs. Naggleton made no reply, and kept her eyes fixed upon Fanny's portrait, just hung over Edith's mantle-piece—the portrait Fanny had given Edith on the occasion of her visit to Jules's poor victim.

" As like," says Mrs. Naggleton, at last, " as like as two peas is, or three eggs to three of 'em."

" Which?" said Teddy, imagining his missus was suddenly struck comical.

" As like," said Mrs. Naggleton, slapping her knee, " as like *as* like—don't you say so, Teddy?" .

" Which?" again asked Teddy.

" That there lovely face in that there frame, to that dead and gone dear—our Jemima."

"Which our girl died at seven months," said Nag., " and this here young woman in the frame which seventeen she is if a day she is."

" But," says Mrs. Naggleton, " but sitch it would have been our gal to be—if to be it had been that she'd lived."

"What!" asked Naggleton, amazedly disgusted that Mrs. Nag. should make a spectacle of herself before a lady, for the showman had no doubt that Edith was a lady, "what! judge what a gal shall be growed hup by a portrait in a frame!"

" Which," returns Mrs. Nag., " the child is father o' the man, and why not woman—that is mother of her?"

Naggleton had not viewed the matter in this light, so he hid as much of his face as he could in the saucer he held.

But Mrs. Naggleton could not forget the portrait, which she averred over and over and over again, was "certainly jest" what her dear darling would have been "if not taken off suddenly, me dear, with her teeth."

Mr. Nag. was going to say that it would have been remarkable indeed if the cherub in question had been taken off without her teeth, but he held his peace, and in order to do so nearly bit a mouthful out of the egg-shell china cup.

" If a pusson," said Mrs. Nag., after drinking more tea, cup after cup, than she had ever known, had not the husband of her heart kept an account by tying knots on a bit of string he found in his pocket; "if a pusson 'ud lend it to one other pusson to carry in a carrywan, why that there show 'ud be a paradise indeed."

Ultimately Mrs. Nag. got into such a state of fluster with the portrait, the tea, and Nag. kicking her under the table, that she was near fainting.

Now Edith was a good-hearted girl, and at last she looked up and said, " Mrs. Naggleton—I *will* lend you the portrait—till you come again."

"Oh, me dear, I hope you don't think I want for to ask for it," says she, whereupon Nag. gave her such an indignant kick for her humbug, under the table, that she showed him the bruise a fortnight after.

So Mrs. Naggleton, by dint of perseverance, got her portrait—just as we may all get the end of our ambition if we *will* it so, and have the sense to strive.

Let us pass over that little parting—the sorrow of Edith to quit her child, the agitation of Mrs. Naggleton, and the good-hearted comfort of the showman himself.

The caravan set out that very night, for there was an important fair to be at the very next morning.

On joggled the show.

It has been said that the vehicle, as a bedchamber, was divided into three portions; in one of which, at one end, slept, cuffed, and kicked, the dwarf and the Albanian, in another at the other end reposed Mrs. N., Tiny, and the nfants, while in the centre Mr. Naggleton, himself, snored his seven hours away, when the wheels had ceased to go and "Betsy" was at rest.

Now on this night the showman had determined that they would travel all night, and as Betsy, though the best of mares, could not reach the destined village without Mr. N's guiding hand, the showman had agreed to have no sleep that night and "take it out" on the following one.

So Naggleton being outside the caravan, Mrs. N.,—all her community being in bed, and Tiny's legs as usual sticking through the curtain which hid her from Mr. Naggleton's view—Mrs. Naggleton, we say, sat down in the middle compartment and determined to enjoy a good look at the portrait.

Now when she came to this determination, the caravan had left the town behind it, and had reached the heath upon which our story began.

The caravan had rarely ever travelled by night, and this novelty struck Mrs. Nag. as she made up the fire, pulled the little round table to her, and took out the portrait from the handkerchief in which she had carefully wrapped it.

Perhaps Mrs Naggleton had been looking at the portrait ten minutes, when she shook her head and determined to seek sleep.

"Let me see," she thought, "till I can find the artist as can copy it, and if it cost the price of Betsy I'll have it. I'll put it away with Puddy's joos.'

And thereupon Mrs. Naggleton dipped under the bed and brought out a trunk, whence she produced the identical jewel-box which has been spoken of so often.

She had just opened this treasure and fingered one or two exquisite diamonds, when the caravan suddenly stopped with such a jerk that Mrs. Nag and the table were really capsized.

"Some people's fools," says Mrs Nag., and she was about to add something more, when—*crash!* the door of the caravan was sent in, and the next moment a pistol was pointed at Mrs. Naggleton's broad breast.

She would have screamed if she had been able, but she had no power, and the diamond emblem she held on one finger so shook by her trembling, that it caught the highwayman's eye at once.

As for the dwarf and Albanian, they woke with the noise, scrambled out of their blankets, and no sooner saw the pistol pointed with deadly effect at their lady-chief, than they immediately retreated into the extreme corner of their snuggery and clung to each other as though they were the dearest friends in the world, and as though the dwarf never gave the white Albanian such an eye as made that fair creature the most blackguardly of shown people.

But not so with Tiny. She came forward with a bounce, smack through and under the calico curtain—she looked a giantess breaking out of a cotton prison, and when she saw the pistol she only flinched once, and then came forward with one stride to the side of her "missus."

The highwayman was so tickled with the sight of this maiden, who in her night costume looked like a whitewashed monument topped with a goggling mask, that he burst into a laugh and put up his pistol.

"What's thee want?" asked Tiny.

"Well, if I wanted *you* I should have enough anyhow," said the highwayman.

"Doant ee be a fule," says Tiny, "and tell us what 'ee want, a sturbin' honest folks in they honest beds."

"Here, lady-fair," said the highwayman, "take the horse and tie him to the shafts, not too near the gentleman in the ropes, or they may fight."

"All right, captain," said a voice, which, while masculine, seemed to have something feminine in it.

The next moment the highwayman jumped lightly into the caravan.

Mrs. Naggleton flinched, and dropped Fanny's portrait to the ground; but Tiny held her ground like a fine young Yorkshire giantess as she was.

"You'll excuse me, sir," says Mrs. Naggleton, as she inwardly took an oath that if ever they escaped with their lives, that this should be the first and last time the caravan was "out of a night,"—"you'll excuse me, sir, but is the gennulmum in the ropes my poor husband?"

"Can't swear he's your husband, my dear," returned the highwayman, "because *I* hadn't the honour of being present at the wedding; but the gentleman in the ropes is the individual who was driving your carriage, my dear, and he can't object to being tied with his own ropes by my friend, who's a most gentlemanly person, I assure you."

"You'll excuse me again, sir," continued Mrs. Nag., "but p'raps the gentleman aint tied 'em too tight; and you'll excuse me even once again if I remarks that me and Naggleton was married in the church in Covent Garden Market, sir—yes."

The man at the last words started, but made no answer. During Mrs. Naggleton's appeal he had been examining the jewels, doubtless thinking them stage trinkets. Suddenly he started again as he saw a *coronet* engraved on the inside of one of the bracelets. He went to the door, and saying to his companion, "Here, just come in here—you can tie up your horse."

Within a moment or so, during which Tiny had unsuccessfully looked about for some means of knocking off the highwayman's head while it was turned away, the second robber entered the caravan, a voice as he did so saying—"I say gennulmem, use her easy; 'cos why, she aint accustomed to the wisits of—of—of sitch gennulmem as you. Easy, Betsy—don't stagger; if you go down, what's to become o' me, a strapped to one of my own shafts?"

Could any observer have seen the two highwaymen, there could have been no doubt that they were the same couple of companions who had entered Old Jabez's respectable tavern, as detailed in a former chapter. The one was Strong-arm Will, the other the slim, half-effeminate highwayman, to whom the mysterious stranger had spoken in declaring that Gentleman Jack still lived.

"There, lady-fair," (which was the name the smaller of the two highwaymen went by), "I never saw you make up to a wench yet—now what do you say to this one ;" and he thrust his whip into Tiny's ribs.

"Hands arf," says Tiny, "or it 'ull be hands on."

"I say, look at this swag," said Strong-arm Will, pointing to the jewels.

The second highwayman took some of the jewels up.

"These handcuffs," said Will, taking up one of the bracelets, "are no faker."(a)

"They l ok real," said the smaller highwayman "they are—they're worth being lagged(b) for.",

"Gad—somebody's cracked a case (c) to find these sparklers. Only think of finding this swag nested amongst show-sneaks. Perhaps," said Will, lowly, "they're fly." (d)

Turning to Mrs. Naggleton he uttered one of the utterly incomprehensible pass words of the time, "Fly a crow to York ?" he asked.

"Sir," asked Mrs. Naggleton.

"Is the nam (e) awake ?"

"Which, sir—the baby ?" asked Mrs. Naggleton.

"They're duffs to fly,"(f) said Will, and began pulling all the remaining jewels from the box.

"Oh! dear me, gennulmen, I don't know what you gennulmen mean, but if you want to know about them there paltry jools—they was the jools of a hactress — she died, poor thing, at Bow Street lock-up—she did, indeed, gennulmen."

The smaller highwayman, who was called "Lady-fair" started as he heard this communication, and asked rapidly, "Did you find her on the London Road, near Hounslow."

"Yes, sir."

"And these are the jewels she wore?"

"Yes, sir."

"*His wife*," Mrs. Naggleton heard the highwayman mutter, and he dropped the jewels he held in his hand; "*I would she had left a child behind her, I would ruin it.*"

"Well, what else have you, me dear, in the caravan ?" asked Will.

"Lor, sir—there's on'y the dwarf and the Albanian, and which I hear their teeth a-chatterin' at this werry identical moment—and, I say, sir, yer don't think the gennulman in the ropes is a stiflin', do yer—cos I don't hear him open his precious lips, an we was married in Common Garden."

"Kim up, Betsy," said Naggleton, responsive to his wife's appeal, but the mare was quite unable to do anything of the kind, for with a

(a) "Faker "—counterfeit.
(b) "Lagged"—transported.
(c) "Cracked a case"—committed a burglary.
(d) Acquainted with the thieving fraternity.
(e) "Nam."—Means man. The word is simply spelt backwards. This mode was very common.
(f) "Duffs to fly."—Do not know the thieves community and their language.

bit of rope taken from his pocket, the second highwayman had tied the forelegs of that animal together. The caravan was jerked, that was all.

"Hullo—here's something else," said Strong-arm-Will, kicking before him the portrait of Fanny, which Mrs. Naggleton had dropped upon the ground, and then picking it up.

Mrs. Naggleton said afterwards, that the highwayman fell backwards as though he had been shot, the moment his eyes fell upon the portrait. He sat down and buried his face in his hands. "Have you any brandy here?" he said, after a few moments.

"Law bless yer," said Mrs. Naggleton, "are you ill," all her fears going from her directly she saw the strong highwayman trembling like a weak child, "I've some whiskey, if that'll do—and praps you'll allow the gennulman in the ropes to have a glass as well."

"Where did you get this portrait ?"

"Sir, it's Fanny's."

"I know that—did she give it you ?"

"No, sir," said Mrs. Nag., "and it's not been given me—ony lent by the lady that Fanny give it to, because it's like our blessed baby—but you don't want to hear about that, and I do hope you won't steal—that is, take the portrait, because it's ony borrered, sir."

"Where is Fanny ?" asked the highwayman, his face still covered.

"Lor, sir—she's very bad a-bed. You know she—she, poor thing, thought she was the lady of a great lord, and she was really much wuss, and that's it, sir."

"What is his name, the villain ? " asked the highwayman.

"La, sir, I don't know—ony know he's a great lord—a hearl."

"If I find him," said the highwayman, "he will never live to break another man or woman's heart. Look here, woman, I'll not touch those things," pointing to the jewels; "but I must have this portrait."

"Lor, sir, them there jools aint wuth thutty shillin', and my honour's wuth more nor thutty shillin'—so pray give me the portrait."

"It shall never leave me," said the highwayman, thrusting it into his breast, and rising as he spoke; "and I swear on it, never to cease sooking this man's life."

"*If he only had a child by that dead woman I would ruin it,*" Mrs. Naggleton heard the smaller of the two highwaymen repeat.

At this moment little Perdita began to wail, and Mrs. Naggleton, conscious that Lady Milly *had* left a child in this world, immediately and unguardedly said, "*Her* child, sir, died within a day of the poor lady herself."

Something in Mrs. Naggleton's face told the secret to the highwayman, who ran to the corner whence the cry had come.

But Tiny flew after him, and with one backhanded blow she forced the robber back.

"Leave my child be," she said.

"Yours?" asked the robber.

"Oh, yes," said Mrs. Naggleton, seized with

an idea "yes, Tiny's had twins; you know she's jined in holy matteromoney with the dwarf—yere Bob, come out and own yer wife."

"All right, missus," said Bob, and that was all.

"If it were," the younger highwayman muttered, "if it *is* – I will ruin him by her; patience, patience—my wrongs *shall* be avenged."

"Come, Will," he muttered aloud, "let us go."

The highwayman Will seemed quite overcome by Fanny's portrait. "Good bye," he said, leaving the jewels of the Lady Milly lying on the table, "I m your friend, my good woman, and may some day help you Come, DEATH," he continued to his companion, "let us go."

"Good bye, also," said the man called Death, "You will see me again, perhaps often. Do not start; I shall not rob you."

The next moment both the highwaymen were on their horses, and soon the show folk had the pleasure of listening to the lessening sound of their horses' footsteps.

Then Mrs. Naggleton tumbled out of the caravan, and helped by Tiny, the Albanian, and the dwarf, she untied "the gennulman in the ropes."

"Well," said Nag., shaking himself upon his release, "that's about the tightest fit I ever had on. I spose they've hooked our Puddy's jools."

"Lor, no, Nag.; which way some people cuttingly *is* fools—which leastways not *you*, Teddy, this night of nights, and they've left em; and the way they went on about them trumpery almost made me think as them trumpery was real."

CHAPTER XXXII.

THE MARRIAGE.

THE fashionable church for marriages was opened and ready for the marriage party.

Numbers of people crowded into the building, one after the other, and the church was almost full.

"Lor a' massy main," says the beadle to the pew opener, "this here feller is one of the tiptop lords, reglar top sawyer he is, and lor a mussy, what guineas you will get, Mrs. Mangles, and what guineas I shall get and praps a dozen, any how *my* rent's paid—and here they are, mar'm."

At this moment up came a carriage and from it stepped two gentlemen—Lord Alchester and Mr. Natherton.

"Gad," said one. "we're here before the noble bridegroom himself."

"Then I think it ought to score one for us in favour of the bride."

They had not walked up and down the church front half a dozen times when the Earl of Milray descended from his carriage.

He was magnificently dressed.

His coat was of pale pink velvet, much braided with silver, and his waistcoat and breeches were of white satin. His shoes were fastened with magnificent diamond-encrusted buckles, and his sword was ornamented with the same precious gems. His hands were covered with white gloves.

Carriage after carriage arrived bearing company of the highest in the land, and the passages of the church were filled with rustling silk, velvet, and satin.

At last came the bride and her mother.

Constance was exquisitely dressed in white lace, beneath which the diamonds glimmered like the reflection of stars from the surface of a quiet pool.

She was very pale and for the matter of that, Holgarth looked still paler than he usually looked.

She bowed to Holgarth on seeing him, and then awkwardly turned towards her mother.

For somehow the young creature had already begun to suspect her future husband. Her suspicions were as vague as the sighing of a summer breeze, yet still they existed. Perhaps it was in consequence of the terror and dread Edith still showed when Holgarth's name was mentioned, or when any reference to him might be made.

As the grand company placed themselves about the altar, a slight noise was heard at the door, but it did not attract the attention of the marriage party, but those not so deeply interested in the ceremony, remarked the entry—first, of a soldierly-looking man, the opposition to whose admission on the part of the beadle, was the chief cause of the slight disturbance which took place at the door.

The soldierly-looking man, however, pushed his way in.

He was almost immediately followed by a couple of men dressed dashingly enough, but with an odd devil-may-care look with them which gave them an unsual air, one was an immensely strong-looking fellow, the other a slim, womanly looking man.

These individuals were followed by a man with black curling hair, a terrible, cold, cruel, and yet intellectual-looking man. His hands were very white, and the nails long and delicate like claws.

The ceremony commenced. Then sounds the voice of the minister, "If any man among you know of any great cause or impediment why these two should not be joined in holy matrimony ye are now to declare it, or for ever after hold your peace."

The pause which always has followed, and does follow, this enquiry and exhortation, was unbroken for a moment or so, during which time the slighter of the two men who had entered the church together, watched the agonized face of Holgarth with a fiendish delight.

It was clear he trembled for himself.

The minister was about to continue, and he had already dropped his eyes upon his book, when a loud ringing voice said, "I forbid this ceremony."

The shudder which passed through the assembly was felt by every one in the building.

It is a terrible thing to hear a man or woman denounce a religious ceremony, and be called upon to prove a just cause.

"Wherefore?" asked the minister.

"He enters the church in a false name."

Holgarth started, but he kept his eyes calmly fixed upon Death. As he first saw her the very clamminess of death broke out upon his forehead, but he had so schooled himself to bear unlooked-for surprises, that almost in a moment after learning that "the woman Death" was in the building he was prepared to battle with her.

He saw all in a moment. He *knew* she had assumed the appearance of a highwayman in order to hunt him down; but after the surprise of the first moment, he did not flinch before the being he most hated and most feared in the entire world.

"This man must be mad," said tne earl.

"Mad as a March hare," added Lord Alchester, taking a pinch of snuff coolly—"gad, Milray, I think I should run him through the body, though we're in a church, if he told me I am not Lord Alchester."

"Mad—no," returned Death, "he is a common highwayman—the man that used to be called Gentleman Jack."

At these words a stifled scream was heard to proceed from one of the galleries of the church. It was the scream of a woman in agony, and yet in joy.

"Let me pass!" the next moment said Edith, for it was she, having come to witness the ceremony from a far off corner—"let me pass!"

The reader can comprehend the reason of her scream.

So defiant had Holgarth been, and so apparently truthful were his pretensions—so weak was she with her proofs, that she had adhered to her determination to cease endeavouring to arrest the marriage of the false lord with the lovely girl whom Edith loved most of all creatures in the world, her only own dear child excepted.

But now, when she had come to see the marriage, which she knew to be a sacrifice—now that she looked upon the poor girl Constance as lost, behold another champion arose in Constance's favour—so suddenly, so terribly, that it seemed like fate itself.

The woman Death, in her undying search after Holgarth, who had injured her and hers in such a manner as forbade forgiveness, had learnt that Holgarth had become a highwayman. She only had known him as a gentleman, and no sooner did she learn this than she took to the road, and soon learnt that he had been called Gentleman Jack.

Hearing Old Jabez say that he was dead, she would have believed that statement, but the German doctor had been at her elbow to tell her Holgarth still lived. This same being had unobtrusively, but with a dead certainty, drawn Death to the church, and then she stood face to face with the man she had sworn to destroy, and not only himself, but all of his, and all who called him friend.

"Gad," said Mr. Natherton, "this Gentleman Jack must be very clever, for he was hanged some months ago."

"No," said Death, "he escaped—the man Jabez will tell you so—he who keeps the inn on the heath."

"Why, my man," said Natherton, "I went to Tyburn myself and saw the scamp hanged, and right well he deserved it—the blackguard."

"Let the marriage be stopped," said Death, "for proof. I say he was resuscitated—brought to life after he had been hung in chains. Let the innkeeper be brought forward."

The minister looked awkwardly about—the denouncer seemed to speak with terrible energy and assurance. Of course, as the aristocratic minister of the day, he knew the entire particulars of the new earl's accession to the title, and the strange tragedy which had ushered in that event. Turning to the gentlemen about he said, "You, gentlemen, know this to be the earl, do you not?"

"Certainly." "There cannot be a doubt about it." "It is beyond question." Such were the greetings which saluted the inquiry.

"Is there anybody here who has been with the earl for many years past?"

No one answered.

"Is there anybody who knew the earl before he came into the title?"

No answer for a moment, and if possible, Holgarth grew still paler as he said, "Reverend sir, let me point out that the vessel in which my troop sailed, is a wreck, the men all dead or slaves—I only, by a lucky chance, escaped sailing with my regiment—and as I never much mixed with company, owing to the brand upon my birth, and which I was able to move

only a few months since, it is clear that men in my regiment, or rather troop, not being able to be produced, I am not in a position to prove myself who I am by the gentlemen amongst whom I have lately lived. Yet I dare say some gentlemen here have seen me as Captain Edgar Trevillian, and recognize me as that gentleman."

"I," said Mr. Natherton, "once saw the earl riding at the head of his troop, and I have not the least doubt in my mind, of course, or I should not be here. Allow me to point out, sir," the gentleman continued, "that the personal peculiarities of his lordship are so great that an impostor could not readily be found—in fact, I doubt if a man like him could be found in the whole of the United Kingdom."

The minister bowed.

"As for me," said Lord Alchester, "I was once introduced to his lordship, while he was plain Edgar Trevillian, and though I grieve to say I was unable to say much to him, for it was late when the introduction was made, and I had been drinking, I can positively swear that the earl is the very man then introduced to me as Captain Edgar Trevillian—there can be no doubt about this. As the Honourable Mr. Natherton has remarked—the personal peculiarities of the earl would ensure his identification at any moment."

As the lord spoke, Holgarth pulled up his coat collar, for at this awful instant, when he was dying a thousand deaths, he feared that the red mark round his neck left by the rope might show terrible and destructive above the white satin coat collar.

"I am most perplexed," said the minister. "By my holy office I may not join a couple in holy wedlock if there be the least doubt about an impediment. If there were any one here who knew the earl while Captain Edgar Trevillian—knew him intimately and quite recently as the captain—and after the death of the highwayman, though this latter point is of little consequence, I should not be compelled to do what I am about to do—refuse to continue this ceremony till the identity of the earl is proved." He then added in a louder voice—"Is any one present who knew the Earl of Milray when only Captain Edgar Trevillian?"

"Aye—aye," said a voice from the extremity of the church—"I know the captain; let's come forward."

The speaker was the soldierly-looking man who had entered the church by chance to see the grand ceremony.

He came forward and stood in the midst of the grand aristocratic company — a strange contrast with their magnificent dresses and jewels."

"Did you know the captain?" asked the minister.

"Aye—aye."

"Did he know you?"

"As well as most men in his troop, sir."

"That is to say," the minister continued—"he did not know you personally."

"No, sir."

"How long have you left the regiment in which Captain Edgar Trevillian served?"

"About six months; but I did not leave. I was dismissed the service.'

"Why?" asked the minister, wondering why the government could dispense with such a strong healthy looking man as the fellow standing before him.

"Oh, not for ill conduct, sir: but they said I had a squint which prevented my being fit for a musket, so I got my discharge, sir."

"Then you know the captain, and saw him a few weeks before his regiment sailed in the *Gorgon*."

"Aye, sir."

"Now look about and tell me—do you see the captain?"

The man, who had kept his eyes fixed upon the minister during the interrogation, now turned them on the marriage party.

No sooner did he see Holgarth than he started and said, "Captain!"

The ladies and lords about also started at this instant recognition, and the colour once more came into the cheeks of Lady Harriet and Constance; but the alarm was equally sudden as the dismissed soldier said, "Though now I look again, he *isn't* quite like the captain."

"I have been ill, for a month or so, my man," said the captain.

"Then your honour," said the soldier, "you are changed in your voice as well as in face—though lord, if you ain't the captain, hardly your own mother 'ud tell him from yer, there's such a likeness."

The earl shrugged his shoulders.

"But," the man continued—"there *is* a mark by which I can tell your honour in a moment." Here the man looked towards the earl's right hand, which was hidden behind the white satin skirt of his coat.

"What do you mean?" asked Holgarth.

"So please your honour, I can tell better by your own right hand than by your hair or eyes. If you're the captain as was, you've got a anchor on the back of that there right hand of yours—and now let's look at it, captain!"

"You are mistaken," said the earl; "it is not an anchor, it is a cross;" and bringing his hand forward, he exhibited the cross which, under his direction, the French valet had pricked into his flesh.

"Well, captain," said the fellow, "it's you, sure enough; but I could ha' swore it was a anchor, and not a cross. Beg your honour's honoured pardon for mistaking you, but when a fellow's in the psalm-house, and the minister's afore him, a fellow's like to be cautious in what he says, captain."

"True," said the earl – "pray remember me better by this," and he put a couple of guineas into the man's hands.

"Thank your honour—hope to live to see your honour often. Blow me, if any body imitates yer honour, I'll have at him."

Said Lord Alchester lowly to Holgarth—

"Confound me, I don't remember that cross on your hand, Milray."

"No? Oh, possibly not. I'm generally ashamed of it, and cover it with white paint—had done so this morning, but rubbed the colour off to prove my identity."

"The marriage can proceed," said the minister.

"Forgive my doubts," said Lady Harriet.

"Oh, you *did* doubt me, my lady?" said Holgarth.

The next moment the ceremony was progressing.

Meanwhile where was the unhappy Edith, without whose aid the soldier would never have recognized Holgarth as the captain? Where was she who had instigated him to put the cross upon his hand—who could still arrest the marriage if she but came forward?

*   *   *   *   *

They were married.

No human voice could put them asunder, and she who might have prevented this sacrifice—she who had almost died to have saved Constance from such a fate—lay insensible in the portico of the great fashionable church.

The facts are these. Edith had ran down the stairs with such rapidity to save the friend of her benefactress, that she fell, and striking her head against the jutting corner of one of the monumental tablets which covered the walls, become insensible.

So she lay till the marriage ceremony was concluded—till the lords and ladies who attended the wedding called Constance The Most Noble the Countess of Milray—till the wedding party left the vestry, and turned towards the door of the building.

Now a party of the press-gang were out on one of their shameful excursions on the morning of the marriage, and, attracted by the crowd about the church-doors, stopped, partly from curiosity and partly from the hope of finding one or two "smart active men," whom they could steal.

The marriage party passed down the aisle, past Death, Sir Strong-arm, and the soldier who had identified Holgarth as Captain Edgar Trevillian.

"*He shall die*!" muttered Death, as the bridegroom passed her, and more than one in the semblance of a human being heard the exclamation. He was a tall pale-looking man—in fact, the terrible German doctor who has so frequently appeared in these pages.

"What did you say, Death?"

The slim highwayman started, and said, "Are *you* here?"

"Yes—what did you say?"

"I said he should die."

"Humph! we must all die."

"*He* shall die at once—this day."

"No—no, Death!" returned the tall pale doctor—"no, he must not die *yet awhile*. His children must die and be lost before him. *He* must die broken-hearted at the wickedness of those children."

"I do not choose to wait."

"You are impatient, Death?"

"Who are *you*, to question me?"

"I am no one. Take my advice—spare him; you shall have your vengeance—only wait."

"I will *not !*"

"You shall !" retorted the terrible creature—a kind of red light flashing from his eyes.

"And who are you who dare to tell me to wait?" asked Death, a hand upon the sword she was wearing.

"Bah! you will know some day," said the German doctor, and turned upon his heel.

Within a moment or so after the departure of the bridal party a terrible scene of confusion had commenced outside the church-door.

The German doctor had passed out amongst the first and spoken to the ringleader of the press-gang. The gang, in fact, were moving away, upon the intimation by one of the number that only women and children went to look at "splicings," when the strange doctor accosted the leader of the gang. Their hands touched, and those near might have sworn they heard the sound of clinking coin. Let that be as it may, it is certain the stranger went into the shadow of the church, and stood waiting there.

As he had come from the church, a burly man in the crowd said—"Well, anyhow, *you're* a queer fish to come out of a church, much less go in one—except to be buried !"

"Oh !" returned the German, "this church is so full of vanity and wickedness. the devil himself might enter without fear, and run no risk of being smitten down on the threshold."

And so, when the stranger stood away from the crowd, and in the shadow of the church, several could not help noting him, and saying how cruel and terrible he looked.

The next moment the crowd poured from the sacred building, and in the midst the two highwaymen, and the soldier who had declared Holgarth to have been Captain Edgar Trevillian.

"There them three is !" said the leader of the gang; and the next moment the three were seized by the sailors.

But they had their work with Strong-arm Will. He flung off the men as soon as they touched him; but they were like bull-dogs—did not know when they were beaten—and fell upon him time after time, till at last he gave way under their repeated attacks, and fell to the ground.

Ropes bound his wrists together before he had recovered sufficient strength to oppose the indignity, and when he found himself thus captured, he shook his hands so, that it seemed possible he would burst his bonds, as did Samson of old.

But the sailors fell on him once more, and thrust the giant into a hackney-coach, such as was always in waiting on a gang of these privileged robbers and destroyers of home

The other two victims had offered but little resistance to their captors, for Death had little or no physical strength, and the dismissed

soldier would never have been allowed to quit the army had he been able to overcome three or four picked and determined sailors.

As Death was forced into the coach she saw the German standing away from the mob, and in the shadow of the church.

The stranger scornfully raised his hat and saluted Death.

Her entire frame shook as she watched his triumph.

"I *will* destroy him yet !" she cried; and the next moment the coach started, and she had lost sight of this demoniac man.

Meanwhile he still stood in the black shadow of the sacred edifice. "He shall die—but not yet awhile !" he muttered in German. "He shall die when he has destroyed souls which are now pure, and even unborn !"

CHAPTER XXXIII.

THE MARRIAGE OF JULES.

IT was a week or two after the wedding, and Fanny was once more able to walk and help herself.

The hideous old woman who had been called in to nurse her had been dismissed, and a pleasant little handmaiden looked after her wants.

It was about eleven o'clock in the day, and Fanny was seated before a little rose-tree, which Jules had politely sent up to her room with his compliments, when that personage tapped at the door.

"Good morn, Mees Fanny !" said Jules—"sall you like de roses ?"

"Yes, sir," she said; for she was still, as she was ever to be, broken down and her spirits utterly destroyed.

"But why sall my Fanny say 'sare' to me ?"

"I don't know, sir."

"Mees Fanny—when sall you be villin' to become the Madame Jules ?"

"When you like, sir," returned Fanny.

"Sall you vish to be Madame Jules to-day."

"If you like, sir," she said.

"And sall you vish to haff some one you know to see you to be married ?"

"I should only like one to be here."

"Who sall dat be ?"

"The lady who was so kind to me – Edith."

"She sall come; but she is no lady—she sall be von servant like me. She is de companion to the mudder of me lady de countess."

"Oh, let her come if you can."

So Jules, who, when not in any way opposed, could be as polite a Frenchman as could be desired, declared he would ask Madame Edith to be present at the wedding, which Jules had arranged should take place that morning in Fanny's own room.

The polite Frenchman immediately took a

coach and drove to Seymour house, and obtaining an interview with Edith, easily persuaded that lady, in spite of her aversion to re-enter Milray House, to come and witness the ceremony.

She put a hood and cloak on, and returned with Jules himself, who leaving Edith at the door, and ordering a footman to show her into Fanny's room, directed the coachman to drive to an obscure part of London, the ins and outs of which the Frenchman seemed to know with marvellous exactitude.

Under his direction the coachman drove along street after street of the lowest and most disreputable description.

At last the Frenchman stopped the vehicle, and descending from it entered a house which, even in that quarter, was remarkable for its squalid and dangerous appearance. It looked as though about to fall to the ground—as though rotted by the evil and wickedness it had so long contained.

The Frenchman continued his way without the least hesitation. He ascended flight after flight of stairs, and at last reached the attic floor. Here he tapped at a dilapidated door, through the chinks of which he saw the man of whom he was in search.

The man whom Jules desired to visit obviously did not anticipate any pleasure from the call, for he started and listened for a second summons.

Jules soon struck once more upon the old door.

"Who's there?" a voice answered.

"A friend, Parson Tom."

"A friend," said the minister, opening the frail door; "it's not many friends come to see me here."

"You sall remember me, sall you not?"

"No—I do not remember you."

"I am Monsieur Jules, valet to the late earl."

"Ah, I remember you now," said the minister, offering the visitor the only chair there was in the room, and seating himself on the edge of the bed.

"Mr. Minister, I know all."

"What all?" asked the minister.

"I heard you speak aloud on the night of the marriage."

"What, that of the Earl of Milray and the orange girl?"

"De same. I hear you say dat he is veritable married, an I'm come to ask you to marry de poor girl once again."

"What—is the new earl in love with her?"

"No, Mr. Minister."

"Who is then?"

"I am."

"You!" said the minister, laughing a hollow laugh—"but what can you want me to marry her once again for—there is no need, and my performance of the ceremony is merely valueless."

"No."

"What do you mean?"

"Dat you air a parson, Mr. Tom—a veritable parson."

"How do you know that?"

"You have whispered, dat night," continued the Frenchman—"dat she is really married to de earl; an' when a man speak to himself he speak de truth."

"You villain—you were listening!" the jovial and not too particular minister cried out.

"Nay, monsieur the minister," returned the valet—"I did not leesten, but I could not help to hear!"

"What do you want of me?" the minister continued. "If you come here," glancing round the room—"in the hope of extorting money from me for my conduct on that night, you may go again; for I am as poor as any beggar, ah, and poorer than there is between here and Bethnal Green."

"I do not come for your money," said Jules, shrugging his shoulders—I come to giff de money to you."

"Give me money—why?" asked the minister, starting.

"Because de labourer is vorthy of his hire—and you sall do de labour."

"How?"

"Marry me to de poor Mees Fanny and I sall giff you ten pounds."

"Ten pounds!" said the minister, starting forward.

"Yees—for dat little ting, and anothair."

"What's that?"

"You sall put it on paper dat de poor Mees Fanny was married to de earl, and dat she sall be his vidow vhen she marry me; and you sall prove dat you are de parson."

"No, no," said the minister; "I swear to you that I am a minister, but I cannot prove it. I should have to divulge secrets that I wish—that I will keep in my own bosom."

"But vhat sall be de good of de paper if you do not show, Mr. Minister, dat you are de parson—and I swear dat I vill not use de paper for five years."

"Five years," the minister continued. "Ah! after five years it will matter little to me who knows who and what I am. Let me see—you agree to pay me ten pounds for marrying you and the orange-girl, and proving on paper that I am a minister of the church, and that the ceremony between her and the late earl was absolute and valid?"

"Preceesly," said the valet.

"Well, I agree," said the minister. "When do you desire the ceremony to be performed?"

"At once, Mr. Minister."

"To-day?"

"De bride and her friend avait you."

"Oh! very well," returned the minister—"it matters little to me whether it's to-day or to-morrow;" and, not noticing that Jules put his right hand into his waistcoat-pocket to make sure a paper was there, he went to a little oaken desk in the corner of the bare room, and took from it one or two small papers and a piece of parchment.

"I suppose," the minister continued, as he went to the desk in question, "you wonder why I am in this miserable hole?"

"Yes," said the valet, with a peculiar smile, and once more pressing the paper within his waistcoat-pocket.

"I'm under a cloud—I was answerable for a sum of money—I am forced to pay it, and can't. Pray, how did you find me out?"

"I find all de people out dat I vant," said the valet. "Are you ready, Monsieur?"

"Yes," said the minister, putting on his cassock—"yes—have you a coach?"

"Yes," said the valet, bowing low, and refusing to leave the room before Mr. Minister.

It was always a dangerous sign when Jules was too obsequious.

The minister, whose only name amongst his associates, such as the late earl, had been Tom, did not notice that a man of a low Judaic cast of countenance eyed him narrowly as he got into the coach, which Jules refused to enter till the other was seated in the place of honour—the right hand back-seat.

The coach was driven rapidly towards Milray House, and soon that polluted residence was reached.

Meanwhile, and during the conference between Jules and the minister, Edith and Fanny had been sitting hand in hand, and the poor girl, who had once sold oranges for a living, had made a confidant of the poor lady whose husband had so mysteriously disappeared.

They had sat for some time, when Fanny said—"May I tell you all the truth, ma'am?"

"What truth?—and don't—don't say ma'am: I'm only a servant, like you."

"I am the Countess of Milray!"

"What?" asked Edith, for she herself lay claim, in her own heart, to that title.

"Yes, indeed," said Fanny—"from what Jules has told me, and from what I have otherways learnt, I know that the minister, who the earl thought was only a pretended parson, was indeed a real one; and so, you see, I became the countess."

"Then why, Fanny, are you about to marry his most unpleasant French valet?"

"He forces me to marry him."

"How?"

"I cannot go back to my dear old business," Fanny returned, lowering her head; "and—and I shall be a mother, and my child will be the earl's. I love it already so much, that I must do it all the good I can; and if I refuse Jules I shall be turned into the street, and my child will die with me. Jules swears if my little one is a boy, that he will get him the earldom, and drive away the present earl!"

Edith started.

"Why do you start," asked Fanny.

"Do you know that the present earl is married to a noble lady?"

"Oh, yes; she does not know my tale—either the real truth, nor that which everybody but myself and Jules believes—but she was so kind to me when she spoke to me some days ago,

that I could have flung myself upon her neck—I could indeed."

"She is so kind, Fanny, that if you injure the earl you will injure her, *for she loves him.*"

"*I* could not love him. Do *you?*"

"I—I *hate* him," Edith unguardedly said; then immediately seeing her error, she said—"I hate him because he took Constance—his wife—away from me. We were such happy companions."

A few moments passed, and then Edith, who had been considering, said—

"Fanny, do you believe in me?"

"Yes, indeed I do."

"Do you believe me to be your friend?"

"Yes; your eyes look so kindly on me."

"And have you no friend to advise you?" asked Edith.

"Not one, but you," Fanny returned.

"And will you take my advice in the affair about the earl?"

"I will. I swear, without knowing what your advice is—I swear to follow it."

"Then see here. This man Jules marries you to use your child against the present earl, who is no more the real earl than he who has recently died. Do not start. The present earl is an impostor—the late earl usurped the title from the son of his father's elder brother. Now promise me that you will not deny that your child is Jules's, and all will be well. When the truth should be told I will tell it, every word. Can you trust me, Fanny?"

"With my life, Edith," the orange-girl returned.

"Do not say anything of your determination to your husband; and you cannot break off the marriage, or I would persuade you to, for Jules has *power* over his master the earl, and the earl through his wife can command Lady Harriet, my mistress and my only friend, through whom only could I help you. Fanny, marry this man, but remember in so doing that you do so for your unborn child's sake, and that I will watch over you and it while life is within me. Trust in Edith, say as little as possible, and leave all to me. I, aided by you, will, sooner or later, defeat them all."

The two unhappy women had continued their conversation for some time longer, when the coach arrived, and Jules and the minister made their appearance in the room.

"Who is to give your wife to you, Mr. Jules?" asked the minister.

"I haff a friend," said Jules; and going to the door, called in the individual to whom reference has been made as watching the coach and its inmates as they entered it outside the minister's miserable dwelling.

Fanny started as she saw this individual, but a reassuring look from Edith caused her to recover herself and she stood up.

The ceremony was at once proceeded with, and in a few short minutes Fanny had become once more a wife.

The ceremony completed, Jules saluted his bride in his usual grimly polite manner, and then turned to a table and began a low conversation with the minister, while as to the Jew who had played the part of father he left the room, but the women still heard him on the outside of the door moving first one foot and then the other.

The writing at the table took some considerable time, and Edith, watchful for herself and Fanny, saw several papers pass between the two men, one of which Jules signed, the other being signed by the clergyman.

A clearance being made at last, Jules took from a coat-pocket a purse of money and counted out ten sovereigns upon the table.

"I would rather have one note," said the clergyman, thinking of *some one* in the country —his dear and confiding mother, to whom he desired to send a five pound note.

"Nay," said the Frenchman, "Mr. Minister, vhere you sall be going de notes sall be of leetle value, for dey charge much for de change of de notes."

By this time Jules had locked up the papers he had received from the minister in a bureau.

"What do you mean?" asked the minister.

For all response Jules took from his waistcoat-pocket the paper with which his fingers had played during his interview with the minister; then giving a peculiar whistle he was answered by the Jew, who once more entered the room.

"Dere's your man," said Jules.

"A bailiff!" said the minister.

"A bailiff," returned Jules, smiling, "Mr. Minister, I haf bought de debt of which you speak dis mornin', and I arrest you!"

The minister flung himself upon a chair and buried his face in his hands, "My poor mother! she will starve!" he said.

"Nay," continued Jules, "not if I know it. I sall vant you to liff, an' if you liff in de Fleet Prison undare my own eye I sall see dat you sall liff; and vhen dat you are ill, I sall see dat you go to de waterin'-places. It is necessaire dat you liff undare my eye."

"I shall starve in prison."

"No," returned Jules, "I am rich for one valet. I will giff you one hundred pounds to liff in de prison to be undare my eye; and den you sall send as mooh to you mudder as you sall tink fit."

"Come, Mister," said the Jew, "vot's the use of frettin', that never does no good."

"Jules! you surely won't send this poor man to prison?" said Fanny.

"Why not, my angel?" Jules returned; "I sall vont him to liff, and if he liff not under my eye he sall starve; derefore, I fix him in prison, vhere he sall not starve, and vhere he sall live in clover."

"Do not speak about this business to him, Fanny, you can do no good," remarked Edith.

"Come, Mister!" said the Jew, "I ain't agoin' to stop here all day!"

The broken-down minister said "I'm ready!" then followed the Jew from the room, who saying—"Ladishes and Mister, yer hobediunt,"

and then keeping his eyes on his prey he quitted the room.

"He sall be safe," said Jules, lowly, "he sall be safe till I sall want him to destroy the earl;" he did not think Edith heard him, but she did, and she whispered to her soul—"Wait!"

CHAPTER XXXIV.

THE PIRATE'S RUSE.

IT is now certainly time to return to Captain Edgar Trevillian, the last of whom we saw at the Bow Street lock-up, and flying from the spot under the suspicions of the honest constable on duty.

Edgar Trevillian reached his ship as the anchor was leaving the water.

His men gave a great cheer as he appeared on deck, but the colonel did not receive him with such enthusiasm; and when the young captain asked his colonel in military brevity to grant him leave of absence upon urgent family matters, the colonel very curtly refused him.

In vain in the few minutes which intervened between the appearance of the captain on deck and the swelling out of the ship's sails to meet the favouring winds, did Edgar Trevillian endeavour to awaken the colonel to a sense of the unspeakable importance it was to him to prevent the loss of the papers, which could not be replaced, and without which, all chance of his obtaining the earldom which belonged to him as a birth-right were destroyed for ever.

The colonel was obdurate, and even went to the length of twitting the captain with cowardice.

Thereupon Edgar Trevillian said not another word on the subject of the leave of absence, but simply bowed and asked leave to retire.

Receiving this permission he ran to his cabin, tore open his writing-desk, and wrote a few hasty lines to Edith, telling her the miserable facts of the case, and enclosing a little ring as a parting gift. Almost the last words in the letter were to the effect that he hoped to get a furlough as soon as the ship had landed the regiment.

Running to the side of the vessel he signalled a boatman, who easily pulled up to the side of the *Gorgon*, as it had not yet attained much speed, and flinging the letter and a sovereign together enclosed in a piece of tarpauling into the boat, he bade the man post the letter and keep the sovereign.

Had the boatman only posted that letter all would have been well, and Edith could have proved that Edgar Trevillian left England with his regiment; but the boatman felt the ring within the folded paper, the temptation was too great, and he stole it. He was too cowardly thereupon to post the letter, and burnt it.

So it is that the most important affairs in life turn upon the most extraordinarily simple circumstances. Had not Edgar Trevillian placed that ring in the letter there would have been little chance of its being opened ; and so by this simple occurrence he aided for a second time the success of Holgarth.

The ship continued its way fairly and well, but who can say what an hour may bring forth ?

At this time the Algerine pirates had become the very scourge of the European seas. The Algerians were known to be bloodthirsty, cruel, and defiant—even courageous ; but it became clear that when on the sea their successes were so great that it was impossible to account for them, except by the supposition that each Algerian fought for twenty men, and each man possessed the courage of a lion.

Their successes were miraculous.

It was known that on several occasions Algerine pirates, though few in number, had absolutely overcome the crews of British ships.

All Europe sought and could not find a reason for this wondrous success.

The loss of the *Gorgon* created much temporary sensation ; although it was but natural Englishman tried to forget the fact that a ship containing some hundreds of an English regiment had been taken and destroyed by a ship's company of piratical Africans.

The mode adopted at last became known, and from that time the Algerine pirates ceased to be feared.

The plan was, when the pirate vessel came in sight of the craft it was intended to take, to give the pirate craft all the appearance of a vessel of pleasure.

The rigging was hung with coloured flags, if it were day ; with coloured lamps, if it were night. Many of the pirates dressed in women's clothes, and postured themselves upon the quarter-deck. Parasols were fixed along the edges of the vessel, and music and singing were commenced.

An observation by telescope, if it were day, revealed the forms of the pirates sufficiently as women, but it did not show the scowling faces and watching eyes.

So the unsuspecting vessel, glad of a little change on the waste of waters, would willingly approach the pirate craft.

As the vessels came nearer and nearer, the sounds of the music swept to the ear ; and it was only when the two vessels were side by side, and the crew and passengers of the unsuspecting craft were anticipating a cheerful interchange of friendliness and companionship, that the pirates unmasked and showed themselves in their true colours.

The rapidity of the change was so terrible, that a *panic* was the consequence ; and hence a ship's company, which an Algerine pirateer's crew would never have dreamt of attacking, only too frequently fell victims to a ruse which had something so terrible and diabolical in it that honest men could not comprehend the stern truth.

The mode once made known—and it was ascertained by a cabin-boy floating to the Spanish shore on the spar of a vessel—the Algerians were met on their own ground.

An English ship pretended to advance in the usual unsuspecting way : each man was armed, and yet the pirates only saw the fluttering of several light shawls, and only heard the fiddle merrily yielding the notes of a hornpipe.

The Algerians were surprised in turn—the panic was so great that they fell an easy prey, and almost immediately after the date of this success the Algerian supremacy became a terror of the past.

The *Gorgon* was one of the vessels which fell a victim to the Algerians before the time when the Spanish cabin-boy reached his native shore with the details of the destruction of his ship and mates.

So great was the panic, that though the *Gorgon* "swarmed" with soldiers, little or no resistance was made.

The crew and the companies of the regiment on board were transferred to the Algerian pirate—a vessel of large size—and the *Gorgon* was fired.

It was necessary to fire the *Gorgon*, because the Algerians would have found it impossible to carry a ship of English build past Gibraltar without its being discovered that she was not manned by English hands.

All vessels taken by the Algerian pirates on the west side of Gibraltar were thus destroyed, for the eye of the great rock would have watched them too narrowly to allow the Algerians any safety.

The pirate vessel which had taken the *Gorgon* reached Algiers without any dangers from honest enemies, and was welcomed as being a great prize.

Some hundreds of English slaves was such an event as had never been heard of ; and, as English servants and labourers were more valuable than those of any other nation, they fetched far higher prices in the slave market.

Of the agonies endured by the English in that terrible voyage to Algeria it would be almost impossible to render any true description, and, therefore, it were better left unattempted. They died in scores in the fetid poisonous hold. Some were patient under the curse of their slavery ; others blasphemed, and made their position infinitely more intolerable by rejecting the only consolation left them. More than two or three destroyed themselves in their rage of anger at their slavery ; while others—God-blessed men, in whom hope never died—smiled as they caught a glimpse of sky or sea, and said that while life remained all chance of escape was not gone.

As for Edgar—to know that he had been so near the goal of all his earthly hopes—to know that he had almost touched the birth-right of which he had been deprived all his life—to feel that he had almost touched the blessed state of living in peace with the creature he loved best on earth—his own fair wife—was to dread madness, as he lay in the stifling atmosphere of the horrible cabin. Then, again, another and still more terrible thought overcame him—the unborn child. who now would have no father's care!

But he kept himself calm—he knew that calmness was his only safety. He knew that if he once ceased to govern himself he should be lost, and never more see the land, the England he loved so well.

He was sold, in the market, to an aged pacha, and was removed inland.

The same lord bought several others of the crew of the *Gorgon*, but they were bad bargains, for, with one exception, they died within a month of their captivity.

Meanwhile, Edgar and his companion were cheerful, and therefore well.

Each man knew that to lay down and give up hope never did any man any good, and was, on the contrary, the cause of all the misfortune and misery to be found in the world: so each man held on his way hopefully, and therefore cheerfully.

About six weeks after their imprisonment—

their captivity—had commenced, they were removed to an estate the pacha had near the sea-shore.

As Edgar and his companion, a man named Johnson, saw the expanse of blue water once more, they felt as though their freedom was almost at hand.

They worked as gardeners, and already Edgar had began to pick up enough of the language of the country to comprehend a little of what was said to them.

One day while they were working, Johnson suddenly said—"The very sea doesn't seem to care for the land."

"How so?" asked Edgar.

"Do you not see the current sets towards the north? There is no tide in this blue Mediterranean, but there seems a current in this part, and which seems to set towards the north."

Trevillian thought of this for several days,

and at last he saw something practical might arise from it.

"Johnson," he said, "if the current sets north it would carry a bottle north, wouldn't it?"

"Aye—certain," said Johnson, who had been a boatswain.

"It is but a venture, but I'll try," said Trevillian.

That same evening, when the work was done, and when the slaves were allowed to stroll backwards and forwards on the beach, Johnson took a bottle from one of the outhouses of the pacha's palace, and hid it in the thick bush which surrounded a rock not three feet from the sea.

Next he took a thick, dried palm leaf and cut from it a strip of the size and appearance of the little oblong pieces of this material which the Asiatics use as writing paper, if the term can be used.

He then took his garden-knife, made a slight incision in his arm, and as the blood flowed he dipped into it a dried reed; thus prepared with pen, ink, and paper, he wrote:

"Captain Edgar Trevillian states that the *Gorgon* was taken by Algerine pirates 10th of January, 1770, off the Spanish coast.—Crew now in slavery in Algiers.—Captain Trevillian will double all ransoms paid for self and comrades."

The little slip of palm leaf on which this intimation was written in blood was then put into the bottle, and the mouth was stopped with clay; a piece of a kid glove which Trevillian had was then tied over the clay and strongly fastened.

Trevillian then took a piece of charcoal from a heap of burnt wood, crumbled it, and mixed it with a resinous substance oozing from one of the trees. With this black preparation, which, from its nature, he knew would resist the action of the sea, he wrote in English, Italian, French, and Spanish these words:

"*The finder is prayed to send this bottle to the Horse Guards, England.*"

The bottle thus prepared was then gently launched upon the waters, and Trevillian and his fellow-countryman watched it with anxious faces.

The preparation of this forlorn hope of communicating with *home* had been carried on under cover of the rock to which reference has been made, and the entire operation had been hidden from the observation of the slaves lying and watching about the beach.

The two men anxiously watched the progress of the bottle as it receded from the shore.

It moved away very slowly but very steadily due north.

In the clear light of that splendid atmosphere the two men saw it for an entire hour, till at last it vanished as the night came upon that speck in the distance, which might carry home to England news which England longed to hear; and news which, if she read, would be found traced in the blood of Captain Edgar Trevillian.

"There it goes, Johnson," said Trevillian; "God knows whether it will ever reach the opposite shore, or whether it may not be dashed to pieces against the first rock it encounters; but somehow it seems part of myself which is going from us, and so God speed it on its way. But whether it saves us or not, whether we're here another month or twenty years, let us, brother companion in slavery, keep up a good heart and never give in, but work on and hope to the end."

CHAPTER XXXV.

THE MESSAGE FROM THE SLAVE.

THE false earl had been married some weeks when he entered the Cocoa Tree one morning in his usual calm and self-possessed manner.

Lord Alchester and Mr. Natherton were standing near the stove when he entered, talking lowly together.

"Anyhow," said Lord Alchester—"he received his wife's fortune yesterday."

"And a large one too," Mr. Natherton returned. "They say it's forty thousand, if it's a penny."

"I wonder whether there can be any truth in it?" asked Lord Alchester, "or whether it's only a plant to bleed him?" (a)

"Don't know—here he is."

"Morning, Milray," said Alchester.

"Morning. What's the news? Who lost last night over the cards?"

"Oh, no one gained—nobody ever does—but they say Finchley's paid a bill this morning about which he was going to hang himself yesterday morning. Seen the paper?" continued Lord Alchester.

"Anything interesting in them?" asked Milray.

"Are *you* interesting?" asked Mr. Natherton, using the freedom, it might almost be said the vulgarity, of the conversation of the age.

Milray smoothened his face as he said—"Hum!—the women say so."

"Well, then, the paper is interesting this morning, for your name is made free use of in it."

"The devil. What about?"

"Oh, read it," said Natherton—"and then to breakfast with what appetite you may."

"Oh, I never read," continued Holgarth; "will you read for me. What's it all about? Do they say I've been robbing the mail; ruining a duchess; or damaging a milliner?—what is it? speak out!"

"Oh, worse than all these," said Achester.

"Ah," retorted Holgarth, still speaking lightly, though he began to feel an inexplicable terror spreading over him - "Ah! then it must be something worth reading, indeed, so read away." Then turning to a waiter, he said—"Brandy."

(a) Scheme to procure money.

As he took the glass his left hand felt the top of his necktie.

"By the bye," Alchester continued, "why on earth do you wear your neckcloth so high? The summer is here: it's the fashion to wear one's cloths low down on the neck, and there you always are with your choker up to your ears almost."

Holgarth gave the noble an ugly look, as he returned—"I suppose a man may wear his neckcloth as he chooses, mayn't he?"

"Oh, my dear fellow," returned Alchester, "he may wear two neck ties if he likes; don't lose your temper. Here, Natherton, cool Milray down with the little article about him in the *Morning Chronicle*" (a)

"Here, listen," said Natherton, taking up the paper and commencing to read. "Singular occurrence:—Yesterday, his grace the commander-in-chief received at the Horse Guards a singular communication. It was a bottle, on the exterior of which was scrawled in a kind of black pitch an intimation in Spanish, French, Italian, and English, to the effect that the finder was entreated to forward the bottle and its contents to the Horse Guards, England. The bottle had all the appearance of having suffered much from abrasion amidst stones and rocks; and it was only with great difficulty that the inscriptions above mentioned could be deciphered owing to the pitch having been rubbed off in many places. Upon opening the bottle, which had been corked with clay—a wise precaution, for had a cork been used it would have been devoured by marine animals— a piece of palm leaf was discovered, upon which was written in English and in some liquid of a dark brown colour—which is at present supposed to be human blood, but the truth of which will be tested to-day —a statement to the effect that H.M.S. *Gorgon*, about which so many conjectures were made, was actually taken by pirates, the crew and passengers removed, and the vessel burnt. The communication was signed Captain Edgar Trevillian, who purported to be a slave in Algiers at the date of the communication. The authorities of the Horse Guards have already commenced to institute inquiries; but it is only justice to our readers to state, even at this period of the investigation, that the authorities of the Horse Guards are inclined to view the whole affair as a hoax, and in spite of the favouring circumstantial evidence which has been adduced. Colonel B—, who lived in Algiers for two years, declares the bottle in which the communication reached England to be a genuine Algerian manufacture. He also recognizes the piece of palm leaf upon which the self-styled Captain Trevillian wrote his communication as a morsel of a very common palm in that quarter of the world; and Colonel B— also states that the smell of the pitch with which the directions on the outside of the

(a) At this period the *Morning Chronicle* was the mighty Journal and the grandeur of the *Times* was not dreamt of.

bottle are written is, when warmed, identical with that of a re-in which periodically issues from a common tree of Algiers. The colonel also states that it is believed that a very considerable current is known to exist in the Mediterranean, the movement of which current is from south to north. This statement would account, with allowances, for the discovery of the bottle in question on the southern coast of the Island of Corsica, whence it was sent to England by the care of the English consul at Ajaccio. But in spite of these favouring circumstances in support of the supposition that this bottle does contain a truly miraculous message from an English gentleman now in slavery in the land of Algiers, we have the too terrible assurance, either that the affair is a great deception, or else that if the bottle was really cast upon the waves by an English slave in Africa, that this person has assumed the name of Captain Edgar Trevillian; for this gentlemen, as is well known, did not leave in the *Gorgon*. That vessel had sailed when he reached the river-bank; and miraculous it was for the present Earl of Milray that when as plain Captain Trevillian he reached the river side, his vessel had lifted her anchor. He was saved from a worse misery than death to become one of England's great earls, and the husband of one of England's fairest daughters. Doubtless, Lord Milray will feel it incumbent on himself and his position to throw what light he can upon this matter. How is it that his name appears in the matter? Can he give any clue as to the real name of the writer? Was there a man in the captain's regiment named Trevillian, and who may have possibly been nick-named after the captain? It is certain that his lordship owes it to himself to express an opinion in this matter, and we shall be happy to be the medium between Lord Milray and the public, who will doubtless feel extremely interested in this case."

Mr. Natherton finishing his reading looked towards Holgarth.

"My lord, are you ill?" he asked, for the nobleman was leaning against a chair and swinging backwards and forwards.

The next moment he fell heavily to the ground.

"Quick! undo his neckcloth!" said Alchester, as he, aided by several about him, lifted the fallen man into a chair.

"By Jove!' said Mr. Natherton, "he has fainted; how tight this cloth is."

"Tight—like a rope—daresay that's what has caused him to drop off," said Alchester.

"What shall I do, I can't untie it?"

"Cut it off!" continued Alchester, and the next moment Natherton was cutting through the thick folds of white cambric with a slight penknife.

"There's the last fold," he said, after a few moments' cutting, and the next moment Holgarth's throat was laid bare.

He was dressed in white satin, with the exception of his coat, which was a very pale green velvet; hence, when the last fold of the white cambric cloth was cut from his neck, the deep red mark round his throat showed deep and bloody against the pale and light-coloured dress.

The men fell back from him as though to touch him were death.

And there he lay still and silent as though the hangman's work had never been left undone.

"Why that could never have come from the tightness of the neck-cloth," said one of the gentlemen about him.

"Gad," cried another, "not from the tightness of a cambric neck-cloth, but may be from a hempen one. By Jove! the man looks as though he'd been hanged! He looks just as Tom Rockets, the highwaymen, looked an hour after he was cut down, and when they'd dressed him for his last home."

"He's coming to," said some one who had been narrowly watching Holgarth, whose eyes now began to quiver.

A few moments and his eyes opened. He stared about listlessly at first; but after a time his face grew less and less wild.

The men about his chair did not address him, they merely stood looking on.

Holgarth looked about from one to the other as though unable to account for this conduct.

At last his eyes rested on Alchester.

This lord, as though under some aversion which he could not explain to himself, stepped back, and thereby left nothing to intercept Holgarth's view of his own reflection in a wall looking-glass a few yards off.

He saw in the next moment that the secret he had hidden so successfully was out at last. He as plainly as any man there saw the deep red mark round his neck.

He leapt to his feet with a great cry, hiding the tell-tale mark as he did so with both hands.

"Alchester—Natherton! why did you remove my neck-cloth?"

"It's the thing to do, I believe, my lord," said Lord Alchester, coldly, and taking a pinch of scented snuff; "when a man faints he's generally picked up and as much fresh air as possible given him. It seems, my lord, you've had too much fresh air."

"Alchester!" said Holgarth, "what do you mean by this tone?"

"Nothing, my lord," returned the noble; "and, perhaps your lordship will oblige me by giving me my title should your lordship think fit to address me again."

And Lord Alchester turned coldly away.

Holgarth sat down in the chair from which he had started, and felt as though all his new-born honours and dignities were falling from him.

He seemed to have no power to assert himself. As though his life was arrested and he could do nought of his own will and power.

At this moment the group was joined by the tall, black, curling-haired German doctor, of whom so much mention has been made.

His appearance excited no surprise, for he was a constant frequenter of all the gaming and chocolate houses in the west-end of the town.

"What is the matter?" he asked.

"Lord Milray has had a fainting fit," said one of the gentlemen about Holgarth's chair.

"In consequence of the news in to-day's Chronicle," said another gentleman.

"It is astonishing to me," said the doctor, "that his lordship should be moved by such a trifle. I remember when I knew his lordship in Germany—he was plain colonel then, and was absent on leave—I say I remember nothing moved his lordship to fear them: not even when the rascally banditti put a rope about his neck, and hanged him for several minutes. I certainly remember that Lord Milray exhibited no evidence of fear whatever under the hands of those robbers of the Black Forest."

"Oh!" said Lord Alchester, immediately, "then that accounts for the red mark round his neck?"

"Why, gentlemen," continued the doctor, "has he never told you the tale?"

"Never," returned several voices.

"Indeed!—I suppose he did not care to praise himself. I did not know that the rope of those accursed banditti had left a mark. Is his lordship any better?"

The doctor, approaching Holgarth, then took his wrist and felt his pulse.

The very action itself seemed to instil new earthly life into the weakened body.

He sat up at once—his old calm defiant expression came into his face, and he placed his hand upon the hilt of his sword.

"My Lord Alchester!" he said.

"My lord?" returned the noble.

"Your lordship," continued Holgarth, "desired, if I addressed myself to you, that I should remember your title—I have done so; and now I ask your lordship the meaning of your insult?"

"My dear Milray," returned Alchester—"pardon me. What possessed me to take such a fancy I do not know, but I seemed to be under the impression that you were not one of us—let us say no more about it"

Milray nodded.

"I'm sure," said Natherton, "a man who can stand hanging by banditti without shrinking—by the bye, doctor, you must give us the entire history of that affair at dinner—need not be hurt at an unpleasant word or two."

Holgarth looked blankly at the speaker when he referred to the banditti—for he had not heard the calm explanation of the German doctor; but they did not construe the look into anything against the earl.

"Can't tell why I fainted, I'm sure," said Holgarth, "suppose it was the heat of this place; as for the newspaper business, I hope you fellows won't suppose me weak enough to be affected by that?"

"I tell you what, Milray," said Alchester,

"the best thing you can do is.to go home and lay by for a little; you're shaken somehow!"

"Well, I don't feel myself," continued Milray.

"I will see my lord home," said the German doctor, "my lord had better walk, it will refresh him."

"Shall see you in the evening," said Holgarth to the gentlemen about him, and then taking the German's arm he left the place.

"You said you should see those hopeful gentlemen in the evening," said the German, after they had moved some steps from the club house.

"Well—I shall, shan't I?" asked Holgarth, looking in alarm at his terrible and mysterious companion.

"No."

"Why not?"

"You must leave England."

"Why?"

"England is not safe."

"Not safe!"

"No!" continued the doctor, "your secret is out too defiantly. The woman Edith knows it—the woman Death will soon know it—and the suspicions of the world are upon you. Remember the message from the slave!"

"The message from the slave!—but I can prove by the papers——"

"Can you prove by your handwriting?"

"What do you mean?"

"Captain Edgar Trevillian once sent a challenge to Lord Harry Evelyn; that challenge fell into Lady Harriet Seymour's hands last week. The handwriting of that challenge has been compared with that of some letters the woman Edith holds, and they are identical!"

"Well, what then?" asked Holgarth, who leant still more heavily on the German's arm.

The doctor did not seem to feel the weight of the false earl.

He continued—"Can you write like those letters?"

"No; can that matter?"

"Yes, the woman Edith is about to denounce you as an impostor. Aided by these letters, her testimony, your inability to imitate the handwriting, together with the fact that the handwriting on the bottle and the fragment of palm-tree leaf within it, is similar to that of the letters to which I referred; and I think I need not say that things look black against you."

"Why did I not kill her?" muttered Holgarth?"

The doctor heard him—"It might have been done; but the time is past. I cannot aid you to write as the captain writes. That is beyond even my power; but I know how to defeat them all—the judges, and Edith, and even the woman Death!"

"Death!" said Holgarth, "I thought she was kidnapped by the press-gang?"

"So she was," continued the doctor, "but she declared her sex and was released. She is watching for you."

"Curse my ill-fortune!" cried the mock nobleman, more miserable at that moment than he had been at any period of his life—even that last night before his execution, and when the hours flitted by so rapidly.

"Ill-fortune?" said the German, "good fortune, you mean!"

"How do you explain that?" asked Holgarth.

"How; have you not just received forty thousand pounds?"

"My wife's fortune? yes."

"Well," continued the doctor, a mocking smile spreading over his countenance, "spend that!"

"But you say I am in danger."

"Yes, in England; in much danger."

"What would you advise me to do? Oh strange and mysterious man, who seem to have mixed yourself in my life incomprehensibly—for why I cannot tell."

"I——like you," the German said, slowly.

"You have saved my life several times — why?"

"I like you," the German returned once more.

"If—if you are that terrible being I one thought you, what object can you have in saving my life; my life gives me time in which to repent. Why do you not cast me into your kingdom in the midst of my wickedness, my lying, and my destruction?"

"If," the German returned as slowly as ever, "if I were he whom you think me to be, I should say—Gentleman Jack will never repent, though there may be moments when he is mad that he is so bad as he is: and, therefore, Satan need never fear to lose his prey. But in real sober earnest I am a man, like yourself. I have taken a liking to you, and I must watch over you. I say you must leave England!"

"Must! you seem to order me."

"Nay, I but spoke as a friend interested in your welfare."

"And I will leave England," continued Holgarth, as though under a spell.

"To-day?"

"To-night. I will leave London, and tell Lady Milray I shall not probably see her for years."

"Oh! you must tell Lady Milray nothing of the kind," said the German doctor.

"I can't follow your meaning."

"The countess must go with you."

"What! abroad?"

"Yes; you can still have mistresses."

"Poor Constance!" said Holgarth, who in the short time he had lived with Lady Harriet's daughter had grown to love her as much as such a selfish wretch as he could love.

"Why, I am still speaking in your interest," said the German. "I mean you to return to England, and enjoy your own when this miserable affair of the message from the slave has died away. Why, what would the world say if you separated from your Constance? It would say Lady Harriet had judged you a traitor, and so had drawn her daughter from your arms. Yes, Lady Milray must accompany you to the Continent."

"Where shall we go?"

"What better place than Paris?—it is gay, careless, and not too particular if a man have money. Go by a false name, and when you can safely return to England I promise you you shall return—no matter how long hence it is."

"But—but you might die!"

"Bah! my family is long-lived," said the doctor, a more terrible smile than ever passing like a cloud across his pale earnest face; "now listen," he continued, "you must leave London to-night, taking with you Lady Milray, the valet Jules, and his wife Fanny. You can go to the city, get her ladyship's fortune in banknotes: and then having done so you must write a letter to the paper for publication, stating that the vexatious rumours likely to arise by the affair of the bottle and its message has induced you to retire to the Continent till the public can be disabused of the infamous fraud which has been put upon them and you. This will colour your flight, which, when once achieved, you are safe. In the action the woman Edith will bring against you cannot go on if you are not present to be served with the judge's notice. See you—you *must* leave England, and in quitting it leave as good a character as you can behind you."

"Great Powers! you seem to know all things, man," said Holgarth.

"You will follow my directions?"

"I will obey *your orders*," said the highwayman, "for you know you order me, and I *must obey you*."

"Good day," said the German, calmly, "I shall soon see you again," and he turned away.

Holgarth did not hear him mutter—"The devil's children on earth are not harvested till they have sown the seed of damnation in many young hearts, which might otherwise rest pure and uncorrupted.

CHAPTER XXXVI.

THE FLIGHT.

WHEN Holgarth reached his palace-house he knew by the look Jules gave him as the valet pretended to be passing through the hall, that he must speak to "me lor."

Past the bowing footman went the miserable lord of the mansion, and called to Jules to follow him.

"Well, what is it?" asked the highwayman, when he and the valet had had the door of a morning sitting-room obsequiously closed upon them by one of the richly attired footmen.

"Me lor, *she* is here."

"Who?"

"De Lady Edith."

"Where—where is she?"

"Oh! me lor need haff no fear; de Lady Edith haff not seen me lady de countess: me lady de countess haff not left her room, and me Lady Edith is in de great drawing-room, valking back and forvards, back and forvards, like de tigress!"

"Has the countess seen the morning papers?" asked Holgarth.

For all answer Mr. Jules calmly pulled out the prints in question from his pocket.

"*You*, then, have read this accursed affair about the bottle?"

"Every word, me lor."

"Do you think any of the household have read it?"

"Me lor, except Mistress Panetty, dere's no von dat can read."

"Good! Pack up all you want to take with us."

"Vhere is me lor going?"

"Abroad."

"To de beautiful France?" asked Jules, rapidly; the first look of joy appearing on that face which had been joyless for many years.

"Yes, France."

"Me lor is afraid to stay in England!"

"I choose to leave it till this accursed affair is blown over."

"Who goes with me lor?"

"Your precious self, of course; your wife, and the countess."

"Sall you tell Lady Harriet?"

"You're too curious, fellow!"

"I speak in de interest of me lor!"

"You will be ready by dark; let a travelling-carriage be at the stable-gate at seven."

"Me lor command."

Holgarth turned haughtily away; for let him take this credit that he was no coward, that his defiance rose with his difficulties, and that he showed it by his manner to his valet, whom he knew was the possessor of evidence which would, if communicated, certainly hang him.

Indeed, Holgarth felt an inclination stealing over him to brave even the German doctor, but the fear of those terrible dark cold eyes, was too great to allow him to make the determination.

Reaching the head of the staircase he entered the drawing-room, and there stood Edith waiting for him.

"You have come at last!" she said.

"Yes, my lovely Edith. I am proud that you should pay me another visit at so early a period after the last; to what am I indebted for this honour?"

"The news!" she answered laconically.

"Of what?" he returned, smiling.

"Why, that from another part of the world comes the message that you are not what you say you are?"

"Bah! I do not take notice of messages in bottles."

"Oh! you *have* read the news?" Edith returned, smiling coldly.

"Yes, I am a gentleman, and all gentlemen read the news. And pray, fair Edith, what news are you going to add to that of the paper?"

"This!—the time I waited for has arrived. I will unmask you! Aye, raise your gloved hand to your wicked mouth, *that* will not stay my words!"

"You think you can prove yourself Lady Milray at present then?"

"I think I can prove you *not* to be Lord Milray!"

"Bah! I defy you!"

"And *I*," she returned, "will make you cringe to me!"

"How, fair Edith?"

"Can you write as Edgar Trevillian?"

"Bah!" he banteringly returned, "who can prove the writing on the palm leaf is Edgar Trevillian's."

"Ah," she returned, suddenly—"you admit now that you are not he?"

"Yes. Why need I hide it from you, fair Edith? The man who loves hides not one single truth from the woman he loves. I love you!"

"And I," Edith added, "abhor *you* in return."

"That is a mere idea of yours," he said; "you know you fancy me!"

"If *my lord* will allow me, let me proceed to the purport of my presence here."

"To be sure, fair lady. How can you prove the blood-writing on the palm-leaf to be Edgar's? It is blurred, and has run, and can scarcely be deciphered."

"Edgar Trevillian wrote an Italian hand—every 'H' was crossed twice, instead of once in the ordinary way—and his letters to me are written with all the 'H's' double crossed."

"But suppose I say that *you* have contrived the writing in the bottle."

"Then," she added, "there is a challenge sent by Colonel Trevillian to a gentleman still in existence—and *I have it*."

"Who is this gentleman?"

"He is dead."

"Then," Holgarth continued—"how can you prove that the letter is what you say it is."

"Oh, leave that evidence to me."

"Great Powers!" thought Holgarth to himself—"how thoroughly the German doctor anticipated this interview. Who is he—who can he be?"

As he thus thought, he once again raised his right hand to his mouth, as though to hide the working of the muscles of the face. The hand was still gloved, for in the agitation of the interview with the German, the valet, and Edith herself, he had forgotten to bare his hand.

"You veil your face once more," said Edith; "it is a pity your countenance is not as fair as your glove."

"I can remove my glove," he said, smiling, as he remembered the cross—and he did so.

She started as she saw the blue-black cross on the back of the white hand.

"You see," he returned—"I have unpainted my hand, and show the cross I was ashamed of, but which saved me in the church."

"*The cross!*" she cried, her face lighting up with an extreme agony of delight — "*the cross!*"

"Why do you rejoice?" he stammered. "Surely by this mark I conquer you—you do not conquer me!"

"*I do*," she returned. "Edgar Trevillian has an *anchor* mark on his right hand—not a cross."

"You—you *said* a cross," the highwayman said, completely overpowered by the discovery.

"Yes; some good angel must have put the word into my mouth. Villain, you have destroyed yourself! Edgar Trevillian has often told me that he was found in infancy by means of the mark—this anchor—which was named in the printed bills issued for his recovery. I have even one of these bills; and *now*, you wretched impostor, who conquers? I told you I would conquer you, and I have. You bear a marvellous likeness to my husband, but you could not deceive a *wife* for more than a moment. You are in my power: do as I bid you, and you shall not suffer—do *not* do as I bid you, and I ruin you."

He was by this time quite pale and weak; he saw himself foiled indeed—saw there was no chance of returning to England after the affair of the bottle had blown over.

"What do you propose?" he asked.

"This. To acknowledge your forging of my husband's self; to let your wife return to her mother, for I know that already Constance is an injured and miserable wife; and to go away, after giving me the certificate of my marriage, which you say you hold—how, I do not know."

As he sat before her, trembling and overpowered, a voice seemed to whisper in his ear—perhaps she has the papers with her—kill her—thrust your sword through her, and all will be well."

He looked up, and a devilish courage seemed to possess him.

"Edith, have you the papers with you that you talk about?"

"Why do you ask?"

"If you could show them me, I—I would give you your marriage certificate, and you could take it away with you."

"No, I have not the papers with me—for a sheep does not guide her lambs into the wolf's den."

A sudden flash of rage overpowered him. "Do you know," he said, laying his hand upon his sword—"that I could slay you as you stand before me?"

"To what purpose? I have left a letter of explanation on my room table. If I do not return, Lady Harriet will find and open it, and then Lord Milray will be pronounced a murderer."

"But if I hide your body?"

"I was seen to enter this house. I have spoken to your people—to your housekeeper. I defy you to kill me, if you value your own life!"

The next moment the click of a sword dashed

into its sheath was heard, and Edith once more breathed.

Then again a voice seemed to whisper in his ear—"Make love to her, destroy her if you can!"

The next moment he was at her feet. "Edith—Edith, I love you; I have pretended to be your enemy, for I thought you would not return a passion for a man who had done you so great a harm. I love you with all my heart and soul! Fly with me—fly to another land, and let us forget this, and all it contains!"

Edith started as he took her hand, and wondered to herself as she felt a kind of thrill pass through her, and as she felt her extreme repugnance to Holgarth leave her as it were. She seemed as though she pitied him, and looked towards him with a gentle countenance, such as she had never believed she could wear when looking upon a man who had ruined her fair name and outlawed her child.

As he saw the change, he continued, "What is the world without love—nothing. Love itself is a universe. Listen to me. Let us fly together—let us leave the puny loves we've known: your's for the weak Edgar Trevillian—mine for this meek Constance. I will die for you, Edith, if you love me: one hour of love for me, and I will consent to forego all further existence. Edith—Edith, your glance is turned from me once more! Look on me—look on me!"

Still with the inexplicable feeling of pitying the man at her feet—still with the mysterious half-delight in his touch still full within her, she looked at him once more.

Then she saw the *devilish* gaze upon her face; his countenance had changed from the passive one she had always known, to an expression of powerful hate, defiance, and splendid cruelty.

In that moment her own true nature returned as she cried, "Protect me Heaven!"

As she spoke, the man at her feet was cast as it were from her, and he fell to the ground.

And then once more she felt all the repugnance towards Holgarth that she had ever felt.

"You have conquered me, Edith," he returned—"and I agree to your proposals. I leave Constance with her mother—I will leave England—and—and I will give you the certificate of your marriage."

"You will do well," she said; "I will be a merciful enemy if you do not drive me to extremes—if you do not drive me to drag you into a court of justice, where I would not see the husband of the daughter of my sole benefactress—the woman who saved me that life which is within me but to foil you, and tear the mask from your face."

"See," he said, going to a beautifully inlaid desk which stood upon an ebony table in one corner of the room—"I am about to give you this certificate." He put his hand to a secret spring; it flew back, and he took a small parchment from it. "Here it is," he said, offering it; and as she took it she smiled calmly upon him.

"Depend upon it," said she, "it is never too late to be honest. You cannot remain in England—you dare not. Leave it—and I promise you as much to live on as you can want. Take the advice of an honest woman—wickedness never *lasts*. It may for a time, but it's not for ever." Here she took his hand, and this time, instead of Edith once more experiencing the terribly gentle feeling towards this man which she had experienced but a short time before, she conferred upon *him* a gentle if but momentary feeling of sorrow and remorse.

But a few seconds and he was the same heartless, hopeless man again.

"Good bye," she said, "for the present. I shall return in a few hours, and with Lady Harriet."

"At what hour?" he said.

"Seven," she returned.

"I would rather you and Lady Harriet called at nine."

"As you will," she added; and placing the precious certificate in the bosom of her dress, she turned and left the room.

"I have worked upon his better feelings," she thought to herself, as she rode home. "He is true and earnest in what he says, or he would not have given me this certificate of my marriage. I owe it to myself to place my son in his proper place, but at least I save Constance, who, married to a man who bore a false name and title, is surely entitled to a divorce."

Edith, clear-headed as she was, did not think that perchance Holgarth had given her the certificate as a blind to his designs.

This was the case. He thought if he threw her off her guard he would prevent her from destroying his schemes.

No sooner had the coach in which Edith was driven away been lost in the distance, than he called for his horse, dashed into the saddle, and rode at a tremendous rate into the city.

He went down to a broker, and in a few curt words bid the man of business sell the stock he put into his hands.

"My lord," said the broker, who had already done some business for Holgarth, "are you aware of the sum these papers represent?"

"Yes—£40,000."

"And you desire to sell this stock?"

"Yes—I will take it in hundred pound banknotes."

"But," said the man of business, who could not comprehend the conversion into cash of so much security, and who coupled this odd demand with the news of that morning in which the name of Lord Milray was mentioned— "but, my lord, the market has fallen; you will lose considerably by the transaction."

"No matter—sell," said the mock nobleman; "I suppose the Bank can as well pay forty thousand as one?"

"Assuredly, my lord," said the broker, and, bowing, left the nobleman while he went to transact the business.

Before Holgarth left the city it was known all over Change that he had sold an enormous amount of scrip; and various were the comments upon the act.

But Holgarth cared nothing for comment or opinion, and he rode back westward with an immense bundle of bank-notes in his pocket.

It was growing dark as he entered the grand street in which his princely house was situated.

"Jules," he said, as he entered — "is all ready?"

"Yes, me lor."

Holgarth then went into his wife's room. She had been ill all day, and had not risen from her bed.

"Constance!"

"Yes, Edgar," she returned, moving her eyes towards him.

"You must get up."

"What do you mean?"

"Important business calls me away from town—and you must come with me."

"But, Edgar, I am almost too ill to remove!"

"No matter—I say you must get up."

She raised herself upon her elbow, but she was so weak that she fell upon the bed again almost immediately.

"No woman's tricks!" he said, savagely. "You are not so ill as that. You can, and you must dress, and leave town with me to-night!"

"I—I cannot," Lady Milray replied.

"You *shall!*" her husband returned, grasping his wife's right arm; and, from the way in which she flinched from him, it was only too clear that he had been in the habit of striking her.

He had struck her within a week of her marriage—he had struck her, apparently, for no fault, fancied or real, and as though the demon of cruelty alone prompted the act.

"I will send Jules's wife to you," he said.

"Why not my own maid?" asked the unfortunate wife.

"I have turned her out of the house," answered Holgarth.

"Why?"

He hesitated for a moment, then he answered —"I caught her stealing."

"Oh! impossible — only last week she returned me a ring which she had heard me say I had lost in the street, and which she had picked up in the house."

"Don't contradict me!" he returned, raising his hand; and, seeing his wife shrink from him, he knew he had conquered, and quitted the room.

That evening, at seven, a carriage stood near the stable entrance of Milray House. The horses had been harnessed as noiselessly as possible, and the baggage had been packed with equal care to avoid noise.

By the faint flickering light of a lantern, four persons came noiselessly over the yard.

"Where are we going?" asked Constance— one of the party—clinging to Holgarth.

"No matter," he returned: "a good wife follows her husband, and asks no questions."

And, opening the door, he roughly lifted the unfortunate lady into the vehicle.

He followed her immediately; and Jules and his wife — the unfortunate Fanny — followed their master and mistress.

Thus the carriage was rapidly driven away.

But some obstruction at a near corner arresting its progress for a moment or so, Holgarth impatiently looked from the window to see what.

The German doctor, lightly raising his hat with his white, long, cruel hand—

"Good travelling!" said the mysterious man.

And the next moment the coach rolled away on its dark and mysterious journey.

CHAPTER XXXVII.

MRS. NAGGLETON IS AWAKE.

MR. NAGGLETON affected the fairs about London; and, as it is very clear he couldn't attend all the fairs in England—there being about six hundred—many of them lasting three days—why, he had a perfect right to choose what district he liked; and so he was never more than sixty to a hundred miles from London.

He never went in the north of England—he used to say "their lungs was too much" for him. He meant thereby, that not only could the men in the north shout, but that they shouted to such purpose, that he could *not* honestly compete with the north showmen; and as Naggleton—poor simple soul—would not *dishonestly* compete, why, the consequence was, that he kept in the south.

For instance—many years before he fathered Perdita he was at a fair near York. He then had the dwarf, the Albanian, the Harmadiller. and Mrs. N. on stilts; and he said so. And yet he got no custom. For the neighbouring showman, a real downy Yorkshireman, actually took the run by swearing he had two dwarfs, two Albanians, two Harmadillers, and a round dozen of snakes.

Of course people like to get as much for their penny as they can, and so poor Naggleton was deserted; although it was a fact that *his* show was infinitely more important than his neighbour's; for the opposition had only got *one* dwarf, *no* Albanian, and the armadillo was such a failure, in consequence of just stopping where he was placed, and never moving a peg, that he might have been cut out of wood; whereas Nag's armadillo was very lively—would, as we have seen, try to rush between people's legs and upset 'em, and would go round for bits of apple and nuts, which, as Naggleton always said, proved "as how he was more nor a Christian nor some hottentotinish people thought of him."

And yet the Yorkshireman succeeded best. Bless my soul, his impudence was amazing! When he was all in to begin, and was so full that he had to swear at his success, he marched out the dwarf in a red gown and his own hair. The dwarf went round and picked up some halfpence and then retired behind the curtain. The showman then put down the apathetic armadillo, and there it stood without a movement; but the showman didn't speak because he wanted to give the dwarf time to dress for the *other*. Then, when the people were very tired with the stony armadillo, he accounted for it by saying he was *thinking!* Suddenly when the dwarf coughed the Yorkshireman knew all was ready; so the scaly armadillo was picked up, shoved away, and on came the dwarf again in blue pantaloons, a red wig, and a horrible limp to make the deception more perfect. This individual was declared to be the brother of the last; and the limp, which made this little curiosity hobble like the devil on two sticks, was declared to have arisen from a fall which happened to him while endeavouring to "resky a hinfant from a house on fire." This statement of course moved the sympathies of the young women in the show, who had come with their sweethearts to the fair to be merry; and they wept profusely when the dwarf did a comic dance in which, seeing the effect his limp had already produced, he made that imperfection tell out so splendidly that when the rogue went round for half-pence once more, every young woman in the vehicle would have considered herself degraded if she hadn't dropped a copper; and, at one round, this Asmodeus made fifteen pence halfpenny, which was immediately torn from his pocket directly after the entertainment was over by the knowing showman.

As for the Albanians they were declared to be *ill*, one always being like the other. And he asked the visitors, "Could they reasonablery hexpect a hill man to show up?" and as they couldn't they didn't murmur, though they might perhaps think it was hard to be told that they should see a lovely white-haired youth, when the proprietor well knew that he was between the blankets; but the good effect of the dwarf who had saved the "hinfant from a house on fire" had not worn off; though, as it was necessary to send the audience away with laughing faces, the knowing showman burst into a comic song which was so good that everybody was tickled, and came out showing his or her teeth, which in conjunction with the chorus "Ri-tididee-tididee-ee," which the rustics outside heard made the show fill again as fast as it was emptied.

Meanwhile, poor Nag was doing nothing, though he knew *his* penn'orth was infinitely superior to that of his rival; and yet, although he knew that—although he found out the humbug of the two dwarfs—although he could have dispersed the history of the limp and the hinfant to the winds—he hadn't gumption to do anything of the sort, and only looked dismal over the business.

Says Mrs. Nag—"Nag, challenge him to perduce the two dwarfs, ask him to show his Halbanians; and jist put the harmadiller against his!" But Nag would do nothing of the kind; and says he to Mrs. Nag—"Jenny, this yere's our first dose in Yorkshire, and this yere's the last!"

However, the Yorkshire showman rather suffered towards the end of the fair, by adding an imaginary learned pig. The audiences, continuing to be moved by the limp, endured the absence of the Albanians; but not even *two* comic songs could compensate for the absence of the pig, which was declared to be asleep—and would they have the "hinyermanity to vake him hup?"

The rustic audience had never stood on ceremony with an ordinary pig: therefore, why so with a learned?

So a reaction set in in favour of Naggleton; but it was too late in the day—the harvest was nearly over; and so, while the rival show-people had a comfortable meal of tripe, onions, and strong ale, Nag and his people went to bed on a cool repast of bread-and-cheese and table-beer; and the only comfort they had, perhaps, was the consoling one that it agreed with them better than richer and more satisfactory fare.

So, after that one trial, Naggleton never went into the north.

Well, on the night when Holgarth, panic-stricken, fled from town, the Naggleton caravan was pulled up at a little village overlooking Dover and the brave broad British Channel.

It was about three o'clock in the morning, and a very pretty condition was the caravan in.

The armadillo had always been the most peaceable of animals for fifteen years. He had been pulled about by children; big rustics had held him up by the flank, "to see what he would do;" old ladies had stirred him up with their umbrellas; and he had always been as peaceable as a lamb. Yet, all of a sudden, he . had flown, and in the middle of the night, direct upon the dwarf's right shin—fixed his four teeth deep in that curiosity's flesh, and refused to yield his hold.

The dwarf, naturally objecting to such a style of attention, immediately dashed out of bed, and screamed that the devil had got hold of him.

The Albanian jumped after the dwarf, to help him, and was immediately knocked down by his amiable friend.

Thereupon, Mrs. Naggleton and Tiny, considering manly protection the first law of nature, dashed insanely, and regardless of consequences, under, or over, or through, or somehow past the curtain which intervened between them and their lord and master, and fell upon that individual, who was dreaming that he heard thunder.

This gentleman, bouncing up under the avalanche formed by his wife and the young giantess, knocked them various ways: the chairs and table immediately went rattling about, and the babies set up such an alarmed roar, that, as Naggleton afterwards said, it really seemed as though the Old Gentleman himself *was* at the bottom of it.

The agony of the family was terrible; for the dwarf did nothing beyond jump about, and shriek—"He's got me tight, and he'll get me tighter! Oh! the devil! the devil! the devil!'

Under these circumstances Nag was so agitated that he could not strike a light for a long time: first he hit his fingers instead of the flint, and then he caught those members between the flint and the steel—till he really didn't know where he was.

At last the tinder caught fire, the sulphur caught the heat from the tinder, and a blaze was got, and the lamp was lit.

Then the truth came out. There the armadillo was; and all the bumping, pulling, coaxing, and threatening in the caravan—to say nothing of a handsome mutton-chop—would not induce him to let go his hold.

"Cut his head off!" says the dwarf.

But this was proceeding to extremities.

"Send for a doctor!" says Mrs. Naggleton; and thereupon Tiny, who loved the dwarf, and had an intense respect for the power of that little gentleman, flopped out of the show, and was soon ringing at the village doctor's.

When this functionary arrived the dwarf flew to him as a deliverer—the armadillo still holding on, and scuttling behind the unfortunate little man.

"Anyhow, there's no blood," said the doctor; and thereupon the armadillo, as though the secret was out then, and there could be no further need of display, let go the dwarf's shank, shook himself coolly, and marched off. He turned round once, as though about to charge the shin once more, when the dwarf gave him a kick—but he seemed to think better of it. Then, suddenly seized with an idea that to run was the thing, he bolted into his blankets; and, when examined five minutes after, was found to be deep in the sleep of innocence.

He never broke out again—he never showed his teeth again—and, after a time, he was relieved from the ignominy of the chain with which the dwarf insisted he should be chained up every night, as the only means of his being able to continue his engagement as dwarf with Edward Naggleton, Esq.—as the little man himself put it.

However, the doctor was not to be called out of his bed for nothing, and so he prescribed a little quieting medicine for his small patient; and he did this with such an air that the dwarf looked at his shin once more with an alarmed look, as though there really must be some harm done though he could not see it; all in fact that was to be seen consisted of four very red marks, the result of the fast hold the armadillo had held with his four very blunt teeth.

The medical man was preparing to leave the show when a vehicle of some kind, which the entire party had heard approaching for some time, suddenly stopped just outside the Naggleton establishment; the next moment a whip was beaten on the door.

"Ho, there!"

Naggleton opened the door.

"What is it?"

"Where is the doctor of this village?—can you tell me?—I want him at once!"

"Here am I!" said the gentleman in question.

"Quick!" said the stranger, "a fainting lady wants reviving.

"Bring her into the air," said the medical man, and he immediately went to the door of the carriage which had stopped so suddenly.

Mrs. Naggleton was never the woman to be behindhand in a case of duty, so she was soon at the other window of the carriage.

"Poor dear," said Mrs. Nag., when the lady had been removed from the vehicle, "she's as pale as death!"

The next moment Mrs. Naggleton saw the countenance of the other female who had been in the carriage. She started; she knew that likeness.

"Stand aside!" said he who appeared to be the master, to Mrs. Naggleton, and she doing so she had an opportunity of plunging her hand into her pocket and bringing up from its depths—where it was habitually kept since the affair with the highwayman—the portrait which she had borrowed from Edith.

"Herself!" she said, and held up the miniature in the full light of the two carriage lamps, which had been removed from their sockets and before the eyes of Fanny, as a kind of introduction to her.

For the carriage was that in which Holgarth, his wife, Jules, and Fanny had left town.

"Edith!" said Fanny, involuntarily.

"Herself," says Mrs. Naggleton in return.

The fainting woman, the unhappy Lady Constance, shivered as she heard the name. Slightly raising herself she said—"Edith—who knows her?"

Mrs. Naggleton made no answer, but she stooped down, and Constance read the words: "I do," in her face.

"Tell her—tell her—not to—not to forget me!"

"Doctor," said Holgarth, rapidly, "enter the carriage with us; we must pass on to Dover or we shall lose the boat."

During the slight commotion of replacing the unfortunate lady in the carriage, Fanny found time to elude the watchfulness of her French husband; and she whispered to Mrs. Naggleton—"We are going into France to stay there!"

"All right, my dear—Edith," returned the showwoman, "she shall know."

The next moment the carriage was driven on, and Mrs. Nag. was alone in the road shaking her head and wishing there was "no harm in it."

CHAPTER XXXVIII.

THE DISCOVERY.

THE carriage had left Milray House two hours, when Lady Harriet's carriage drove to the door.

Edith had told all to Lady Harriet—had proved to that lady the justice of her claim to be Lady Milray—and had painfully shown to that lady that Lady Constance had been the victim of an unprincipled villain.

Then she added that she had seen the false Lord Milray, and that he had agreed to yield Lady Constance once more into her mother's keeping, and consented to go away upon the payment of an annual sum.

Then Edith, determined to reveal all, told Lady Harriet that she had learnt the mock earl had cruelly illused his position as Constance's husband; and added, that to save Constance from *herself* was Lady Harriet's duty.

Lady Harriet was terribly overpowered by the facts Edith placed before her, but she recognised as truth the argument Edith held, as, putting herself under her protégée's directions, she bade her do with her as she liked.

Lady Harriet's carriage drove rapidly to Milray House, and soon Lady Harriet was looking up towards the windows which she knew lit Constance's ordinary sitting and bedroom.

"Edith, there is no light in her room!"

"No!" said Edith—"and yet I know she has been ill, and not down stairs all day."

"Why does not the man knock at the door?" asked Lady Harriet.

At this moment the footman came to the window.

"Me lady, the door is hopened; a very vierlent pussen wants me lord; and, me lady, me lord's gorne"

"Gone!" said Lady Harriet, starting—"open the door!"

Obedient to her desire the door of the carriage was opened, and she was lifted by the stalwart servant, rather than helped, to the ground.

Leaning heavily on the man's arm she ascended the steps, and stood upon the threshold.

"Where is Lord Milray?"

"Me lady, me lord is not at home," said one of the Milray footmen.

"Where is Lady Milray?"

"Me lady is also from home."

"He lies!" a woman said, coming forward.

It was the terrible woman named Death, who had resumed her feminine clothing. She looked, if possible, even more worn and determined than when she first appeared in the house of Edith's father.

"Who are you?" asked Lady Harriet, clinging to Edith, who was standing near her.

"No matter!" returned Death—"that is not the question. I say this lacquey-fellow lies when he says that Lord and Lady Milray have left the house—and I will see *him!* I watched Lord Milray, as they call him—he's no more a lord than I am—I watched him into this place four hours ago. I swear he has not left the house since, for I have watched for him, as I have a right to do. As for Lady Milray, *she* is ill, and cannot leave the house."

"I repeat," continued the footman, "that neither Lord nor Lady Milray is at home."

"Let me pass," said Lady Harriet; and, as the footmen fell back, she moved towards the staircase.

"Madam, let me come with you," said Death—"I entreat, I implore you, let me come with you!"

"No," said her ladyship, who still clung to Edith's arm, and who instinctively fell away from the touch of Death's hand—"no—remain here! But I promise you that if Lord Milray is here, you shall see him; and not only shall you see him, but he *shall* hear what you have to say to him."

"I will wait," said Death; "you will find him."

And she sat down in one of the hall chairs, and looked sternly before her, her face absolutely set with undying purpose and revenge.

Lady Harriet slowly ascended the staircase, still leaning on Edith's arm.

"He is here!—he is surely here!" said Edith. "I think I saw the working of all that is good —even in such a man as he—in his face as I left him: he surely has not deceived me!"

"And my poor daughter's fortune—if *he* is gone, it is gone!"

"Lady Constance's fortune!" said Edith, starting—"I thought it did not pass into *his* hands for a week to come!"

"Indeed, Edith, he came into possession of it yesterday."

Again Edith started. Was it possible that the message had arrived only a day too late? Was it possible that he had stolen away with his wife's fortune?

The footman going before, carrying the branched lights, here stopped at the drawing-room doors.

"Open them," said Lady Harriet.

All was desolate! The great clock ticking ominously on the shelf was all the sound which saluted them.

"Light us to Lady Milray's own rooms," said Lady Harriet, placing her hands upon her breast. "How my heart is beating!" she continued to Edith—"my old complaint seems redoubled to-night!"

Arrived at Lady Milray's rooms, the doors were thrown open.

All was equally dark and desolate as the drawing-rooms.

"Constance!" said Lady Harriet.

"Constance!" the poor mother repeated, calling more loudly.

Yet no answer!

"Constance!—my daughter, Constance!—answer me!" said the agonised Lady Harriet,

REVELATIONS OF A JAILOR.

stretching her hands towards the dark black suite of rooms.

"Madam," said Edith, "do not show your agony before the servants—all may yet be well—or they may talk and create a scandal."

"True—tell them to go."

Taking the branched candlestick from the powdered footman, Edith desired the man and his companion to retire.

"Come, Lady Harriet," said Edith, as she closed the door upon themselves—and very mournful was the echoing sound caused by this action—"come Lady Harriet, the sooner you know the entire truth the better you will be able to bear up against it."

"True," said Lady Harriet, tottering forward; and had Edith been less agitated, she might have remarked that the lady's lips had grown black, and that her eyes were lustreless.

The two women walked softly to the adjoining bedroom. Then once again Lady Harriet called her daughter by name. Still her only answer was mournful silence.

By this time they had reached the dressing table.

In placing the branched silver candlestick, which she still carried, upon the table, Edith overthrew a cushion, and the next moment she started as she saw a folded paper lying in such a position that it must have been placed under the cushion. Edith bent down and read—"Please take this letter to Lady Harriet Seymour — for pity's sake and the love of Heaven."

"Dear madam," said Edith, taking the paper, "see—here is a letter in Lady Milray's hand-writing."

The mother started: then, in a faint thick voice, bade Edith read it.

This she did.

The letter contained the following words :—

"My dearest mamma, whom perhaps I may never see more. He bids me follow him, and I have no power to disobey him. Where we go I cannot tell. Whether he will let me write to you I cannot tell; but if we are parted never to meet again, dear, dear mamma, I and my unborn child will never cease to bless and pray for you. Good bye. He will be here directly, and must not see me writing. Good bye, dear, dear mother. Your loving, heart-broken daughter, Constance."

There was a silence for a few moments, which was at last broken by a low moan from Lady Harriet.

"He has gone," said Edith; "gone with Constance's immense fortune; and once again in hoping to do all for the best, I have caused a catastrophe!"

"Edith, give me that letter!" said Lady Harriet, calmly.

It was surprising to see how calm and strong she had suddenly grown, yet still her lips were black—her eyes lustreless.

"Follow me down stairs. I must see that woman," continued Lady Harriet, standing as

upright as a rock, and seizing the candelabrum.

"Madam—Lady Harriet, what ails you?" asked Edith.

"What must ail us all some day, Edith. I know what I feel."

"Lady Harriet!" said Edith, still more alarmed—"you frighten me."

"Follow me down stairs!" said Lady Harriet, moving forward with the energy of a woman all powerful to live a hundred years.

Steadily she went down stairs, down into the hall, where lay the inanimate form of the woman Death, and bending over her a tall dark man, whose white hands were feeling the temples of the poor creature.

"Do not fear," said the gentleman to Lady Harriet—"I am a doctor—a German doctor. Passing by the open door, and wondering to see it open, I looked in and saw this poor creature fall from the chair in which she was sitting to the ground. Being a doctor, humanity and my profession prompted me to step in. It is only a fainting fit; even now she is recovering. Leave the door open," the doctor continued, speaking to the footmen in the calm even voice he had used all along. "Leave the door open the cool air will soon bring her to ; and lift her once more into this chair."

As the footmen did so, the doctor stepped behind the chair, so that as the woman Death opened her eyes she could not see him.

Lady Harriet, generally so gentle and thoughtful for others, was now too much agonized by fears for her daughter's safety to take much heed of the stranger ; and seeing that she was recovering, she turned to the servants, who had hurriedly assembled from all parts of the house, and addressing them, she said—"I—I command any one of you who knows anything of his or her lord or lady to tell me at once all he or she knows."

There was a silence of a few moments, and then a faint voice said—"If you please, me lady——" and then stopped.

The crowd of servants made an opening, and brought to view a trembling girl, who was one of the under housemaids.

"Speak, my good girl ; do not be afraid," said the lady.

"If you please, my lady," continued the girl, "I was in the stable, watching for some one, and—and I saw my lord and my lady, and Jules and his wife, go off in a travelling carriage by the back road, and my lady was so ill that my lord had to lift her into the carriage."

Lady Harriet groaned, and would have fallen to the ground, but Edith caught her and placed her in a gilded chair which was placed by the side of a white marble table.

"Gone!" cried Death, starting to her feet. "Gone! then I am once again foiled. Once again must I seek him over land and sea—never to cease watching for him till he expiate his crimes—never to die till I have forced him to die the worst of deaths—he who had done me and mine such harm that the ruin of a weak woman is a sin which falls into nothingness by the side of my great wrong."

"Edith," said Lady Harriet—"I am dying."

"Oh, no, no, no!" cried Edith.

"Yes. Let no unholy noise, or fright, or sorrow disturb my last moments. Some one fetch me a sheet of paper, and pen and ink—quick, quick."

Not a word was spoken in the pause which followed, and during which several of the servants about ran to fetch the required articles.

"Quick, quick," said the lady; but the servants not returning at that moment, the lady looked rapidly about and saw that upon the white marble table at which she was sitting stood an inkstand and pen.

With some difficulty she raised her hand, took the pen, dipped it in the ink, and wrote as follows, upon the white stone beneath her hand:—

I give and bequeath all of which I am possessed to my friend known as Edith Marlow, (but who is in truth the Countess of Milray,) if my daughter Constance does not return to England within seven years. If she does, all my property is to be taken by her. Until the time when my daughter may return, my friend Edith Marlow is to enjoy all interest of my property.

(Signed)   HARRIET SEYMOUR.

"Witness this," said the dying lady to those about her. Edith did not hear the words, for she saw her benefactress was dying, and she had cast herself on the ground near her

"*I* will witness it," said Death; and she wrote her trembling name on the white marble

"Some of you," said the lady, "also place your names here."

Two or three of the servants immediately placed their names beneath this unusual will.

Then the German doctor stepped forward smiling a cold smile, and he said—"Let me also witness this will."

As he took the pen the dying lady said lowly "God bless all here. Kiss me, Edith."

As the words passed the dying lips the pen fell from the doctor's hand, and he stood pale and trembling before the lady.

The next moment Lady Harriet Seymour fell back dead; and as she did so the doctor turned and fled from the house.

www.ingramcontent.com/pod-product-compliance
Lightning Source LLC
Chambersburg PA
CBHW081156170626
46813CB00009B/3208